SCENTING EVIL

SCENTING EVIL

A Thriller

Based on the Case Files of a Crime-Solving Clairvoyant

D.J. Adams

CAPITAL BOOKS, INC.

22841 Quicksilver Drive

Sterling, Virginia

CAPITAL BOOKS, INC.
P.O. Box 605
Herndon, Virginia 20172-0605

ISBN 1-892123-71-1 (alk.paper)

Library of Congress Cataloging-in-Publication Data
Adams, D. J.
    Scenting evil : based on the case files of a crime-solving clairvoyant / D. J. Adams.
        p. cm.
    ISBN 1-892123-71-1
    1. Southern States—Fiction. 2. Clairvoyants—Fiction. 3. Kidnapping—Fiction. I. Title.
PS3601. D37 S34 2001
813'.6—dc21   2001037485

Printed in the United States of America on acid-free paper that meets the American National Standards Institute Z39-48 Standard.

First Edition

10 9 8 7 6 5 4 3 2 1

For Bob,

Who taught me that life and love go on,

and that sailing is relaxing

and chivalry and honor among men still exist.

A Note from the Author

Like Lindsay Freeman, the heroine of this book, I am a clairvoyant who works with law enforcement agencies to find missing children. Lindsay's involvement in this case is much like my own in a very similar case almost twenty years ago.

Then, as in the story told here, terror struck the heart and soul of a small southern town. Then, as in the story told here, two very brave little girls were kidnapped from their homes and brutalized by a psychopath very much like Roman Marsh. In that case, I was the clairvoyant who brought the children home. In this fictional account, Lindsay Freeman does the job.

Scenting Evil, then, is based on actual events and people. But I have changed or altered the names of all of the characters, including the criminal, and the sequence of events to protect the innocent families and children concerned. This book, like the true crime upon which it is based, is a story of violence, rage, torture, fear, love, and redemption. But it is a novel.

For many years now I have worked on many such heart-rending and terrifying searches for missing children. As a clairvoyant, I have the ability to see into the hearts and minds of people—good and bad. Using this ability, I have been able to help law enforcement agencies find children who have been taken from their loved ones, just as Lindsay does in these pages. But from this work, my mind has become burdened with too many ugly memories of vicious attacks on peaceful, unsuspecting families.

Can you imagine what it's like to be afraid of your own memories, scared to let yourself go back and rethink your past? Most of the time I live in that state of mind.

In this novel I have forced myself to go back and remember all that happened so many years ago. My eyes stray to the bulletin board hanging in my office. I see the precious faces of the girls I helped to save whose photographs hang there. There are photographs of their family members as well whom I came to know and the fine law enforcement agents who worked on this case with me. There hangs a recent birthday card sent to me from "Penny," now an adult. Shining glitter covers it and little stars wrap around a tiny angel. The feeling in the air and the mere image on the card take me back in time and I can almost smell the Penny of long ago.

It was a case just like this one that threatened to make my ability as a clairvoyant too public and to expose my family and me to unwanted publicity and even persecution. Then, I made the decision to become anonymous. Now, I find that my memories are threatening to overwhelm me. So I've chosen to fictionalize my cases, starting with this one, as a way to be heard while protecting myself and those I've helped. This fictional town, these fictional families, and I have all gone on with our lives. Our scars have given us character.

Scenting Evil is meant to give hope and courage to those who may suffer from tragedies like this. I wish I could say that this is the last of its kind, but even as I write, I'm working on the case of another child whom someone has stolen, another family ripped apart. In this case, too, I hope that my clairvoyance will help us find the missing child. I hope also that my readers will understand the responsibility that comes with this God-given ability, and respect it, as I have come to.

—D. J. Adams

CHAPTER 1

Roman Marsh raised his head from sleep.

What was it that woke him this time? He always wondered about that. Was it the things that go bump in the night or the sounds that stir your conscience as you sleep? Groggily he tried to focus his eyes as well as his mind. He let his head hit the pillow again and lay looking up at the ceiling. He growled long and deep in his throat. The kind of low rumbling you hear that makes the hairs on the back of your neck stand up and makes your skin tingle with a fear of danger. He had practiced this until he had it right, and now it was second nature to him. It was one of the things that gave him pleasure.

Roman lay there with his body slowly coming to life and the comfort of relaxation leaving him as the tension slowly eased its way back in. The hand resting above his head clenched tightly into a fist. His mind wandered through the avenues of his desire, searching for the things that gave him pleasure until the thought hit him like a bolt out of the blue. The adrenaline started racing through his body, waking him up completely.

"It's out there," he said out loud to no one but himself.

Or could it be that the tiny being on the floor heard him? Rolling over quickly, he pulled the mini blinds roughly away from the window. The sweat that covered his body glistened in the light of the full moon. He forced the muscles in his arm to work the window up. Raising his face to the warm moist June breeze that came through the opening, he inhaled deeply. As his senses came alive he started to tingle all over. He let the feeling run through him from the roots of his hair to the tips of his toes. His throat constricted and his chest tightened. He wanted it to be tonight, he needed it, he even prayed for it, to whatever beast it is that a man like him prays. The scent that he needed was in the air. Blessed Be, there it was! He let the rumble in his narrow chest continue and enjoyed the vibration as it tingled within him. He glanced at the clock—1:38.

He let his head fall back to the pillow, letting the feeling continue to caress him. The night breeze blew in the window, and the coolness of it made his body erect. His mind wandered over the past to the day he'd had and what was in store for him tonight.

"Oh, you are crafty," he whispered to himself.

"Run, run, as fast as you can, you can't catch me, I'm the gingerbread man." He giggled in the darkness as his hands went to work on his body.

Feeling the rushing sensation overtake him, he surrendered to it and the sweet ecstasy only he could bring to himself. His stomach grumbled as he worked his body into a frenzy of sensation. He was hungry, but food was not his desire. In his mind he could see and smell his prey. His flames danced with desire as little Marcie Anderson lay perfectly still in the corner on a pallet of dirty blankets under the rocking chair, pretending to be asleep. She dared not lift her head.

CHAPTER 2

Penny Ware played with her friend Ashley outside the gate.

Even though this was forbidden and they both knew it, they tested fate as most seven-year-old girls would. Besides, the sidewalk was longer and wider out here, making it a better place to play. With all that room, you could really get a swing on the pebble you had to place in the little square outside the gate.

Her parents' only child, Penny was a bit spoiled and self-centered. Her long blonde hair was usually pulled back into a ponytail. Her sweet face looked as if it was molded from peaches and cream. The only thing that needed tweaking was her personality. Time and maturity would take care of that. Bill and Justina, her parents, loved her just the way she was.

Ashley Griffon was Penny's best friend. The two girls had known each other since they were two years old, when the Wares had moved to town. Now, the two girls played hopscotch outside the gate, drawing on the sidewalk and taking turns jumping the number of spaces. Light tresses of hair blew in the gentle breeze, and giggles and squeals of laughter could be heard drifting through the warm evening air.

Ashley threw her rock to the next square. She took the stance and counted out loud as she jumped.

"One, two, three, four," she said as she landed on each square. Penny laughed and clapped her hands as she watched.

"My turn, my turn," she said jumping up and down, her ponytail bouncing with her movements.

Inside the house, Justina Ware felt a chill run up her spine. She grabbed a dishtowel from the counter top.

"Oh my God," she whispered as she wiped her hands and ran through the house, then flew out the front door.

Seeing the two little girls playing outside the gate, she lunged at them. They were playing like any other children, only they were outside the safety of the yard. Justina threw open the gate and pulled both girls roughly through it—fear, anger, and desperation flashed across her face.

Her heart pounding, she felt her blood run cold as she thought of what could have happened and what had happened ran through her mind. Trembling uncontrollably, she shook both girls roughly. She felt tears sting her eyes as both little angelic faces looked up at her in fear. They didn't understand; there was no way they could. This had never been so serious before. They were small children, just seven years old. They were also the targets of a madman. She pulled them both to her and wrapped her arms around them as she knelt to get closer, holding them tightly as if that alone could protect them.

Looking them straight in the eye, she spoke slowly. "Never, ever, ever leave this yard or any other yard without an adult. Do you understand me?" she asked, gripping their arms tightly for effect.

They didn't understand, but knew that it must be important, so they both nodded and said "Yes, ma'am," as tears ran down their cheeks.

Justina stood straight up, wondering if inside the gate was really any safer than outside since, after all, the horrible tragedy had happened inside the gate. She glanced around, surveying her surroundings, and for the first time since coming to this small town she had the uncomfortable feeling that someone was watching them. She pulled the girls closer to her legs and ushered them back inside the gate. Latching it as she went, she again glanced in different directions, thinking that she would have Bill put a lock on the gate when he got home.

Justina wiped away the tears of each child as well as her own, using the dishtowel she still clutched tightly in her hand. She felt terrible, and she was angry that someone had robbed this sleepy little town of its security, angry for bringing them all to this moment. She bent down and kissed the tops of the two little heads below her.

"It's getting late. Let's take Ashley home," she said, looking around suspiciously. "Wait here and I'll be right back. I just need to put this up," she said as she held the dishtowel up for them to see.

Justina walked as Penny and Ashley skipped along beside her. Walking, skipping, and laughing as they went, they had no idea what a pretty picture they made. Justina's mind drifted for a few minutes, back to an earlier time, when a child was safe. They had come to this town when Penny was two years old so they could raise their daughter without fear. *A smaller city was supposed to be safer. Now, every parent in this small town was faced with this fear, this nightmare. The poor Andersons, what must their evening be like?* This town had all the right things. Neat little houses all in a row with flowers and shrubs decorating their yards. A small southern town where everyone knew everyone else had been her dream. Where children of different families grew up together so that Penny would have someone close, since at this time it didn't appear they would be blessed with any more children of their own.

As the three walked past the silent Anderson home, they all slowed to look at the house. Tonight it was much the same as it had been since the Wares had moved to the town. There was one difference though: Marcie was gone. Janet Anderson was the portrait of anguish as she sat just inside the window in her rocking chair, rocking and waiting. Justina waved and tried to smile at her. Her heart was hurting for her friend who now had only agony as a companion. The troubled house had an eerie feel to it.

As they looked at the house, Penny leaned over and whispered to Ashley. "Marcie is gone."

"I know," Ashley whispered back. They hurried past, trying to avoid being touched by the town's worst tragedy, as if it could rub off on them.

Justina saw Barb Griffon come out of the house and stand on the porch as they approached. They exchanged a look and Justina hugged her. They knew what the other was thinking, and they also knew how important it was to keep their children safe. Each mother loved the other child as well as her own. Enough to die for if need be.

"Jus," Barb said as Justina and Penny turned to go. "Can Hal drive you and Penny home?"

"No, sweetie, it's okay. Really, we need the night air and some time to be normal. Thanks anyway."

Barb watched them turn and head back in the direction of their home, praying silently that everything was in fact, at least for tonight, normal. Barb and Ashley stood on the porch and waved as their friends walked hand in hand back toward home.

This was a time both Justina and Penny enjoyed—the early part of the evening when there was still light outside, but the sun had started to go down. They strolled with fingers entwined and chatted about homework and school plays, mother and daughter in a rare warm moment when love is so obvious.

He stood in the nearby shadows of the trees and watched them as they strolled along together. The trio had walked right past him, the two little ones playing and laughing together. Now he watched as the remaining two headed in his direction after leaving the child with the dark hair with her mother. When he had been so rudely awakened, he'd been angry, but now more than twelve hours later he knew why. His senses had been right then, and they were right now. This moment was meant for him to see. The scent in the air had not led him astray. This was why the winds had stirred him. Here was his reward for listening.

He giggled to himself, an almost hysterical sound, as he glanced up into the sky, sniffing lightly, and waiting for the right scent to hit his nostrils, but it never did. It really didn't matter, there was still time. He just wanted to watch them for now. He hummed a tune to himself, his own little tune he had adopted as a small child. *Run, run as fast as you can, you can't catch me, I'm the gingerbread man.* How perfect life was, Roman thought, that happiness could come on an early evening breeze.

Roman watched them, loving the way Penny's ponytail swayed in the breeze and the light scent of baby powder that drifted from her as they walked by. She was the one, his baby come home to him. He turned to let his eyes follow them down the street. They seemed oblivious to his presence, totally engrossed in each other. He had time, he thought to himself, time and patience. He built the moment in his mind. He saw the scenario and loved the climactic moment he envisioned. Ducking his head and stepping back further into the shadows of the large oak tree, he tingled all over. This time, this situation, would be his finest ever.

CHAPTER 3

In the large house just down the road from where they strolled, the Andersons were suffering the agony every parent prays never to have to go through.

You fear it, you talk to your children about it, you even threaten them with consequences. But you never really think it will happen to you. Little seven-year-old Marcie Anderson was missing. Taken from the front yard of her home and no one heard or saw anything out of the ordinary.

She had been outside playing with her dolls, just as she did most afternoons, and in the flash of a moment she was gone. The only trace remaining was a pretty pink sweater and her toys, left where she had last been seen. There was no sign of a struggle and no one to say what had happened. In the blink of an eye, life for this family and this town had changed. How could this have happened and why?

Janet thought back to the previous day as tears flowed freely down her cheeks. She and Marcie had argued over her hair. Janet had fussed with Marcie's hair until it hurt and she had pulled her head away.

"Ouch, Mommy, you're hurting me," Marcie had cried.

"Sometimes it hurts to be beautiful," Janet had told her daughter.

"I don't want to be beautiful. I want to be like the boys."

Her mom had laughed at that. "Your father and I waited for years for you, little girl," she had chided, "and we will not give you up for some boy. Besides, we have boys, remember? This whole town is filled with boys."

She and Mac had three boys, and she loved them just as much as she loved Marcie. But they were older, and Marcie had come along at a time when Janet felt old and used-up. Marcie had saved her from feeling that she was no longer needed. Mac had loved Marcie from the moment he found out Janet was pregnant. He just knew this was going to be his little girl, in fact had named her almost the day Janet had shared her news with him. He had been right. Janet was a hero for giving birth to a baby girl, and she felt needed for the first time in years. The boys—Jayme, seventeen, Colton, fourteen, and Vance, twelve—all looked just like Mac. Marcie looked like Janet, another reason to love her so. She was Janet's baby and her second chance at life.

Marcie was a beautiful child. Her long chestnut hair that fell to her waist was pulled back into a half ponytail with a pink bow, the rest hanging in soft ringlets. She had been wearing pink shorts and a white top that day. The sweater had been abandoned on the porch with the other reminders of Marcie's absence. "She needs a sweater," was all Janet Anderson had said in days, since the day she had called to her daughter to come inside and there had been no answer. She sat in a rocking chair in the window and waited for them to bring her the news they had found her child. Just sat and rocked and waited, her misery apparent through the clear glass pane. So apparent in fact that no one could bear to drive down the road, let alone walk by. All but one.

Roman watched Janet from the shadows after Penny and Justina had gone by and thought about sweet Marcie. He needed to remember to go and feed his little pet and to stroke her soft skin a time or two. He watched as Janet prayed for the safe return of her child, her head bowed, hands clasped, lips moving in silent prayer. *I will take care of her for you, Mommy, I will stroke and powder the skin of the precious little pet. She is mine now. Blow her a kiss in the wind and say good-bye.* Roman stood there in silence remembering his bittersweet adoption of Marcie.

CHAPTER 4

Roman let his thoughts drift back in time.

Not back in time really, just a week ago, but to him, with the sensation being so real, each day had been a lifetime and pure heaven. He thought about the evening that he first saw Marcie. She had been playing out in front of her house, jumping rope with her friends, singing "Skip to My Lou." A plan had formed in his mind that day. She could come to live with him, she needed him, she would love him, and she smelled so wonderful. He would rescue her from family life.

He walked past the three little playmates and said, "Hello." Without changing their singsong tone of voice, the three little girls had greeted him. Even now he could hear the faint distant echo of childish voices that had sung, "Skip to my Lou, my darling, hellooo, and good day to you, sir," as he stood there in the fading evening light outside the Andersons' home and watched the misery of Janet Anderson.

Roman remembered how Marcie had looked him directly in the eye and smiled, her little brown pigtails jumping in time with her feet. The scent of her had stayed with him, long after he had walked away. He remembered it was then that he had decided to make her his. She was so sweet, and the eye-to-eye contact they had shared was so filled with meaning. To him, she seemed to call out, "Take me with you."

His mind danced forward to the following day when he had waited all day for her to come outside to play. He reminisced about the time that he stood, watching the house, hidden in the trees across from the Anderson home. The anticipation had built in him to an elevated level, one that he almost couldn't stand. He could almost feel it again now. She had come home from school that day and raced into the house with small books in hand, the kind they gave little girls with long hair and a sweet smile. He heard her calling out to her mom that she was going outside to play, and out the door she had come, all sunshine and glitter, chewing on a cookie. He remembered the feeling that had washed over him as he watched her and how he had walked down the street in the opposite direction so he could appear on the same side of the street she was on when he was ready.

He had walked around the block several times. He remembered the old woman the next street over had started to look at him funny. He hated old women like that. They always smelled of makeup and perfume. *Shit, she must be thirty-five years old,* he thought. She had stood and watched him on her front porch. He tried to smile at her and say hello but it caught in his throat. He'd turned right, the opposite direction of the way he wanted to go, to throw her off just in case she had any bright ideas like calling the police or someone else. That would've ruined everything. He was too close, things were going too right, and that sweet scent had been everywhere in the air then just as it was now.

Roman had slowed his steps until he'd reached the cover of a large magnolia tree that hung over the fence in Marcie's yard, offering him a hiding place until the time was perfect. Marcie had still been outside alone when he had come back around. Before he reached her, a small boy, older than her but still just a kid, had come running out of the house and grabbed her ponytail, yanking it hard.

Marcie had turned where she sat and let out a loud cry. "Stop it, Vance!"

Roman had felt rage boil within him and he had wanted to tear the kid apart. The kid had run off, shouting "Cry baby" over his shoulder, leaving the front gate open for Roman.

Thanks, kid, Roman had thought, not that he wanted to use the gate to get in, but getting out with it open would be easier. Marcie had sniffled, wiping her nose on the back of her hand, and gone back to her toys. Roman wanted to reassure her that she would never be treated like that again, she was going to be his pet in just a short time.

He'd watched as her mother had come out of the house with a sweater and a glass of something in her hand. She'd bent to say something to Marcie, but he couldn't hear her. It didn't matter; nothing really mattered but Marcie. Roman remembered the sun fading fast, and he had been where he could see and hear her. That day had been so much like this day, the smell in the air, the time of day, and the low afternoon light. Roman had been close enough to touch.

He remembered getting *the feeling*, just as he was now, and how just like now, it was not the time or the place. He couldn't afford to get lost in it just yet. He needed the scent in the night air, and he was waiting for it to over-take him. The evening air had shifted just as he knew it might.

Roman thought back to that time again. He remembered shoving his hands into his jacket just as Marcie picked up the sweater her mom had brought out. She had twirled it in the air above her to sling it about her shoulders when her friend had come to the gate. Ashley had stood just inside the gate opening, talking to Marcie. They chatted as little girls do and giggled about something silly. He'd heard the lilting laughter as it had drifted across the evening air.

The scent of something had been in the air that night too. What was it that made him so aware? He'd watched the two little girls talking at the gate and recognized the other girl from the day before. She was precious, but he had his pet chosen. Still, this one would've been easier. She was, after all, outside the gate, and she'd had no chaperone with her. He could've simply followed her home and started up a conversation about "Skip to My Lou." Roman had given himself a good mental shaking. No, he had made his choice. Ashley had no idea how close she had come to being the one; no one did, not until much later.

Roman remembered sliding over the fence behind the big magnolia tree. He had taken out his pocketknife and picked up a stick from the tree that had fallen to the ground and began to whittle it. He'd huddled close to the trunk of the tree so no one could see him. He remembered struggling with his desire. He'd stood there watching the two little girls talking sweetly at the gate, his eyes staying on Marcie. His heart had been devoted to her, and his plans had been made.

Roman stirred himself from these memories. He enjoyed this one so much that he conjured it often in his mind. He loved rolling around in it and feeling the sensation of the day. He could see the position where he had stood, watching Marcie, before she had come to live with him. He looked up again and saw Janet Anderson wipe a tear from her eye. She seemed to be rocking faster and faster and as he started to look away he saw her pitch forward and put her head in her hands. In that moment she looked so much like Marcie that it forced Roman back to his memories.

Marcie had been the perfect one for him. She'd smiled at him; they had made eye contact. He knew she wanted him. Ashley had left the gate open and run off in the same direction she had come from, and Marcie had returned to her toys, sitting there at the end of the porch near his tree. She still had the sweater, and when she'd passed him, he had known that the sign had come. The scent had come from the sweater, sweet and smelling so like a baby as she had tossed it aside to lay on the porch. He was caught up in the moment and the movement of her. His body had been alive with a tingling sensation and he remembered rubbing his hands up and down his front and backside. He'd stood there with his eyes closed and let the wind drift around him as he'd listened to her playing right there in front of him, her sweet little voice filling the air and creating a cocoon around them. He'd let his head fall back and his hands take him to that blissful place of release. At his release Roman had known at that time that he would take Marcie with him. The napkin in his hand had fallen to the ground as he zeroed in on the unsuspecting child.

Roman was startled as he looked around him and realized where he was. The hour had grown late and he wondered how long he had been there. Glancing at his watch he realized it had only been half an hour, even though darkness had fallen. His memory did that to him from time to time. Once he started the memory process, he knew he had to finish it, otherwise there was no satisfaction, and he needed the satisfaction that going over his perfect memory would bring him. He looked again at Janet in the window. She was sitting upright with one of her sons at her side. Her hand was on his cheek and she was speaking to him. Roman saw the gentleness in her. He thought of Marcie and knew that she could be that gentle in time. She was so precious to him and he longed to be precious to her as well. Roman wanted the memory again. He wanted to think about it as if it were happening again for the first time. He forced his mind to replay the day just as it had happened.

He had hummed softly. In all his presenting, he had found that this was the best way—hum a tune that was familiar. So he did. *Skip, skip, skip to my Lou, skip to my Lou my darling.* Marcie lifted her head at the sound. She looked in his direction, and when she saw him hiding there by the tree she stood and headed toward him. He looked down to the evidence of his desire and stepped in her path. Not yet, it was too soon for all that. He bent his head to her and whispered, "Hello." Marcie leaned into him to hear what he was saying.

"My throat hurts so I have to whisper," he said. He had her when she started talking to him, and he knew it.

"Does it hurt a lot?" Marcie asked. Roman had nodded yes and croaked out in a hoarse sound. She felt sympathy for him and offered him a drink.

"My mommy always gives me juice when my throat hurts. You want some of mine?"

He took the glass and drank like a man dying of thirst, inhaling the scent of her. Life was probably pretty good in this house. He could smell it. They loved their children, unlike his childhood. There had never been love or under-standing for him, and no one had ever brought him a sweater and a glass of juice. He would tell her all about this when the time came, and she would love him and soothe his troubled spirit. She could be his mommy.

He took her hand and started walking toward the gate. For just a moment she had held back, and he hummed the little song again and whispered, "Let's go play hopscotch."

That was it. She went willingly to the gate and out the opening. He walked her to the spot where she and her little friends had played just a short time before. The chalk drawings still on the sidewalk called to him. He jumped the squares like a pro and Marcie did the same. There was no one there to see him with her. It was the dinner hour, just the way he had planned it. They talked of her friends and she told him that Penny lived down the road a bit.

"Let's go see if she wants to play too," Roman suggested.

They walked, hand in hand, toward Penny's house. He felt the fear rise up in him and knew this was the only way, but he hated the panic that each child felt when he did this. He had placed his car between the two houses. Close enough to use force, if necessary, until he made her understand, and close enough to walk to if she just came along as she was doing.

As they neared the car, he held her hand tightly in his. She started to become scared; he could tell by the way she looked at their combined hands and then at him. He had loosened his grip, but just enough to ease her mind. They had talked about Penny's mom and playing jump rope. Penny was the best in class at double Dutch. She explained that this was a certain kind of rope game. Just as they neared his car, he reached down and pulled her to him, grabbing her waist and whisking her off toward the car. She started to cry and kick her feet. Just as he jerked the door open and shoved her inside, she fainted in terror.

Roman wondered if she was okay, and if not, what would he do, where would he get another pet so soon? He thought once again of Ashley Griffon. She must be home by now. Maybe if he hurried . . .

Marcie moaned as he pushed her over the seat, and he ran around to the other side of the car. As the door closed behind him, he heard Janet Anderson in the background, calling for Marcie.

"She's not coming in tonight, ma'am," he said more to himself than to anyone else, since little Marcie Anderson was out cold next to him on the seat in her white top, pink shorts, and no sweater.

Marcie lay there looking precious, her hair a mess, but still so sweet-smelling. She was so lovely and so soft with no clue as to what lay ahead of her. He would powder her daily and feed her sweets to keep her sweet. She was his beauty. He ran his hand over her bare legs and across her tummy that was now exposed. She had the softest skin he had ever felt.

Marcie's skin called to him and he wanted to taste it just one time before she woke up. He knew that the fear would be in her eyes when she woke up, and fear made a person smell and taste funny. He pulled down the road that was the closest since he knew that he couldn't wait any longer to touch her and himself.

Stopping the car but being very careful to avoid the streetlights, he turned off the car lights and let the engine idle. He ran his hand over her legs again, and she moaned softly. He undid his pants and stroked himself again as he bent to lick her leg. He tasted her. She was as sweet as a Georgia peach. He let his head roll back and felt the sweet release that only he could give himself. Blessed scents, he was in love again. He headed his car toward home, tossing the napkin out the window as he went.

Roman was startled from his memory by the lights of an oncoming car that jolted him back to the present day and time. His body betrayed him as he stood there in the streetlight. He saw a man drive up to the house and park. He walked purposefully to the door and went inside without knocking. Roman saw Janet lean forward and her mouth move. Then she began to cry again and the man went to her and wrapped her in his arms.

"Nope," Roman said out loud with a giggle in his voice, "he didn't find her."

Roman realized he had been lost too long in his memory. The scene before him was mesmerizing so he just stood there in the darkness and watched. He saw Marcie's parents try desperately to console each other. He thought of her softness and wondered if that is what they missed about her. She was like rabbit fur, like cotton candy or silk, the softest thing he had ever felt. Well, almost; that other little pet had been soft too. He let his mind drift back to his other pet. Her skin had felt like silk too. He wondered where she was now. They had left her in a train station tied up in the bathroom so she couldn't get away. Her leash had been tight but not too tight and she had been well trained during the time that he and Reese had her.

He thought back to his brother. Reese had always been a difficult person. He was violent. He was gone now, though, gone far away. Roman was glad, Reese scared him and he was glad to see his brother go. Still, the way he went bothered Roman sometimes. But there had been no other way. He would never have gone on his own. Maybe some time in the "behave yourself hole" would do him some good.

Roman shook himself like a dog shaking water from its coat. Roman wanted the memory of Reese to go away. He wanted to remember Marcie and how she had come to him. Rubbing his fingers together as he stood in the shadows of the night, Roman once again returned to the memory of their first night together.

Marcie had started to awaken. Roman could tell she was confused and scared. She had no idea where she was and thought maybe she was having a bad dream. She called out to her mommy. Mommy always made things better, even bad dreams. What came to her ears was the sound of a man's voice and he was grunting softly.

"Daddy!" she had cried out in the dark to her father.

Feeling something soft stroke her skin, she had relaxed, and then drifted off to a peaceful sleep, completely unaware of the danger she was in. Roman had carried a sleeping Marcie into his home, wrapped in the soft blanket that just minutes before he had used to stroke her soft little legs. She had snuggled up close to him and rested peacefully in his arms. *How sweet and easy they were to please at this young age before the world got hold of them and turned them into vicious bitches,* he thought.

He longed to turn a light on so he could see her smile in her sleep, knowing that she felt safe in his arms, but that would wake her and he wasn't ready for that. He needed time so he could explain to her where she was and that he was going to take good care of her. He knew fear would cross her face, and he wasn't willing to part with this sleeping baby in his arms yet. He couldn't bear to have her pull away from him, not when she felt so good. He loved this little pet already, and he wanted her to love him too. Time would take care of that. He knew that in time she would love him as much as he loved her. Or else. He never wanted to think of what the "or else" was, but he knew from his past that the "or else" was a bad thing. He had heard it many times in his youth. He had survived it and Marcie would too.

For Roman Marsh memory was a powerful thing. He loved it almost as much as he loved the very thing that caused the memory. Again the little ditty rose from his throat: *Run, Run as fast as you can, you can't catch me, I'm the gingerbread man.*

CHAPTER 5

Mac Anderson watched his wife cry and wiped the tears from his own face.

He had heard the police say that if Marcie was not found in the first twenty-four hours, the chances of getting her back were next to none. She had been gone a week now, and they were no closer to getting her back than the day she had been taken.

She was the light of his life. A precious gift from God, one he had never taken for granted. He had not taken the time to pray, he realized for the first time since this had happened. Oh, he had said things like "God, please," but he had not really gotten down on his knees and poured his heart out to God. This thought hit him like a ton of bricks as he watched the misery cross his wife's face. Could it be that God was waiting for him to humble himself? If so, he would do that right now. Janet glanced up at him and a weak smile lifted the corners of her mouth. She loved him. He knew this better than he knew his own name, and right now she was hurting so badly, he could stand it no more.

Mac crossed the room and knelt in front of her. Putting his head in her lap, he said softly, "I put the boys to bed."

She just whimpered and laid her head on his. She knew that he was hurting just as much as she was, but she was unable to help him. Her pain was that severe. They clung to each other for a while, then Mac stood and put his hands on the sides of her face, looking deeply into her eyes.

Finally he spoke. "I promise you, if it's the last thing I do, I will bring her home."

She looked up at him and for a fleeting moment she believed him.

He walked to the front door and, pulling it open, turned to her and simply said, "I'm going to church," and left.

Janet sat there in total misery.

CHAPTER 6

Roman Marsh stood across the street and watched.

The feeling of elation was almost overwhelming. He even shed a tear. He was the cause of this misery; this was his payback, his opportunity to get even for all the things adults had done to him during his childhood. He ran his hands up and down his body, letting the nerves in his fingers tingle with the sensation, like when you run your hands up and down on rough fabric. Roman loved that feeling. Shoving his busy hands into his pockets, he had found victory and he was going to savor it.

He was going to follow Mac. He wanted to see him brought to his knees. The man was big and proud, and little Roman was going to see the big man crawl. He ambled through the streets, a safe distance behind Mac, and let his mind wander. He wondered at the possibility of this new town. What could he accomplish here? Where was he headed in his quest for the perfect scent? He wondered who he was. Where had he come from, and why did they never want to hold and inhale the sweet scent of him? Who were his parents, and whatever became of them? He knew for certain what he would do if he ever found them, but he also knew that he would never look. He was their loss and that was their shame, and now he was going to show them all what they had given up. Someday, they would read about the wonderful baby smell of him and know all that he had accomplished in his life and what they had made him do.

He strolled down the street toward his new intended. He had looked up once or twice as Mac had stopped in front of him. They were standing outside the house of the other little pet that his sweet baby had played with. Roman wondered what her name was. He would have to ask his pet when he got home. He looked at the little house with the pretty curtains all neat and clean. The house was dark for the most part, except a single light in what he thought must be the family room. *Were they in there watching television together?* he wondered. The thought made him almost sick to his stomach since he knew what would happen when the TV was turned off. He paused for just a second and inhaled deeply, breathing in the scent of the house.

"Ah," Roman said out loud as the sweet scent again stirred him.

He stood there for a moment and envisioned the moment of sweet pleasure that he knew this house and its inhabitants would give him soon. A dog barking in the distance stirred him, and he was jolted back to the present as he realized he was standing in the streetlight. Roman looked up just in time to see Mac turn the corner and hurried after him.

Mac never knew Roman was there. Head down and going through his own mental meandering, Mac never thought to check behind him. This was such a safe town, no one ever thought to look, until now. He wandered down his street and past the homes of his friends and neighbors that just a week before he had taken so much pride in. Mac loved this town.

He walked to the church instead of driving his car. He needed time to find the words he wanted to say to God. He needed the night air to help clear the misery from his mind. He inhaled deeply the sweet scent of magnolia blossoms. With his head down, he wandered, twice looking up to realize he was on the wrong street. Making his adjustments, he finally found himself outside the church.

Looking up, he asked, "God, are you ready for me?"

The answer seemed to come, because he felt that old familiar pull that beckons you inside and then makes you feel as if you belong, gently chastising you for not being there sooner. He pulled the door open, and the smell of God hit him full in the face, that musty scent of hymnals, candles, and promises. He staggered against the door, and despite the promises he had made to himself on the way, he crumbled to the floor a mass of emotion. He lay there for a long time, letting the tears fall as sobs wracked his body and the emotions overtook him. He sobbed for his baby, for his wife, and, finally, he sobbed out in anguish for himself, begging God for an answer.

Pastor Johnson found him there, lying on the floor over the threshold, the door half open. Carl Johnson knew this family. He had baptized them and their children. He knew what brought Mac to church this evening; everyone in town knew, and he could no more have turned him away than God himself. He knew this night was special, and he knew that God had brought Mac here, just as God had delayed him from his dinner.

His stomach grumbled in protest, but he whispered, "Hush. We are about to do God's work here."

Mac let himself be lifted as Pastor Johnson found a strength in himself belying his age. Mac seemed as light as a feather as he pulled him up from the ground.

"Mac," he said gently, "while this is the house of the Lord and even the floor is blessed, I think it's best you came inside."

Pastor Johnson pushed the door open, and as he did, he looked up and just to the right of the door. Standing across the street and just barely out of the light was the lone figure of a man. He could have sworn that he saw the faintest glimmer of a smile on the man's face.

But he did not have time to think about that now. One of God's children needed him to listen and to advise. He was not all that sure he could. This would be his greatest challenge as a minister.

CHAPTER 7

Roman Marsh turned with a smile on his face and left the church, thinking to himself, *Hurts, doesn't it Dad?*

He had followed Mac from his home. It had just happened that way, he really had not intended to, he just wanted to see where he was going. *Was he running to a mistress for comfort or did he have some other dark secret like we all do?* He wanted to see Mac fall apart, and he wondered at the course he had taken. *Where was he going?* His route had seemed to make little or no sense to Roman, and he had looked up and turned, looking around at his surroundings. He had then twice made a turn and headed back in the same direction he had just come from.

Roman chuckled to himself. "Misery sure makes one do funny things."

Watching from across the street, he saw Mac stand in front of the building and look up as if waiting for something. What could that be? He knew that others found comfort in these places, and he too had often come to buildings like this looking for comfort, like when he went back to the orphanage looking for his mother. Or when Reese had to go away. He knew they had prayed to the Blessed Be in these places, and there had been many a time when he had, as a small child, been forced to sit on his hands while the others prayed.

Who was this Blessed Be? Why had It never come to save him as a small child? No one powdered his bottom and kissed him good night when he was little. No one brought him juice and a sweater and now everyone needed to suffer as penance.

He wanted the whole world to suffer. Suffer for him. Suffer for Reese.

So many times in his life, he was told to pray to the Blessed Be, but who was that and just what was he supposed to say? He found out soon enough that he needed to be quiet and put his head down to avoid the whipping that was sure to follow if he didn't, but he was never told who the Blessed Be was.

Roman turned and headed for home and his sweet baby pet. Did she miss him? "Of course she did, silly," he whispered to himself.

Mac talked for hours to Pastor Johnson. He bared his soul and begged for forgiveness, promising to give more and do more for the church and others, if God would only send his baby home. He didn't really care what he had to do. He just wanted her home. Pastor Johnson tried to explain God's way to this grieving father.

"Mac," he said gently, "you know that God does not work this way. Pray for the strength to get through this, and ask him to give the law enforcement officers the wisdom to do their jobs, but understand that God will not interfere with anyone's free will."

Mac did not understand. He and the good pastor prayed together for a miracle. He prayed with his hands clasped, and his head resting on them, because he was too weak to hold it up any longer. Pastor Johnson left him there at one thirty in the morning to go home to his own bed. He understood the distraught feelings that motivated this father, but there was nothing that he could do. This was between Mac and God, and he left them to it.

CHAPTER 8

Captain Tony Miller sat at his desk, but the inactivity was killing him.

He slammed closed the file that he was reading on other scenarios of lost and missing children. This one seemed so different, and yet his cop mind reasoned that a missing child was a missing child. This was different only in that he knew for sure that a stranger had taken her and where she had been when she had been taken. Still no ransom had been asked for; actually, there had been no demands at all. He couldn't stand this anymore.

He stood and shouted to anyone who cared to listen that he was going home for lunch. The office quieted, everyone turning to look at him. He stormed out of the office. He barely made it to his car before the tears of inadequacy streamed down his face. He wanted and yet didn't want to know what this little girl was going through. Was she still alive? What the devil was he going to do to bring her home? He drove his new squad car around the Town Square.

Two weeks ago, hell, a week ago, this car had been big news. Everyone had turned out to see it. Now it seemed stupid to have been so excited over something so trivial. It never ceased to amaze him how fast things changed when you least expected it. He wanted the days of just a week ago back. What he wouldn't give to be on patrol and cruising down the Andersons' street at six o'clock on that Tuesday evening. He would have busted that guy and then taken him back to the station, locking him in a cell with every father in this town for just five minutes. He would have let Mac Anderson at him first, and then, he would have taken what was left of him.

Thoughts like this traveled through his mind at a rapid rate. He couldn't control it and he really didn't want to. He eventually got around to thinking about his own police department. The police force, if you could call it that, of this little town was small and in need of some revamping. They needed a lot to even begin to get started: a new computer, some radios that really worked, and more men to assign to this situation that was fast getting out of hand. Tony had been with the force the longest, and he knew they were out of their league.

His wife thought what they really needed was the help of a clairvoyant. Ideas like hers came pouring into the station constantly. The phone rang all the time, people just walked in, and someone had even left a note on his patrol car. Everyone had a solution but nobody had any clues. Everyone had seen a strange person here and there. Hell, he didn't know what to do. He had never dealt with anything like this before. Who was this guy? Where did he come from? These were just two of the questions that ran through Tony's mind. This guy was a fucking nutcase and the whole situation made everyone's skin crawl. The whole town was looking at Tony, waiting to see what he was going to do. Damn funny thing for them to do because he didn't know what the hell he was going to do. Stick his head in the sand maybe. That was the only thing he could think of at this moment.

Tony drove through the town that was his home and stared out the window, his hands tightly gripping the steering wheel and his face absorbing the afternoon sun. He thought about the day that Marcie had disappeared and tried to recall all that had happened that day.

Tony was the first officer on the scene after the call from the Anderson home. At 6:45 on a quiet Tuesday night, Janet Anderson called, hysterical and screaming that someone had taken her daughter.

"My baby, my baby" was all that the dispatcher could make out of what she was saying. After several minutes of trying to calm her down, the dispatcher agreed to send someone over.

Tony volunteered. "Never mind, it's on my way home, I'll take it," he said on his way out the door.

Grabbing his hat, he had ambled toward his car and thought, *Wonder where that kid has run off to?*

What he found made the hair on the back of his neck stand at attention. Janet Anderson was still screaming, and Colton, the middle son, was looking everywhere for his sister.

A neighbor, Beth Wilson, was there, trying to calm Janet down. Mac Anderson pulled into the driveway like a maniac, with gravel flying everywhere and a look of fear in his eyes, after getting a call at work from a frantic neighbor.

Janet held a picture of her daughter in her hands along with a sweater and a rag doll. The doll just hung there like a limp omen as she staggered to her husband and collapsed against him.

She looked up at him and cried out in anguish, "They took her, Mac. Oh God, they took our Marcie. Please do something, please, Mac," she moaned in loud wails.

"I will, baby. Tony and I are gonna do something," Mac said as he placed a large arm around his wife and pulled her to him, as if that by itself could offer comfort.

Tony reached into his new patrol car and, grabbing the radio, hollered into it, "Get me some help out here at the Andersons' on the double."

Tony walked over to Mac and Janet and with his hand on Mac's elbow ushered them both toward the house and away from the driveway that he knew any moment would be filling up with cars.

"Janet," he said softly, "tell me what happened."

Janet looked at him for a moment in stunned silence. "I called her to come in and she didn't, Tony, that's what happened. I have been around the block, called all her friends, we have checked the house and the backyard, she isn't here."

Her words were getting louder and louder as she rambled on with an almost vacant stare in her eyes.

Mac held his wife close to him. He listened to the words spilling from her, since this was the first time he had heard what happened as well.

Tony asked if Janet had checked the child's room.

"Yes! Do you think I'm stupid, that I would have called the police without checking everywhere? Tony, she's been gone since six o'clock. Do something!" The wail in her voice was returning.

Tony felt uncomfortable under her stare. He took a step back and looked down at his watch; forty-five minutes had gone by.

Most of the officers who had arrived after Tony's call for backup stood there in shock, looking at him and wondering what to do.

Mac stood there, holding his wife and looking at everyone in disbelief. Finally he shouted in a lion's roar, "Somebody do something, NOW," scaring everybody into action.

Tony felt foolish at that moment. He still believed Marcie would turn up, that she had just wandered away and any moment she would come around the corner. But he had to investigate, just in case. *Gosh,* he thought, *just in case what?*

"Okay, let's go over everything, leave no stone unturned. Jordy, go door to door and start asking questions. Find out if anyone knows anything. Take Billings with you. And be careful. Preserve any and all evidence, and watch where you walk. Don't screw this up, guys. Now get moving."

The officers moved off with gloves and flashlights in hand and evidence bags in their pockets and made a thorough search. Things started to unfold, getting progressively worse.

Everyone from family to next-door neighbors was questioned repeatedly. Then the Andersons were questioned individually. Tony knew that eventually bank records and business contacts would have to be inspected if this thing continued to go the way it seemed to be going. Personal questions were asked. Was anything wrong at home? Was Marcie unhappy about anything? The family doctor had been called for Janet and he too was questioned. When Mac became angry, Tony pulled him to the side.

"Mac, this is customary. Hold on, okay?"

Mac just glared at him. "Hold on, shit, somebody needs to find my kid."

"We're doing what needs to be done, just bear with us here," Tony had reassured him.

They were asked all the questions that rub on the wrong side of the nerves of a parent with a missing child. More clues were needed, but no one had any real idea of where to go for them. Some of the officers had started to search the house and the neighbors' houses for blocks around.

As they searched Marcie's bedroom, Janet had to be sedated. Tony would never forget the sound of her screams and the low moans that escaped her lips, before the sedative took hold and transported her to a place where feelings wouldn't hurt so much. He could hear them as he watched the officers as they had searched the little room. Lifting the little ruffles on Marcie's bed and peering into her drawers made most of the officers feel as if they were invading her private space. He could tell just by the looks on their faces.

Then a shout came from outside. They had found something. Mac beat everyone to the door. An officer stood near the tree by the front gate just inside the yard and he was looking up.

Everyone heard Mac gasp the words, "Dear God, please, no."

Mac couldn't stand the thought of his baby hanging in the tree. He had always feared that tree since Marcie loved to climb it. He held his breath and turned away just long enough to brace himself for the news.

By the tree, just to the left of where Marcie had been playing, were signs that someone had been there. There were shavings of wood and large boot prints with some rather odd markings that marred the dirt. There was also evidence that the man had stood and watched the child for some time and had brought himself to what appeared to be sexual release before he had taken her.

The officer by the tree had followed the tree line from as high as he could see and then had hunkered down in a squatting position at its wide base. Gloves were on his hands and the pencil in his right hand was pushing around what looked like a crumpled napkin or tissue.

Tony walked over to where he was, squatting next to him. The officer pointed out several things. There was a napkin and its contents. What appeared to be some form of body fluid covered it.

"Bag it," Tony instructed.

This was not the sort of thing you wanted to tell the parents of a missing child, especially a female child. There were several footprints in the dirt around the base of the tree; something in them caught Tony's eye. He looked at the shoes of the officer closest to him and then he looked around him at all the other shoes in the area, including his own, just to be sure. There was something different about one set of prints.

Tony called Will Jenkins over and pointed at the prints by his feet.

"Will, what do you make of that?" Tony asked.

Will was a crime scene photographer. Retired from the big city, he had settled here to be near his favorite fishing hole. He moonlighted with Tony's department to occupy his time with something other than fish. His wife said he needed a job, so he did what he could to help in the few times he was called out. This was one of those times.

Will hunkered down over the spot and moved his pencil pointer over it lightly so as not to touch the soil but to help his mind trace the image.

"Looks like toe caps, but I haven't seen them in years. They're a dress thing for the shoe that a few men wore years ago, but like I said before, I haven't seen them in years. Most men never wore them or have ever heard of them for that matter."

"Can you make an impression of them for me?" Tony asked.

Will nodded "Sure thing, right away."

Tony looked at the wood shavings and the baggie with the napkin in it. He stood and took several officers aside. "Let's keep this just between us, okay, guys? This doesn't need to get out just yet."

They nodded their heads, agreeing it was the thing to do.

Mac had been relieved that Marcie was not hanging in the tree. The question was, where was she? If someone had taken her, where to? Who was he, and did he mean to do her harm? Mac's mind worked frantically, thinking of all the possible scenarios. He found himself wanting, for the first time in his life, to do bodily harm to another human being. Tony watched the emotions play over his friend's face and heard his words; he felt they were his words as well.

They would wait for a ransom demand and in the meantime set up telephone taps and wires.

"Make the calls, get it arranged with the judge," Tony said to his sergeant.

"You got it, sir," the sergeant said as he hurried away.

Tony watched each officer head to his patrol car that night and knew that the ones who were married with children of their own wanted to call home.

Meanwhile, neighbors had ushered the Andersons inside and closed the doors as reporters arrived. Snapping pictures and asking questions, they seemed to have no regard for the family, even in this small southern town where everyone knew just about everyone else. Tony always wondered how they knew when something happened. Did they have a nose for news after all? He wondered if someone had tipped them off. This was not a lights and siren call, after all.

He had originally thought that Marcie had just wandered off. When the call came in, he had calmly walked to his patrol car, slid behind the wheel, and took the time to buckle his seat belt. Now he felt guilty about his complacency. If he had hurried, could he have caught the perpetrator?

Four hours later, with very little to go on and no ransom request, he had driven away and left the Andersons with their new misery, and no little girl to put to bed. Only an empty bedroom with pink ruffles that hung gracefully to the floor.

Tony would never forget that day. He felt helpless and when he caught the son of a bitch he was gonna make him pay. For now, he had no clues, and with nothing to go on, he could do nothing but wait for the lab to come up with something or, worse yet, for something else to happen. He had a cop's instinct that the wait wouldn't be all that long.

The FBI had been called in to help, and while he hated that his town was under that kind of scrutiny, he knew he needed the help. Times were changing in this one-horse town, and he hated it.

With a heavy heart, he headed his squad car slowly toward home. He needed his family, and the need to see to their safety was quickly becoming overwhelming. Precautions had to be taken now to keep the other kids safe, especially his Becky. He knew he could never live without her.

The Millers had the same number of kids as the Andersons, and two of them, Jayme and Vance, were in the same class as his boys, Mike and Jerry. Becky was only five, just a baby.

"Please God," he said out loud, "please keep my family safe from this." Somehow he knew that night that this was a prayer of futility for everyone in this town. A crime like this had never happened in his town before, and he had no idea where to start. Tony remembered thinking he was gonna make damn sure it was never going to happen again. Or at least he hoped not.

CHAPTER 9

Tony needed a break, but he had no idea where one was going to come from.

He just couldn't let this case go unsolved, no matter what. As the patrol car pulled alongside his modest home, Tony sat and stared at it. His memories had given him a multitude of emotions—guilt, fear, anger, just to mention a few.

He studied his home. It felt good to him, as if it had never been violated and was totally clean. He cleared the front door of his house and listened for the normal sounds heard during the day. Summer sounds that everyone was home and life was as expected, noisy but normal. The sounds did not let him down, and he yelled out a hello.

Squeals of laughter filled the air as Becky came running around the corner, her cotton socks sliding on the hardwood floor. She slid to a stop by banging into him, and he stooped to pick her up. He snuggled her close and buried his nose in the crease of her neck as her pale brown curls fell over his nose. This was his baby. The youngest of four, she was the apple of his eye. First they had had three rough and rugged boys and then this tiny ruffian came along and stole not only his heart, but also that of everyone in the house.

Mike, Aaron, and Jerry treated Becky like one of the boys, but lately they had all chosen to stay home a lot more than usual and play with her.

The boys were older and they knew what was going on in town. Mike was friends with Jayme Anderson. Jayme and Mike had talked that same day about all that had happened. Jayme felt like it was his fault, since Marcie had wanted him to take her to the park and he refused.

"One damn time," he had said in tears to Mike, "one damn time that I don't give in to her and look what the fuck happens. This is all my fault. If she doesn't come home, how am I gonna live with myself?"

Mike had sat with his dad that Tuesday night and told him what happened. He knew the way Jayme was feeling wasn't right, and he had tried to tell him, but the kid wouldn't listen.

"Hindsight is a powerful thing," Tony had said, as he watched the promise come over Mike's face that he would always be there for Becky. Unspoken, but there just the same.

Now Tony watched his sons, all three of them, come around the corner and saw the look on their faces.

"Any luck, Dad?" Mike asked.

"No." This was scaring them too.

He tousled their hair, each one in turn, and asked, "Where's your mom?"

They all said at the same time, "On the computer," and snickered.

Tony put Becky down and she ran off with her brother's hat, much to his dismay. She loved the attention she was getting recently, not knowing why the boys were around so often to play with her, but loving it just the same.

Tony rounded the corner, and there his wife sat, face glued to the screen—his homecoming queen. He smiled at the intensity on her face and wondered what she was reading. He walked up behind her and stroked the back of her head.

Claire smiled up at him. "I knew you were coming home today. Lunch is in the kitchen."

He laughed at her and asked, "How did you know that?" This was probably only the third day in his entire career that he had come home for lunch.

She just looked at him and said, "I'm your wife, it is my job to know you, and that's something that I do well."

"Yes, you do," he said, as he folded his arms around her neck. "Give us a kiss."

She stood and faced him. As she kissed him, he held her just a little too tight, causing her to step back and ask if he was okay.

"Yeah, but this thing with Marcie is so hard to deal with. Some nut comes into our town where nothing ever happens and takes one of our kids from her own yard. We have no clues to go on, nothing, and I just can't stand it. What if it were Becky? What the hell would we do?"

She held him close to her and tried to give him some of her strength. He cried softly on her shoulder, and she let him, wondering at this man who was her husband. He was so much to her and their kids. A man of strength and character, he laughed easily, and he had a lot of friends. Everyone liked Tony Miller—the man, the cop, and the dad. His tears burned into her heart. Before, she has seen him cry only at the birth of their children and the death of his father. These days he cried openly in front of everyone. Claire loved him more for it and the town felt honored to have him because of it.

He stood there holding her, then asked her what he should do. She had an answer, but she knew he was not going to like it. She gently stood back from him and looked him in the face.

"Tony, I know that you do not believe in this, but please hear me out."

"Oh, Claire, not that again, this is serious stuff. This is a child's life we're talking about."

"Tony, please, just come and read this article. Just read it with an open mind and you'll see there are people out there who investigative agencies use to find missing children."

He allowed her to pull him into the living room and seat him in his favorite chair. She shoved the article into his hands, then nodded at it.

"Your mom brought this by earlier today, hoping that I could talk you into reading it."

He looked at her as if she had two heads. Shock was an understatement.

"You and my mom working on me together!"

The truth was, Claire and her mother-in-law never had gotten along very well, and after Tony's dad died, it had gotten worse. Ruby, Tony's mother, often seemed to go out of her way to make people miserable, and Claire was her favorite target. People often patted Tony on the back at functions where both women were present and shook their heads in understanding and pity.

He couldn't fathom this transformation. These two women had not gotten along since Claire refused to use olive green as her wedding color. That had been nineteen years ago last September. *What in the world could have brought this about?* He held the paper, but it was secondary in his mind to the shock at this new partnership.

Claire rattled the article in front of him. "Read that. Then I will tell you what else I've found out about it."

He focused his eyes for a minute and turned to read the article though he couldn't help looking up at her from time to time. For nineteen years he had tried to make his mother and his wife see that they wanted the same things in life. He wanted to share a happy family life with them both, and here was an article, a piece of paper that had done what he could never do.

"I'll be damned," he muttered to himself, shaking his head.

He held the article in his hands and glanced through it. This was silly. No one could do this sort of thing. He had heard the television commercials for the 1-900 telephone lines and always thought those people were nuts and so was anyone who put faith in that sort of thing. Besides, isn't this stuff of the devil? He looked at Claire, and the look on her face told him that she wanted some kind of statement from him. He stood up and threw the paper on the coffee table.

"This is sacrilegious," he said, "and I'm not gonna have any part of it."

Claire grabbed the paper and pointed to it. "Tony, listen to me. This woman has been on talk shows, and she's on the Internet."

"Oh, I see, that makes her honest and the real thing, right?"

"No," she said, "but she has helped hundreds of people. Come look at this with me, over here on the computer."

She pointed to the place where she had spent the better part of two hours before he had come home. Tony looked at it, almost afraid to go near it. Hell, he thought, it's not a monster. She pulled him again by the hand and he let her. This was becoming a habit with them, he thought for a second, her guiding him through life. She pulled out the chair she had been sitting in just a short time before and pushed him into it. She bent over him and stared clicking the mouse. He couldn't follow the cursor on the screen, and the blur it made as images whizzed past made him dizzy.

All of a sudden she stopped and said, "There."

"Where?" he asked laughing.

She didn't think he was funny and pointedly told him so.

Pointing to the screen she said, "Read!"

He knew he didn't want to risk the wrath of this woman who was trying to make a point. The one thing his daddy had told him never to do was to poke fun at a woman on a mission. Boy, he had said, if you want to grow to a ripe old age, just do as they tell you and won't nobody get shot, mainly you. Tony had chuckled at his father's words.

So he looked at the screen, and there before him was a pretty young woman with dark hair and bright green eyes. She looked normal enough, no beads around her neck and no scarf tied around her head. No crystal ball that he could see. He was instantly intrigued. He started to read the biography before him. When he finished, he looked up at his wife and wondered when she had gotten into this. He'd always known she was smart, a hell of a lot smarter than he, but the way she handled the computer was almost better than how she handled him and that was quite a compliment.

Now before him on the computer screen was someone who might be the answer to his problem. The woman looked normal, sitting with hands folded beneath her chin, smiling for the camera. He wondered who had been sitting next to her and had been cropped from the photo.

If this was for real, and he was not all that sure it was, there were some very famous people in this woman's past. She took clients, only by referral, and she never did psychic shows or anything like that. He wondered just how far she would be willing to go to prove herself. Could she stand up to some scrutiny and would she be willing to? Because he was gonna check her out and if she was a fraud, his investigation ought to bring it out. If not, well, then he would apologize to her and hope that she would still be willing to help.

But first things first. He was going back to the station to make some calls. Surely if she was all she said she was, someone in law enforcement knew her, or at the very least knew about her.

He stood up with a look that Claire knew. He was on a mission and may not make it home tonight until way past the kids' bedtime, and hers for that matter.

"Kiss the kids," she said as she handed him a sandwich wrapped in a paper towel.

He turned and with a sheepish look on his face headed back in her direction and took her in his free arm, kissing her like he hadn't in years.

"Wait up for me," he whispered huskily in her ear and snuggled into her neck.

She giggled, knowing that when he finally came home, she would have been asleep for hours. No matter, he always woke her up to tell her about his day. Tonight she would be ready for him.

Tony left again with the first smile on his face in days, maybe even weeks. He counted back on his fingers; nope, days still. His children played outside, Becky with her army of brothers ready to defend her if the nutcase came their way. He pondered the perfect picture they made. How had he been so blessed? God only knew.

CHAPTER 10
Tony's next few hours were spent researching.

He read materials at the library and had his secretary, Paula, who was also a dispatcher, look some things up for him on the Internet. She gave him a funny look when he had her enter some words to search but he offered no information. The look on his face told her now was not the time to pry. He spent a weary five hours digging for information and then called it a day.

As he left the library that evening, he drove around the streets of his town. It all felt normal to him on the surface. He couldn't understand how something so bad had not affected things. He drove up and down the familiar streets just as he did most evenings before he went home. He was dedicated to this place, his roots were here. It was complacency, he realized, that made one insensitive to the slight changes in the air. For far too long this town had had good luck. There had been no killings, no robberies, no rapes, and certainly no kidnappings. He felt the differences now, now that he knew what could happen.

He turned his cruiser down the Andersons' street. He slowed as he approached the big house that had so much anguish in it that pain seemed to radiate from its wooden frame. Pulling over to the curb, he stepped out and pulled the handle on the mailbox. What he found was just what he thought he would find—nothing. He looked at the house and could see Janet in the window, rocking in her favorite chair. It made the hair on the back of his neck stand up. He waved and tried to smile as he got back in the car. Janet had sat forward for a moment, but as Tony got back into his car and drove away she let her feet resume the only motion that gave her any comfort. In her arms was a small rag doll wrapped in a pink sweater, which she held close to her breast. Tears slipped down her face and still she rocked.

Tony made his way home. Too sad and too weary to do anything else he fell asleep in his uniform on the living room sofa.

CHAPTER 11

Two more days passed and still nothing, no sign of the girl, no ransom note, no clues—nothing but frustration.

Tony had finally made a call to the FBI, and they were sending someone. To be honest he needed their help, even though he hated to admit it. They knew this stuff, and they had the manpower. Maybe it was better to defer to the pros. But Tony felt disappointed that he couldn't bring Marcie home. After all, the Andersons were his friends; his family sat next to them in church most Sundays. And he felt frustrated. Having the FBI agents would cause utter chaos and he hated chaos. He liked order and simplicity. He liked being in control.

Late into the night, Tony sat in his favorite chair parked in front of the TV. He watched the sun start to rise and listened to the high-pitched sound as the station left the air and he felt miserable. Tomorrow was another day. The days seemed to drag by since frustration and anger filled them, but mundane things continued on too and that made them go by fast. The "no news" factor was a pain in the butt. He had said it too many times lately. "Sorry, no news" was becoming something he said even in his sleep. Around 5:00 in the morning he found his way to bed. Climbing in next to Claire, he pulled her body up against him.

CHAPTER 12

The next morning, sure as spring rain, the phone rang.

Tony made a grab for the phone from the bed and pulled the receiver under the covers in time to hear Paula holler at someone in the background about not putting something somewhere as he said hello into the phone.

"Hello," he said again. He heard nothing but background noise.

"Hello," Tony yelled a third time into the phone.

"Oh sorry, sir. I hate to wake you up, but we need you down here right away."

"Why?" he asked indignantly pulling the covers over his bare bottom.

"Sir, there are men here and they are putting stuff everywhere. They say they are from the FBI and that you called and requested immediate help."

Tony groaned and nodded his head. *What good does that do? She can't hear my head rattle, but if she could . . .*

"Be right there," he said.

"What?" Paula hollered into the phone.

Tony hollered back, "I said I'll be right there," as he slammed the phone down.

Claire rolled to her side. "What's up?"

"FBI all over my office," he said. "I have to go."

"Is this about Marcie?"

"Yeah."

Tony showered and dressed in record time. As he made it downstairs, he looked around at his family as Claire handed him the first of many cups of coffee he would consume today. Kissing her briefly, he touched each of the heads of his kids.

"Mike," he said as he headed out the door, "hang out close to home today, okay?"

"Sure, Dad."

Fucking guy comes into town and takes somebody else's kid and I have to give up mine and they have to give up their free time. This sucks. He was pissed off too early in the day. This was gonna be a bad day.

These thoughts, and knowing that the FBI was invading his office, put him in a foul mood. By the time he reached his office, he was steamed. Walking through the door, he simmered on low burn, the steam rapidly rising. Who did these guys think they were? He was ready to lash out at them.

As he cleared the front desk, a man in a suit came from behind it and held out his hand. Tony looked at it and then slowly took it in his own as he shifted his coffee cup.

"Captain Tony Miller," he introduced himself to the young man. "I run the show around here. What, may I ask, are you doing behind this desk?"

"John Hanks, FBI," the agent responded. "Sorry to barge in on you like this, Tony, but we have been sent here to help. I hope we can work together."

Yeah right. From the look of things at this moment, you guys have succeeded in fucking things up as bad as a can of worms. Tony nodded at the room around him with a questioning look in his eye that seemed to mingle with the anger that was still apparent.

"It's Captain Miller to you, kid. Is this your idea of help?" Tony asked abrasively as he looked around the room.

"No, sir," Hanks said as Tony surveyed the room once again, "but we had no idea where to put this stuff. It seemed to me that no one here knew we were coming. Were you aware of it, Captain?"

"Yeah, I knew you were coming, I just didn't know it would be today. *You* can take this stuff out to the garbage for all I care, or back wherever it came from. I requested help, not all this *stuff*, and while I will admit that we do need help here because we are out of our league, I do not want all this stuff cluttering up my station house."

"Sir, this is very high-tech equipment and it will be valuable in finding Marcie Anderson, if it isn't too late."

Tony glared at Hanks. "It isn't too late, and don't you forget it! You got that?"

"Yes, sir!" Hanks stammered.

"Just what is this stuff?"

John Hanks was young and excited, and he knew he was walking a fine line with this hard-nosed cop who seemed to be having a bad day. He busied himself showing Tony what the instruments did and how they would, or could, help in finding Marcie. Tony walked with him quietly for the tour but John could see that the chief was taking it all in. The agent tried hard to make it clear that he was here to help and that this stuff was here to help him do just that.

Finally, Tony stopped the tour with a single hand held up in a "stop" position.

"Hanks," he said, his voice gradually getting so loud he could be heard over the noise of the already confused station, "this is real nice *stuff* you got here. I'm real willing to have some help on this one since we have never been through this before, and we hope to hell never to go through it again. I will extend my help and my men and even my dispatcher, but I will not, do you hear me, I will not, share my office!" he boomed. "Do you understand me?"

"Yes, sir," Hanks said, taking a few steps back and shaking his head in affirmation.

"Good!" Tony shouted. With that he walked past Hanks into his office and slammed the door.

The entire room was quiet. You could have heard a pin drop.

"Well, gentlemen, I tried to tell you," Paula said.

Hanks looked at her. "You also said he was a nice guy."

"He is. Give him a minute and he'll come back out here and apologize."

Sure enough, Tony opened the door. Sheepishly he said, "Hanks, I'm sorry," and then he closed the door again. The room was filled with quiet, smiling faces.

"See, I told ya," Paula said.

Hanks nodded and smiled too, feeling for the first time in twelve hours that this was going to be okay, no matter what happened.

Tony sat at his desk feeling like a jerk. Hanks looked like just a kid and he was probably scared to death. *Shows you how much the fucking outsiders cared about Marcie. Hell, they didn't even send someone with experience. They sent me a pup wet behind the ears.* He was gonna call someone, that's what he was gonna do. He picked up the phone and dialed a number. The voice on the other end said, "Good morning, Federal Bureau of Investigation, may I help you?"

Tony hung up the phone. *Shit! Give the kid a chance. Let's see what he can do.* Tony stood and walked around the desk. Pulling open the door, he growled out Hanks name. The kid turned to look at him.

"Yes, sir," he said.

"We'll talk in a bit," Tony said, and shut the door a little more gently, but still with an authority that said "do not enter." He felt like a jerk, and he wanted a cup of coffee. Reaching for the phone, he dialed the desk.

"Paula, bring me a cup of coffee and a new attitude, will ya?"

"Yes, sir," she said with a smile in her voice.

Paula walked into Tony's office a minute later with a cup of strong black coffee, just the way he liked it, in her left hand and one for her in her right hand. Tony saw it instantly, and he knew what was coming.

"Okay, let's have it."

Launching right into it like he knew she was going to, whether he wanted her to or not, she said, "Tony, we've been together through thick and thin, and you know I don't ever butt into your business."

"No," Tony said sarcastically, "not you, Paula."

She smiled, knowing full well that she did, but she always started these little pep talks like this. "We need help here, this guy is real smart, and he's cute too. Did you get a look at those cheeks?"

"No," Tony said, knowing darn well that she meant the cheeks that were located at the southern end of his body. "That's your job, Paula."

"Yes, you're right, but they're so cute I thought that you might have noticed for me," Paula said in her usual ninety-to-nothing rate of speech.

He smiled for the first time that day. "You're right, Paula, we do need sweet cheeks around here to help. He kinda dresses up the place."

"Where should I put him, sir?"

"Put him in the storeroom," he said dryly.

"Tony!" she said with a threatening tone to her voice.

"Oh shit. Okay, put him in the office next door."

"Good, I already have."

He looked at her with a knowing glance. That's what he figured; she ran this place no matter what anyone thought, even him. She stood up to go.

"But tell him to be quiet."

"Yes, sir."

"Paula," Tony said, as she headed toward the door. She turned to look back at him.

"Yes, sir?"

"Thanks for the attitude adjustment," he smiled, the second one of the day.

She nodded. "Anytime sir, anytime."

"Now send Hanks in here."

"Yes, sir," she said again as she closed the door.

Hanks must have been outside the door waiting, because as Paula closed it, he walked in. "You wanted to see me, sir?"

Tony pointed to the empty chair. "Have a seat."

Watching Hanks take the chair vacated by Paula, Tony said, "I'm sorry about this morning, you just caught me unaware. I knew you would be coming, but to tell you the truth, I expected someone older, someone with more experience."

"Sir, I graduated at the top of my class, and I have had some experience. I've worked more then twelve abductions and over one hundred missing persons."

"Well, good for you," Tony said. "You're about one hundred and eleven up on me cause this is my first one, and I hope my last."

John knew how Tony felt. He felt the same way every time there was a new one, another child taken. He nodded at Tony. "Sir, with your permission I'd like to help."

"Thanks."

For the next two hours, Tony and John talked about the day that Marcie Anderson had been kidnapped. Notes, reports, and evidence that had been taken at the scene were gone over again and again. People were discussed, even scrutinized. Finally they were done. John stood and shook Tony's hand. "Thank you, sir."

"John, dispense with the sir, please, it makes me feel old."

"Yes, sir, I mean, sure thing, and Tony, by the way, did you realize that

Paula runs things around here?" John said pointing with his thumb to the outer office.

"Yeah, I did, a long time ago," Tony said with a smile on his face and one in his voice.

With the information that Tony had provided, John went to his new office with an eerie feeling in the pit of his stomach and the story still fresh in his mind. Something about it bothered him more than just the usual kidnapping, if one could ever be considered usual.

That day was a flurry of activity unlike anything this small town had ever seen. Plaster casts of footprints were made at the Andersons', under the big tree, just inside the gate, where the man who had taken Marcie had stood. Even though they were a week old, they were still in amazingly good condition, since the area had been roped off and no one had been allowed to go near the spot. DNA samples were taken from the tissue and the surrounding area, and more people were questioned. No one had seen a thing, and by the end of the day, John felt as bad as Tony did. He had met new people, some would be friends and some he didn't think highly of, and still others he would forever be in awe of. How did they learn so much and where in your head did anyone store all that information?

He had been chauffeured all over town and then told that he needed to find his own way. He'd even been spit at. Well, not really; someone had been dippin snuff and his foot had gotten in the way. At the end of his first day, John sat at his desk and literally shook from exhaustion. He really wanted to show Tony what he could do. So far it hadn't been much, but this was only his first day.

He ordered more phone equipment and special cameras for watching the house, even during the night. It was a known fact that most kidnappers who didn't demand a ransom hung around watching the house of the victim to see what kind of havoc they were wreaking on the lives of its inhabitants. All of this was taking a good deal of time to set up and get in motion, and he was beginning to get discouraged.

A knock on his door brought him around and out of his mental wandering. Looking up, he saw Tony standing outside the door watching him. He waved him into the room and gestured toward a chair.

Tony came in and slid into the offered chair. He looked tired too.

"Anything?" he asked.

"No, not a damn thing. This guy leaves no signs other than the ones that we have found already. If he has any priors, I can't find them. He walks into a town this size and takes a kid. Then he disappears as if he had never been here. I want to know why he took her."

"Do you? Do you really?" Tony asked.

John looked at him with a level stare and then shook his head in the negative. "No, I just want to catch this bastard and hang him by the balls."

"Me too," Tony said as he stood and left the building.

This was the pattern for the week. Phone taps were set up. Pictures of the house were taken. And everyone who came and went anywhere around or near the Anderson house was interviewed. Mac's employer and the people he worked with were questioned. People from the church, even the pastor, were raked over the questioning coals. No one knew or had seen anything out of the ordinary or had any ideas about Marcie or the man who took her.

The fact was that she was gone. No ransom had been demanded. No one had contacted the family or the police and no one had a damn clue what to do next.

The week marched on slowly for everyone, especially the Andersons.

CHAPTER 13

Roman headed to the junkyard to feed his little pet and to see how she was faring after the day's strong heat.

Lately, she had been sullen and despondent, crying for her mother and father all the time. He was tired of it. She no longer smelled good, and she would not eat what he brought her. At home, she recoiled from him when he came near, so he had brought her here to teach her a lesson. If she was going to act like a junkyard dog, he would treat her like one.

Walking through town, he felt a sense of elation because he had a plan. He knew what he would do to make her happy again—he would get her a pet. It had been his plan all along anyway to do that eventually. He had really wanted more time alone with her, but if this was the only way to make her happy, well, then he would get her one that she knew and liked, and he had that pet all picked out.

When Marcie first came to him, she wasn't always afraid. When she awakened, she would cry a bit, but that was because he was new to her. Finally, with a little coaxing, she had come around. He told her that her mom and dad had sold her to him, and that was why he had taken her. He promised to take good care of her and to rock her to sleep every night, just like her mommy did, and to kiss her too, just like daddy did, if she would be good.

Things had gone well for the first few days, but then one night as he was tucking Marcie into bed, he brushed her skin with his fingertips the best way he knew, and she got scared. Things went badly that night. He did not get to touch her and to powder her the way he wanted without her crying. Once she started crying, she wouldn't stop for hours. He hated that, so he hollered at her to stop. But she cringed away from him and cried harder, wailing that she needed her dolly and she wanted to go home.

He chased her across the bed and the room that night, into the farthest corner. She lashed out at him, biting and kicking. When she landed a strong blow to his groin, he doubled over in pain. Gosh, he thought, as he slapped her face, are girls born knowing to do that? She had to be taught right now never to do that again. The lesson she learned that night would stay with her forever; he was sure of it.

Marcie had never been hit before, not like that. Daddy had spanked her one time for throwing a glass of milk at Vance. He'd been teasing her with a noodle at the dinner table, so she threw milk at him, glass and all. She hit him too, and that made the fact that she was punished worth it. This was different though. She knew that Daddy loved her; he had cried at the spanking he gave her. But this man just stood there with a mean look on his face, then had jerked her roughly over his knee, pulled her pants down, and smacked her hard. The stinging slaps sounded loudly in the room. Marcie cried most of that night.

This was not at all what Roman had thought would happen when he took her. This was not the way he had worked it all out in his mind. He would try one more time tonight and see if she would be good. If so, then he did not need the other pet yet. This one would do fine for the time being.

He approached the junkyard from the back gate. As he fished the flashlight out of his pocket, he thought of Marcie. He walked with determination toward her tiny prison. There, far into a field of cars, back where the worst cars were kept, was his destination. Few people ever came back here, and he felt safe, like he was among his own kind—the rejects of life. He had been here many times before, trying to coax a stray kitten or two to come to him, but they never got close enough. They were born wild; that was something he understood. He too had been born wild, abandoned by his parents, just like cats abandon their young after a few weeks, when they are no longer cute and cuddly. His mother had left him and walked away, never looking back.

He had learned a lot from those cats, great lessons about life. They ate and drank what they needed, slept when they wanted, and appeared to have no need for most people. That was the best way to keep from being hurt.

About a hundred feet into the yard, he stopped before an old abandoned Mercedes with the interior still in pretty good shape, save for the rain damage. Most of the parts were missing since people had come when it was still in the front and taken what they needed, leaving the rest. The owner of the yard had hauled it back here to be forgotten. Just like he was forgotten. He had always wanted a Mercedes, and now he had one.

Roman lifted the trunk lid cautiously, and there lay little Marcie Anderson. He realized that he had been holding his breath, and he let it out.

Marcie whimpered, just a little, at the sound of his approach and bit down hard on her lower lip. She had promised herself that she would eat anything he brought this time. She wanted to go home, she wanted to play with her friends. She did not want this man to touch her again, but she had no idea how to keep from crying when he was near her. She knew, though, that she had to try because he had taught her what he would do if she did. There was a bruise on her cheek still, evidence of his lessons. As he lifted the trunk lid, she tried to smile at him, her little mind racing ahead to what he might want her to do. What would keep him from being mean to her again?

Roman had been afraid she was gone, either found or escaped.

Although he thought he had scared her too badly for her to try to escape. He had tried to scare her enough before he left but he wondered about the power of fear sometimes. The trunk had been tied so that it could be left open just a bit. The back seat of the car was missing and there was some air for Marcie, but the seat brackets had kept her from escape. Marcie could have tried, but Roman had scared her so much she never thought to test him. She had stayed in the trunk all day, in the heat with only that little breeze, and watched the cat playing and the dirt blowing around, but she never left the trunk. He scared her and she knew that he could be mean if she pushed him.

He stood there with a flashlight in his hands, looking at her. When he saw her smile, he beamed.

That was it, she thought, smile. Smile like you are smiling for the camera. She'd had her picture taken one time when she had not felt good, and try as she might, she just hadn't been able to smile. So Mommy, standing off to the side, had told her to smile like she was eating chocolate cake. Marcie had broken into a big grin and the lady had taken her picture; it was the best one she had ever had taken.

Marcie smiled again at the man and lifted her arms to be picked up, hoping he would not hurt her. She was trembling and wet with sweat.

This was better, he thought, she almost seemed happy to see him. He reached forward to touch her and realized that he needed to give her a bath. She was dirty, and she didn't smell good anymore. He stroked her cheek, and she shivered just a little. That was the plan: bath, food, and a good night's sleep in a soft bed, and the pet would be better and would welcome his touch. He gathered her up in his arms, and she let him, as he carried her back to his house just beyond the yard. He liked the way she felt in his arms, the little bottom pressing against his forearm and the weight of her resting against his chest. He could feel the desire building in him, but he needed to do things first. Desire was for later, after he put her to bed.

He walked with her for a time. He barely felt the weight of her even though she was a good fifty pounds. She seemed smaller to him lately, and he wondered about that. As they crossed the field to his home, he whistled to her a happy tune that he knew she recognized. *Skip, skip, skip to my Lou, skip to my Lou, my darling.* She just let her head fall and drifted off to sleep, letting the night breeze caress her and enjoying the air that swirled around. She never wanted to go back in the trunk again.

He carried her into the house, leaving the lights off, and set her down. She cried out in the dark, clawing frantically for him, and he reached to pick her up, feeling her fear of the dark. She let him, because her fear of the dark was worse than her fear of him. He loved the fact that when she was scared she reached for him. That was the way, he realized, to get her to come to him, keep her scared. A plan was forming in his mind, but there were still things he needed to do tonight.

He crossed the room to open the door to the bathroom and switched on the light. Setting her down on the toilet seat, he ran her bath, and somehow, the whole thing seemed so normal—like a father running his daughter's bath. Roman added bubble bath that was pink and pretty and smelled like magnolia blossoms. The label on the bottle said so. For Roman, it was the scent that sent him flying, up, up, and away.

Marcie sat there looking at her feet. She wanted her mommy and daddy. She didn't want this man to touch her again. She wanted to go home and wanted her daddy to beat this man up. When she got home, she would ask him to. She punched one small fist into her other hand and viciously kicked her feet as the tears started to fall down her cheeks. Roman mistook her tears for fear of the dark, and he gently touched her little cheek, saying soothingly, "I'm here, Marcie. I'll take good care of you. You won't ever have to do anything that you don't want to ever again."

She sat there and let the tears fall. As the bath ran, he talked of his childhood and tried to get her to tell him about school and her friends.

Roman Marsh had been raised in an orphanage that had a philosophy about raising children that he had not agreed with. No pretty families came to take him home. The ones that did come, Roman didn't like. He did not want to do things like brush his teeth or wash his hands until he was ready. His nightmares were of spankings and threats, of church, and the Blessed Be that would punish you if you didn't say your prayers and do as your parents told you. He would holler at his foster parents, whoever they were at the time, that they were not, in fact, his parents. He had been passed from foster home to foster home. Then, when he was nine years old, he met Reese.

"What's a foster home?" Marcie interrupted.

Roman's face clouded over, and he gritted his teeth. "It is a store where kids are kept till somebody wants one. A bad place with no love, not like I love you," he said as he stroked her cheek.

Marcie instinctively jerked back. Roman grabbed her arm hard, and she winced in pain.

"I'm saving you from the foster home," he continued, "from being beaten up everyday because you ain't their real kid. You're different and they don't never want you to forget it. I ain't gonna force you to eat food that you don't like, like they did me. I didn't get no cake, no candy, and no soda pop. Where people, bad men, touch you bad. Where me and Reese were touched till we fixed that asshole. I don't want anyone to touch you that way."

Roman was shaking in anger as he ranted and raved. He could see that he was making Marcie scared of him again so he took a deep breath and tried to calm down. Still, he wanted to share himself with her, so he told her that he grew up near here with his foster mom and dad, after his real folks had given him away when he was a young boy. He knew they did this because he had smelled bad. Roman told Marcie about the many times he had been called a bad seed and told that was why his parents had left him.

He mimicked the voice that taunted him. "You're a bad seed, Roman Marsh, just a bad, bad seed."

Marcie felt sorry for him because he looked so unhappy. She bet he missed his mommy and daddy, just like she did. Maybe they were two of a kind, no mommy or daddy that wanted them. *Mine sold me, and yours just gave you away.* She touched his shoulder gently with her tiny little hand. She felt sorry for him now, wanting him to get that mean look off his face. That snarl always scared her and it made her jaw hurt when he gritted his teeth like that. He looked up at her touch and smiled. This is the way. Be nice to him and he will be nice to you.

"Didn't you have any friends?" she asked him.

"Friends," he said, "no, no friends. Only Reese."

"Who is Reese?" Marcie asked in her little girl voice.

"Reese is my brother. In foster homes you have lots of half brothers and sisters but that don't mean nothing. He was mean. He had to go away. He did some mean things and I had to make him go away. I put him in the 'Behave Yourself Hole," Roman was speaking but it seemed more like he was talking to himself rather than to Marcie.

"Tell me about your friends, Marcie," he asked, more to get her to talk than for any real desire to hear about them.

Marcie told him all about Penny and Ashley. They were her best friends. They played hopscotch and jump rope and they always stuck up for one another against Amy Jo, who was mean to them all the time. They loved to play with their Barbie dolls most of all. They had pretended just the other day that Barbie was getting married, because Ashley's mom had gotten a new wedding dress for her Barbie. Marcie wanted one too, but her mom said she had to wait until her birthday.

Roman watched the animation in her pretty little face as she talked. He was fascinated by the twisting of her little fingers as she carried on her one-way conversation, all the while keeping his body under control, trying to hide his erection. He loved the sound of her voice. Its sing-song was like the tinkling of a sweet bell. He drifted off to another time, long ago, when another voice had sounded like that as he placed tape across her mouth and left her tied to the washbasin in the train station. Where was she now? He still had her hair in the keepsake box under the bed.

He shook himself again. He needed to stay in the present. *Friends* had been the word, and he needed to remember it to keep her talking to him, so that he could be happy.

Marcie was crying again, he realized when his mind came back to her. Losing track of his thoughts made their progress backslide, just like a forgetting Christian. He knew that backsliding was wrong. *Can't let wrong happen again.* He looked at her with a start and wiped her eyes.

"Friends," he said quickly, nodding his head.

At that she looked up. Friends had been the key word, and he saw that in her eyes. She needed a friend, and that was what he was going to get her. His pulse quickened and he let the plan take shape in his mind again. He told her that her little friend from down the street would come over to play in a day or so, if she was good. She smiled at him, and this was an honest smile. She was happy and began telling him about all the good times she, Ashley, and Penny had.

"Like the time," she started, "that Penny ate all the malted milk balls in the carton. We knew she was gonna get it. We tried to think of a way out. Her mom was gonna be mad at her, she just knew it. Penny and me sneaked away to the corner store. It was only five blocks away. We took a box of malted milk balls and left a note. The store manager called our mommies, and we both got in trouble. We laughed about it later, but that day it wasn't funny at all."

She was laughing, and doubling over with joy at the memory of it.

Roman was enchanted with her. He thought, *This is why I have her, to help me create a life where things are sweet all the time.*

She continued. "Then there was that time Penny and I tried to get a kitty. We wanted to keep it to share in the clubhouse we made from a box my daddy gave us. It was supposed to be a secret, but my brother Vance told my mom and she came to see the kitty. She said it was dirty but that we could keep it outside and that she would help us feed it. The kitty lived there with us for a long, long time and my mom and Penny's had to buy food for it. Penny is always thinking up fun things to do to make people smile. She makes me happy. I bet she could even make you happy too," Marcie said.

That innocent tale sealed Penny's fate.

CHAPTER 14

So Roman Marsh decided to take Penny as a pet for Marcie.

He would do anything for Marcie—but for now, a bath and powder. She let him take her clothes off, and he closed his eyes so as not to see her naked. He was gaining her trust and he wanted to keep it.

She liked that and felt better. Maybe this was not so bad after all.

Roman put her soft warm little body in the tub. She played with the tub toys. The little rubber duck and the sponge were almost like ones she had at home, and just for a minute she wanted to cry again. Marcie was so sweet, Roman thought, so sweet and pure. His heart was so full of love for her. Finally he had love, real true love. His thoughts were running away with him to a dangerous place. He tried to pull himself together, with his hand over the erection growing stronger inside his jeans. He was breathing heavy, like he had been running, and he wanted to be as far away from her at this moment as he could.

He would not touch her like that. He had been touched like that as a little boy, touched by Reese and touched by his foster dad. He knew it hurt. He would not hurt his pet. It was different when she was asleep, but when she was awake, it was wrong. He steeled himself and bathed her roughly, making her cry out a time or two. He could see the look of confusion on her face. He knew she was wondering what she had done to make him act so rough, but he couldn't help himself.

She didn't want her hair washed, but he dumped a bucket of water on her head till she choked and gagged in the rain of it. He lathered her head, and then the water again. This time, she was crying. Her tears angered him. Didn't she know what he was holding himself from, saving her from? Didn't she realize how much that would hurt him if he had to do that to her? No! He would not do that. No matter what, he would not. He lifted her out of the tub and began drying off a crying Marcie with the soft towel.

As he did, his mind went back to his childhood and the man who had taken it from him. His foster father had bathed him, and Reese too, and they both saw the look come into his eyes when they were little. Roman had been ten, insisting that he could bathe himself. He had been nearly drowned by that man, and then carried into the bedroom and thrown on the bed. His bottom had been forced in the air and slathered with Vaseline for the assault that he would never forget or heal from. All the while Reese, who was thirteen and powerless to help, had looked on.

Marcie cried out, and Roman realized he had rubbed her skin almost raw. It had the look of a raspberry. He shook himself and gathered her up in his arms, carrying her again to the toilet seat. Letting her stand on top, sniffling and confused, he let the towel fall to the floor as he shook baby powder all over her. He let her rub it in, while he walked away.

She wanted her clothes and her soft jammies, the ones Grandma made especially for her. She couldn't understand why her mommy and daddy gave her to this man, but she felt sure that they would have given him her clothes too. They didn't have anyone else to give them to unless they got a different little girl. Maybe one that didn't cry when she got her hair done. Marcie made a promise to herself that, if she ever got away from this man, she would promise her mommy and daddy she would behave if they would let her come back home.

Roman threw her one of his tee shirts, explaining that it was just until he had clothes for her. Her mommy and daddy wanted to keep her clothes for the other little girl they would get to replace her. Roman knew they would replace her; they had always replaced him when he was little. Marcie's eyes welled up as her own worst fears were voiced out loud. Her heart hurt at those words. Roman told her he would wash her clothes out in the morning and let them dry. Did her mommy and daddy want another little girl? What did she do? Whatever it was, if someone would just tell her, she would tell Mommy and Daddy that she was sorry and never do it again, so that they would let her come back home.

Marcie followed Roman into the living area. Unsure of what to do, she just stood there with bare feet and wet tangled hair looking at him. Waiting for him to tell her what was allowed. He turned on the television softly.

"Sit there." He pointed at a mat on the floor.

Marcie thought it looked like Rusty's old mat. Rusty had been Daddy's dog that died last year. Daddy had said the dog died of old age and it was then that Marcie started to worry about Grandma. She was the oldest person Marcie knew.

Marcie sat on the floor watching the TV, while Roman put her dinner of sweet rolls and hard candy on a piece of paper. She ate and then drank water from a plastic cup. Marcie did not remember what she watched on TV that night, but she drifted off to sleep and dreamt of her daddy, crying out his name. In her dreams she ran to him and he scooped her up in his arms. He loved her still, and she was happy. A funny little smile crossed her face as she slept, and Roman was pleased at this as he watched her. Had he only known what her dreams were about, he would not have been so happy.

Roman scooped up a sleeping Marcie and put her in his bed and went back to the living room to fulfill his desire. The room was dark except for the light of the television set. His shirt clung to him, still damp from Marcie's little body after her bath. He tugged at the moist fabric but he never thought to take it off. He sat in his chair, forcing it into a reclined position, then let his memories travel back to the scent of her in the tub and the way her skin had felt. Standing up again, he turned off the television, walked to the bathroom, and retrieved the towel he had dried her with. Returning to the living room he let the desire roll through him. He sat up again, and then slowly and as quietly as possible he wandered to the door of the bedroom and listened to her breathing. She was sound asleep.

Standing at the foot of the bed, Roman watched her. He longed to sleep like that. He was almost jealous of her because she had the ability to sleep like an innocent baby. He had never been that innocent. Not even in his youth. He crossed the room to the side of the bed. Reaching forward, he touched her foot. The skin was so soft and her breathing so heavy that he let his hands give him pleasure.

He relieved himself of the tension that had been inside him since he had carried her from the trunk, since she had pressed her bottom on his forearm on purpose. She had wanted him to do it to her. He knew what little game she was playing. She was teasing him, teasing his body with her little innocent one. That word played over and over in his mind—innocent . . . innocent . . . innocent. What was it supposed to mean to him? He knew she was pure. She was so young, she had to be pure, unless her daddy did it to her. He needed to check, but she seemed so sweet and so demure. She looked down at the right time and up at the right time. She didn't know anything about the ways of life yet. No, he was pretty sure she was still pure. But if she wasn't, well then things between them were going to be different. That was for sure.

But she loved him, she trusted him—he just knew it. If she awoke one more time and caught him doing this to himself, she would be scared again, just like the last time, and he didn't want that to happen. Not now, when they were getting so close. She was at a crossroads with him, and he didn't want her to go back to the fear she had for him before. He also did not want her to leave him—ever, even when he decided to give her a choice, even though that was years away.

Marcie had awakened when Roman had picked her up and now she lay very still, trying to keep her breathing deep and even so he would think she was asleep. She remembered one time, on the way home from a party with her parents and brothers, when she was tired and wanted to be carried in. So she had pretended to be asleep, and her brother Colton had made fun of her, saying that she didn't sound like she was asleep. She had been breathing too hard, like she had run a marathon, so she knew what she had to do this time. She heard him at the foot of the bed. She didn't want him to touch her. She wanted to cry out, but she did not want to go back into the trunk for crying. So she lay there, breathing deeply, and pretended to be asleep.

He touched her leg, and she wanted to pull away from him. Why, oh why did her mommy and daddy give her to this awful man? What had she done? What was she going to do? She held her tongue between her teeth and cried inside. She wanted to go home. She even wanted her brothers. She missed her friends and her toys. Maybe if she was really good, he would take her to play with Penny or Ashley at their house and she could call her mom and dad and beg to come home. She heard him groaning at the foot of the bed, and she wondered what was wrong with him. He always did this when she was asleep. He seemed sick, but she didn't care. She hoped he would die. She would go to her grandma's house and live with her. That is what she would do, and she would never have to see this man or Mommy and Daddy again.

Grandma always wanted her. She had always called Marcie her precious little angel, and Marcie believed her.

At that thought, she started to cry. Roman thought she was having a bad dream and went to the side of the bed to comfort her, hurriedly buttoning his pants and stuffing the wet shirt inside them. Running his hands nervously up his chest and over his head, he then brushed the hair back from her face, which was buried in the pillow. She rolled further onto her side so he could not touch or see her. She was still asleep, or so he thought, lost in dreams.

"Shhhhh, little one," he cooed. "I will go get your friend Penny soon to play with you, and we'll all go and get you both some new clothes."

When she quieted, he thought she must love the sound of his voice just as he loved the sound of hers. But what she really loved was the idea of Penny coming to play. Penny always knew what to do. Marcie seemed to drift off to sleep, and Roman went outside for some night air and to catch his breath. This parenting was hard work.

Marcie lay there listening as Roman walked out the front door. Slowly, she lifted her head and listened.

"Mr. Man, are you there?" she called out.

She waited for an answer. Nothing came so she sat up just a bit more. The fear in her was real and the last thing she wanted to do was to have him in there with her again. Straining to hear, she leaned more toward the living room. Slowly she sat all the way up and peered around the doorway. She couldn't see him or hear him. She had heard the door close, but where was he? Marcie slowly slid from the bed and walked softly to the living room door. He wasn't there. She let out a loud sigh as she headed for the door.

"Maybe I can get to Grandma's house."

As Marcie reached out for the doorknob, she paused to listen again, her ear to the door. Withdrawing her hand she went to the window to see if he was just outside. She moved the curtain aside as carefully as she could and looked out into the night. Her eyes had already adjusted to the darkness, and with the light in the yard, she was able to see far into the yard but couldn't see anyone out there. Slowly she walked back to the front door and reached for the doorknob.

Immediately she jerked her hand back as pain bit her fingers. The jolt was sharp and severe. Marcie cried out and grabbed at her wounded hand with the other one. Tears poured down her face as she ran back to the bedroom, flung herself on the bed and cried until she finally fell into a troubled sleep.

CHAPTER 15

Tony drove through the streets of town as he usually did when he had a lot on his mind.

He thought of all the information he had gathered in the last few hours about psychics. After all the hours of reading he called a friend that he had gone to school with in New York. Talking to Marc had made Tony feel somewhat better, and then he wanted some air to get it straight in his mind. He couldn't go home just yet. He played the conversation with Marc over in his mind. Marc said his department used a clairvoyant a while back, and she had been good, really good.

"Let me check on this and I'll call you back."

"Yeah, make it quick okay?" Tony told him.

Tony had let the receiver fall gently back into the cradle. He thought about his conversation with Marc. It gave him a good feeling, a feeling of not being alone. Someone else in the same profession had been here before. Tony trusted Marc to do what he said he would. Tony needed a dictionary, he wanted to look up the word clairvoyant. What a word, what the hell was the definition of that word anyway?

Now Tony drove down the street that little Marcie had lived on. *Oh shit, I've got to stop saying that. Had. It's like she's dead or something, which she is not.* He tried to convince himself he believed she was still alive and unharmed. The truth was she had not been seen in nine days now, and this was taking way too long with no clues whatsoever. What was a detective supposed to think with no clues and no eyewitnesses? Nobody new in town, and no one remembers seeing someone drive out of town at 6:45 P.M. in the middle of the week. *Shit.* He wanted to believe that someone would come forward and say that they had seen something, anything. *Please God.* He pounded his fist against the dashboard of his new squad car.

"I feel so fucking helpless!" he said out loud. Lately Tony felt as if he was always waiting for something to happen.

When his radio crackled, the sound scared him out of his own thoughts. He heard his name come across it. He reached forward and grabbed the radio, feeling the tension and the butterflies in his stomach start to flutter about in a frenzy. Pressing the button, he said, "Captain Tony Miller here."

"Captain, you have a call from New York. Can I patch it through?"

Tony let the air he had been holding in his lungs out. "Sure." He heard Marc Holbarth on the other end and his body began to relax as he answered. "Hey, Marc! How are ya, did you find out anything?"

"She's for real, and she has worked for the FBI in Washington, New York, and California on several cases; she does this on a regular basis. The girl is the real thing, with a great success rate, all but one time."

"What happened that one time?" Tony wanted to know since his cop brain had to ask.

"Law enforcement screwed it up," he said. "They waited too long, the kid had been dead about three hours when they found her, and that sent the clair home on the run. She cried all the way to the airport. Hey, Tony, if they had gone where she said, when she said, they would have found the perp having his way with the kid, but she would have been alive—unless the wacko did the kid afterward. You never know in this business."

Tony shuddered at his colleague's brusqueness and tried to listen to what he was saying. *Shit, the city could make you hard. Thank God I live in a small town.*

Marc went on. "I feel like this clair is the real thing and might be just what you need."

"Marc, what's this 'clair' thing that you keep saying?"

"Oh, it's short for clairvoyant. That's what we call 'em and there is a difference between clairs and psychics, just so ya know."

"Yeah, what's the difference?" Tony asked.

"I'm not really sure, but bet your bottom dollar she can tell you."

"You ever meet her?"

"Yeah," Marc chuckled. "Nice tits, hourglass figure, the kind your wife won't want you to spend time with."

Tony chuckled. Same ol' Marc. "Really, Marc, did you meet her?"

"Yeah, I did, she seems real normal. No chanting or walking around talking to the air or shit like that. She just held things and talked to people and every now and then when someone wanted to test her and think a question to themselves she would look at them and say, 'I don't work that way.' Totally blew them away with that one. Hey Tony, remember Ron Gerald?"

"Yeah," Tony answered.

"Well, she nailed his affair and told him that his wife was going to catch him before she went home tonight. We all laughed and old Ron just stood there with his mouth hanging open. You see, his wife had been taking a class, so when she would have usually been at home, she was out that evening. He was getting together with his 'girlfriend' on those evenings. Well, we all just roared at that. He took off running for the parking lot as the phone rang. It was his wife and she was going to her mother's. You could have heard a pin drop in that room. It was totally cool. The old bastard, he deserved to get caught. He always thought he was better than everyone else. Turns out he was porking this girl over on 40th Street and she was married to a cop too. Small world, huh?"

"She knew all this?"

"Hell yeah! Man, she just stood there and looked at us then, and we all just hung our heads. She said, 'Now gentlemen, and I use the term loosely, can we get to work?' Well, none of us wanted her to look at us that closely, so we were sure ready to 'go to work,' as she put it."

"Did it work?"

"Well, we did just about everything she wanted. We drove her here and there and took her to meet the parents of this little girl. Not all that little, she was twelve, but small and petite. She was cute as a bug's ear. We met the teachers again and the friends who had seen her last, everyone who had anything to do with her at all, from the coaches to the pastor of her church.

"We knew she was on to something because the kidnapper started calling us at the station threatening her and stuff like that. Shit, she was never scared. She just kept pushing us to go to this field. We made plans to do that the next morning, but we got an anonymous tip about 5:00 A.M., saying the child had been seen being dragged into an abandoned warehouse on the south side. So, instead of doing what she wanted us to do, we played cops and robbers and stormed the warehouse. Nothing—not a damn thing.

"Across town in an apartment that this clair had seen in her mind was a child being murdered. She came unglued on the way there, and when we found the kid three hours later, she swore that she could hear the guy laughing and she ran home, almost literally. It was a bad scene. I hurt like hell that night. I was an awful lot greener than I am now, so I went out and I got stinking drunk. So, my friend, if you call her, know she is hard-nosed about finding dead kids. She won't pull any punches with you. She's gonna call it like she sees it. She's one tough bird."

Tony asked, "You know how to get in touch with her?"

"Yeah, I thought you might want that number."

Marc gave Tony the number and hung up, but not without saying, "Tony, good luck man. I know this sucks."

"Yeah, it sucks, Marc. Thanks a lot. I'll let you know what happens, and I'm sorry I had to call you so late."

CHAPTER 16
Tony hung up and let Marc's words sink in.

A dead kid. Could his town take that? He had no idea, and didn't want to find out. He headed home, down Main Avenue, letting his mind wander. When he came to a stop sign, there before him was Mac Anderson, staggering as if he were drunk.

"Damn," Tony said to himself.

He was not sure he could handle this right now. As much as he wanted a break from this for a while, it was clear he wasn't going to get one. Tony turned on his flashing lights and pulled up to Mac.

"It's two in the morning, Mac. What are you doing out here?"

Mac was crying. He let the weight of his body lean against the squad car. Tony felt it shift when he did. Mac looked terrible.

"Tony, what are we going to do? Where is my baby?" The sound of his voice was so pitiful it made Tony's heart hurt.

Mac's anguish washed over them both. Tony leaned across the seat and pushed open the passenger side door. "Get in, Mac," he said.

Both men wiped their eyes and ran their hands through their hair almost in unison. They couldn't have done it better if they had tried. Sniffling loudly, Mac climbed in. They sat for a moment in companionable silence.

Mac wanted Marcie back and Tony understood—completely. There were no promises Tony could offer that didn't sound hollow, even to his own ears. Mac looked at Tony as he pulled away from the curb. Then he cried, right out loud, sobbing out his pain as he leaned forward and let the dashboard take his weight. Tony drove, and Mac cried. There was nothing to say. What do you say to the father of a missing child? Finally, Mac's heart-wrenching sobs slowed enough for him to talk and he turned and looked at Tony again.

"I've been to the church. I couldn't think of anything else to do. Janet just sits in that chair, rocking back and forth, holding Marcie's sweater. I'm telling you, Tony, I'm ready to sell my soul to the devil himself, or anyone else for that matter, to get my little girl back. No ransom request, nothing at all from the man who took her. She's so sweet, so pure, you know, Ton?"

Tony could do nothing but nod.

"What are we going to get back? A body, a shell, what?"

Tony had no idea but these were things that he too wondered.

"Mac, have you ever heard of the police using psychics?"

Mac looked at him. Finally he replied, "Yes."

"Well, Mac, I've found one who's skilled in this sort of thing. To be honest with you we seem to need some help here. We have nothing to go on, no one has seen a damn thing. I've talked to everyone I can think of to talk to. I've wandered these streets and followed up on every single silly lead, in the hopes that one of them might pan out."

Mac let this sink in. The concentration clearly showed on his face. They drove in silence for a few blocks, until Tony pulled up in front of the Anderson home.

Mac turned to look Tony in the eye. "Just get her back for me, Tony. I don't care how you have to do it, just get her back."

With that, Mac got out of the car, closed the door, and headed toward the sidewalk where the girls had played just a week before. Remnants of chalk could still be seen on the surface. As he drove away, Tony watched him stagger up the stairs to his front porch, not from drink but fatigue and that feeling of being whipped. Tony headed around the corner toward his own home and the warmth of his wife's body. He had a chill that ran the length of his spine. He needed Claire and he hoped that she needed him. *God help me,* he prayed as he climbed the front porch stairs of his home just as Mac had done a few minutes earlier. *God help us all.*

Mac didn't need his key to get in. No one had bothered to lock up. Janet was still sitting in her rocker, just as she was when he left hours ago. She was asleep, with her head falling to the side. On her face he could see the traces of tears that had dried on her cheeks. Mac bent and lifted her gently into his arms. She was as light as a feather. She must not be eating anything, but he understood this. When was the last time he had eaten anything? He wondered about the boys—how were they faring? He would check on them after he tucked Janet in.

She moaned softly in his arms. "Mac?"

"Yeah, babe."

"You've been gone a long time. Are you okay?"

"I'm fine Jan, go back to sleep."

She rested her head back on his shoulder and drifted off to sleep again. He wondered just how many of those sedatives she had taken tonight. If that was the only way she could rest, then so be it. He didn't give a damn. He might take one himself tonight. He laid her down in the unmade bed and pulled the covers over her. She had not made beds or even dressed herself in days. She just sat and rocked in that damn chair. He was going to have to get some help in here tomorrow, somebody who wasn't so torn with pain that they couldn't function.

Turning off the light, he turned to look back at his wife. *How the hell had this happened?* Mac felt so sorry for her, sorry for them all. Janet had never, in twenty years, left the beds unmade. Even when their children were born, she had arranged for someone to come in each day and tidy up. Dinner had always been ready. She was the perfect wife and mother, this was the perfect home. Mac had always wondered how she did it. In fact, he was in awe of her most of the time.

Now he was afraid for her. He knew the pride she took in her house, and knew that the untidy atmosphere was a real symbol of her depression. No one from the outside world knew that, for most or her life, Janet Anderson had suffered from severe depression. That would not have been socially acceptable. She kept her secret well. But when Marcie was born, the depression had lifted and she'd smiled a lot more. He'd even heard her singing in the kitchen a few times. The house itself sang with the baby in it. Funny, he realized, they always called Marcie the baby, even after she no longer was. He headed slowly down the hallway toward the boys' rooms. Each step was a chore. This is a big damn house, he thought to himself.

When he peeked in Jayme's room, there on the floor asleep were Colton and Vance. Jayme lifted his head from the pillow and made a sudden move.

"Who's that? I have a gun!"

Sure enough, he did, pointed right at his father's chest. Mac felt fear run through his body.

"Jayme!" Mac said quickly. "It's me, Dad."

"Oh, Dad, I'm sorry. What are you doing?"

"Just getting home," Mac replied. "What the hell are you doing with a gun in your bed? Have you lost your mind? Give it to me!"

"I'm scared, Dad. I just need it to make me feel safe, like I can do some-thing if something else bad happens. It's not even loaded."

Jayme felt foolish sleeping with a gun that wasn't even loaded. But having it to use as a threat for an intruder did make him and his brothers feel better. He looked at his dad again and sat up on his elbow. "Mom needs you, Dad. You should try to be home more."

"I was here!" Mac caught his tone of voice. "Oh, Jayme, I'm sorry. I went to the church. I needed to pray and talk to Pastor Carl."

Jayme and Mac did not have an easy father-son relationship.

"I'm sorry too, Dad," Jayme said. "I just hurt so much."

Mac looked at the two little boys sleeping on the floor. "What are these two knuckle-heads doing in here?" He chuckled.

"They come in here every night now. They're scared too."

Mac just nodded. "Get some sleep, son." He turned to go.

"Dad," Jayme called out.

"Yeah, son."

"I love you."

Goose bumps rose on Mac's arms. "I love you too, Jayme."

Turning one more time, he closed the door softly and headed back downstairs. *A gun? Is that what this family had been reduced to by this fucking psychopath that took people's kids? It that what you called someone who did this sort of thing, a psychopath?* That was not what he was going to call him when they caught him, that was for sure. He was going to call him dead!

Mac sat at the kitchen table and ate some food he had scavenged from the refrigerator. He realized there really was not much left in the house to eat. He was going to have to get someone in here tomorrow, for sure. If he could just remember to get up and to breathe tomorrow that is. Lately those were the hardest things he had to do. Mac wandered to the sofa and lay down without taking his shoes off or cleaning the dishes off the table. *Shit sure has gone to hell in a hand basket.* Then sleep claimed him.

CHAPTER 17

Tony drove home in silence except for the dispatch radio that made an occasional crackling sound.

He welcomed the sight of his house. As he put his key in the lock, the loneliness of the night settled on his shoulders like a cloak. He wanted companionship. He wanted to see that his babies were all safe in their beds. His arms ached to hold those he loved, feeling the wave of desperation that came with that desire.

Desperation hurt. He hung his cop's hat on the hook in the hallway that was there just for him. He loved the way Claire made a home. She was always doing little things like that to let him know that he was the reason that this home existed.

He paused in the doorway between the front hall and the den. There standing before him was the most beautiful vision he had ever seen. The perfect image of woman, mother, and wife anyone had ever known. His wife, Claire, was offering him a drink in one hand, dinner on a tray, and a smile to warm his weary heart. She stood there in the soft light and Tony realized again that she was like tonic to his soul, but his stomach grumbled as the smell of the food met him, and he realized that he had not eaten a thing all day.

But food was gonna have to wait. He needed to hold her, and the picture she presented in her long black lace nightgown made his blood boil and his loins stir. How had she known he would need her so badly tonight?— Hell, it was almost three in the morning.

She always seemed to know. Like this afternoon, she had known he was coming home. How did she do that? He wanted to hold her so badly that he could barely move. The man in him needed her, the woman. The husband in him needed his wife, and all that she offered. She was a vision, and he almost didn't want to move so that he could store this moment in his memory for life. A beautiful woman of forty-two and the mother of four, she was graceful and elegant to him. Her body had taken pregnancy in stride and she had only become more striking with each child. His desire for her never failed.

He crossed the room and took her in his arms. She smelled of soap, water, and a light dusting of powder. He buried his face deep in her neck and stroked her hair. It was so soft, and he wondered what time she had gotten up to be here for him. She wrapped her arms around him and held him close.

"I'm not going to ask how your day was," she said. "I know how it went. I'm here now and if you will let me, just for a while, I'm going to take all your cares away. I'll give them back to you later to worry about but for now you need to just let me love you."

He couldn't argue with her, he didn't want to. He nodded. She led him to his favorite chair. Pushing him down, she knelt in front of him and took off his boots, one at a time. He watched her, amazed at what he saw in her. She was still in love with him after all these years. He reached his hands out for her and she gently held them in hers.

"Eat," she said, handing him the plate, warning him that it might be hot. He took it and to his amazement it was. She had gotten up and warmed him a plate; this woman, after twenty years of marriage, still catered to him. She handed him silverware, a napkin, and switched on the stereo. Leaving him to his dinner, she headed for the bathroom. Running the water in the tub and pouring in sea salts to relax him, she wondered what his day had been like. She knew that tomorrow he would tell her. This was the pattern when he was stressed, although she had never seen him this stressed. She laid out fresh towels and his robe that smelled of fabric softener.

Walking back into the living room, she saw he had wolfed down his food. He must have been hungry. Tomorrow she would address his eating habits, but not tonight. Tonight he needed love and understanding. Taking his hand, she coaxed him into the bathroom.

He stood there looking at her. As his hands went to the buttons on his shirt, she pushed them away. She unbuttoned his shirt and let it fall to the floor. His belt, pants, and socks followed. He stood there in his underwear looking at her.

They both grinned for the first time and he said. "Now what?"

Claire said, "Never mind that yet. Get in the tub."

"Yet," he said. "You mean as in right this minute or not at all tonight?"

She giggled and pulled his shorts down around his knees. He wagged Mr. Happy at her like a dog wagging his tail. She had named it that on their wedding night and somehow it had stuck. She broke into laughter and he joined her. It felt so good to laugh and to enjoy her company. She splashed water at him and he scooped her up and stepped into the tub. Her squeals could be heard throughout the house so he kissed her into silence.

Usually when they made love, she was a moaner, so he'd had to explain to his oldest son early on what was going on. They thought he was hurting her. That had been a day. The memory of it made him smile. Tonight he wanted her all to himself, even if more than three fourths of the night was gone. He would take what he could get. She squirmed in his arms. Wet and warm, she wiggled and giggled.

"Be still, woman," he said, "or this is gonna take us no time at all."

She sat still in his lap and felt the proof of his words. Had it been that long? She could not really recall the last time they had really made love. They had a thing they did every other night or so but lately there had been no time for true lovemaking.

She wrapped her arms around him and kissed his warm, soft lips. He deepened the kiss with passion. Taking the soap in her hands behind him she lathered him up while his kiss continued. He chuckled low in his throat.

"Afraid you're going to make love to a dirty man?" he asked.

"No, I just know that you need this. And my plan is to spoil you so that I can have a new dress that I saw yesterday."

"Buy it," he said.

They both laughed again because they knew a dress was not what she really wanted. What she really wanted was to ease his mind for a while. She washed him off as well as she could with him teasing and kissing her all over.

"Enough, woman," he growled.

Standing up with her in his arms, he stepped from the tub. Without drying off, he carried her to their room, and ever so gently, laid her on their bed. His lips never left her and his hands started that old familiar journey that took them both to readiness. She longed to feel that wave of sensation that came over her every time he took his time like this. He knew this woman and what she liked and tonight he was gonna do it all. His lips burned a trail down her stomach and his hands followed. He loved her with his body the best way he knew how. Twenty years of learning about her and he still longed to be the only love in her life. The only man who would or could bring her to such ecstasy. She cried out his name with release and he lost himself in it. His moment came right behind hers and he held her to him.

Breathing hard and sweating, he whispered, "I love you."

"I love you too," she said, her hands brushing the sweat from his face.

They clung to each other and drifted off to sleep.

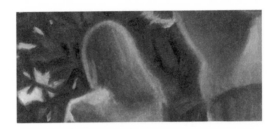

CHAPTER 18

Tony awoke the next morning with the feeling someone was watching him.

As his eyes tried to focus from the deep sleep, he caught a slight movement out of the corner of his left eye. He assessed the situation. His leg was thrown over Claire's leg and his entire hip and buttocks area was exposed. Not to mention anything even remotely attached to that area of his anatomy. He lifted his head to the sight of his youngest child poking her finger at him.

"What are you doing to Mommy?" Becky asked.

"Hmm" Claire murmured, starting to rouse too.

Becky sat on her daddy's side of the bed and asked another question. "Mommy, why are you sleeping on Daddy like that? You look like worms in the flower bed!"

Claire sat up with a start and grabbed for the covers. Tony's anatomy had been caught in a bad position, and he shrieked in pain and doubled over. Claire glanced at him in concern, and then realizing what had happened, she laughed. Becky was still expecting answers from her embarrassed parents as her father sat up and pointed to the door.

"Out," he said trying to hide his grin, "and next time KNOCK!"

Becky's lower lip started to tremble as she backed toward the door. "You hurt my feelings," she cried.

Claire gave Tony a look that quelled any morning plans he might have had. He lunged forward and scooped the precious child in his arms. She squealed with joy, as he tickled her and rolled her up in the bedclothes. Grunting and growling like a dog, he tumbled her all over the bed. Becky loved when her daddy did this and her squeals of laughter could be heard throughout the house.

Soon the bed was full of kids ranging from five to seventeen. Everyone was laughing for the sheer fun of it, and the picture they made belonged in a family magazine. Mike, the oldest, had realized immediately what was going on when he entered the room and saw his dad's bare bottom partially hidden under the sheets. He grabbed a giggling Becky and hoisted her up to his shoulders.

"Got caught, huh?" he winked as he went out the door. "Glad you got you a little, Dad. Maybe now you won't be such a grump."

Tony threw the pillow at him laughing. "Hey watch it, you're talking about my wife here."

"Yeah, well, she's my mother, and we're all starving. From the sound of things earlier this morning, even you two must have worked up a good appetite." He ducked again as the pillow whizzed by his head and, with Becky atop his broad shoulder, scooted out the door.

When Claire raised a hand to cover her mouth, the look on her face told Tony that she was embarrassed the kids had heard and seen so much. He laughed at her. Tackling her about the waist, he pulled her to him on the bed.

"He's a young man, Claire. Better he see it here than half the places I learned it." She batted at him with her free hand as the phone rang.

Claire answered it the gracious way she always did, in a voice saved just for that moment. "Good morning," she said sweet and softly as she made a move for her robe.

Tony grabbed the robe and stuffed it under the covers as the voice on the phone asked for Captain Tony Miller.

"He's right here, Paula," Claire said in her strongest southern drawl as she handed the phone to him and lunged for her robe. Tony stuffed it farther under the covers, tempting her to come back to bed to get it.

As Tony reached for the phone, Claire grabbed the covers and yanked them back, exposing both her naked husband and the robe. Finally, he surrendered it and took the phone.

"Tony here," he said.

"Captain?" Paula said into the receiver with a smile. Realizing she'd interrupted something from the sound of things at the other end, she held her hand over the mouthpiece and giggled.

"Yeah," her boss said, trying to sound gruff.

"We have a woman who insists on seeing you right away and she won't be put off. She says it's important, that she's been waiting for days for someone to call her back."

"What does she want?"

"She says she saw a man walking around the neighborhood the day the little Anderson girl was taken and that she's been calling all week and wants you there now. She sure sounds put out, sir."

"Get me her address and tell her I'll be there as soon as I can. If her calls have really been ignored, I hope whoever took those calls knows that his or her ass is seriously on the line. You make sure that message gets around the station house before I get there, okay, Paula?"

"Oh, I will sir. Believe me, I sure will," Paula answered.

He hung up without saying good-bye, throwing his legs over the bed and heading for the shower.

Afterward, when Tony reached the kitchen, the smells of breakfast and the sounds of his family tickled his senses. He loved this crew. Patting his wife on the fanny and kissing his kids good-bye, he grabbed a handful of bacon.

Stuffing it into his mouth he said, "I gotta go," and headed out the door.

In less than a minute his head appeared again around the corner of the crowded kitchen.

"Hey, Mike," he said, and was about to add more when his son interrupted.

"Yeah Dad, I know. Don't worry, I'll be around here all day."

The fun of the morning, the normalcy of it all was gone, and again there was a kidnapper in their midst. Tony nodded his head and disappeared. They all watched him go, wondering when he would be home again.

CHAPTER 19

When Tony arrived at the station ten minutes later, he walked in on a heated argument between his dispatcher and one of the patrol officers, Robby Henderson.

It seems the patrol officer had taken a call on Friday evening from a Rose Muella. She lived just two blocks from the Andersons and she'd been calling since the weekend. She had gone out of town on business the evening the kidnapping had taken place. She called as soon as she got home and read the local paper. Tony just glared at the two of them.

"Shit," he exclaimed, directing his question to the young cop. "Shit, shit, shit. What the hell were you thinking, or is thinking not something you're paid to do?"

"Sir," he said, "I took the call, but the woman was babbling all crazy and stuff, and I thought that she was confused or drunk or something. We've gotten a lot of those calls, and none have led anywhere. We've checked out over fifteen this week alone. That's a lot of wasted manpower if you ask me."

Tony stood there with his mouth hanging open.

"Oh well, damn it," he said. "Fifteen, you say. I just cannot believe all that work between ten officers and two dispatchers. Shit. No wonder you didn't get to check that out. But while we're on the subject, let me make this perfectly clear: I didn't ask for your opinion, and we check out everything, absolutely everything, do you hear me?" Tony was shouting by this time and the young cop took several steps back.

The young patrolman realized from the deadly look in Tony's eye that he was in trouble. Tony stepped forward and grabbed him by his shirt, lifting him almost off the floor.

"I have cried my eyes out and puked my guts up over this little girl. Last night I helped a friend of mine, her father, home because he was so distraught over the abduction of his little girl that he couldn' t make it alone, and you think it is too much trouble to check out one more call? Get your hat, buddy, we're going for a ride," he said as he shoved the young, scared officer from him.

All eyes in the station house were on them as Tony looked around.

"Get back to work," he shouted. Everyone instantly looked elsewhere, anywhere but in his direction. Some felt sorry for Robby and some felt that the rookie needed the lesson. Tony was a fair man but he didn't tolerate slackers or hotshots, and Robby acted like a hotshot most of the time. He would be a good cop in time, but to be a good cop you had to learn your lessons and this was a biggie. Most of them had been there with one captain or another. Many had been there with Tony Miller, whose philosophy was "Do your job, shut your mouth, and go that extra mile." They all knew it. There was no room here for glory-hound cops.

Tony headed for the door where Paula was waiting with a piece of paper in her hand. "Go easy on him, Tony, he's young," she said softly.

"He won't be after today," was all Tony said as he grabbed the paper from her outstretched hand and went through the door.

Robby was on his heels, scared to death. Paula gave him a look and smiled slightly. It was gonna be a red-letter day for this kid. He would either make it or he wouldn't and this was the day for that decision to be made.

CHAPTER 20

As Tony drove to the address on the paper Paula had handed him, he looked at it repeatedly as if it might disappear before his eyes.

His cop intuition told him this was something more than just a goofy call from a drunken woman. He glanced again at the rookie sitting next to him and for just a brief moment felt sorry for the young man. Tony was going to teach him a lesson and make sure that he got it right, so this never happened again. He had to learn that every call was important until you were sure it was not. Tony pulled the car up to the curb in front of a modest home just two blocks away from the Andersons. *Two blocks—damn, this was the closest lead they had gotten in the whole week.*

Rose Muella watched them from the window as the police car came to a stop. *About damn time.* She watched the two men get out and say something to each other. They shifted in their pants like men do and she grinned. *Well, that's better than doing the panty dig thing. I'm going to wait until they ring the bell and then I'll get up.*

Tony and Robby climbed the concrete steps of the porch, and Robby rang the bell. Standing there waiting, they both felt foolish, since they had seen her in the window watching them. *What was she trying to prove?* Tony began to wonder if this was going to really be anything. Rose opened the door and looked at the men before her. They looked at her, a pretty woman, thirty-eight years old, a divorced mother of two, the report had said. Her children were with their father for two weeks since she was traveling a great deal for work.

Pushing open the screen door, she said, somewhat frostily, "Come in."

As they entered, both assessed the room. Pretty, frilly, but clean with an orderly type of mess. Books everywhere and a computer turned on but with nothing more than the screen saver flashing. They slowly scanned the room.

"Everything in order, gentlemen?" she asked pointedly.

Both officers cleared their throats and paused.

"Ma'am," Tony broke the silence. "You called the station on Friday evening and said that you had seen a man in the neighborhood on Tuesday evening. Why did you wait so long to call?"

Although he knew the answer, this was his way of taking control of the situation. Rose impatiently told him she had already told his dispatcher that she had been out of town.

"And why did you take so long to respond?" she countered.

So much for control; no one was going to control this one.

"Yes, ma'am, I know you told her, but can you tell me?" He smiled at her and that seemed to help. She gestured toward the couch and they all sat down. Her living room was decorated in a flowery, colorful style that made it obvious that a man did not live here. There was no La-Z-Boy in the living room with a table nearby for that much needed beer at the end of the day. Both men felt a little uncomfortable on the feminine couch, but they shifted and waited for her to explain. Suddenly she stood up and offered them a drink.

Robby looked at Tony and smirked before saying, "No thanks."

"Do you mind if I do?"

Both men shook their heads no, then watched her walk into the kitchen and open the refrigerator door. Pouring herself some tea from a pitcher, she explained, "I've been suffering from a sore throat, and the medicines I've been taking have been drying me out."

Tony laughed out loud, and Robby looked down at his hands.

"What's so funny?" she asked.

Tony told her. "Young Robby here thought you were a drunk."

Robby sat embarrassed and felt the need to explain. "Your voice was so fuzzy the night that you called in that we didn't take you seriously."

"We have been bombarded with calls about this," Tony added apologizing.

Rose could have been offended but she wasn't. "I've been really busy with work and all and I couldn't take time off so I had to take the medicine. I guess it does make me sound funny."

She smiled as she sat down next to Tony on the couch.

"So what did you see, ma'am?" Tony asked as he nervously adjusted himself on the couch.

"Well," she said, "the dog next door keeps taking my paper, so I was out on the front porch waiting for the paper boy to bring me a replacement for the one I didn't get that morning. I wanted to read it on the plane that evening. I never used to call, but I was paying for the dog to chew it up so I decided what the heck. Anyway, this young man walks by and I really didn't pay much attention to him the first time except to think that he was oddly dressed for this day and age. The second and third time he went by, he seemed so distracted that I started to watch him. The fourth time he passed me I really started to worry that he was casing my house. You know, with traveling and all, lots can happen."

"Yes, ma'am," Tony agreed. "He walked around the block four times?"

"No, he would walk to the end of the street and look down that way and then he would sometimes head that way, but a couple of times he turned and came back by my house. His head was down and his hands were in his pockets the whole time. Once he caught me looking at him. He stared right up at me and you know it scared me. Something about him scared me. He seemed to have something heavy on his mind."

"What way?" Tony asked.

"What?" Rose said.

"You said he looked 'that way.' What way did he look?"

"Oh. He looked in the direction of the Andersons' house. You can almost see it from here. If you stand on the far outside edge of the curb, which is just what he did."

They both looked at her and there seemed to be a question in their eyes.

"Yes," she said without a question being posed. "I went to look and sure enough you can almost see the Anderson house from there."

"That is very thorough of you, Mrs. Muella," Tony said.

"Mrs. Muella is my ex-mother-in-law. Please call me Rose."

"Well, Rose, that is very thorough of you," Tony repeated.

She looked him straight in the eye and said, "I've had almost a week to be thorough, Captain."

"Point well taken. What did he look like?" Tony asked.

Her memory was amazing. Her attention to detail and her ability to put it into words left him wondering if she would teach his officers to do the same.

"He walked with his head down so at first I did not get to see all that much. Just that he had long hair, not long really but longer than guys his age are wearing it."

"His age?" Tony asked.

"Eighteen or nineteen years old."

Tony's mind shut down. This was not the work of a teenager. *This was the work of a man that could plan things out and then carry those plans to fruition. No kid could do that.* He listened to be polite, but his mind discarded this one.

She continued, and something in her voice made him sit and let her talk. She wasn't going to be put off anyway.

"He had neat, clean clothes and he seemed to have an educated air to him. I would have thought nothing of it if he had just gone by one time or even two."

"Just how many times did he go by, Rose?" Robby asked.

"Several, at least four that I saw, who knows how many before I came outside."

"That does seem strange." Tony nodded.

Rose continued. "His hair was so neat and he was so, so . . . tidy, that's the word. Have you ever met someone who was too neat, too well put together, so that they almost made you feel uncomfortable, like you were dirty?"

They just looked at her. There really was no need for an answer since she was talking more to herself than to them.

"He had on a striped light and dark green shirt that was tucked into his dark brown pants and a brown woven belt with a brass flat square buckle. His shoes were brown and they had something shiny on the tips of them. "

That caught Tony's attention. No one knew about the kidnapper's shoes but him and Will Perkins, the crime scene camera guy, who had taken a picture of the impression left in the dirt. Tony had decided to keep that detail from the press. He had seen it in the dirt at the Andersons' house, an imprint of something that his grandfather had probably worn on his shoes. A shoe tip protector; for lack of a better word, it was called a toe cap.

"Rose, what was it exactly that he had on his shoe?"

She looked at him and thought about it. "A shiny piece of metal that covered the tip of his shoe. Why?"

"Did he have on boots?" Tony asked.

She thought about this too. He noticed how careful she was to get things straight and clear in her mind before she answered. He liked that.

"I think they were half boots."

"Really, why?" Tony asked, looking at her intensely.

"Well, they covered more than a shoe did since I don't remember seeing any socks, but there was no line in his pant leg halfway up the leg and boots do that, you know? I never date a man that wears boots because that looks so tacky unless, of course, he is a real cowboy and he wears them with blue jeans. Jeans do wonders for the male derriere," she said with a serious face.

Tony and Robby said at the same time, "I'll have to remember that," and they all laughed.

"Rose, back to the thing on his half boots."

"So you agree with me then?" she asked.

He said he might but would not commit. He really didn't need to. She could tell when she had mentioned the toe thing on his shoes that she finally had his attention. Prior to that he was just doing his job or being nice, she was not sure which.

"Well, it was shiny and had a brilliance to it. It was silver. That gave the neat and tidy thing a real boost, you know?" she said, looking at them with intense persuasion in her eyes.

They just looked at her waiting for her to go on.

"He was mumbling something to himself on the way by, but I couldn't make it out. He just kept on saying something that sounded the same over and over. He had a watch on too. A plain one but nice just the same. He looked out of date to me."

Tony asked, "How much do you think he weighed?"

"About one hundred and fifty pounds."

"Hair?"

"Brown. I didn't get close enough to see his eye color."

"That's a good thing if this is the guy, Rose," Robby told her. "He might be dangerous or he could have acted out at the moment."

"Also he is left-handed," Rose added suddenly.

"What?" both officers exclaimed.

"How do you know that?" Tony demanded.

"Well, he wiped his face and smoothed his hair a few times and it was always with his left hand."

"Rose, is there anything else you can tell us about him?" Tony continued.

"Yeah," Rose said. "If he took that little girl, he's sick."

"We know that, if this is the guy who took little Marcie Anderson."

"It's him," she said firmly.

"How do you know that?" Robby asked.

"It's my job. I'm a professional people watcher of sorts because I'm a talent scout for a major film company. I hide out in this little town to raise my children away from the big city and Hollywood."

"Rose, you are amazing," Tony said. Robby nodded in agreement.

CHAPTER 21

After thanking Rose, the two men left and neither said a word until they reached the car.

"Captain," Robby said. "I'm sorry."

"Not yet you're not, but by the end of the day you will be," Tony said with a promise in his voice.

Robby felt a burning sensation deep in his stomach. "Are you going to fire me, sir?"

"No, I did something like this too when I was your age and new to the force, a hotshot with a name to make for myself. A senior officer taught me the lesson that I'm going to teach you, a very valuable lesson, and when I'm done you'll wish I had just fired you."

They pulled away from the curb. Tony too had a sick feeling in the pit of his stomach. *My God, if Rose was right, this was just a kid.* He tried to remember what his hormones were like as a kid. He was scared now, really scared. This kid, if he was the one, was warped and twisted, and he had the hormones of a teenager. He himself had been an animal at eighteen. He'd just met Claire, and they had spent most of the time at the drive-in, in the back seat of his old car. Oh shit, he thought, and wiped his hand over his face.

"Captain. Captain?" Robby was trying to get his attention.

"What, kid?"

"Sir, what is the shoe thing? What was Rose talking about?"

Tony thought about this. Did he want to share the information with this kid or not? He wasn't ready to yet but felt he needed to tell him something.

"I can't say right now. Give me a day or so, okay?"

"Yes, sir," Robby said. "Where are we going sir, if you don't mind my asking?"

"No, I don't mind. We're going to see the Andersons."

With that, Robby knew why he had felt the dread. He had been off duty when the call came in that Tuesday. He heard enough about it, though, and he sure didn't want to go there. How did you tell your superior officer you didn't want to do something? You didn't. You just sat there and shut your stupid mouth, and the next time a call came in, even if it was a damn cat in a tree, you would do something about it.

CHAPTER 22

Tony drove the two blocks to the Andersons' house using the path Rose said the man had looked down.

Down Avenue A to 3rd street. Two blocks and then across the street was the Andersons home. He pulled up to the curb and looked at the house. Robby felt tense and afraid. He didn't want to go inside. It was as if the house had an illness and he didn't want to catch it. His stomach churned, wanting to be anywhere but here, even fired. Tony got out and looked in the car window at him.

"Coming?"

Robby nodded and got out. Both paused to look at the window where Janet Anderson sat in the rocker.

"Weird," Robby said.

"Yeah, she just sits there holding that doll and little sweater and rocking, waiting for someone to tell her something. Mac isn't much better, but he is functioning."

They walked up the steps together and rang the bell. Janet never moved. Jayme opened the door and recognized Tony.

"Yes, sir," he said.

"Can we come in, Jayme?" Tony asked.

Jayme stepped back. "My dad's not home and my mom just sits there."

"Yeah, I know," Tony said. "It's okay, we just want to ask her some questions."

"Have you found my sister?" Jayme's voice broke with fear.

"No, son, we haven't, but a woman a few blocks over saw a man the day your sister was taken and she has given us a pretty good description of him."

Tony walked over to where Janet was sitting and knelt in front of her. Taking her hands in his, he called her name. She looked up at him and tears came to her eyes again.

"Tony," she whispered, "have you found Marcie?"

"No, Janet, we haven't found her yet, but we will. When we do, I promise you I will put her in your arms myself."

She nodded her head and whispered, "Thank you."

"Janet, I need to ask you something. I realize that I have asked you this before, but do you remember seeing a young man walking around here lately. He's about eighteen or nineteen?"

She stared at him blankly and then slowly it seemed to register. "A young man?" she asked.

"Yes, a young man," Tony said slowly, dealing with her as he would a small child.

"A young man took my baby?"

Hope fell from his face. He thought she had recalled something.

"We're not sure, but a man has been seen in this area on the day that Marcie was taken, and the person who saw him said he was acting strangely and looking in this direction."

Janet jumped up from her chair, knocking Tony to the floor. Robby and Jayme jumped back a few steps. Janet started screaming and waving her hands about as her head shook from side to side. She was shrieking with a crazy look in her eyes.

"A man takes my baby and you won't do anything. You didn't do anything. Why, why, Tony, why won't you go get her back for me? I just want her back, I'll give you money. Do you want money? We have money, Tony, really we do and I'll give it all to you, I really will," Janet said as she frantically crawled around searching for her purse while trying to hang on to Tony's shirt.

She was crying loudly and then the moaning started as she pitched herself forward. Falling on top of Tony, she clung to him and tore at his clothes. Jayme jumped up and made a grab for her at the same time that Robby responded. They both grabbed her and pulled her off Tony. She was shaking her head back and forth and screaming at the top of her lungs.

"Mom, stop!" Jayme's cries penetrated the room, hitting Mac straight in the heart as he walked in the door.

Mac ran across the room and grabbed her in his arms. Looking at Tony, he said, "What?"

Tony stood up and straightened his clothes as he held his hands up and looked at Mac. Tears were in his eyes as he leveled them at Mac, and he saw the look on his face.

"No, Mac, it's not what you think. We came by here today because someone saw a man walking around here the day Marcie was taken."

"Thank God," was all Mac could say. He picked Janet up in his arms and started to carry her to their room.

"No," she moaned as she pointed, "please . . . the rocker by the window so I can wait for her."

"No, Janet. She will be home soon, but for now you need to rest. She will need you to care for her when Tony brings her home."

Janet heard Tony's name and whispered, "Tony promised me, Mac. He's gonna bring Marcie home."

"Yes, sweetheart, I know."

Mac put her to bed and went back downstairs. He looked at Tony and Robby, shaking his head.

"I'm sorry," he said. "She's not herself these days and I don't know what to do for her. Hell, I don't know what to do for me." Mac looked terrible.

"Mac," Tony said. "This is Robby Henderson. He's going to be working with me on this."

Mac shook Robby's hand and motioned them to the sofa. They all sat while Mac watched them closely.

"What brings you here, Tony? I mean if you had anything to tell me, you would, right?"

"A neighbor of yours remembers seeing a man walking around here the Tuesday evening that Marcie was taken."

He lowered his head at these words. Tony could not bear to look at the pain in Mac's eyes. *He hurts, and I'm powerless to help him.*

"This neighbor gave us a very good detailed description of the young man. We're going to investigate it further, but we wanted to know if anyone around here had seen anyone like this guy that same day."

Mac listened, and when he was sure Tony was finished, he asked the question both Robby and Tony had feared he would.

"Why did she take so long to come forward?"

Tony cleared his voice, trying to find the words to answer.

Robby interrupted. "Mr. Anderson, sir, it's my fault. The call came in when we were bombarded with calls about this. The woman sounded drunk and crazy so I chalked it up to that and did nothing. I'm sorry, sir. If this turns out to be anything, I personally will resign from the force. Please forgive me . . . I had no idea."

The kid was almost in tears. Tony was proud of him. Mac sat there and looked at him. Finally he broke the uncomfortable silence.

"Robby, I want to be mad at you, but I can't. I just want my little girl back. You do whatever it takes to get her back."

"Sir, you have my word, as an officer and a gentleman, that I will do everything in my power to bring your daughter back to you."

It was a grave statement, but taken just the way it was meant.

Mac looked at Tony. "Why didn't she call the police that day while he was out there stalking my baby?"

Tony answered truthfully. "I have no idea. I guess she was busy or thought it was nothing. She did say that he was well dressed and clean-cut. Very tidy were the words she used. He must have done or said something to alleviate her fears about him."

"What are we going to do now?"

"We'll have a sketch artist from the FBI prepare a drawing and try to find this guy for questioning. We'll also ask other people in the neighborhood if they've seen him or remember anything like this happening. That is where we will start, but Mac, I feel we're on to something now. We have some place to go and something to do. To tell you the truth, we were all running out of ideas."

All but one, Tony thought to himself. They stood to go and shook hands, all of them thinking separate thoughts. Robby had an intense desire to do whatever needed doing to make things right. Mac wanted Marcie back, while Tony wanted someone to fix this mess.

CHAPTER 23

Jayme waited until Tony and Robby had left and then walked into the room where they had been sitting.

Looking at his father, he saw for the first time an old man.

"Dad, can I talk to you?"

Mac looked up at him. "Sure you can. What's up?"

Jayme sat uncomfortably on the edge of the sofa. He clasped his hands together tightly and looked at them. Mac could see that something was on his mind.

"What's up, Jayme?" he repeated, getting worried.

Jayme's eyes filled with tears as he looked at his father. The teardrops began to flow slowly at first, then turned into a wretched sob. His shoulders shook with emotion. His father went and sat by him, holding him for the first time in more than ten years. They sat together, father and son, and both cried for a few minutes.

Finally, Jayme spoke.

"I'm so sorry, Dad, I really am. I didn't know that someone was gonna take her."

Mac felt a tingle go up his spine. "Jayme, what are you talking about?"

"Marcie, Dad. She wanted me to take her to the park last Tuesday, but I had plans to go with the guys to Josh's house for some one-on-one. She asked me and starting crying when I wouldn't take her."

Mac relaxed. "Jayme . . . son, this is not your fault. This is no one's fault."

From in the corner, they both heard it at the same time . . . sniffles from a small nose that was running as quickly as the tears. Looking in that direction, they both saw Vance at the same time. Mac motioned him forward and wiped his eyes.

"Not you too?" he asked gently.

Vance nodded. "I pulled her hair when she was out in front."

Mac gathered him in his arms and put him in his lap.

With an arm around each son, he said, "Boys, this is not your fault. The fault lies with no one living in this house. Do you hear me?"

They both nodded solemnly.

"Where's your brother?"

"He's upstairs. He's afraid to go outside," Jayme told him.

"Go get him and meet me in my room."

The boys took off, and Mac headed up the stairs behind them. Pushing open the door, he saw Janet, lying there and staring at the ceiling. She looked at him as he entered.

"Janet, we have to talk."

She sat up as tears filled her eyes.

"I'm so sorry, Mac. I lost it. I'm so embarrassed."

"It's okay. Tony understands, since most of the time I think he feels like doing the same thing. Janet, we have another problem."

"No, Mac, please no more." She was crying softly as she rolled to her side and curled into a fetal position.

Mac gently sat down on the bed and said in a voice that let Janet know he would take no argument, "Janet, I know that you hurt, we all do, but we also have three sons who desperately need us. They hurt so badly that they are hiding in Jayme's room with a gun."

Janet sat up then and turned sharply toward him. "A gun, oh my God, Mac!"

"They're scared, Janet, and they live in a house that's fallen apart. You can't seem to do anything but sit in that window and cry. They need you, we all do," Mac said as gently, but firmly, as he dared.

The boys were just outside the door waiting to be called in. Janet held her hand to her mouth.

"Oh, my God, I'm so sorry, Mac. I was hurting so badly. I'm sorry."

"It's okay, but we have to get ourselves together for them."

Mac opened the door and called the boys in. They watched their mom as they sat by her, on the edge of their parents' bed. Jayme put his arms around her, and she laid her head on his shoulder. He was big like his father, strong, and still something in him was just a little boy, especially tonight. She cradled him close to her. The other boys joined in and Janet kissed each head. Yes, she did have three sons who needed her still, no matter how big they were.

Mac stood up and faced his family, one shy of being complete.

"We have got to stand together here. We need to get out and talk to people and find out what they know or might have seen. We need a plan of action and we all have to work together to get Marcie back. This may be up to us, you know, because the police don't have a lot to go on."

Colton looked up at his father and said, "She's in the junkyard, Dad."

Mac looked at him startled. "Why do you think that, son?"

"I had a dream that she was there in a car, and a man was talking to her."

Janet started crying again, and Jayme nudged his brother roughly with his shoe.

"She is not!" Jayme said, wanting to quiet his brother. "He woke me up the other night with that one, Dad. Sorry."

"Yeah, and you pulled a gun on me," Colton whined.

"Silence!" Mac said sternly, gaining everyone's attention. "Stop fighting among yourselves and get out there and look for her. She is alive, and she needs us to bring her home. Jayme, give me the gun. No one is coming into this house, especially if this family remembers to lock the doors before they go to bed at night. We need to start mingling and talking to anyone that will listen. Janet, get out a picture of Marcie. Let's make some flyers of her and get your buddies together to circulate them. You boys have the best resources out there in your friends. Talk to them and get them to help you look. Look everywhere and don't think that anything is silly, okay?"

The boys all agreed and Janet pulled them to her again and kissed them all.

Could it be that as a family they could make a difference? Only time would tell. Janet stood up. For the first time she had hope that maybe someone would see Marcie's picture and help find her or know something about her. Surely someone had seen her by now. They all group-hugged like they hadn't in years.

Mac said, "Let's get some food in that kitchen. We can't work on an empty stomach."

Now united as a family, with a plan, they moved into action with the kitchen first on the list. Mac stood and watched them go downstairs, hoping that this show of force would help. He didn't know what else to do. They were all dying of inactivity. He needed them to help him move as well. All he could think of now was that he hoped he was right.

CHAPTER 24
Roman and Marcie spent each day the same.

He threatened her each morning, telling her she had to be quiet all day, stay in the house, and not go near the door. If she disobeyed, he would put her back in the trunk. Then, he kissed her good-bye and sat outside for an hour. One hour every morning, he sat on the log outside and watched to see what she would do. She never left the house—for fear of the trunk and Roman's rage. Every night they ate dinner together, and he washed her body. Then, he forced her to watch him wash his.

"Cleanliness is next to Godliness. We must be sure it's done and know how to do it," Roman would say repeatedly.

Tonight was no different from any other since she had been with him, except that this night he said he had a surprise.

"Go and get cleaned up, wash your face and hands. Wait . . . I'll come with you," Roman said, as she headed for the bathroom.

He stood next to the toilet and watched her urinate and then wiped her bottom. She cringed each time, but their routine never changed. When she was done and Roman was satisfied that all had been done according to his specifications, he took her hand and led her into the kitchen. There on the table was a brown paper bag. Marcie looked at it in anticipation, as any child would.

"Go ahead," Roman said, "open it."

Marcie reached for the bag and peeled it open. Inside was a shiny blue bowl. She looked up at Roman, not really sure what to do or say.

"Do you like it?" he asked, smiling at her.

"It looks like my dog's bowl. It's very pretty. It's for me?"

Roman nodded. "Yup, it sure is. Now you have your own bowl to eat from—no more paper plates for you. We're family now."

Marcie wanted to say this was a dog's bowl, but she somehow knew that would be the wrong thing to say. She hugged it to her chest and smiled as she rocked back and forth. She had something that was all hers. Roman was pleased. He led Marcie to the counter where he put her evening cupcake in the bowl. She looked at the cupcake and then at Roman.

"Don't we have anything else?" she asked in a small voice. "I'm kind of tired of cupcakes."

Roman felt anger at her words and told her to just eat it and be happy that he let her eat such things.

"I never got those when I was a kid," he said.

Marcie ate her dinner while Roman ate his. Then together they cleaned up the kitchen and headed back into the living room, Roman to his chair and Marcie to her pallet. She fell asleep on the floor and he in the chair.

Sometime in the night Roman awoke and carried Marcie to her corner bed in his room. He tucked her in gently and kissed her good-night, then turned and went back to the sofa. Roman thought she would come to love him and be content with her life, but lately she was showing signs of unhappiness. He wondered why. She had not been back to the trunk, because every day she had been so good and not caused him any trouble. She ate what he put on her plate, and she did what she was told.

The next morning, Roman awoke stiff from sleeping on the couch. He remembered the thoughts that had gone through his head as he drifted off to sleep. Maybe today was the day. Marcie made him happy, so as a reward he could bring her another surprise. She loved surprises, and it always made him feel good to make her smile at him. He hardly ever felt rage anymore. The two times he had felt the rage come over him were not her fault. Still, she was unhappy. He could tell by the look on her face and the way she carried herself that something was wrong. *Maybe she misses me when I'm gone all day? Maybe she gets lonely? She needs a pet. Today is the day.* He kissed her good-bye at the door and as usual she presented her cheek just as he had shown her how to do. Today, he caught her as she looked down and wiped a tear from her little cheek. She seemed thinner today too.

"I will bring you a pet today, if you want one," he said to her as he was leaving.

She looked up and smiled through her tears.

"That would be nice," she said.

Yet, somehow he felt that her response was just because he had trained her well. Roman grabbed her shoulders and squeezed. Marcie winced and cried out in pain, trying to pull away. He shook her till she cried out.

"What's wrong with you?" he demanded.

Marcie' s fear made her speak out honestly. "I'm lonely and I want my mommy. Please get my mommy for me and let me see if she will let me come back home."

Tears ran down her face, and she hugged herself, rocking as she stood there. He shoved her from him and she fell to the floor. As he loomed over her, she scrambled for the cover of the recliner.

"You ungrateful little bitch!" he screamed. "I feed you, clothe you, and you want your mommy?"

He sneered as he kicked her bare foot that she had left exposed. She cried out in pain and then bit her lip.

"No!" her wails pierced the air. "Please, I'll be good. I'll be really good, I promise."

"Too late, it is too late!" He walked around the small house, screaming and throwing things. "You want your mommy? Well your mommy doesn't want you! You should be glad that I took you in or you would have to live on the streets. Do you hear me, Marcie? Do you want to live on the streets like the other dogs and cats with no one to feed them or keep them warm? Do you want to be dirty and sleep in the rain? I could throw you out, ya know?"

Roman continued screaming until Marcie hid where he could not see any part of her.

Finally, he stormed out the door screaming, "You won't get no pet from me today, no siree, no pet, no pet!"

But he was only gone a moment before he came back. His anger wouldn't let him leave that way. He was mad and it was her fault. So much for her not being the cause of his wrath. So much for getting her a surprise to make her smile.

Roman's wrath terrorized her into obedience. Marcie knew that he would rant and break things and then go off to wherever it was he went all day, sometimes late into the night, leaving her alone with nothing to eat. She also knew that the house had better be clean when he got back or the screaming would start all over again.

She hid her face, crying softly. "God, please let Mommy and Daddy change their minds."

She felt Roman's hands, clawing for her, and she screamed as loud as she could. He grabbed her face in his hand and squeezed it hard.

"Shut up!" he screamed at her. "Shut up or I will hit you right in the mouth!"

Marcie bit her lip and tried not to cry. She shook with the energy it took to control herself. Her sobs diminished to a silent shudder as he stroked her hair.

"There now, it's okay. We do these things from time to time. All families fight. I love you still," he whispered in her ear. "Do you love me?"

She wanted to pull away from him and go out the big door, running away from him, but she was too scared. Instead she nodded and said, "Yes."

He sat her on the floor and looked at her. "Feel better now?"

She looked up at him and nodded.

"Good," he said. "Now will you behave today?"

She nodded again and went to the corner, where she was to sit until he got home. Curling up on the cloth that was on the floor, she laid her head on her arms and did not look up again until he was gone. Then, she lifted her head at the click of the door, and his head reappeared around the door as it swung open.

"I'll bring your friend home with me tonight." Then he closed the door.

Marcie finally smiled a genuine smile. She sniffed and wiped her nose on her sleeve. Penny was coming to play with her tonight. She could hardly wait.

CHAPTER 25

As Roman watched the house from the log where he sat every morning, he wondered what she was doing in there.

She must be sitting on the floor and doing what she was told. She was a good pet and he loved her. All was forgiven.

As he lay on the couch the night before, plans had formed in his mind for that evening. He knew he needed something for Marcie to do during the day and he knew too that having her own pet would be good for her and good for him. He could stroke and powder the new pet too, just the way he did with Marcie. Marcie was learning to be neat and clean. People did not keep themselves clean enough these days, but he was teaching her it was the only way to live. Marcie' s pet would learn that too.

He stood and headed off in the direction of the shop. He didn't like this work. It was dirty and nasty, but a job was a job and he would carry his own weight. No welfare for him; that was wrong. Every American needed to do his share, make his own plans and carry them out alone. That was the American way, he told himself. He knew this was true. It had been beaten into him since he was old enough to walk. Each foster family had told him that. He knew that good people often took kids from the home, but he had never been lucky enough to be chosen by one of them. Some of them even had cake and ice cream at night.

Roman knew how to be a good American and he was gonna do just that. He had plans to make, that was for sure.

Roman walked with his head down, the way he always did when he was deep in thought. Heading for the dreaded job, he wondered what he would do for the rest of the day. How was he going to keep his mind on his work when he had so many other things he would rather be working on? He needed time to get his thoughts together anyway. Things like this took planning and luck. He didn't like it when things didn't go right. It ruined everything and made him angry. He wanted to have his way today and make Marcie smile. He wanted to see her pretty white teeth and smell the happiness on her.

As he walked in the door of Bobby's Auto Salvage Yard, the smell hit him of old cars, wrecked and abandoned with grease and oil oozing from them. He hated that smell but he knew it was worse in the yard itself.

Bobby looked up at him and smiled. "Hey, kid, how are ya this morning?"

Roman hated Bobby and the way he talked. He was so common. Bobby stunk. Actually, he reeked from years of being in the car salvage business. His nails were permanently dirty and his clothes were worse than that. Roman would have burned them in the back yard if they were his. People judged you by the way you looked and smelled; he'd been told that all his life.

Roman looked at Bobby even though it disgusted him. "Fine, and you?"

"Can't complain. Don't do no good anyway, nobody'd listen if I did," Bobby replied with a chuckle.

Bobby was known for minding his own business. He didn't carry gossip and disliked those who did.

"You need some dirt on those hands of yours, boy, some grit under those fingernails. Give you something to eat for lunch later."

Bobby laughed at his own joke, and Roman, knowing that was expected of him, laughed too. He covered his mouth, just as he had been taught as a small boy, so that no one could see the dark hole of his mouth. He wondered to himself why, if it was so bad, didn't everyone else cover their mouth? He wondered about a lot of the things he had been taught.

Roman walked around and punched the time card as Bobby continued. "Hey, kid, I need to go pick up some cars with the flatbed. Can you handle things alone this morning?"

This was the break that Roman wanted.

"Sure I can, Bobby, and I'll do a good job too, you'll see, you'll be so proud of me."

Bobby looked at Roman and thought how eager the young were for praise and respect. Roman was young, but he'd been on time every day for the last three months and had never made a mistake, except for that time he had locked the keys in an old junk car. That had been a day. Roman had walked around all day just about in tears, terrified of the repercussions. Bobby had felt bad for the kid and given him the rest of the day off. That had been about a week ago and he'd been perfect ever since. A little strange maybe, but on the whole a good kid.

Even though Roman hated Bobby and the way he smelled, he wanted his boss to be proud of him just the same. He needed to show that he could do anything, no matter what it was. Roman' s chest swelled with pride at the thought of being in charge and being alone so he could make all the important decisions, like who got what and for what price.

Bobby stood up, leaned forward, and slid the keys to the yard gate across the counter.

"Open her up for me, will ya, kid?" he said as he unfolded the morning newspaper so that he could read it. The story of Marcie Anderson was still front-page news. The headlines told a bleak story of no clues, and the article below it asked anyone with any information to call the police department. Bobby read just the beginning of the story. His heart went out to the Andersons even though he didn't know them. He couldn't imagine going through that. If the son of a bitch who took that child were in front of him, he would pound him to a pulp.

When Bobby said as much to Roman, the young man just looked at him. Bobby thought that maybe he hadn't heard about the kidnapping so he pointed to the paper on the counter.

"Yeah," Roman said, "I read all about that. Sad, huh?"

"More than sad. That sicko needs his freaking head adjusted and I'm just the man to adjust it for him," Bobby said as he punched one fist into his other palm.

Roman felt disgust for Bobby and the emotion was starting to get out of control. "What time ya leaving, Bob?" he asked.

Not only did Roman Marsh hate Bobby, he also had Marcie Anderson, and he had planned her abduction sitting right there with Bobby in the same room. Now, he was planning something new, a pet for Marcie. With Bobby gone for the morning, it would be easier to make his plans.

Roman smiled to himself, and Bobby smiled back at him. He was proud of himself. Bobby trusted him; even though Bobby repulsed him, it was still an accomplishment. He couldn't wait to get home and tell Marcie. He might try to sneak off and tell her at lunchtime.

Bobby heaved his large frame out of his chair. He picked up his keys from the desk near a large container of coffee, which he grabbed as well.

"I'm gone," he said to Roman. "Take care of the joint." Out the door he went, hitching up his pants.

As Bobby climbed into the large flatbed wrecker, Roman picked up the telephone. Dialing the number he had just looked up in the yellow pages, he waited for an answer.

"Gaglan Elementary School," the voice said.

"Hello, what time does school let out today?"

"Pardon me?"

Roman asked again. "What time does school let out today?"

"Sir," the voice said, "there is no school today. School let out for summer vacation last Friday and the first summer school session hasn't started yet. Can I ask who's calling?"

Roman slammed the receiver down. He was mad now, storming around the small junkyard office, kicking anything in his path. This was going to ruin everything. How was he going to know where Penny was and when she would be there? He hit the wall just as a customer came in and looked at him.

"I have those days, son," he said grinning. "Try not to let it bother you too much."

"Yeah, but lately," Roman said, "they're happening too often." He took a deep breath to calm himself.

"So what can I get for you?"

"I need a door handle for a '69 Ford Mustang and the mirror for it too, passenger side front door."

Roman handed the man a screwdriver and pointed to the only useable Mustang in the lot.

"That's all we have that has anything good left on it, sir, but you're welcome to what you find on it."

The guy walked outside and over to the car. Roman watched him just in case he had been lying and was there to spy on him. The guy had a dangerous smell to him. But as he bent over the Mustang Roman returned to his thoughts. What was he going to do now? He needed a sign that this was going to be okay and everything would work out. He promised Marcie and he didn't want to let her down. He needed time to think of something.

The man came back inside, interrupting his thoughts. Roman watched him as he came to the counter.

Trying to smile, he asked, "Find everything okay?"

"Yeah, I got it, thanks. I need this for a car I'm giving my wife for her birthday on Saturday. We drove out to the country last year and found this Mustang in an old man's garage. It was in pretty good condition except for this," he said, holding up the objects in his hand, "and some missing belts, little things like that, so I went back later and bought it and have been restoring it ever since then. She has no idea."

Roman couldn't have cared less. His mind was on a scent that had drifted through the window about that time. The man continued to talk, totally unaware that Roman's mind was in another place.

"Buddy, hey, buddy. How much do I owe you?" the man asked, jarring Roman back to the present.

He looked at the objects the man had and made a calculation on the machine on the desk.

"Twenty-two dollars, sir," Roman said.

"This stuff costs a lot, doesn't it?" the man said. "I guess when you restore these old ones that's what happens. Will you take a check?"

"Yes sir," Roman said, "if it's local and you have the proper identification."

"Got that," the man said as he pulled his wallet from his back pocket.

He stood at the desk and wrote out the check as Roman let the scent fill his nose again, raising his head in the air and sniffing to try to get as much of it as he could. Roman felt almost euphoric, the feeling starting to get the better of him as he tried to hurry the man along. When the man handed him the check and laid his driver's license down on the counter, Roman stood stock-still. This was too good to be true. Here before him was Bill Ware, who lived on Third Street. That was the street that Penny and Marcie lived on.

Roman checked the address just to be sure. *Yep, just three doors from Marcie's old house. The sign, this was the sign that everything was going to be okay.*

Roman looked up at the man. "Hey, you live on the street that little girl that's missing lived on. I was just reading about it in the paper."

"Yeah," Bill said, "she used to play with my little girl. We're all upset over it. We've never been through anything like this before."

"Do the police know anything yet?"

"No, there are no leads, no one has seen or heard anything," Bill said, shaking his head.

"That's a shame," Roman replied.

He took the check and handed Bill Ware his license back as he smiled the secret smile of evil waiting to happen.

CHAPTER 26

Nancy Gale hung up the phone at Gaglan Elementary, then sat looking at it for a moment.

Something was wrong with that phone call—it gave her an eerie feeling. This was not a school day and any parent with a child here knew that! Summer school hadn't started yet, so it couldn't be that either. She glanced at her desk and the newspaper with the story of Marcie Anderson. The feeling in her heart wouldn't let her do nothing. She quickly picked up the phone and dialed the police department nonemergency number posted on the sticker on her phone.

"Police department, nonemergency line, this is Barbara Tharp. How can I help you?"

"This may be nothing, but I just got the strangest call," Nancy said.

"Who is this please?"

"Oh, sorry, this is Nancy Gale at the elementary school and I just got the strangest call."

"Yes, ma'am, you said that. What did the caller say to you, ma'am?"

As Nancy told the story of the call, Barbara's mind raced to Robby Henderson's failure to follow up on a call. That was not going to happen to her—no way.

"Let me send someone to talk to you, ma'am, just to be sure there is nothing to this," Barbara said in her calmest, most efficient voice, even though she was shaking.

"Okay. Do you think it's anything to be concerned about?" Nancy asked.

"We never know and it's better to make a report than not. An officer will be there shortly."

They both hung up and felt nervous for the same reason—Marcie Anderson.

Barbara's hand shook as she picked up the microphone and pushed the button.

"I need an officer to go to Gaglan Elementary School," she said.

The microphone cracked and a voice came back to her. "This is Captain Miller. What have you got, Barb?"

Her voice shook at the sound of his.

"Sir, the secretary just called from the elementary school. She got a call from a man wanting to know what time school let out for the day."

Normally this wouldn't have been a big deal, before Marcie's kidnapping and before school was out for the summer, but now things had changed in a big way.

"I'm on it," Tony said, turning his car toward the school.

A second voice came on the line. "Sir, this is John. Mind if I join you?"

"Yup, meet you there," Tony responded.

"Shit!" John threw his microphone down on the seat next to him. Grabbing for the town map, he searched for the school. *Asshole. He knows I don't know where the damn school is.*

In the car, Tony chuckled to himself, and Robby wanted to know what he was laughing about.

"He doesn't know where the school is and he's too proud to ask."

Robby laughed too, a nervous laugh, knowing full well that this joke or something a whole lot like it could be played on him some day. He was curious to see how John would handle this one, being a hotshot FBI agent and all.

But John found the school on the small town map quickly and headed his car in its direction. He was actually closer than Tony so he chuckled to himself as he pulled into the driveway and saw Tony's car coming around the corner. Tony and Robby saw him at the same time. They looked at each other and shook their heads.

"Smart son of a bitch, isn't he?" Robby said.

"Yeah," Tony muttered under his breath.

John leaned against his car, smiling at them. *Gotcha.*

The three walked into the school office together. Nancy looked up from her desk, and seeing all these men in uniform she realized the seriousness of the situation.

They greeted her and for more than an hour asked her questions about a thirty-second conversation. She could remember it and the approximate time, but not much more. The sounds in the background and the way his voice sounded were things she never thought to focus on.

The men took their leave and talked outside. Tony's first thought was to try to contact someone at the local telephone company to see what they could come up with. John knew this was a dead end. He knew the limitations of phone calls that had already happened. What they needed was a phone tap. But what was the point now? The caller wouldn't call back. He already had his information. There was little that could be done about this call but if they could think ahead, who would this guy call next? John was running through things in his mind. The fear was mounting in his heart as a thought came to him.

"Maybe this guy is planning to take another kid," John said with strong conviction in his voice. "We need to be more aggressive. We need phone taps and that sketch from the sketch artist and we need it now!"

"Let's get it done," Tony said.

They all looked at one another and the fear was obvious in each of them.

"Why do you think that?" Robby asked.

Tony looked at the young cop. "He calls a kid's school and wants to know when school is out. What? Do you think he wants to bring Marcie back and drop her off at the school?" Tony said more as a statement than a question.

Robby felt foolish. "No, sir, I guess not."

"Let's ride around, look for anything that seems out of the norm. Whatever normal is these days," Tony said.

They left, going in different directions, but feeling the same feelings, Tony and Robby in the squad car and John in his own car. There was a feeling of unfinished business that seemed always to hang in the air, or maybe it was the feeling that something was coming—something sinister.

With plenty of daylight hours left, they rode around the small town with its tree-lined streets and quiet houses filled with precious families. They seemed to drive for hours, looking up first one street then another. They had no idea what it was that they were looking for, but both Robby and Tony felt that they would know it when they saw it. That didn't happen, and at nine o'clock Tony dropped Robby off in front of the station. "See you tomorrow," he called.

"No, sir, I'm off tomorrow," Robby said loud enough for Tony to hear.

Tony stepped on the brake and then backed up to where Robby was standing.

"Son, I'm not off, so you're not off. We are on until this is solved."

"Yes, sir." Robby knew that he deserved it and much more. Instead of firing him, Tony was just going to teach him a lesson. "See you in the morning, sir."

"Good night, Robby," Tony said as he drove away.

He felt bad for treating the kid that way, but he had a lesson to learn and Tony was going to make damn sure that he did.

CHAPTER 27

Lindsay Freeman sat in front of her computer for the tenth time that day.

A single mom, she was currently balancing her full-time job at the hospital with part-time work for an astrology web site, doing readings online. The web site was a good place with dignity and quality; everyone there wanted to bring something to it and to see it grow and do well. Dignity was the hardest thing to achieve in the metaphysical world. So many people sought help but few wanted to admit it. This, however, was a place where everyone with some sort of metaphysical gift had a home. A rare place to fit in. Clairvoyants were rare people. There were people with many types of other gifts working on the web site as well—clairvoyants, psychic intuitives, tarot readers, those who read runes, and some who did astrological charts. There was a little something for everyone and most had a reason for their gift. Lindsay's was trauma.

At the age of seven, she had found herself knowing things no one else seemed to know. It started back one summer when a drunk driver crashed into the car carrying Lindsay, a friend, and the friend's mother to a picnic. Lindsay's friend hadn't survived the accident, and Lindsay suffered severe head trauma.

What seemed like only moments after the cars collided, Lindsay awoke with a terrible headache. What she didn't realize was that she had been in a hospital for more than a month. The fog was lifting slowly as she came back from wherever it is we go when we are unconscious. Her head hurt, her mouth was dry, and she felt stiff and sore everywhere. A feeling of heaviness seemed to consume her body.

She lay still and let her eyes adjust to the light. Then in her clearing vision she saw her mom. Lindsay could see the worry and joy at the same time on her mother's face and she could feel the tenderness of her mother's hand as it held hers. Lindsay felt confused. Her mom reached over and grabbed something next to Lindsay's head on the pillow. A voice came over the speaker.

"Can I help you?"

"My daughter is waking up. Can you send for the doctor, please?"

"Yes, ma'am."

Soon a man in a white coat appeared and smiled at Lindsay. "Well, hello young lady," he said. "You gave us quite a scare. I'm Dr. Jenkins and you're in the hospital. It seems you've had a rather nasty collision between your head and a window. How do you feel?" He was shining a light in her eyes as he spoke.

At first Lindsay croaked out something incomprehensible. Her mom held a glass of water to her mouth. Lindsay saw her glance at the doctor and he nodded. Looking down at it, she felt confused and then things started coming back to her. She took a sip of water.

Swallowing, she looked at Dr. Jenkins and said in a hoarse voice, "Your wife won't need surgery."

The doctor took several steps back as her mother looked on.

"How did you know that?" he asked as shock registered on his face.

"I don't know. I can feel it, and hear it in you I guess," Lindsay said.

"What do you mean, you can feel it in me?"

"I mean, it's what you're thinking about, or something like it. Is that wrong?"

"No, it's not wrong. She's is having tests in the morning at this hospital. The only thing is we just found this out this afternoon and we haven't told anyone. How did you know?"

"I don't know. I just do," Lindsay answered.

That answer was to become a common one for many years. Lindsay eventually received training in her gift, some good, some not so good. Learning to function with it and even to use it to help others was a long-standing challenge. Talking was the hardest thing for her. Too many times after the accident she had said the wrong thing, disclosed too much or let someone's secrets slip out at the wrong time. Once she stopped talking altogether for two years and needed help from different sources to learn to be socially acceptable again. Lindsay learned over time to feel others out before telling them about her ability for fear they wouldn't like her or, worse yet, they would fear her. Friendship was an especially hard thing, since she was never sure whether people liked her for herself or for her ability.

Now thirty years later, Lindsay had learned to live with her gift—though sometimes it felt more like a curse than a gift. There were days when she felt like a prisoner, like her life was not her own, and no matter how much she longed to be like everyone else, it was not to be. She hung on to her memories of childhood before the accident, of what it was like to be just like everyone else. In later times she was thankful that she had been chosen to have the gift. Thankful that her mother had been so patient, so willing to do what was needed to get her the help and training she needed. Thankful for the job she now had that could be an outlet for the endless information she received, whether she wanted it or not.

As she looked at her computer screen, she could see her son, Jack, out of the corner of her eye, bouncing around the living room, wanting something to eat and something to do. He was six years old with blond hair and bright blue eyes.

"Come on, Mom! You've been there all day. Let's go ride our bikes and get something to eat, wanna?"

He watched her, knowing she was going to do it, his face bright with expectation. He was just waiting for her to move. Lindsay stretched her back and her arms, smiling up at him. He was so cute as he stood there looking at her.

"Okay," she said. "Let me finish this one and we'll go."

Jack plopped down on the floor and began to pout. "I wanna go now, let's go now."

"Jackie . . . ," Lindsay said with a warning in her voice.

The tone was threatening, but they both knew she didn't mean it. He giggled at her, and she reached out to mess up his hair. She had been online all day, doing e-mail readings for the endless supply of people who came for help with broken dreams. Lindsay admired the woman that built this company for the strength she had. She finished what she was doing and stood up, stretching and realizing just how sore she was.

"Okay, Jack. Let's go. A bike ride and a burger sound good to me too." She grabbed her keys from the counter top in the kitchen. He was up in a flash and out the front door. She was right behind him as the phone rang. Pausing to look at it, she felt no urgency, and decided to let the answering machine grab it.

"Hi, Lindsay, this is Kay. I just wanted to see if you were home. Call you later."

Lindsay pulled the door closed with a smile. She knew she shouldn't be using her gift this way, but she really couldn't help it. Besides, her son and the burgers were waiting and she was hungry!

Jack and Lindsay rode their bikes through their small town, past old, established homes intermixed with the occasional new one. Those look so out of place, she thought as they passed by. They rode with the wind in their hair, without a care in the world, save where to get a burger. Laughing and joking, they were good friends with a common need for each other's company. It was warm for this time of the day, but June is always warm. With the kids out of school for the summer Lindsay was hoping to spend more time with Jackie outside, doing just what they were doing now.

Lindsay's mind raced ahead as it always did. Jack needed a physical sometime before school started, and Melissa, her youngest daughter, was being a real handful for some reason. In fact, Melissa had been a handful for a while and showed no real signs of getting it together any time soon. She was a beautiful child but wild as a March hare. Lindsay was worried about what the year would hold for her. Her other daughters, Marie and Lea, were older than Melissa by four years. They seemed to have a knack for getting their act together and keeping it that way. They could usually figure things out for themselves. Lindsay was crossing her fingers that Melissa would settle down as she got older.

Jack's voice interrupted her daydreaming.

"Hey, Mom, are you coming? You must be getting old," he said loud enough for those they passed to hear him and laugh.

Lindsay had let her mind and her son get away from her. She laughed as she sped up and passed him. "Come on, slow poke," she hollered. "I'll show you old."

Jack sped up, laughing as he raced to catch up to her. They laughed and made silly faces at each other as they rode into the Dairy Queen parking lot. Putting their bikes down and running inside, they ordered a dinner of burgers, fries, and sodas, then they sat outside and ate in the warm evening air.

Back home, after storing the bikes in the shed, Jackie asked, "Mom, what movie are we gonna watch before we go to bed?"

"I don't care, just not wrestling."

Jack thought for a moment. "How about *Star Wars*?"

"Sounds good. You get the movie and I'll get some ice water."

On the way to the kitchen, Lindsay noticed the light on the answering machine was blinking. She paused to look at it. Something felt unnerving as she reached for it and she almost pulled her hand back. *You're being silly, just listen to it.* Pushing the button, she felt a chill creep up her back. She'd had a feeling a few days before that something was coming. It had haunted her until this moment. Now that it was here, she felt terror settle around her shoulders.

"Ms. Freeman, I hope you don't mind my calling you at home. We got your number from a friend of my husband's. Well, not a friend really, more like a colleague. My husband, Captain Tony Miller, is the officer in charge of a missing child case and he got your name and number from a fellow officer. He's someone you've worked with before so I felt you might help us. Can you call me back? My name is Claire Miller."

The message went on and on, but Lindsay knew what had happened. A child was missing, that was all that she needed to know.

She looked up to see her son standing there. He knew this was bad. He was young, but he knew what his mom did. He knew that she helped people whose children had been kidnapped. They stood together, Lindsay's arm protectively draped around her son, listening to the voice of Claire Miller.

Jack looked up at her. "Are we still going to watch the movie, Mom?"

"No, son, you go ahead. Get in mommy's bed and I'll tuck you in. I'll be there soon."

He knew there was no way she would come now, unless he cried, but he felt sorry for the lady who had called. Lindsay tucked him in and helped him say his prayers before kissing him goodnight.

"Mom, we're okay, huh?"

"Yes, Jackie, we're okay. Watch your movie and try to go to sleep."

She hit play on the VCR, and *Star Wars* came on the screen. Closing the door softly behind her, she headed back to the answering machine. She hit play again and as the message played she jotted down the phone number. After listening to the rest of the message, she dialed the number.

"Hello," said a female voice.

"Hello, this is Lindsay Freeman. I received a message on my answering machine this evening from a Claire Miller. Can I speak with her, please?"

"Oh, my goodness, this is Claire Miller. How are you, Ms. Freeman? Thank you so much for calling me back. I just cannot believe I'm actually talking to you."

"I'm fine, thank you. I understand you have a missing child and your husband is the police captain in your area," Lindsay said patiently.

"Yes, yes he is," Claire said. She was so excited she could barely contain it.

"Mrs. Miller, can I speak with your husband, please?"

"Oh yes, I mean, no. He isn't home now, but he'll be here later tonight. He always comes home eventually."

"Can I reach him at the station?" Lindsay asked.

"Oh, well, he really doesn't know that I called you." Claire was stumbling over the words.

Lindsay listened for a time. She was tired and trying very hard to be patient, but that was wearing thin. Feeling that she wasn't getting anywhere, finally she said, "Mrs. Miller, can you have your husband call me about this little girl?"

Claire just sat there with her mouth hanging open. She had never spoken to a clairvoyant before and she was amazed not only at how normal she sounded but also that she had known that the missing child was a girl.

"Hello?" Lindsay asked.

"Yes, um, oh, yes, I'm here. How did you know it was a little girl?"

"It' s what I do. Would you please have your husband call me? Thank you for your time. Good night."

Lindsay hung up the phone feeling bad for being so curt, but the information she was getting about the child made her impatient. Sometimes Lindsay realized that she could be a little abrupt. However, time and experience had taught her to be somewhat hard-nosed with people. She had to protect herself. Still, she had instantly liked Claire Miller. She had a down-home quality that was hard not to like.

Lindsay sat down in the chair by the phone to wait. Propping her feet up on her desk, she let the visions she was getting flow over her. Even though she'd done this many times before, she always had to remind herself she was in her own home and safe. As she closed her eyes, she felt the presence of a man around her. She could almost see his face and smell his breath. She had never picked up scents before. This was a new sensation for her. Her fingernails gripped the side of the chair as a shiver ran down her spine. Fear was in the room with her. This vision was no different than any other had been. A demon was still a demon.

Lindsay heard this man growling. The sound seemed to come from somewhere deep inside him, where his pain lived. She felt a fear in her, a fear for the child this man had in his control, and a fear for all children while he was still out there. She knew sleep would not come easy this night.

CHAPTER 28

Justina hung her head over the toilet and vomited for the third time today.

She wiped the cold sweat from her forehead and then her mouth with the cool washcloth she was relying on for comfort. She ran her hand through her hair and sank down on the floor. She was shaking and wondering what on earth was wrong with her. The convulsions in her stomach started again. Again, she lurched forward vomiting. *What on earth? The last time I felt like this was when . . . oh my goodness!* She ran her hand across her still-flat stomach. *A baby, could it be after all these years?*

She and Bill had wanted another baby after Penny was born, but it had not happened. Now she was afraid to hope. She stood, shakily, and let her body catch up with her. She staggered to the bedroom and over to the desk. Picking up the calendar, she glanced at the month. This was June already; she was amazed how fast time was flying by. *When was my last period?* She flipped the pages, looking for the red pencil mark.

June went by, then May—her hand went to her mouth. "My gosh," she said as April came into view.

April, that was almost two months ago. She felt a sense of elation take over as she stood there looking at the red marks.

"I'm pregnant," she said out loud to let the feeling sink in.

Just then she heard a gasp at the door behind her. She turned slowly to see Bill standing there, tears coming to his eyes, a questioning look on his face. Justina had been so caught up in her own emotions about the possibility of the pregnancy she hadn't even heard him come in.

"A baby?" he whispered.

Justina nodded. She walked over to him and he held her close.

"I think so, I mean I haven't had a test, but I think so," she said.

"Thank God, a baby," he said.

The tears on their cheeks mingled as they held on to each other. Bill took her face in his hands and looked her in the eyes.

"Let's not tell Penny until we're sure, until the doctor confirms it, okay?"

Justina nodded, covered her mouth, and ran for the bathroom. Bill watched her go concerned, but smiling and feeling pride swell in his chest. *A baby. Good job ol' boy.*

CHAPTER 29

Tony climbed the three steps of his porch and walked to the door.

Just as he reached for the doorknob, it was jerked open by Claire.

"My goodness, what is it?" he asked as he pulled her into his arms. "Are we going to do this again?"

She giggled and squirmed in his arms. "Come inside, I have news."

"What put a bee in your bonnet?" he asked her. "Are the kids okay?"

"The kids are fine. Becky is sleeping and Mike is working on something in the garage. The boys are watching TV. But listen, Tony, you will never guess what happened! Never in a million years will you get this."

Tony stood there looking at her. Finally he raised his eyebrows in a questioning way.

"What, Claire? Just tell me. I am tired and hungry and I really want to take a shower, not play twenty questions with you."

"I talked to her!" Claire said. "She is so nice. Tony, wait till you meet her."

"Who?"

"Lindsay Freeman. I called her just to see what she would say and she was so nice."

Tony felt anger rising in his chest. "How did you get her number, Claire?"

"Oh, I got it from your desk at work. Didn't Paula tell you I came by today?" she asked, ignoring his anger.

"No, she did not, and what were you doing going through my desk?"

"Well, I wasn't going through your desk really. I brought you lunch and I wanted to write your name on it when I put it in the kitchen, so I was looking for paper and pen. Don't be mad, sweetheart, I just couldn't stand it when I saw the number. I had to call her; I only wanted to hear her voice."

"Well," Tony asked, his anger dissipating in the face of her childlike excitement. "What did she sound like? Did she have weird music playing in the background and chimes going off?" He raised his hands and wiggled his fingers.

"No, she did not," Claire said defiantly, planting her feet and putting her hands on her hips. "She was very nice, and she sounded just like me."

"Oh, brother. That's just great."

Claire stamped her foot, and he laughed at her. "I'm sorry, sweetheart, I was going to call her anyway. I did some checking, and some people I've worked with have seen her in action. They say she's very competent, though a little blunt at times. To be honest, she may be of help, and anything at this point is better than what we have. I just don't want to be laughed out of a job."

Claire hugged him and handed him the phone.

Tony looked at it for a moment. "Can I have something to eat first?"

"Oh, honey, I'm sorry," she said, heading toward the kitchen. "I'll get you something right away."

"Something," Tony said, "I want *something* all right . . . normalcy, that's what I want."

"The number is right there on the desk, if you want to call while I get your dinner."

Tony looked at the piece of paper. *What the heck,* he thought and dialed the number.

Lindsay picked up the receiver on the third ring. "Hello," she said sleepily.

Tony realized he must have awakened her and started to hang up.

"Captain Miller? Is that you?"

"Yes, I'm sorry to wake you."

"No, it's okay. I guess I fell asleep here at my desk. I've been waiting for your call. I spoke to your wife earlier. She's a very lovely woman."

Tony realized he didn't really know what to say to her.

"Just relax," Lindsay said, "and let the words come."

He started talking then. "I got your name and number from another cop. We used to work together a long time ago and we went to the academy together. He said you helped out his department some time ago when they had a missing child and that you're pretty good. I myself find it, uh, you know, a little, uh . . ." Tony stammered as he realized that he had almost insulted the woman he was calling for help.

"Strange," Lindsay offered.

"Yes, sorry, but I do. I've never met anyone like you claim to be. To be honest, I don't really believe in it. To me life is about science, and this is not science."

"That's okay, Tony," she said. "That happens a lot. I too find it a little strange, but I live it. Can you tell me the name of the little girl who is missing?"

"Marcie Anderson," he said. Tony wasn't going to give her any information that she didn't ask for. He wanted to see what she could tell him.

"Is she seven years old?"

"Yes, she is."

"Does she have brown hair?" Lindsay continued as images of Marcie started to come to her.

"Yes, again."

"Has she been missing about a week, maybe just a bit more?"

"Yes," Tony said.

"She comes from a large family and is very close to her mother, is that true? Her mom has the same color hair as she does and there are brothers, lots of brothers. But she is the only female child, is that right?" Lindsay was on a roll. The words were coming faster and faster as images of Marcie and her family filled her mind.

Tony was amazed. "You have them pretty much down to a tee. Has someone else called you about this family or do you have relatives here?"

Lindsay ignored him. She just kept right on with her questions, not even listening to the answers until she felt something new and different, different from the Anderson child. "She seems to have something blonde about her hair. What is that?" Lindsay asked. To her it felt foreign.

"I don't know. I see her all the time, but I've never noticed anything blonde about her."

"Really, well let's go on. All of a sudden I feel an only child, one whose mother is pregnant?"

"No," Tony said, "she's not. She's one of four children, and her mother is an older woman. Marcie was a change-of-life baby for the Andersons."

"Do you know what this could mean? I feel two conflicting situations here."

Tony shook his head. "No, our situation here is pretty cut and dried. Someone took Marcie Anderson from in front of her house around six P.M. on a Tuesday evening more than a week ago, and we have no leads."

"Hmmm, this is strange. One child seems to be from a large family and the other—well, I feel that she's the only child of a small family and the mother is newly pregnant. Tell me this, officer, do they live on a street that is tree-lined and the name is a number?"

"Yes, the Andersons do, but there's only one child."

"Is the Anderson house just one story?" Lindsay asked.

"No," Tony replied, "the house is two stories and Marcie's bedroom is upstairs."

"I'm sorry, that's not what I get at all. First, I get a picture of her being taken outside, but then I see a sleeping child being taken from her bed. This is confusing to me. I guess maybe I'm not the one to help you. I'm so sorry."

"Thanks for your time. You were right on several things. Thanks again for taking time to talk to me."

"You're welcome, and if I can help, please feel free to call me. I'll do what I can even if it's not much," Lindsay said, really regretting she couldn't help.

Tony hung up and sat looking at the phone. *That was spooky,* he thought. *She was right on the money with so much, and then all the sudden, she got off and that was that. Well, it was worth a shot.*

Claire brought him a tray with a warm roast beef sandwich, chips, and a large glass of milk.

She looked at him. "Well, how did it go?"

"It went well for a while, then she got off track. She seemed to know so much, but all of a sudden she asked if Marcie had something blonde in her hair and was Janet pregnant."

Claire looked at him and stroked his hair. "I'm so sorry, honey. I had hoped it would help."

"I know you did. Thanks for calling her," Tony said. "She seemed so right about so much of it. Ages, family structure, looks, all that. It kind of bothers me. She was too right; something feels off. She knew the street name was a number and that it was tree-lined. She knew Marcie was seven and had brothers. She thought initially that Marcie had brown hair, which she does. She was on the money, Claire, until she asked about an only child, the blonde in her hair, if her mother was pregnant, and if they lived in a single-level home. So she was half right and half not. Damn, I had just started to get excited thinking that I might get some help and now I guess not. This sucks." Tony looked at his plate. Food had lost its appeal.

Lindsay sat in silence, staring at the phone. *I missed something, but what is it?* She had a feeling there was something she either was not getting or she had missed altogether. Could it be that something else was coming? She was so afraid of not being able to warn others when crisis was upon them. As she stood up to go to bed, something shiny caught her eye, something at the toe of her shoe. She stooped to see what it was, but the image was gone.

I must be more tired than I thought. She wandered off to bed to cuddle with Jack. The movie was long over, and she could tell he had reset the sleep timer. The screen hummed blankly. She switched it off. *Ant races . . . that's what Jackie called it when the little dots raced across the screen.* She lay still in the dark and tried to go to sleep. The nagging feeling that she had missed something stayed with her until she drifted off. The last time she glanced at the clock it was 1:30 in the morning.

She dreamed about shoes and shining things attached to the toes. For some reason the dream scared her, and she sat up in bed. Breathing hard, she felt the fear subside. *What did shining things on the tips of shoes have to do with anything?* If she could, she would call Tony Miller tomorrow and find out what he knew about shiny things on shoes. The one thing she knew for sure was that this was somehow connected to him. She would have to check the pages on her desk for doodlings. Maybe she had jotted down the number, or perhaps she could check her answering machine to see if Claire Miller had left it. She never thought it could be concerning anything other than the Marcie Anderson case. She lay down again and drifted off to a peaceful sleep.

Tony and Claire were dreaming their own dreams as well. Tony saw someone coming toward him in the light of the streetlamp. The only thing he could make out were the tips of the man's shoes that glowed an almost fluorescent green. The man seemed to be pointing at him as he walked away backwards. In his dream, Tony started chasing the man, but no matter how hard he ran he couldn't catch him.

Claire dreamt that she was at the airport meeting Lindsay Freeman. She was waving and waving at the airplane as the tiny passengers came down the stairway. Her arm hurt because she had waved so much. She woke up with her arm in the air waving frantically. Tony was sitting up beside her, shouting for someone to stop.

CHAPTER 30
Roman Marsh was sleeping soundly when the scent woke him.

He opened the mini blinds and pushed the window up further. The scent was there for sure. It was time to go. He looked to the side of the bed. There sleeping on the floor on her mat was Marcie. She was softly snoring; every now and then, she would call out something that he could not quite make out. No matter. Tomorrow when she woke up she would be a happy pet again, soft and yielding. The thought of that gave Roman such a feeling of elation that he almost laughed aloud.

He dressed quietly in dark clothes. He didn't want to disturb her and have a scene at this late hour. He had things to do, things for Marcie, things she would not understand but would love just the same. She never moved and he stroked her hair for being a good girl.

Roman carried a small bag under his arm as he went out the door. He walked through the junkyard and down the streets he was beginning to know. He kept his head down, staying in the shadows of the trees, out of the direct path of the light. He alternated between running and walking as he made his way to his car two blocks away. Walking up to it, he saw something on the windshield. A ticket! He had gotten a ticket for parking in a no parking zone!

Damn the luck. Fuck them, I am not going to pay it. He crumpled it up and threw it on the sidewalk. Getting angrily behind the wheel, he grabbed the window handle and rolled it down quickly. With his head out the window, he sniffed furiously, waiting for the scent to hit him. He started the car and drove through town. He was heading in the direction of the neat family homes on a closely tree-lined street.

Roman stopped his car in the shadows and got out. He could see his target just beyond the next set of tall bushes. With his pocketknife in hand, he walked to the side of the house opposite the glow from the street light.

I should have brought a B-B gun to shoot that light out. He sniffed the air again. There was that sweet, blessed scent that he needed. As he inhaled, it filled his lungs. This was the night. Now he knew why he had been so rudely awakened. Roman let his fingers slowly travel over the screen on the window. He felt the texture of it and laid his face up against it but he couldn't get a feel for her room.

This was not it, he thought, because he remembered Marcie telling him you could see the backyard from the bedroom window. He moved around the corner to the back of the house. There was a window with no screen right by the swing set. He quietly walked to it, ready for anything. The hair on the back of his neck stood up and he could feel goose bumps travel up and down his arms. He was under the adrenaline rush he knew so well at times like this.

Crouching below the window, he held his breath for short intervals and waited for his breathing to settle back to normal. He needed release. He was so excited, and he needed to free the live animal force within him. Roman knelt next to the swing set and rested against the red wagon that sat in the yard waiting for someone to come out to play. He let his hands go to work on his body. Feeling the tingling of his skin, he opened the front of his pants and brought about the desired response.

Breathing better and feeling the aftermath of his freedom, he went back to work. *I love this*, he thought to himself. *This is what I was made for. This is what I was bred for by whoever my breeder was.* Roman went to work on the task at hand.

The window gave way rather easily after he slid his knife into the seam of it. Sliding and working it forward, he felt the catch give way with the slightest pressure. He pushed it to the left. It was that kind of window, and it opened wide. He looked into the little room that seemed filled to the brim with things he could not quite make out. Different shapes and sizes greeted his eyes, but nothing dangerous. This was, after all, a pet's room.

What amazed him the most was the sweet, warm smell of the room. He climbed inside and listened. He could hear the heavy breathing of someone sleeping nearby. Moving so softly he almost could not hear himself, he made his way over to the bed. Standing at the side of her pretty bed, Roman watched Penny Ware sleeping. She was his prize, his intended. He stroked her skin, letting his fingers travel up her bare leg. She was dressed in short pajamas that had ridden up in the night-wiggle of sleep. He touched her bottom and patted it affectionately. She was shameless in the way she slept; he would have to teach her better. She was so precious he felt tears come to his eyes.

Penny must have sensed someone else in the room and started to awaken. Roman panicked, fearing this would cause complications he wasn't ready for. The scent was in the air, this was the night, and nothing could stop him now that the scent was there. He had to go forward or the scent would abandon him. Slamming his hand down hard on her mouth as she let out a scream, he knew that he had hurt her. Her eyes wide and wild, she kicked and thrashed about in the bed and tried to claw his fingers away. He reached for her and shook her roughly with his other hand.

"Stop it right now or you'll be sorry. Do you hear me? Do you want to go and play with Marcie?" Roman asked.

Penny shook her head yes, and tears came to her eyes. Roman started to take his hand away and Penny inhaled a large breath. Just as she started to scream, Roman hit her hard in the face, knocking her instantly unconsciousness. He stomped his foot in frustration. Why was this happening to him? The scent had betrayed him, even when he had done all he was supposed to do.

Roman was in a state of panic as he raced around the room. He listened at the door for sounds. Hearing nothing, he ran back to the bed. As he passed the window, the scent once again caught him, calming him almost instantly. *She is sleeping like a baby*, he thought.

He walked around her room looking at her things, touching her toys and opening drawers. He let the silky feel of her things soothe his feelings. Taking the bag he had carried with him and opening it on the bed, he loaded it with things little girls need: toys and clothes, shoes and hair things as well. The bag was heavy when he was done, but looking at Penny sleeping, he knew that her slight frame would be no weight at all.

He dropped the bag outside the window and went back to Penny. Looking at her, he saw something trickling from the corner of her mouth. Roman bent and stuck his tongue to it. *Blood*, he thought, and he shoved her roughly. *She was fine*, he thought to himself. He was mad at her again for making him hit her like that. He would teach her, just as he had taught Marcie. He looked again at her sleeping form. Wiping the blood from her face with the sheet, he lifted her into his arms. *She's tiny*, he thought, *so small and defenseless*. He would protect her from everything and everyone. He made his way out the same way he had come in, except for one thing. This time he had a heavier load.

CHAPTER 31

Bill Ware heard something that stirred him from sleep.

He thought about it and realized it could have been a car starting. He let the sleep clear from his mind and wondered if the people next door were having their baby tonight. He turned over and felt for the warm form of his wife. She was there right beside him where she had been for years. He thought about the baby that might be coming. *What a surprise this was.* After years of trying, then just when they had quit, Justina was pregnant. He hoped it was true, and was praying for it.

He realized that he had lain awake too long. Sleep wouldn't come again easily, and now he had to go to the bathroom. He glanced at the clock next to the bed. "What the hell am I doing awake at 2:14 in the morning?" he whispered. He slowly got out of bed and walked across to the bathroom; a night-light lit the path for him. He felt a chill in his bones as he stood there, taking care of nature's call. The house was cold even to him, and he knew Justina and Penny would be feeling it soon.

Walking to the door and slowly pulling it open, he heard Justina say, "It's cold in here. Will you check the thermostat?"

"Will do," he called back over his shoulder, smiling as he went. Did he know his girls or what?

"Check on Penny too, will you," Justina said as she pulled the covers closer.

"Yes, dear, I will." Thinking in just a few months, God willing, they would be checking on two babies. His family was growing and he loved the thought.

He checked the thermostat first and found that it had been set on seventy-two degrees, great for him but not so great for his girls. He turned it up. Next, he walked down the hallway to Penny's room. Opening the door he let his eyes adjust to the light that was coming in from outside. The window was open and Penny's bed was empty. He turned to look down the hall at the bathroom she used. *No light there.*

He walked the short distance to the living room to see if Penny was in there watching TV. She was going to get it if she was up at this late hour after having been put to bed. Bill was upset with Penny because lately she'd been showing a little more independence in ways that were starting to get out of hand. It was time to settle that issue right now, he thought to himself as he turned the corner into the living room.

But Penny wasn't there either. Bill checked the doors. Finding them all locked, he felt the first waves of fear take hold as he raced back to her room, his heart hammering away in his chest. He could see Penny's still vacant bed in the glow from the street light. He ran to it, stumbling over toys he knew had not been there when he had tucked Penny in earlier that night.

Oh my God, his mind was screaming while he was trying to be calm. He reached the bed and felt the coldness of the sheets. Turning around and racing for the light switch, he stumbled again over the toys that should not have been there. The light blinded him temporarily, causing him to shield his eyes before turning around. Bill felt the fear boil up in him. He was afraid because he knew, in the harshness of the bright light, what he was going to find.

He turned slowly. There before him was the open window and the stained bedclothes. The sight of the sheets trailing out the window removed any hope that Penny was in another part of the house. Bill let out a groan that started in the pit of his stomach then slowly turned into a howl. He sank to his knees and put his head in his hands, rocking back and forth. The images that he had seen were forever burned into his mind. He struggled to get himself together for only one reason. From somewhere far away he could hear Justina calling his name. He began to get slowly to his feet, using the frame of the door as support.

Then Justina reached the door of Penny's room. When she looked inside, she released a heart-wrenching scream that made Bill's blood curdle. He grabbed her, holding her close. She had seen it too. In her mother's heart she knew that Penny was gone. She melted in his arms, and he slowly laid her on the floor. Still kneeling over Justina, he turned again, just to be sure he had seen what he did not want to see. Just in case it was a nightmare, and he was going to wake up.

There, just under the open window, was a good sized spot of blood that had been smeared on the white sheets of the bed his daughter had been sleeping in just a short time before. He had tucked her in himself, only he had not checked her window. He had let someone take his child.

Bill started to shake and then the tears of agony came. He knew he had to get up. He needed help. He needed to take care of Justina. He got to his feet and picked up his wife. Carrying her to the sofa, he gently put her down and then grabbed the phone. Dialing 911, he waited for what seemed an eternity.

"911, what is your emergency?" the calm voice of the dispatcher asked.

"This is William Ware. I live at 1202 Third Street and I need the police," he said in an amazingly calm voice. "I need the police and an ambulance. My wife is unconscious and my daughter is missing."

Once the necessary business was accomplished, he lost it. Maybe it was hearing the words that shook what little bit of control he had. The dispatcher heard him start to cry. She tried hard to keep his attention.

"William," she said in a calm voice, "listen to me. I need you stay with me, okay? Keep the phone by your ear and listen. William, are you there? William?"

There was no talking and almost no sound except for the heart-wrenching sobs of a man in pain. The dispatcher knew what to do. She grabbed her microphone. "All units in the vicinity of the 1200 block of Third Street, please respond to a 911 call from the Ware residence at 1202 Third Street."

There were only two cops out there, but both ran for their cars outside the restaurant. *Shit, there goes dinner for the night,* they both thought. The dispatcher made the next decision on her own, grimly picking up the phone. Dialing Captain Tony Miller's residence in the middle of the night was against the rules, but tonight it would be unthinkable not to.

Tony reached for the phone and slammed it to his ear. "Okay," he said, "this better be important."

"Yes, sir, I believe it is."

"What have you got, Rachel?" Tony asked in a no-nonsense tone of voice.

The dispatcher winced at the sound of his voice. "Sir, William Ware called 911 and requested the police and an ambulance at his residence. He said his daughter was missing and his wife was unconscious."

Tony was on his feet, with one leg already in his trousers. "I'm on my way. Send an ambulance," he ordered.

"One is on the way, sir."

"Did he say anything else?" Tony wanted to know.

"No, sir, crying is all I can hear now. I lost contact with him just after his request. I can hear him in the background, crying still, sir, but he won't answer me."

"I'm just around the corner. Tell him I'll be there in a minute."

Claire was sitting up by this time, and Tony was fully dressed as he hung up the phone. "What's wrong?" she asked.

"Penny Ware is missing" is all she heard as Tony ran out the back door to the garage. Lights and sirens filled the air as he sped down the block, and she could hear the tires screech as he made the corner. She got up, dressed, and ran down the hall to wake Mike.

"Mike, wake up," she said as she shook him. He was instantly awake.

"Mom. What's wrong?"

"Penny Ware is missing. Go get Becky and let her sleep in here with you and the boys," she said. "Don't let anyone in here but Dad and me, do you understand?" Then she too ran out the back door and to the garage and her tires screeched as she turned the corner.

Tony was the first one on the scene with the ambulance and two patrol cars right behind him. Running up the two steps to the front door, Tony tried the doorknob. Finding it locked, he put his shoulder to it and it gave way. There on the floor was Bill Ware leaning over the couch and Justina. Tear-filled eyes turned to look up at him as Tony grabbed Bill's shoulders.

"Tony," Bill sobbed, "he took my baby. He hurt her or worse before he left here with her. He took her from my home. It is my job to keep her safe. Oh my God, he took my little girl." He laid his head back on Justina's chest.

Bill was falling apart fast, and Tony needed him. He pulled him roughly to his feet and shook him.

"What happened and when, Bill? I need to know. Show me the way."

The ambulance attendants had arrived and were taking care of Justina as Bill turned to them and said, "Be careful, she might be pregnant."

Tony's mouth went dry. "What did you say?" he asked Bill as he grabbed his arm, halting his progress down the dark hallway.

Bill looked at Tony. "Jussy might be pregnant. We didn't want to tell anyone till we were sure and told Penny."

"Okay," Tony nodded. "Now show me the way, Bill, and tell me everything that happened,"

Bill seemed to come through when he was needed. The house was filling up fast. Claire comforted Justina and rode to the hospital with her since Bill was needed at home.

The lights and sirens had awakened most of the neighborhood and people were starting to mill about. Suddenly Mac Anderson's large frame filled the doorway. Tony and Bill stood looking at him. Mac came forward and put his arms around Bill. "Hang on, buddy, we're going to be okay. Just hang on."

Bill laid his head on his friend's shoulder and cried. "What are we gonna do, Mac, what are we gonna do?"

"We're gonna get her back, we're gonna get both of them back. That's what we're gonna do and we're gonna be strong and not make any mistakes. Are you with me?"

"Yeah, I'm with you," Bill stated.

The three men went through the house as Bill described the night's events. But when they came to Penny's room, he hung back.

"I can't go in there again," he said. Tony and Mac nodded.

Tony steeled himself for what he would find. He rounded the door, and he saw it immediately. The room was a mess. The drawers were open, and things had been taken out carelessly, dumped here and there. The window was open, and he could see a sheet was trailing out. His officers were out there working in plain view.

Tony called out to them. "Be careful where you step, don't cover his tracks. When you're done out there, come in here. And get Will Jenkins on the phone and ask him to get out here double quick."

Just at that time, a sound was heard in the hallway, and John came running around the corner. He was mad as hell. He looked Tony right in the eye.

"Why wasn't I notified?" he demanded.

"This isn't about you, John. A child is missing."

"This is my case too!"

Tony grabbed him by his lapels, shoving him against the wall. "I said this isn't about you. My friend's daughter has been taken, and God only knows what has happened to her. You want to help, then help. Otherwise shut your mouth or I'll will shut it for you."

John shoved Tony's hands away and smoothed his shirt.

"We'll talk about this tomorrow," he said. Then he saw the fear and anguish in Tony's eyes. John instantly felt like a jerk. "God, man, I'm sorry. I was wrong to come barging in here like that. I just want to be included so I can help. That's all."

Tony patted him on the back. "I understand," he said. "We're over here."

Tony pointed to the bed and the window. They both saw the blood at the same time.

"Sweet Jesus, will you look at that," John said. Tony and John walked to the bed but as they reached out to touch the red spot, they both pulled their hands back.

Tony called outside the window for the lab people to come in the minute they got there.

"They're on their way, sir, I'll send them right in," someone responded through the window.

Suddenly a cry went up from the group of officers out back. Tony and John rushed toward the rear of the house, looking for a back door. Mac was sitting with Bill when they went by.

"Back door!" Tony shouted on his way by, and Mac pointed to the left. John saw the door at the same time. They both ran through it. Officers were standing by the bedroom window, looking down in the dirt. There were shoe tracks everywhere, but a high concentration of them could be seen in one spot. A light was shining on a child's wagon and the tracks that were near it. Tony and John stepped up to see together.

There it was again. Proof that only a man could have done this terrible thing, because only a man could produce the evidence that was on the tissue and the child's toy. The marks in the dirt from the man's shoes were so much the same that Tony knew them before he studied them. He pointed out the outline of the toe caps to John.

"We found these same markings at the Anderson home too," he said as he traced the outline with his pen.

John carefully examined the impression. "What is it?"

"Those are markings from toe caps. Men wore them years ago to dress up their shoes. This guy dresses a little strange. Did you read the report from Rose Muella?"

John nodded. "His age scares me a little," he said.

"Me too," Tony whispered.

They both stood up and walked back to the house, leaving the findings outside to the other officers. The lab guys had arrived and were inside. John and Tony headed straight for them, wanting to be there while they worked. The house was a flurry of activity, more than it had ever seen, for the worst possible reason.

The scenario played on in Roman Marsh's car. Traveling down the road toward his home, Roman passed police cars and an ambulance. The police cars elated him, but the ambulance worried him. What if the police cars were not about him? What if no one knew yet what he had done? There should be no reason for an ambulance, unless of course . . . the thrill hit him like a bucket of bliss. What if the parents had heart attacks and died at the scene? That would be blissful. He would then be important. Penny would need only him then for the rest of her life. What if they killed each other in blame for Roman's deed? That would be euphoric.

Roman had to know. The suspense was killing him. He turned to look at Penny in the back seat. She was still out cold. This distraction was a godsend for Penny, even though she didn't know it. There were a host of things that Roman would be doing to her if she'd ben awake. She needed to be taught to sleep like a lady even if she was only a pet. Lady pets must sleep with dignity too. Roman would teach her though, since it was obvious that her parents didn't care enough about her to teach her such refined things.

He wiped the blood from her lip again and tossed the napkin from the window as he turned the car around. Penny was still out, but she moaned a little as Roman straightened her clothing and the blanket he had taken her in. *She is so cute,* he thought. He wanted to powder her. She smelled so good. He bent his head toward her to get a better whiff. Inhaling deeply, he let the air stay deep in his lungs till they were near bursting. Then he slowly let it out, only because he had to. He resented that his body would not let him hold it in longer.

He was getting lost in his thoughts and needing to find a dark road when the sound of sirens rang in his ears again. He shook his head like a dog and tried to concentrate on what he was doing and where he was going. The curiosity was killing him. He had to know where they were going and what was going on. Most of all, he needed to know if it was about him.

Turning the car to the right, he drove in a large circle so he could come up behind the Ware home. There it was, the chaos he had created with his own hands. He smiled and sat there, letting the feeling wash over him. The ambulance was just leaving and he knew that this was all for him. He felt important and included. *It feels so good. I'm important to a family unit.* He smiled again. *This is so good. I'm so happy.*

Roman brushed a tear from his eye and started the car moving forward again. It was time to go home and feed his and Marcie's new pet. He stroked the hair of his newest pet and prayed to the Blessed Be that she would be a good pet so that he would not have to discipline her. Surely the Blessed Be would answer his prayers.

CHAPTER 32

Around the corner from where Roman Marsh had sat with Penny, a disgruntled neighbor stood by the road glaring in the direction of the departing taillights.

Hershel Owens hated litterbugs, and he cursed out loud as he stared at the tissue Roman had thrown out the window. Quickly, he grabbed the pencil and paper from his housecoat pocket and wrote down the license plate number.

He shook his fist in the air. "Damn litterbug," he shouted. It was bad enough that all those damn sirens had robbed him of the little sleep that he got, but now someone dared to drive down his road and throw trash out the damn window. Hershel had had more than enough. "I'll get you, you'll see. I'm gonna report you to the police, that's what I'm gonna do." He stormed inside and dialed 911.

"911, what's your emergency?" the dispatcher asked.

"This here is Hershel Owens over on Fourth and Elm streets. This guy is throwing trash in the street, and I want something done about it. I work hard in my yard every day, and some yahoo drives down my road in the middle of the night and throws trash along the curb. Now what are ya gonna do about it?"

The dispatcher took a deep breath and counted slowly to five. "Mr. Owens, I'm sorry that someone threw trash by your house, and I will take a report and have someone come by to talk to you later today. But that really is not an emergency now, is it?"

Hershel was really mad now. "Missy, you think I got nothing else to do but clean up after someone that don't even live around here? I work hard to make this a nice house and a nice yard. Maybe citations should go out to those who don't, but I won't get one of those cause my stuff is always neat and clean. You tell that fancy pants captain of yours that Hershel Owens wants to talk at him right now." Hershel was shouting into the phone.

"Sir, I can't do that. Captain Miller is working on something very important right now, but I will have him come over as soon as he is free." Rachel responded with all the patience that she could muster.

"You do that," Hershel shouted and hung up.

Rachel made a note and taped it to Tony's office door. This really was going to be a bad night, she thought to herself as she walked back to her station.

The sun was coming up just as, one by the one, the cars started pulling away from the Ware home. Tony had armed them with detailed lists of instructions, and John had recruited a group of trained men from Tony's staff to work with him. Robby was among that group. Raymond Ross, the sketch artist, was going to meet with Rose Muella that day and get her version of what this man looked like. Damn good thing, Tony thought, because that was all they had to go on. No prints other than boot prints that seemed to be a size nine. That could be any one of a million men.

Tony was tired and frustrated, working now on about three hours of sleep. How did someone eighteen or nineteen years old become a professional kidnapper? Was he a kidnapper or a child stealer?

"Lord, please just don't let him be a child killer," Tony whispered to the heavens as he headed for home.

Mac Anderson went to his house and got out his car to take Bill to the hospital to be with Justina. Janet was sitting at the kitchen table with a cup of coffee. She was dressed in clean clothes, and her hair and make-up were done for the first time in more than a week. She looked up as Mac came in.

"Penny?" she asked.

"Yes," Mac nodded. "Justina might be pregnant and Bill's really worried about her. I'm going to take him to the hospital to be with her. Is that okay with you?"

"Sure it is," she said. "Stay with him as long as he needs you. The kids and I will work on the flyers for Marcie. I guess we should start some for Penny too. Even in a town this size we don't know everyone. Maybe someone has seen Marcie and will see the flyers and call."

Mac smiled and touched her shoulder. She seemed so much better with something to do for her daughter.

"This isn't just about us anymore, is it, Mac?" she asked softly.

"No, sweetheart, it isn't." He kissed her good-bye and whispered as he left, "I love you."

Janet went back to her job and prayed softly that God would intervene.

Tony made it home almost the same time that Claire did. When she arrived, he had just walked in and was rummaging around like a crazy person through the things on the desk.

"Damn it," he said as little pieces of paper hit the floor. "Where the hell is it?"

"What?" Claire asked, as she came in. "Are you okay?"

"No, I'm not okay. We have some fucking weirdo out there taking our kids, and I can't find a damn thing on this desk and my head hurts like hell. Would you be okay if you had to deal with this?"

He was screaming at her, but she knew he didn't mean it. He was angry, hurt, scared, and frustrated. She put her arms around him, holding him for a brief second before she reached into his shirt pocket, pulling out the number he was looking for.

"Looking for this," she asked as she held the paper in the air.

"Oh, Claire, I'm sorry," he said, tightening his grip on her. "This is making me crazy. I feel so damn stupid. Why didn't I see it last night? Lindsay Freeman told me, but neither of us realized what we were seeing. Besides Marcie, she saw a blonde girl, an only child living in a single-level home with a pregnant mother. That was Penny. Justina is pregnant, although no one is sure yet, and Penny does have blonde hair. I could have prevented this if I'd just listened to you and to her. I have to call her. We need her here."

Tony reached for the phone as Claire said, "Tony, it's 5:30 in the morning and it's only 4:30 where she is."

Tony looked at the phone. "Claire, I have to."

Claire gave him the paper and went to make coffee.

He dialed the number that was already beginning to feel familiar. She answered almost immediately.

"Hello, this is Tony Miller."

"Hello," she answered. "I was expecting you to call but not quite this soon. Can I ask you a question?" she said in a hurried voice.

"Sure. I can see that I didn't wake you."

"No," she laughed, "I don't sleep much."

"I need your help again," Tony said.

At the same time she asked, "What does shiny things on the tips of shoes have to do with this case?"

They both stopped talking and silence filled the air.

Then Tony said, "You first," and sat silent.

Lindsay repeated, "What do shiny things on the tips of shoes mean to you?"

"The man we suspect of taking these children wears something on the tips of his shoes called toe caps. Men used to wear them all the time. They're a dressy thing."

"Captain Miller, you just said *these children*. What do you mean by that?"

"You were right last night when we talked," he said. "We just didn't know it yet. You said the child was in her bed or outside. Both have now happened. You said a child with blonde hair and brown hair. Again, both things are right. You also said a single-level house, and last night Penny Ware was taken from her bed in a single-level home in the middle of the night. Her mother is pregnant and no one knew it till last night. So you see, you were seeing the second abduction in process. If I had listened to you, I could have prevented this." He was quiet and she could hear the grief and defeat in his voice.

"Tony," she said, "this is not your fault. From what I'm getting at this moment, there was little you could have done. He had this planned out in his mind well before he did it. Had I been there, I could have seen it, but that's not the point. We must move forward now. Something is different this time, Tony, what is it?"

"This time," he said slowly, "he hurt the child in her bed."

"No, he didn't rape the her, if that's what you're thinking. He seems to have held her mouth, and she bit her lip I think. That's all."

"That's all?" Tony wanted to holler, but he knew that was a blessing.

"Is there some blood, Tony, just a small spot?"

"Yes," he said, "about the size of a silver dollar, along with some smear marks."

"It's from her mouth. She's going to be fine, if that's the worst thing that happens to her."

Tony felt relieved. "When can you come here?"

"Let me make some arrangements," she said. "I'll try to get a flight out later today."

"Our office will pay for everything, and you can either stay with us or we can get you a room, whichever you prefer."

"I'll stay with you and your wife, if you're sure that it's no inconvenience," Lindsay said.

"None at all. My wife may drive you crazy, but you're more than welcome. I'll have tickets ready for you when you let me know your schedule. But Ms. Freeman . . ."

"Yes?"

"Can you come as soon as possible?"

"Sure I can."

He hung up the phone.

Sitting in the semi-darkness, Lindsay thought back to another time when this same thing had happened and the situation had not gone well at all. She felt the terror rising up inside her, boiling in the pit of her stomach as the images swept fiercely through her mind. Her mind rebelled and she felt tears sting her eyes.

Images of the tortured child she had found in that awful basement in Chicago assaulted her. She saw the blank eyes that had cried out just hours before she and the police barged through the door of this rundown building. She saw the long red line that had been carved through the poor baby's body, the one that had ended her life and suffering at the hands of a depraved animal. She felt the little body in her hands as she had then and heard the last little bit of air escape the lungs as she had that day when she had scooped the tiny child up in her arms, mindless of the blood that oozed out on her own clothes. She had held that child and cried then. She did not want to go through that again.

Lindsay realized that the child she felt herself holding was actually the receiver of her phone. She placed it in the cradle and tried to control her breathing, struggling to block the images before they became more real. Moaning out loud, she rocked back and forth in the chair as she fought her way back to the present time and a new situation.

This would be different. This time she had the support of the people she would be working with, and she had already proven herself to them. Still the image of the tortured child hung in the back of her mind. Each time she let herself relax, the images fought their way to her conscience. She had to get a hold on herself. She needed to get up and move around. Again another night with little or no sleep. She was going to be a zombie at the end of this day.

She headed for the kitchen and the coffeepot. As she stumbled through the darkness, images of that long ago tragic night floated in her mind, but she seemed to have a handle on them. That was, until she opened the refrigerator. The light spilling out onto the floor reminded her of the light that had spilled into the room where they had found the little girl. She felt her mind let go as she sank to the floor. She wrapped her hands around her head and lay there on the floor crying out her anguish at not having been on time, not being persuasive enough with the authorities and not being able to breathe life back into that tiny soul. The light of the refrigerator lit her as she lay on the floor in her kitchen, now safe from the rest of the world. The only demons that threatened her now were the demons of her own memory.

She felt the room shift as she was dragged back from that time and place by the presence of someone else in the room. Her daughter Marie knelt beside her and placed a hand on her shoulder. "Mom, are you okay?" She looked up at her daughter.

"I let myself in while you and Jackie were gone. I hope you don't mind."

Lindsay straightened herself up and looked at Marie for a moment as she tried to get her bearings. "No sweetie, of course I don't mind. I'm sorry about this. I got a call this evening about a missing child and it brought back some bad memories for me."

Lindsay stood and made her way to the coffeepot as Marie headed for the overhead light.

"What are you doing here anyway?" Lindsay asked.

"Jerry is out of town and I hate staying there by myself. I thought I would come and keep you company, just in case Jack was with his dad. But when I got here no one was home. Still it feels better here than at my house and besides you have stuff to eat." They both giggled.

"This will always be your home. Come whenever you want, but stay out of the refrigerator." They both laughed again as the coffee brewed.

"Mom, you want to talk about what's bothering you?" Marie looked hard at her mother.

Lindsay reached over and touched her daughter's cheek. "It's a missing child case or actually missing children now," she said. "It seems to be bringing up a lot of old memories and I just had a hard time with it for a few minutes. I'm okay really."

"Are you going to go?"

"Yes, I have to."

"Do you want me to keep Jackie?"

"If you will." Lindsay was grateful. She could always count on Marie.

"Of course I will. You be careful and call us and let us know what's going on, okay?"

"It's a deal." Lindsay sat there in the early morning hours and wondered what the next few would hold. A new case always put a kink in her plans, so when she started doing this work she had learned not to make plans. It had been hard on her children, but life with a clairvoyant parent is always hard on the kids. There are few things that they get away with. Secrets were almost always exposed in this family, and she smiled to herself as she thought back through the years about some of the things they had tried to pull. She loved them and she hoped that never in their lives would they not love or need her. She sat forward and realized she was stalling. She set the coffee cup down with a determined bump.

Standing up she walked to the desk area and reached for the phone book. Looking up Continental Airlines and dialing the number, she felt her stomach tighten. She listened to the recording and pressed the appropriate buttons in response to the computer voice she was listening to. Gosh she hated those things, "I miss the old days," she mumbled to herself.

"Good morning, Continental Airlines, may I help you?" the voice asked. It caught Lindsay off guard and she had to pull herself back from her thoughts.

"Uh, sorry, you caught me daydreaming. I need to make reservations for a flight, please, round trip."

"Okay, what is your destination please?"

Lindsay gave her the information.

"I can get you on a flight out this evening at 7:35 P.M. from Chicago O'Hare. Will that work for you?"

Lindsay looked at the clock; twelve hours. Yes that would work just fine for her, but she was not so sure about the children she was leaving behind or the ones that she was going to find. She accepted the flight and wrote down the numbers.

"That will be fine, thank you. Can you confirm that for me please?"

"Sure I can, I just need your name and billing information and when you would like to return."

That was always the hardest part about making travel arrangements like this. One never knew and airline companies always wanted a date and time. Lindsay said "I have no idea yet. Is there any way to work around that?"

The line was silent for a moment and then the voice said, "You don't know when you're coming back?"

"Nope, sorry."

"Let me check with a supervisor and see what we can do. I'll just be a minute."

Lindsay used the time to make a list of all the things that had to be done before she left. People who needed to be notified and things she needed from the store to make sure Jack had all he needed while Marie was taking care of him. He had a hearty appetite, and she didn't want to put that expense on Marie and Jerry.

The voice said, "Hello," as if for the second time.

"Yes, sorry, I guess I was daydreaming again," Lindsay said.

"Ms. Freeman?"

"Yes."

"We can book that for you with a tentative date, but we need some idea of your return date if you can give us one. There will, however, be a fifty-dollar fee on your return trip ticket if you change that tentative date."

"That's what I thought," Lindsay said. "Okay, let's do that."

She gave the required billing information as she was directed and began writing down her itinerary for her daughter and so she could let Tony Miller know when she was coming.

"Thank you very much, Ms. Freeman, for doing business with Continental Airlines. We look forward to serving you again. Enjoy your flight."

She hung up the phone and went to talk to Marie. Now it was time to let Tony Miller know when she was coming so that he too could make his arrangements. She dialed the number and waited. A sweet little voice answered the phone. "Hello."

Lindsay immediately saw the face of a small girl with brownish-blonde curls all over her head and a face like a cherub.

"Hello, is your daddy there?" she asked.

"Yes, ma'am."

"Can I speak with him please?"

"Yes, ma'am."

Then Lindsay heard nothing.

"Hello," Lindsay said again.

"Yes, ma'am," the child said again.

"Sweetie, can I please speak to your daddy?" Lindsay asked with a smile in her voice.

"When do you want to talk to him?" the little voice asked.

"Now, if that's okay," Lindsay said, smiling to herself. She knew that the child was playing a game with her, so she said, "Can you tell your daddy that this is police business?"

"Yes, ma'am, I can. Should I do that now?"

"Yes, sweetie, if you will. This is very important."

"Okay," and with that the phone hit the table with a loud clank and she heard, "Daddy, telephone."

A few minutes later a female voice picked up the phone.

"Hello," Claire said into the phone.

"Hello, Mrs. Miller, this is Lindsay Freeman. Can I speak with your husband, please?"

"Of course. Tony's in the shower. Give me just a minute to take the phone to him."

"Thank you, that's not necessary," she said laughing to herself. "I don't really need to interrupt his shower."

"Okay, I'll have him call you. Can I relay a message?"

"Yes, if you would. Tell him my flight is booked and I will see you all this evening around 9:50 P.M. your time."

"Oh, okay, and will you please consider staying with us?" Claire could not help herself, she just had to ask.

"Yes, if you're sure I won't be a bother," Lindsay said.

"No, oh no, no bother at all, we would love to have you and I will make sure that the kids don't get in your way," Claire stammered. She looked around her house and thought of all that needed to be done before Lindsay came to stay with them. Maybe Louise from across the way would help her clean and get the room ready.

Lindsay wondered sheepishly who would protect her from Claire. She giggled at the thought.

"We'll be there to pick you up this evening," Claire said.

"Thanks again, Claire. I'll see you then. Oh, and Claire, I'll be wearing a navy blue pantsuit."

"Okay, that will make you easier to spot in the crowd. See you tonight."

An hour later Lindsay was in the shower, trying to keep thoughts of the two little girls away. She sensed that they were traumatized even as she stood and let the water run down her body. What was the man doing to them? Where were they and how was she going to get through the next few hours?

She hated to travel in an enclosed area. Being a clairvoyant she was a victim to others' thoughts when she was cooped up with them. People thought the strangest things when they flew. Most of them had fear at one time or another, making her scared most of the time. She needed to remember to bring a book so that her own mind stayed busy. She stepped out of the shower and patted her skin dry.

She longed for the nap she knew she couldn't have till her flight, if it was possible even then. She reached into her closet for clothes that would see her through the next few days. As time slipped by, she packed and made arrangements: paid the bills, did the grocery shopping for the kids, locked the office for the week and left a message with the answering service, and then made a list for the kids to take care of along with numbers where to reach her, just in case. Her family always came first, and she tried to make sure that everyone she worked for knew that and understood. This was one issue that she would never bend.

At five o'clock that evening she headed for the airport and an uncertain event. Her bags were on the seat behind her, and the kisses were still wet on her cheeks from the family she left safely behind.

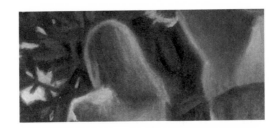

CHAPTER 33
Marcie lay on a blanket on the floor and waited.

She had finally cried herself to sleep, the tears leaving tracks as if needing to prove they had been there. The bang of the living room door had jolted her awake, although she hadn't realized what it was at the time. She lay as still as she could and waited for some other sign that the monster had returned. Sometimes she dreamed she was the princess in the tower who was kept there by the troll that lived under the bridge. Some day her Prince Charming would come to rescue her.

The bumping sound started again. Marcie trembled in her makeshift bed. It seemed to be muffled this time, but she knew for sure that he was back. Something wasn't right though. Marcie tucked her head back into the crook of her arm and pretended to be asleep. She was afraid to look up for fear that he was there looking at her. She didn't want to see him or for him to see that she was awake. Her body shook with fear. It could have been the cold if the weather was different, but the night was hot and balmy as the Deep South could be this time of year.

There it was again, a bang. Lifting her head just a bit, Marcie tried to squint her eyes in the darkness to get a look just beyond where her eyes could see without raising her head anymore than she already had. The sound seemed to come from inside the house one moment and then outside the next. Marcie knew there was nothing out there other than Roman unless it was a wild animal or a dog or something like that. That she could deal with; anything was better than the wild animal that lived here with her. He was the creature she feared most. She knew he was near, but she didn't know what he was doing this time.

She was so afraid. All she really wanted was to go home. She missed her mom and dad. She even missed her brothers. Her first few days here Marcie felt she was in a bad dream, but now she knew this was real. She just didn't know why.

She listened closely, but she couldn't hear Roman breathing from the bed. She couldn't hear his deep snores or the grunts and groans he made in the night. She knew he was in the living room but what was happening out there? Maybe her mom and dad had changed their minds and come to get her. With that thought Marcie felt hope stir inside her heart. She lifted her head ever so slightly, just enough to get her ear off the blanket that she was lying on. She heard someone talking now, but the sound was faint. It sounded like Roman and she knew from the sound of his voice that he was mad, real mad.

One time when she had first come to be with him, she had woken up in the middle of the night to hear him outside in the yard. He was walking around in a large circle, screaming. She had looked out the window that time, something she would never do again. He had come running into the house, yelling at her for spying on him. He had been so angry that night that he had taken his clothes off and done that thing to himself that he always did when he was mad. Marcie hated to see that. She hated what it did to his face and how his body strained from what he was doing. He was hurting himself, though Marcie thought he deserved it.

Roman always made Marcie go and wash her face and hands when he did that to himself. "Get out of here, go wash your dirty face and hands," he would scream at her. Marcie ran for the bathroom and scrubbed her face as hard as she could. She would cry, but she always did what he told her to. Marcie prayed the whole time for her daddy to come and beat him up for being mean to her.

Again Marcie heard a loud sound. She was pretty sure that he was in the living room. Who was he screaming at and why was he was walking around in a circle waving his arms in the air?

Slowly she inched her body off the ground. She peeked over the bed and saw to her relief that she had been right and he wasn't there. She sat up and let her eyes adjust to a light coming from the living room. She looked at the window, longing to go peek out there and see what he was up to, but she was too afraid to move.

She didn't want him to come into the room where she was, but more than that she didn't want to go back into the trunk of that old car again. The trunk was an ever-present threat. A tear ran down her cheek. She was so afraid and confused. Sitting up, she hugged her knees and rocked in the darkness, and longed for home. Would someone please come and take her home?

Suddenly she realized his ranting had stopped. She felt the fear get stronger in her and she stopped rocking, straining again to hear where he was. She heard footsteps that were moving fast and sounded angry as they came toward the house. Marcie realized that Roman was running in and out of the house. "I wish he had a mommy who would punish him for that," she said to herself.

As the footsteps came closer to the room, Marcie lay down quickly and pretended to be asleep. She tried to control her breathing, so that if he got close to her he wouldn't be able to tell she was faking. She heard the bedroom door open on its creaky hinges. The little carpet that was always by the door made a slight whooshing sound as it was pushed roughly away and he stepped into the room.

He didn't turn the light on, but she knew he was there. He stood in the doorway, but she couldn't hear him or understand what he was doing. He shifted on his feet and then the bedroom door closed and she was alone again. Marcie trembled as her tears flowed freely.

He was angry; she could tell that by the way he walked. He sounded like Daddy when he was mad at one of her brothers and someone in the house would say, "Boy, are you gonna get it now," but it was never her. She was never afraid of her dad.

Now Marcie heard a new sound coming from the living room. She sat up just a little bit, ready to lie down suddenly if he came toward the door again. The sound was like a crying, whimpering sound. She listened closely and then she heard him and she knew what he was doing.

Roman took a deep breath and grabbed handfuls of his hair. At the top of his voice he shouted, "SHUT UP. Stop that crying and be a good pet or you go to the dog pound, do you hear me?" He pulled his hair till it hurt and then he stomped his feet in rapid succession on the floor. He was having a temper tantrum, but he couldn't help it. His precious new pet was being bad and he had no idea what to do with it.

Her taking had been so good, so sweet, and she had smelled so good as they had driven through the dark streets. He had prolonged the drive home so he could have her all to himself and not have to share her for a while. He had enjoyed those precious moments with her. That was before she had awakened, before she became the screaming, crying little bitch that she was being now. Roman felt reality slipping away from him. The pet had control and he hated that. No one took his control and no one controlled him. He needed to get control again and this little pet wouldn't let him. It cried and hollered back at him. He had slapped it a time or two and now it was crying again. He grabbed his body all over, pinching himself, pulling on his skin and tearing at his clothes. He spit on the ground and jumped up and down. He needed to take control back from her. He wracked his mind trying to decide what to do.

"Reese, where the hell are you when I need you?" Roman shouted into the night air. He looked at her lying there on the sofa. Her hair was a mess and it stuck to the tears on her face. Her clothes were rumpled and she had her thumb in her mouth. She was watching him, but he could see that she was both scared and something else. Defiance showed in her eyes. She was actually mad at him! Roman was shocked by it.

That pushed him over the edge, and he stormed toward her, grabbing her little body by her hips and turning her over his knee as he sat roughly down on the couch. In one motion he tore her pajamas from her. She struggled to get away from him as he slapped her bottom and she refused to cooperate. The more Roman fought her, the louder she cried.

Somehow the mind knows just how far to go and when to back down, even in the very young. After a few minutes, Penny stopped struggling and cried softly to herself. Roman felt the change in her. He spanked her a few more times before pushing her roughly from him and onto the floor. "Look at me," he said softly.

Penny turned her head in his direction and sniffled loudly. He was looking down at her and glaring. "Behave yourself or you will be sorry," he said in a threatening voice. She was trembling, crying and choking on her own tears. She turned her face away from him.

"Look at me if you want to be good," Roman said again. Penny refused to turn to him. He felt the rage coming again, braced himself, and pulled at his penis through his jeans.

"LOOK AT ME," he shouted at her, "or you will go in the trunk, do you want to go in the trunk?"

Penny hiccuped and turned her head in his direction. Roman had thought for a moment he was going to have to spank her again, just to get her attention, the way his foster dad had done to him. It worked; he knew that from his own experience.

He felt her eyes on him. Roman stood and walked around to where she was lying on the floor. He turned to face away from her and opened his pants wider, shifting his hips just a little to let his pants fall to the ground. He stood there with his back to her and his buttocks exposed and masturbated. He had control again.

Penny watched him in horrified fascination. She saw his head fall forward and watched his body start to sweat and jerk. When he reached his release, he looked over his shoulder at her. Penny threw up and Roman laughed. Yes, he had control again.

Marcie had heard it all. Seeing nothing and hearing everything, her imagination had run wild on the floor in the corner where she had learned to live. She thought that he had killed whatever he had in there with him, and she cried out loud at the mention of the trunk, not being able to stop herself. "Please don't let him put anyone else in the trunk, please," she cried softly to herself.

In the living room, Penny cried too, lying on the floor in her own vomit with the rag clutched in her hand that Roman had thrown at her. He felt in control again for the first time in hours. Life was sweet and justice was his. "You just have to show some animals how to live," he thought proudly.

Inside Marcie tried desperately to stop crying. She held her hand over her mouth and choked back the sobs, but she was afraid she had been too loud. She knew there was no way that he had not heard her. She waited for him to come and she didn't have to wait long.

The Roman that opened the door and stood there looking at her was not one that she wanted to see. She really didn't want to see him at all, but this Roman was even worse than the other one. His eyes were glassed over and he seemed to be drunk.

He walked over to where she lay on the floor and nudged her gently.

Something happened to him in that brief moment. He felt himself drift off into another place and even as he felt that happening, he knew he was losing. He struggled to regain all that he had worked so hard for. All those years of struggling through therapy and counselors and foster parents. He had finally learned to fool them all, and now here he was losing his grip because of a pet that would not obey him.

He looked down at Marcie. This was his sweet pet. This was his best baby. He loved this pet, and he bent and stroked her hair as he dried the tears on her cheeks. She had been crying for him. He had been gone too long, and she had missed him or perhaps been worried about him.

He felt renewed anger at the pet in the other room, the one who had taken him from his precious baby. It was all her fault. His Marcie would make her behave. She would teach the new pet how to act and what was expected of her. He lifted her in his arms and she knew to snuggle or he would be mad at her. She cringed but buried her head against his neck.

Roman sighed and lifted her easily and carried her toward the living room.

"I have a job for you, my sweet baby," he said.

Marcie looked up at him. "What it is?"

"I want you to train our new pet."

Marcie thought about what she had heard and was afraid for any animal that he had captured. What did he do to it to make it cry like that? At the same time, the child in her was elated at the thought of having a pet, something to cuddle with and to love.

"We have a pet?" she asked in a little-girl voice.

"Yes," Roman said, "and you get to teach it all sorts of things and make it behave. Can you do that?"

"Oh yes, I'm good with animals. My mommy always says that I'm gonna make a great vet, uh, pet doctor. Where is the little pet?"

"In here," he pointed to the living room toward the couch.

Now Marcie could see a semi-naked Penny Ware lying on the floor, her hair all messed up, her bottom exposed, and a rag in her mouth. Penny's eyes were pleading. Marcie threw her head back and screamed.

CHAPTER 34

Lindsay was already aboard the airplane when in her mind she heard the screams.

She jumped up in her seat as she cried out, "NO!" in a long agonizing scream.

The passengers around her stared, and the flight attendant quickly made her way down the aisle. Lindsay sat down, embarrassed.

The attendant placed a hand on Lindsely's shoulder and looked her in the eye. "Are you okay?"

Lindsay looked up at her and shook her head just a little, trying to remember where she was. "Yes, I'm fine. I just had a nightmare. Sorry to have scared everyone."

"It happens. Can I get you anything?"

"A glass of water would be nice, thanks," Lindsay said. The flight attendant smiled as she went to get the water.

Lindsay put her head in her hands. Oh God, please, please don't let the screams be for real. But she knew that she had heard the screams of the children. First one, then the other. She knew they were still alive, but she couldn't tell what condition they were in. She was afraid to look more deeply, for fear she would not be able to control herself. If she had been someplace where she had some privacy, it would be different, but not here aboard the airplane like this. She needed a place where she could be alone so that what she saw she could take her time dealing with. She also needed to get to know each child individually so that she could tell one from the other in her feelings.

But for now she needed a distraction so she could get through the flight. With an hour to go, she needed someone to talk to. She looked to the left and the right of her.

The woman to the right was totally engrossed in her book, and the man on her other side was asleep.

The flight attendant came back with the water and asked how she was feeling.

"Better now, thanks, I just had a bad dream, I guess," she said again. "Maybe I'll just read for a while."

Lindsay picked up her book, but she had a hard time concentrating. Eventually she got through a paragraph or two. This flight was going to be a true nightmare. Lindsay just let it happen.

CHAPTER 35
Justina Ware rolled to her side in the hospital bed.

She was in terrible pain but she couldn't for the life of her remember what had happened. Her body hurt and she felt the dried tears on her face. She reached a hand up to brush them away. As she did this Bill's face loomed before her.

Taking her hand in his, he whispered, "Feel better, babe?"

She nodded, but she couldn't remember what she felt better from. Her nod had been automatic. She looked into his eyes and saw the fatigue and the worry there. Something had to be bad, but what was it? Panic started to grip her and she looked at him again. "Bill, what happened to me? Am I okay?"

Bill looked down as Justina went through the events of the day in her mind. He could almost see her thinking. He knew that in just a short amount of time she would know. He tried to prepare himself for it. Just as she stumbled across the realization that she was pregnant, her hand went to her stomach.

"Oh, my God, no, please tell me we didn't lose our baby. Bill, please tell me."

Bill looked at her, not sure what to say. She was crying and her hands were working over her stomach muscles and she moaned, out loud.

"At least we haven't told Penny yet. She would have been so disappointed," Justina said.

Bill realized that Justina had blocked out Penny's kidnapping. She thought she had miscarried. He couldn't tell her, he just couldn't.

She was crying uncontrollably now and Bill took her hands from her face.

"Jussy," he said, "we didn't lose the baby. The baby is fine. You are fine. In fact, the doctors have confirmed that you are pregnant."

She looked at him, afraid to believe it. "Then why am I here?" she asked. "If I'm fine and the baby is fine, why am I here, Bill? What's the matter? You look terrible and I feel terrible. Please tell me."

Just then the door opened and the Dr. Loomis walked in.

"Hi there. How is our patient?" he asked.

"I'm fine and I want someone to tell me what's wrong," she said as she started to sit up. The bump on her head made her wince, and she felt the pain from it all the way down into her shoulders as she raised her hand to touch the sore spot.

"Ouch, what happened to me?"

Bill looked at the doctor and motioned him outside the room.

"Jus, we'll be right back, okay?"

"No, I want to know what happened to me, and I know the two of you are going into the hallway to discuss this and not tell me the truth when you come back. Bill, please tell me."

"I will, Jussy, just give me a minute, okay? Let me talk to the doctor and please believe me when I say the baby is fine."

"Okay, but doctor," she said as she pinned him to the wall with a stare that would take no argument. "Tell me is my baby okay?"

"Mrs. Ware, the baby you carry is fine," he said. The sound of his voice must have convinced her because she let them go with no further argument.

Bill and Dr. Loomis walked into the hallway. "Doctor," Bill said, "she doesn't remember what happened. What do we do?"

"Yes, I realized that almost immediately. I think for now let's just go along with it and buy some time before we have to tell her."

Bill nodded his head. "I agree, maybe something will turn up. Maybe someone will find Penny and Marcie."

The doctor shook his head. "This is a terrible thing to have happen here. Are there any clues?"

"No, none as of yet but it's only been a few hours. Tony Miller is a good man and I think he has a plan." They talked for a few minutes more.

Justina lay in the hospital room alone. She was trying to remember the day. *Why am I here, what happened?* She tried to rethink the evening and all that had taken place. They had had dinner, and she had done the dishes and put them away. She remembered thinking that she would be sick in the morning so she wanted it done. She didn't want to have to face it tomorrow when she felt bad. The evenings were going to be her time to get things done. She had bathed Penny and set out clean pajamas for her. Penny . . .

Oh my God, Penny . . .

Justina's hand flew to her mouth as she let out a blood-curdling scream. She remembered the open window in her daughter's room. She remembered the blood-red spot on the bed.

The door burst open, and Dr. Loomis and Bill ran into her room as Justina's screams rolled through the hallways of the hospital. Her eyes were filled with terror and she was shaking from head to toe. She rolled her head back and forth as if the image that played through her mind was too much to take lying still.

Bill grabbed her and held her close as the doctor pressed the button that would call the nurses. They could hear them running down the hallway. Bill tried to hold Justina close, but she jerked away from him and screamed right into his face.

"PENNY . . ."

Bill pulled her head to his shoulder and rocked back and forth. "We'll get her back, baby, I promise we will. Please, Jussy, for our baby, calm yourself, please."

She crooned low in his ear as he held her to him. "My baby, oh Bill, our little girl. Please tell me no, Bill, please," she cried out in anguish as a nurse pushed a needle into her arm that would take her to a place where Penny Ware and Marcie Anderson were not missing.

CHAPTER 36
Tony Miller was waking up.

He had needed that nap badly, but he now felt disoriented and out of sorts. His eyes felt like he had sandpaper for eyelids. Ordinarily he never slept during the day, but then he didn't often suffer from lack of sleep at night. He looked across the bed to see what time it was—2:30 in the afternoon. Tony had left word for the sketch artist to see Rose Muella, and he needed to see what they had come up with, if anything.

This case seemed to be a lesson in futility. A team of evidence people were at the Wares' house, making plaster casts of the prints in the backyard, and he was hoping that the lab had something on the tissue they'd found at the Andersons more than a week ago. Tony needed to talk to John as well; maybe he had found something. He wanted to clear the air with John, since they had left things on such a bad note. Emotions run high on this sort of case, but Tony knew that he'd been hard on the kid last night. John was a highly trained officer and they didn't hand out those degrees to just anybody.

"Shit," Tony said out loud. "I need to go kiss ass so I might as well get up and get dressed for the occasion."

He wondered what to wear. Brown would probably be a good color, Tony thought, with a touch of irony.

Claire was in the kitchen with Louise from across the street. The two of them were taking a break from cleaning out the guestroom for Lindsay to stay in. Claire handed him a cup of coffee. "Getting things ready, huh?" he asked.

"Yes, she's an important person and she's going to make a difference, Tony," was all Claire had time to say before the screen door opened.

Tony's mom stood just inside the door, a look of expectancy on her face.

"Mom," Tony said, walking over with his arms outstretched to hug her. She stepped into her son's embrace and looked over his shoulder at Claire.

"Mother Miller, how nice to see you."

"Shit, you called me, you crazy woman, and told me to be here. You didn't even ask, you just told me to get over here. I thought maybe my son was sick and needed some good care," Ruby said with a sneer on her face.

"Mom," Tony said in a threatening voice.

"No, Tony, it's okay. I did that, she's right."

Tony and his mother stood there looking at Claire as if she had two heads.

"You did?" Tony asked.

"Yes, I did. I wanted your mom to know that Lindsay was coming here and to share in it since it was mostly her idea."

"It was all my idea, but it was nice of you to let me know that arrangements had been made. When is she coming?" Ruby asked.

"Tonight," Tony said. "But we have work to do, and I promise you both this: there will be no bickering back in forth in front of her or I will get her a hotel room and pack you two off to Mother's house to put up with each other."

They both nodded, knowing he was too tired to argue. Besides he had that look, the one that said, "No argument."

Tony looked tired, scared, and like he needed to sleep another twelve hours.

Food, Claire thought, he needs to eat. She headed for the refrigerator at the same time that Ruby pulled sandwiches out of her bag. She hugged her son, telling him that this was for him and all those other fine boys who were working for him.

"Go find that bastard," she told him.

He kissed his wife and mother and was gone. The three women watched him go and wondered what this day would bring. Claire wondered what time he would make it home. She was hoping to go to the airport to meet Lindsay Freeman with him.

Ruby looked at the other two women and said, "Let's get it done," as she motioned them into the kitchen.

CHAPTER 37
Mac and Bill sat in the hospital waiting room, talking.

They had gone over the two different scenarios so many times they had each of them memorized. To anyone who might have seen them, they looked like two ordinary men sitting there talking, sharing time together. In fact, they were doing just that, but the thing they shared was more than friendship. These two men wanted to find the man who had kidnapped their daughters and kill him. They agreed that if the opportunity came up, one of them would do it. There was no other way to live with this. Both men feared for their daughters but Bill's daughter had bled in her room. What did that mean? Had she been raped at the age of seven?

Bill stood up and ran his hands through his hair. He couldn't stand the thought of that. Every time he went home, he stayed away from Penny's room. Mac's cleaning woman had gone over and changed the sheets on Penny's bed and straightened the room. Still Bill couldn't bring himself to go in there. He couldn't face any more bad news just yet. Not when so much hung in a delicate balance with Jussy.

The door at the end of the corridor swung open, and Tony Miller came toward them. "I just left your house," he said to Bill. "We have some new evidence. It's not much, but it's something. The DNA is not back yet from the lab with the smears we collected at Mac's house, but I think this is the same guy."

Bill looked at him. "You think this is the same guy, you *think*. You mean you're not sure. Could there be two animals out there taking people's children and molesting them in their beds at night where they should be safe?"

Bill was working himself into a frenzy as he stood up. Mac stood up too, "Bill," Mac said, "just let him talk. This isn't Tony's fault."

Bill looked at Tony again. The two men stood there facing one another, almost like a stand off. Bill backed down first.

"Shit, Tony, I'm sorry. I don't know what to do. I'm just scared, man, that's all," Bill said as he held out his hand to Tony.

Tony shook Bill's hand. "This is hard on all of us, Bill, but we have to stick together." Tony pointed to the chairs behind them. "Let's have a seat."

At the sound of the door the three of them turned to see John Hanks heading their way. He was smiling.

"I think I have something," he said.

All eyes were on him as he gestured to the chairs. "Sit, guys, this is going to take time. I ran the profile of this nut through the agency's computer and looked for someone younger than thirty. Thinking back to what Rose Muella said about him, I think that we're looking for someone between eighteen and twenty-five. He's white and wanders from place to place."

John continued. "Two years ago there was a situation in an area not too far from here that was much like this one. Someone was taking little girls just like this. Both were found alive, a little worse for the wear, but alive. One of them was found chained to a fence in someone's backyard, suffering from exposure. The other child was found handcuffed to a bathroom sink in a train station. Her hair had been cut short, very short, and she had been pretty beaten up. But," he paused to look at both fathers, "while they had witnessed sexual acts with animals and extreme masturbation, they themselves had not been penetrated."

John waited for some reaction and he didn't have to wait long. Mac Anderson was on his feet again. "What do you mean, *witnessed sexual acts but not penetrated?*" he shouted.

Bill was up, pacing now too, as was Tony. Tony looked at John as Mac asked that question.

John explained, "They had to watch this man have sex with animals and masturbate. I know it sounds bad, and it is, but at least he didn't rape them."

"True, he just fucked up their minds for the rest of their lives," Bill said.

"This is crazy. We're hoping for one kind of torture instead of another," Mac said. His size intimidated John, who backed up as Mac loomed in front of him.

Tony stepped between them. "That's what therapy's for, Mac. You and I both know that when we get them back they're both going to need therapy."

Bill and Mac looked at Tony and John. "Are we going to get them back?" Mac asked.

John thought quickly. He knew that, in spite of the information he'd just shared, cases like this usually ended badly. John looked at them with sadness, knowing in his heart that both sets of parents or at the very least, the Andersons, would soon be grieving. To him it was most probable that Marcie was dead since this man had taken another child. He saw no reason to take two of them if one was still living. People like this usually replace one with another.

Still, there was always hope, so John answered these fathers as honestly and as gently as he could. "We sure are going to give it everything we've got." That was the closest thing to the truth he had.

CHAPTER 38

Janet sat at the table in the dining room and surveyed her surroundings.

The pale yellow wallpaper with the magnolias on it and the tablecloth and curtains that matched seemed to be someone else's now. She felt she had lost her identity when she had lost Marcie.

Thinking back to the day they picked out the furnishings for this room, she remembered Marcie and the good time they'd had together. They had laughed and joked about decisions they made to create a room that Marcie said would be for "special cassions."

Strewn across the oak table now were pictures of Marcie with poster boards and markers to make up the cry-for-help flyers. Marcie had been right; this was a special occasion. Janet felt the tears slip down her cheeks as she thought of her precious child. Her long hair pulled back and that sweet face and the way her eyes would light up when her daddy came home. Janet's shoulders shook as she sobbed out her grief. She spread her fingers over of her memories and thought of Penny and what the Wares were going through. She knew firsthand what this felt like, and she also knew she should get up and go see Jus, but she couldn't bring herself to. She had tried to keep from imagining what her baby was going through, but now the thought came uncontrolled. "Please God," she begged as she laid her head on her folded arms, "please keep my baby safe.

"Please God," she cried, "please don't let him rape my baby girl. Please don't let him abuse her in any way." She clutched her daughter's picture to her breast and prayed for her child to die swiftly if he was torturing her.

Jayme walked up behind her and placed his large hands on her shoulders.

"Mom, Dad's on the phone."

She hadn't even heard it ring. Patting Jayme's hand she stood on shaky legs and headed in the direction of the phone.

"Hi, babe," she said.

"Jan, I'm here at the hospital with Bill, Tony, and John from Criminal Investigations. I wanted to ask you about something."

"Okay."

"I know this sounds strange, but Tony has asked a woman who is clairvoyant to come help us. She's found other missing children, and she has already given him some useful information. What do you think?"

"I think at this time I'll try anything. How is Jus doing?"

"They have her sedated. She's in shock and pretty out of it most of the time. Bill said at first she didn't remember."

I wish I didn't remember, she thought to herself. "Bless her heart, give them my love. And yes, I think any idea is worth trying."

"I think we'll have to meet with her, babe. Is that okay with you?" Mac asked.

"Meet with her, why? I mean, that feels a little spooky, Mac. I'm not sure I want to do that."

"She's going to need to talk to everyone, Janet. She needs to get a feeling or something like that for the girls. We need to do all that we can, okay? Will you do this?"

"Mac, do you want to? Do you think this will do any good? I mean I want Marcie back and I would go to the ends of the earth to get her back, but is this okay, not against God or anything like that?"

"Janet, all I know is that this is what she does. She has helped the police before and we have a chance with her and I want to try." Mac sounded desperate.

"I do too, sweetheart, I do too," Janet said.

"I'll do whatever you think is best. I just want Marcie back."

"Me too, babe, me too."

"Hey?"

"Yeah?"

"Do you think Marcie and Penny are together? Do you think they're both still alive?" She hated to ask, but she just had to hear him say yes. It would help her go on for another few days.

"Yeah, baby, I do. We have to believe that they are together and alive." Mac was trying to sound positive and control the quiver in his voice. "We're going to meet with this woman tonight at the Millers. Look pretty for me and I'll see you soon."

Janet blew him a kiss over the phone and thought to herself how normal that was. She had been doing that for years, and now here in the midst of this abnormal situation she was doing something that felt so right, so normal. He blew the kiss back and hung up. When he turned around, all eyes were on him.

"She agreed," he said.

"Good," said Tony. "Why don't ya'll plan to meet her at the station at 9:00 tomorrow morning? And be prepared. I gotta tell you, guys, it was spooky to hear this woman yesterday and the way she described everything."

They all looked at him as if he had lost his mind.

"What?"

Mac spoke up first. "Tony, I don't mean to tell you how to handle this bud, but I need to hear what she has to say tonight. I know we're all tired but I can't sleep anyway, and I'm sure Bill is not going to get any sleep."

Bill nodded in agreement.

"What, you want to meet with her tonight?"

"Yeah, if we can," Bill said.

"In fact," Mac added, "Can we go with you to the airport to pick her up?"

"Look, guys." Tony was shaking his head. "I understand what you're going through, but this woman has been up since 5:30 this morning and I have put her through a lot already today. She's gotten on an airplane with very little information and she's flown all this way. She's bound to be tired."

Bill looked hard at Tony. "We're tired too, Tony, but my little girl is out there somewhere with that fucking nut. My newly pregnant wife is lying in there suffering. I want some answers and I want someone to tell me whether my little girl is still alive."

Bill looked at Mac and saw the tears in his eyes as he nodded his agreement. He knew Mac felt the same way he did. John and Tony looked at the ground as the moment of emotion threatened to choke them all. John finally said, "I think we should all go. Let's see if she knows who we are. I want to know if she can pick out officers from fathers. Like a test."

Tony looked into the faces of the men who stood before him. He saw right away that they were not going to back down.

"Okay, you win. Hopefully she won't be too tired to talk when she gets here."

CHAPTER 39
Tired was the one thing that Lindsay was not.

As she sat aboard the airplane she played a mental listening game she sometimes played when cooped up with a bunch of people. She listened to the conversation a few isles back. Since she'd given up on the book she'd tried to read and was trying to keep her mind off the little girls, she started feeling the thought processes of two people sitting somewhere behind her. She tried to hone in on it.

A woman was considering a relationship with a man who was sitting next to her. He had been pursuing her at a distance for months and with her recent transfer to his division she was thinking of giving in. Lindsay knew that they worked for the same company and that this man had a position of authority, so she assumed that he was her boss. When she looked inside him and listened to his heart, she found that he was just trying to seduce the woman. He had never given her feelings a second thought. Lindsay felt the presence of another woman to whom this man was bound. The creep was married. *Asshole,* she thought to herself.

She eavesdropped again, this time picking up several conversations on her way back to them. She heard the woman think that he would be a good catch and she was probably lucky to have him. He could afford a large house and a family, two things she wanted in life. The woman must have looked over at the man because Lindsay suddenly felt an incredible urge. Her body tingled and she felt the two of them touch.

Oops! she thought, *I need to get out of this one.* She felt bad for the young woman and tried to look over the seat to get a look at her. She had to stand up and pretend to adjust her clothes to do it. *Good grief, he's old enough to be her father. He should be ashamed of himself.*

As she was sitting back down the elderly man next to her caught her eye and said, "Well?"

"Well what?"

"What does he look like?" the man said.

Lindsay studied him for a minute. No, she could not feel a gift in him.

"How did you know?" she asked.

"Honey, I've watched people all my life. I'm intuitive, not clairvoyant but intuitive. Now you must be clairvoyant because I feel it in you. You've fidgeted for this entire flight. You had that little outburst and I knew you felt something bad. At first I was afraid we were going to crash, but you settled down and tried to read and then I felt you tense up. I knew you were listening to someone with that quick mind of yours." He winked at her.

Lindsay just looked at him.

"Okay, I know you heard something back there and it's bothered you in some way. What it is?"

Lindsay giggled. "You're right," she said in a tone of conspiracy. "See that couple back there over the right wing?"

The man stood halfway up, looked around the cabin, and sat back down.

"Yep," he said.

"Well, that nice young woman is thinking what a good catch he would be and he just wants to get her into bed with him. All the time this jerk is married and she is thinking wedding bells." Lindsay paused. "I think they're traveling together on business, and she's not aware of his marital status. The sweet young thing wants a house, kids, and the picket fence and Mr. Hot Pants wants to get laid."

The old man chuckled. "What's going on now?" he asked.

Lindsay listened to them again. The man was telling the woman that he wanted to get to know her better and that this trip, even though it was for business, would be a great opportunity for that. Lindsay relayed the message. The old man had a twinkle in his eye.

"Let's sabotage him."

"Okay," Lindsay said. "How?"

"When the plane lands you walk past her and whisper that he's married. Tell her to check him out first. She may look at you funny, but you'll save her a world of heartache and give him a royal case of blue balls from the look of things."

Lindsay laughed out loud as the captain came on the intercom, announcing that the plane would soon be landing.

"Ladies and gentlemen, we are approaching our final destination and should be landing in about 15 minutes. The flight attendant will move through the cabin and pick up any beverage containers and trash. The weather here is a balmy eighty-two degrees. Thank you for flying with us this evening and I hope that you enjoy your stay. Flight attendants, please ready the cabin for landing."

With that the seat belt signs lit up and flight attendants moved through the cabin one more time.

Lindsay looked at the man next to her. "Thanks for making this flight a little better."

"No problem, little lady, my pleasure. You gonna tell her?"

"Yep, if I can get her away from him long enough."

The man looked at Lindsay and smiled. "Leave that to me."

The plane landed without further ado, and in no time all the passengers were walking down the ramp to the terminal. Normally this was a difficult time for Lindsay because people were touching her and bumping into her, but this time her mind was on the young woman with the wedding dreams.

The old man stood next to her as she looked for the couple.

"There they are," she whispered.

Lindsay and her companion headed straight for them. They were headed for the baggage claim, walking hand in hand. Lindsay walked up behind them and looked at her accomplice. He nodded and moved to the other side of the man.

"Excuse me, sir," he said. "Do you know where I can get a cab?" As the man directed him toward the door not a hundred yards away, Lindsay leaned forward and whispered in the woman's ear, He's married. Look at his ring finger to see if it has a tan line."

The woman turned to look at Lindsay.

Trying to suppress a smile, Lindsay saw her little old friend wink at her and she winked back.

The young woman looked down at her new beau's hand and held it up with her own still attached. There was a tan line where a ring used to be.

"Are you married?" the young woman said, loudly enough for all near by to hear.

"What?" the man answered.

"I said, are you married? It's a simple enough question. Are you married?"

Lindsay and her accomplice laughed as did many others standing nearby.

The man looked uncomfortable. "Well uh, I, uh."

"Yes or no, it really is a very simple question."

Lindsay and her buddy smiled at each other.

The man stood there with the onlookers waiting. "I'm uh," he stammered, "yes, I'm married but we're not happy."

With that the young woman slapped his face and the security guards moved toward them. She grabbed her bags from him and turned on her heel and was gone. Lindsay hugged the little old man and they both broke out in laughter.

Then she turned and saw them. They had been standing there near the wall watching her. She kissed the kindly man on the cheek and wished him well on his journey.

"Will you be okay?" he asked.

She nodded toward four men a few steps away. He looked at them. "I guess so." And then he too was gone.

Lindsay walked up to Tony Miller. "Captain Miller," she said as she stuck out her hand in greeting.

The four men were shocked. They hadn't thought she would look the way she did or that she would know who they were. The truth was anyone could have picked them out. Four men standing together had to be law enforcement or the Mafia, she thought with a giggle.

As Tony took her hand, he felt the calluses on it. He turned it over to inspect it.

"I work in my garden," she answered his unasked question.

Tony greeted her and then introduced the others. She shook hands, and as she came to Mac and Bill she felt the tears. She reached up to touch Mac's face and then Bill's. "Your daughters are alive and together, but this is not the end of it," she said. They watched her, somewhat in awe. She looked so normal.

She smiled. "What did you expect, gentlemen, a turban and a crystal ball?"

They coughed and grunted the way men do when they're embarrassed.

"Shall we?" Tony said as he gestured toward the door. They all left the airport with John and Tony carrying her bags, thinking she must have brought half her wardrobe with her.

She turned to look at them. "No, it's not my clothes. I learned long ago that I can only sleep on my own sheets, so I carry them with me."

Again they blushed to have been caught with their thoughts. Tony thought to himself that they would have to be careful around her.

"Not really," she said out loud.

Tony looked at her. "Can you stop doing that, please?"

"Sorry," she said. "I just need to prove myself to you right off the bat so that you will listen to me when I feel something that may be important."

"I understand," Tony said.

Finally Lindsay said, "It's okay to talk about this?" It broke the ice and for the rest of the ride home they each told their story. Mac first, then Tony, then John, and finally Bill. Lindsay waited and listened. The emotion in the car was so thick that each person felt it to an almost stifling degree.

Lindsay looked at Bill. "He did not rape your daughter. The blood on her bed is from her mouth. He hit her but he didn't rape her."

Bill sobbed into his hands and said out loud through gasps, "He hurt her. I guess one pain is different than another, but he still hurt her. It is my job to keep her safe in her own home, in her own bed and he got to her anyway. Why?"

Mac listened to them, then asked her if she was too tired to work on this tonight.

"No, quite the contrary," Lindsay said. "I'm too keyed up to do anything but work."

Everyone in the car exhaled, letting out air they weren't aware they'd been holding. The men had an urgent desire to know what she knew.

As Tony turned onto a side street, he looked over at John, who in turn looked at Bill and then Mac. Lindsay felt the tension rise. She wondered what was coming next; another test, perhaps? She looked out the window at the line of houses. They were modest homes with yards filled with bushes and flowers. She felt something coming, and strained to get a feeling for it. It felt sinister. Fear was mounting and she could feel danger lurking about.

What was it? She waited till she felt the stirring of someone in the bushes near the car. "Slow down, Tony, please."

Tony did as she asked and looked nervously at the others. Lindsay rolled the window down. She felt the night air hit her face and she listened with her inner ears. All of a sudden she could feel the person responsible for all the pain and suffering.

"Stop!" she demanded and threw the door open as the car came to a halt. Lindsay walked across the street. Stepping onto the sidewalk she knelt down and felt the concrete. Slowly she stood and walked deeper into the bushes and closer to a large tree. She sniffed the air. Baby powder, what did that mean? Baby powder, it came to her as clear as the night sky. She was standing there looking around and sniffing the air as she saw the other images coming to her.

Tony, John, Mac, and Bill were out of the car in an instant, watching her and waiting for her to go across the street. She didn't. She just continued toward the end of the block on foot, staying close to the hedges and fences as if she were trying not to be seen.

All of the sudden she stopped. She looked around and then looked across the street. Her hands flew to her mouth as she ran across the street to a fenced yard with a large tree in it. She ran to the tree and put her hands on it. She could hear him now. "Run, run as fast as you can, you can't catch me, I'm the gingerbread man," she sang in an almost childlike voice.

Mac's knees buckled and he fell to the ground. Bill knelt beside him, and Tony stood with his mouth open, unable to say anything. A passing car shined its headlights on everyone, breaking the spell.

Lindsay staggered forward. "Where are we?" she demanded.

No one could answer her, and she saw for the first time Mac on the ground crying. She ran to him and knelt in front of him.

"Mr. Anderson, are we at your house? Please tell me."

All he could do was nod. Lindsay walked back toward Tony.

"He stood over there," she pointed across the street. "Actually he watched all of them playing. There were three of them and they played together. He spoke to them all, but only Mac's daughter answered him. He chose her to take first even though I think he actually wanted the second child. He watched her again from this tree."

Lindsay walked back to the tree and put her hands on it. She let the images flow as the words tumbled from her mouth. "He stood here in the middle of the day and made his plan to take her. He was tired of walking and wanted to get it done. She was going to be his pet. He always wanted a pet in the yard. So many pets and he wanted just one, he was frustrated by a woman, a little boy, and then another child. Finally he made up his mind."

"Ugh!" Lindsay suddenly recoiled from the tree as if it had shocked her. Her face was a mask of distaste. "He, oh God, he . . ." Lindsay was backing away from the tree as Tony came up behind her. He looked into her eyes but it was too late. She had to say it or live with it herself. She was past the point of control. She looked up at him as tears filled her eyes. "He ejaculated here," she pointed to the ground.

Tony turned to look at Mac. "Yes, he did," was all Tony could say.

Mac grabbed him by his shirt. Tony explained. "Janet was here before and we didn't want to tell you that in front of her."

Lindsay spoke softly. "Mac, be glad, because that's why he doesn't rape them. He knows that it's wrong so he does this to himself to keep control."

Mac was exhausted from all of this. "I need to go home," he said simply.

Tony reminded him that Janet was at his house, waiting for them to return with Lindsay.

"Let's go, everyone," he said.

Lindsay was already walking ahead of them, when they turned to her. She was headed down the street toward the Wares' residence. She felt him again. Stronger this time. He had a plan and he needed to carry it out. He felt desperate now and that bothered her. "Slow down," she said to herself as if she were talking to him. "Take your time here, think this through."

Bill ran after her. Tony ran for the car. Mac loped after him and John was behind Bill. She was running toward the back of Bill's house.

"He's here, right here," she said as she turned the corner. Bill stood still trying to catch his breath. He watched her as she ran her hands over the screen of the window at Penny's bedroom.

"He stood here, and he waited for a light to go out. A light in another room near the far side of the house." Bill remembered going to the bathroom that night. Oh God, he had been there when Bill was in the bathroom. Bill felt the strength go out of his legs as he leaned against the house.

Lindsay put her face against the screen. She played with a frayed edge of the tin. "He stood here on something," she said.

Tony and John looked at her and both said, "Yes."

"He stood on a wagon outside the window and opened it with a pocket knife. He took her from her bed that's just inside the window," John said.

"What else do you see Ms. Freeman?"

"Lindsay, please," she said.

"What else do you see, Lindsay?"

"He was angered by her when she woke up with him in her room. He hit her mouth to shut her up. She was unconscious after that."

They all walked around to the front of the house. The door had been repaired by this time, even though Tony's shoulder still felt sore. Bill reached into his pocket and produced a key to let them in. He hung back, and Mac stayed with him, understanding why he could not go in just yet.

Tony led Lindsay to Penny's room. He turned on the lights, but Lindsay turned them off again. The lights had disturbed the image. She walked into the bedroom. Feeling him in there, she retraced his steps. Tony watched her, fascinated by her movements. He knew this man had taken Penny's clothes and he watched Lindsay do what the kidnapper must have done.

She looked at Tony and John. "He took her out the window with him and then sat somewhere near here and watched you all making a fuss over him. He was thrilled over it. He still hasn't raped them and they are for the most part safe." It was the "for the most part" that Tony did not like.

"Let's go to my house and have some coffee," he said to Lindsay. "My wife and Mac's are there. John is here from out of town and Bill's wife is in the hospital."

Tony held the door open for her as she slipped through it. Down the hall she could feel Justina Ware and the mother and wife that she was. She was pregnant and the baby was a boy.

They met Bill and Mac at the door. As they went through it, Lindsay said to Bill, "Congratulations on your son."

"I don't have a son," Bill said.

"Not yet, but you will," Lindsay said with a smile.

Bill smiled too. The intense mood of the evening was somewhat alleviated. With the hardest part behind them, the passengers of Tony Miller's car again rode in silence, each one lost in thoughts. They had been through a great deal this evening and they wanted to just sit and regroup.

Tony knew this evening was just beginning if he did not take control of things when he got home. Claire and his mom would be all over her. Janet Anderson was there too, and she would have her questions. He knew this was a special event in their lives, but it was also a nightmare. Claire never really understood what he did in his line of work. Yet, she was supportive enough of him to take care of the other issues of their life so that he didn't have to. It was why their marriage worked.

Tonight he was doing something that would entwine the two major factors of his life. Even though he knew it wouldn't be forever, he was doing something he had never done before. He was literally bringing his work home. But he couldn't think of any other way since the whole town was affected and in a small town like theirs, with his friends involved he couldn't imagine holding these painful conversations in the police station. He also didn't feel right leaving Lindsay Freeman at a hotel and sitting there with her all night, telling her all the details of the case. She would have to be brought up to speed in regards to times, dates, and events that had taken place so far. There was no way he could sit in a hotel room with her all night. Claire would skin him alive. So he was taking Lindsay and everyone else to his house and he was going to use the kitchen table as a desk and the room itself as headquarters till this thing was over, as much as he hated it. He had never had the need of a desk or a private office at home because he'd never brought work home before. In fact, it was one of the things that he prided himself on.

The crackle of the police radio pulled Tony back from his thoughts. "Captain Miller, this is Rachel. I have a copy of that sketch from Raymond Ross if you want it."

Tony grabbed the mike from the console. "Rachel, can you have a uniform run it to my house? I'm almost there and I could sure use it for the night's work."

"Will do, sir. Anything else you need from here?"

"Nope, that'll do."

Tony pulled up to the curb. Lindsay looked at the family home where she would be staying. It was warm and inviting, and the little flowers she could see illuminated by the streetlamp gave it a very nice country look. She opened the door and got out. The others followed. As they all shut the doors of the car, the front door of the house burst open and several women came toward them.

Claire looked at Tony and gave him that eye that could stop her children cold in their tracks. Tony glared right back at her. "What?"

"Where have you been?" she demanded. "We've been waiting for hours."

"I'm afraid it's my fault," Lindsay said. "I wanted to see the houses and the streets where the children live."

Tony introduced Lindsay to his mother and Janet and then to his wife. Lindsay shook hands with them all.

Tony ushered everyone into the house. "Would you like some time to yourself?" he asked Lindsay.

She looked at him. "Do you think that's wise?"

"No, but she can be mad all she wants. If you need time, you need time. You're not here to entertain her."

"It's okay, really, I understand. This happens all the time," Lindsay said graciously. "She had her heart set on meeting me at the airport, we look at this as work, not a social function. We've been leaving her out of it, in her way of thinking. Now it's time to be sociable."

Tony was relieved she understood. He showed her to the room she would be using. It was a nice room with flowered wallpaper and its own bath. Fluffy towels hung in the bathroom and scented soap filled the soap dish on the lavatory. The scent drew Lindsay to it.

"I'll give you a minute. We'll meet you at the table in the kitchen." With that Tony closed the door and left her to herself.

She looked around the room and saw all the pink. "Yuck!" She didn't like all that frilly stuff and here she was in the middle of a room that clearly had new pink curtains with a matching bedcover, dust ruffle, pillow shams, and throw rug. She walked into the adjoining bathroom. The scent was there again. It was a wonderful soft scent that reminded her of baby powder. Lindsay looked around the room for the source. Ah, it was the tiny rosettes of soap, also pink. It was too much, and she almost laughed.

She put her things away and then washing her hands and patting them dry with the towel that was, of course, pink, she looked at herself in the mirror. Her face and hair needed some work. She took care of those things and then walked out of the confines of the room to join the others. "Pink," she said out loud to no one but herself.

Lindsay joined everyone at the kitchen table. The kitchen was homey and roomy. She looked around her at the cabinets and the knick-knacks that filled the spaces on the kitchen shelves, and felt her first wave of homesickness. She fought it off as she looked at the others. She didn't need, nor could she stand, to bring anything else into her brain.

When she finished surveying the Millers' kitchen, she looked up to see all eyes on her. They were staring at her, waiting. This she was used to.

"Would you like something to drink?" Claire asked her.

Lindsay took a glass of ice water. She sipped the water and looked around her at the faces. Even though on the outside they appeared quite calm, on the inside she could see they were barely holding it together. She felt for the parents most of all. Bill Ware was struggling with his pain and she could see the images of his daughter's kidnapping running through his mind as he stood near her, trying to be patient. With his arms folded across his chest, he seemed to be holding his heart. She watched the images run through her mind in black and white; the empty room and the open window that had scarred this man. She saw in prism form his glance to the bloody spot on the bed and she heard a woman's scream.

She jumped back from the table, scaring everyone in the room. She saw the looks on their faces as she turned her eyes toward Bill and looked into his eyes. He was nervous having her pin that stare on him. He shifted uncomfortably and looked back at her. "What?"

She looked deeper into him, and then she stood up, pushing the chair back with her legs. She walked around the table to him as the others just stared at her. When she reached Bill, the room was silent. She reached her hand up to touch his face. "You found your daughter missing, didn't you?"

"Yes," he answered as tears filled his eyes.

"You feel responsible for this, don't you?"

"Yes," he said again. "It's my job to keep her safe. I let her down."

His shoulders shook as he bent slightly forward and the tears rolled down his face to drop on the floor. He slumped into a chair as Lindsay put her arms around him and guided him into it. Lindsay knew there was no way this group was going to make it through the next few days if she kept them this emotionally charged. She needed some sleep.

She lifted Bill's chin in her hand. "We are going to get your daughter back."

With that she turned to the Andersons. Lindsay saw their hands clasped together and reached over and touched them. "Your daughter too."

The doorbell rang, breaking the spell. Tony went to the door and returned with the sketch of the man Rose Muella had seen. It was rough, but Rose's eye for detail had captured him to the best of her recollection. Tony looked at the sketch and then passed it around the table.

"He looks so normal" was the thought that went with the picture. Only Bill thought the guy looked familiar, but he couldn't place where he had seen him.

Lindsay looked at it and her mind shut down. She was simply too tired to go on.

"I hate to be rude, but I'm so tired. I need to rest for a while. I'm truly sorry."

"Oh goodness, of course," Claire Miller said as she jumped to her feet. "I'm so sorry. You must think us all so rude."

"Not at all. I know you all need answers. All that I can tell you right now is that your little girls are alive and for the most part safe," Lindsay said. She bid them all good night. Lindsay walked into her room and pulled her linen out of her suitcase. She would need to sleep on her own sheets if she were going to get any sleep at all. She remade the bed and then changed her clothes and wondered about her family. She wondered how they were doing without her.

She climbed into bed, completely exhausted and drifted off to sleep almost immediately.

The kitchen was not quite so calm. Bill looked worn out and he still had to go to the hospital to be with Jussy. He wanted to fill her in on the happenings he felt she could take. He stood to go and the others walked him to the front door.

"Give her my love," Janet said as he pushed the screen door open.

"Will do," Bill said as he walked down the steps. He stopped at the car and looked back at them all standing there.

"What do ya'll think?" he asked. For a moment there was silence, mainly because most of them didn't know yet what to think.

Tony looked at Bill, then Mac. "I, for one, am glad she's here."

"Me too," Mac said. "I'm just not sure that I know how to act around her, that's all."

Janet said, "If she can bring Marcie home, then I'm all for this."

Bill nodded his head and got into the car. He started the engine as the others went back inside. They sat in temporary silence around the kitchen table, thinking to themselves.

Tony turned the drawing of the suspect around and studied it. John leaned into his side and looked on. "What do you think?"

"I'm not sure what to think yet. What I want to do is to get this drawing to every person in the county and see if we can flush this guy out."

"It may not be him, Tony. We have to be careful. We don't want to point the finger at an innocent man. Emotions run high with kidnappings. In a town this size we could cause a lynching," John whispered.

Tony looked over his shoulder and laughed at John's words. "This ain't Mayberry but you may be more right than you know."

"Why don't we circulate a flyer of this sketch and say something like, *Wanted for questioning in the disappearance of Marcie Anderson and Penny Ware?*"

"Yeah, that could do it. We need something else, something to get everyone's attention," Tony said.

Janet spoke up. "We can add it to the flyers I've been circulating for Marcie and Penny. Like an addition at the bottom."

"Hmm," Tony mumbled.

John looked at Janet. "It could work. It's not a statement. It's a request for information."

"I like it!" Tony said.

"I can do it starting tomorrow," Janet said.

Janet and Mac sat looking at John, Tony, and Claire. "What do you honestly think about Lindsay, Tony?" Mac asked

"Honestly, I think it's what we've needed for some time now. I'll admit that I didn't believe in the beginning, but now after all that we've seen . . . I mean, how can you not believe her?"

Late into the night, after everyone else had left too, the light glowed in the Miller kitchen with the sketch of Roman Marsh lying on the table.

CHAPTER 40

Marcie didn't know what to do for Penny, but at least Roman was gone for now.

He had left in a fit of rage and Marcie had no idea when he would be back. After she had screamed at the sight of her friend, Roman had thrown her on the floor. Marcie had crawled to the recliner and scurried behind it. Roman had growled in a loud raging voice about ungrateful pets and stormed out the door.

Since he left all the time, Marcie had grown used to it. She definitely preferred the times when he was away. She could dream and pretend she could eat what she wanted and even watch TV. Her time was her own when he was gone. Marcie could not tell time, but she had a way of knowing when he was coming back if he had gone to work. But this was different because he left in the early morning hours, mad at Penny and her for screaming. When hours had passed and still he didn't come home, Marcie was getting hungry. She didn't want him to come home, but she wanted him to bring her something to eat.

She looked out from behind the sofa. Penny still lay on the floor with her clothes all torn up, whimpering from time to time. Marcie got up from behind the recliner. Her legs ached from sitting in that crouched position for so long. She looked at Penny. She was trying to figure out what to do. She didn't want Roman to come back. She wanted Penny to get up and play with her, but Penny just lay there on the floor as she had for hours. She had pulled her clothes around her, and her crying had lessened some.

"Penny, wanna come and play with me?"

Penny whimpered and closed her eyes. "I want my mommy," she cried in a whisper. "I wanna go home."

Marcie looked at her, trying to think of what to do. "Penny, do you wanna watch TV for a while? We can watch anything you want."

"No, I want my mommy and my daddy. I want to go home."

"This is your home now," Marcie said. "Your mommy and daddy gave you to Roman and you have to be real good now or he will get real mad."

For some reason Marcie's words made Penny mad. She opened her eyes and looked hard at her friend. "Why do you think my mommy and daddy did that? You are stupid, Marcie Anderson. My mom and dad would never do that. They love me."

Marcie was surprised to hear Penny say that. She knew that the only way they could be here was if their own mommies and daddies did not want them anymore.

"Penny Ware, don't you say that to me. Your mom and dad gave you to Roman just like my mom and dad did," Marcie said with her hands on her hips.

Penny sat up and looked at Marcie. She pulled her pajamas closer around her, stretching them over her knees in the process. "Why do you think that?" she asked again.

"Because that's what Roman told me," Marcie answered. "He told me my mom and dad gave me away and he felt sorry for me and took me with him."

Penny shook her head. "Marcie, your mom and dad did not give you away. They think you are kidnapped."

"Kidnapped?"

"Yes, they told the police that you were kidnapped and they are crying. Your mommy sits in the rocker by the window all day every day. The police were at your house and they asked everyone questions, even me and Ashley. They even went into our club house and looked for you."

Penny saw Marcie start to cry and then she felt bad. "I'm sorry, Marcie, I didn't mean to make you feel bad."

Marcie sniffled into her hands. "You mean my mommy and daddy want me to come home?"

"Yeah, your mom is real sad. She cries all the time. We can all see her by the window when we go by your house."

"Then why did Roman tell me they gave me away? He hurt my feelings when he told me that, and it made me cry." Penny didn't know, but she didn't want to stay here with Roman.

Penny was thinking hard. "Marcie, we have to get out of here."

"No, Roman locks the door from the outside and if he even thinks we looked out the window he'll get real mad, and you know what that is like."

"What is that thing he does to himself, that thing that he does to his privates?" Penny asked.

"I don't know. He said his dad used to do it to him when he was mad so he does it to me, I mean us. Just don't make him mad, okay?" Marcie looked at Penny with a pleading look in her eyes. Penny nodded. She didn't want Roman mad either.

As Marcie and Penny looked around them, Marcie gasped as she realized the living room was a mess. "We need to clean this room or he will be really, really mad when he gets home."

"Let him clean it himself," Penny said.

"No way. He'll be mad, Penny, if we don't have the house clean. He told me to train you, to show you how to behave yourself. He'll spank us and then maybe put us in the trunk if we don't clean this house."

They both got up and started picking things up. The room had been clean, impeccably so, and Marcie knew it had better be that way when Roman got home. She picked up Penny's blanket and folded it as neatly as she could. Stuffing it behind the couch she told Penny, "Roman likes everything in its place and you can't make a mess or he will start screaming. But if he does that, then he puts powder on you so it's kind of okay."

Penny looked at Marcie in disbelief. "Why does he put powder on you?"

"I don't know. I think he likes the way it smells 'cause then he walks behind you going like this." Marcie imitated Roman as she walked around with her nose in the air sniffing. Penny laughed for the first time. "Well, I don't want him to touch me," she said.

Marcie grabbed her arm in alarm, scaring Penny. "Never let him know that you don't want to him to touch you, or he gets so mad that he pulls your hair."

Immediately Penny was scared again and the light mood vanished. Marcie took Penny's hand and led her into the kitchen where she got them each an apple to eat. Marcie tried to remember all the things that Roman had taught her in the last week about how to act and what to say and do. She listed them for Penny, who promised to try to remember.

"Don't worry, Penny, you *will* remember or he'll get mad and then you never ever forget," Marcie said with meaning.

As the two girls started for the living room, Marcie ran back into the kitchen and grabbed a rag from the sink. Penny, watching her, got the picture and grabbed the two apple cores from the table and put them in the trash that Marcie had pointed out as she wiped the table. Then together, holding hands, they went back into the living room.

Penny was going to climb on the couch, but Marcie held her back. "We can't sit on the couch, only on special cassions."

Penny asked where they were supposed to sit, and Marcie pointed to the floor.

They sank to the rug together and turned on the TV. Soon Penny was fast asleep. Marcie watched her friend for a minute and then went back to the show. Just a few minutes later Marcie heard him. No matter how quiet he was, she had learned to hear him. She nudged Penny to wake her up as she turned off the TV.

"What?" Penny asked sleepily.

"He's here, shhh."

"Oh no," Penny wailed and she started to cry. Marcie hugged her tight and grabbed her hand in the darkness, dragging her toward the bedroom. Marcie pushed Penny onto the floor and told her to be quiet or he would know they were awake. Penny tried to muffle her sobs as best she could. Marcie lay down beside her and cuddled her close.

"Breathe slow," she whispered in Penny's ear, "or he'll know that you're not asleep and make you get up and keep him company." That was all the prompting Penny needed. She tried to act like she was asleep, but she was so scared. Her little body trembled, and she felt tears run down her cheek into her ear as the front door opened.

Roman stepped into the room. He sniffed the air and felt the calm take over. He stretched in the doorway and then reached for the light. He had done a good day's work and this was his reward: well-trained pets sleeping in their little bed as they should be. He walked into the kitchen and opened the refrigerator. He noticed that two apples had been eaten, and he whirled around to look at the table. He smiled and walked to the trash bin. Reaching inside he felt the apple cores, cold. It had been some time since they'd been eaten. He again went to the refrigerator and took out some bacon and eggs. As he cooked for himself, he wondered where the pets were, even though it had only been minutes since he'd last seen them. He knew where they had better be, if they knew what was good for them. He walked to the bedroom and pushed the door to the side. He was ready to be mad as the anger boiled inside him. But there they were, huddled together where they should be. He was a good master, he thought to himself.

He wandered to the TV and turned it on, then back to the kitchen to finish his dinner. The smell of bacon had made the girls hungry, but Marcie whispered to Penny that she never got that kind of food. Roman had told her it was just for grownups and she had to wait till she grew up to get any of that. They had held their breath together and squeezed each other's hands as Roman had come into the room. Hunger was the last thing on their minds as they waited for him to go away.

The two little girls stayed like that for the rest of the night, calling on the warmth of each other's body for reassurance and comfort. Traces of dried tears on their cheeks, an occasional whimper stuck in their throats.

CHAPTER 41

The napkin lay on the table, the one Roman threw out the window of his car.

Hershel Owens saw him do it. Even though Hershel was scared to death, he had waited until the car turned the corner and then ran to the curb. Looking in the direction the vehicle had taken, he paused and then turned to look behind him to see if anyone was watching. No one was, and he looked down at the ground. The tissue lay there as if it were heavy, resisting the breeze of the early morning hours. Hershel stooped and picked it up, but his hand recoiled as he thought about the ambulance and the police cars and he worried about getting involved. He didn't want any trouble, but he'd heard on his police scanner that someone had taken that little girl and he knew her mother was in a bad way.

Hershel looked up and down the road again. Still, no one was in sight. He reached into his bathrobe, pulled out a handkerchief, and wrapped it around the napkin. He'd seen the old car come to a halt outside his house, and he watched to see what the person inside it was going to do. Sure enough the person was a litterbug. Now Hershel had proof. He wasn't sure what he had proof of, but it was more than that this person was a litterbug, of that he was sure. Then he saw the red blood spot on the napkin, and he knew this was important. He was not so sure yet what to do, but he knew he had to do something.

It had been twenty-four hours since he called the police station. Now the napkin still lay on his table like a bad omen. He stared at it and then at the little piece of paper in his hand that held the numbers of the car's license plate. With a determined movement he put it in a plastic bag and headed off to the police station. "If they won't come to me, I'll go to them," he said to himself.

Paula watched the old man approach the desk. She knew who he was, and she wondered if some neighbors had let their dog poop in his yard again.

"Hello, Mr. Owens, how are you this morning?" she asked.

"I'm good, missy, and no, I ain't here to complain, just in case you want to know."

"Good. What can I do for you then?"

"Someone threw this out their car window by my house the morning that the little Ware girl was taken, and I thought you might want to know," Hershel said, looking Paula right in the eye. She saw that he was serious and he felt this was important. She took the plastic bag with the tissue in it and opened it slowly.

Normally this old man was a complainer. He called the station every time someone's dog crapped in his yard or his paper got wet. He was a real pain. But this time seemed different. She held the plastic bag open in her hand and picked up the napkin by the corner edges. She saw the blood almost instantly. Placing it carefully on the counter, she looked under the desk for an evidence bag, then looked at Hershel again.

"Did you see who dropped this?"

"Yes'em, I did," he replied.

"Can you describe who it was or do you remember anything about them?"

"Older model, two-door, dark car, just one person in it. I think it was a man but it was dark so I ain't sure."

"Really?" Paula asked.

"Yep," was all he said.

"Thanks, Hershel, I mean Mr. Owens. Can you have a seat right over there and I'll get someone to talk to you?"

Hershel turned to look at the uncomfortable bench behind him.

Paula saw immediately that she had said the wrong thing and started to speak at the same time Hershel did.

"I'm going to go home," he said, "and ya'll just come there if anyone wants to talk to me or if they want the other piece of information that I got since no one around here gives a fiddler's hoot."

Paula was already coming around the counter and taking his arm to gently lead him to a softer chair behind the counter. "I'm so sorry, Mr. Owens. What was I thinking? Sit back here with us, and feel like the honored guest that you are. We need more good citizens like you." She was patronizing him and he knew it, but he wanted to sit behind the counter. He wanted to be treated like someone important. Paula wanted him to stay and talk with an officer, and she wanted to be sure that he remembered every little thing they could pull out of him.

Paula immediately got Robby Henderson to talk with him and brought coffee for them both.

This is more like it, Hershel thought to himself.

After Robby took Hershel's statement, he excused himself for a moment. He walked into another part of the station with the plastic bag and the tissue in his hand and held it up to the light. He could see the blood on it and felt a gut instinct that this was related. Could it be that the man who had taken the little Ware girl had thrown this out the window? That had to be too much of a coincidence. Still, after what he'd been through, he would check it out. He picked up the phone on the desk and dialed a number.

Claire Miller answered and handed the phone to Tony, who had a questioning look in his eyes. "It's the station," she said. "Sounds routine."

"Hello, this is Captain Miller," Tony said into the phone.

"Hey, Captain, this is Robby Henderson. A man, a Mr. Hershel Owens who lives over there behind the Ware residence, saw someone drop a bloody napkin out of a car window. He says this happened the other night during all the commotion. He picked it up and brought it inside with a handkerchief and we have it now. He got a look at the car but not a good description."

Tony knew Hershel Owens well. "Get the napkin to John Hanks and have him take it to his lab. Tell him the story and ask him to test it double-quick. Then keep Hershel there. He saw more than you got out of him, I guarantee it. Keep at him till I get there."

"Yes, sir," Robby said.

"Damn, barely eight in the morning and the crap has started already. Do you think things will ever get back to normal around here?" Tony said to Claire. She was up and in a bathrobe.

"Tony, do you have to talk like that? This is not the station house, you know."

"I'm sorry, babe, I just hate this and not having a clue what to do, and every twelve hours or so something else happens."

As Tony quickly shared the news with Claire and started dressing, there was a knock on the door.

Claire and Tony said at the same time, "Come in."

It was Mike. "Mom, Dad, I really need to talk to you about something."

His parents exchanged a glance. "Go ahead, Mike, what's up?" Tony said. Claire sat down on the bed.

"Dad, this may be nothing, but Jayme and Carl thought that we should look into it. See, there's this new guy in town and he seems a little odd."

"New guy as in a new high school guy or new guy as in an older man?" Tony wanted to know.

"He's our age, but he's weird. We saw him over near the junkyard."

Mike's parents could hear his concern, and they knew their son was not an alarmist.

"Dad, I just feel that everything should be considered, ya know?"

Tony ruffled the young man's hair. "You're going to be a good cop someday, you know that?"

"Detective, Dad, detective."

"Okay, detective."

"Well, anyway, we've all been looking around, the guys and I, and we saw this guy walking around talking to himself. He was rumbling and groaning and stuff like that, pulling his hair and shouting to himself. He looked like he was really mad about something, so we followed him. When he saw us he stopped and stood there. It was really weird. He was on the feeder road, out by the junkyard. We didn't see a car right there by him but we watched him walk down the road. He started that hollering stuff again.

"Jayme wanted to go and grab him, and I told him that we couldn't do that without reason or we would get into real trouble, but really, Dad, this guy was strange."

"Mike, when did you see this guy?" Tony asked him in the most serious way.

Mike knew this was important, so he thought about the exact time. "It was yesterday afternoon at 3:30," Mike stated.

"Very good," Tony said. "Okay, let me get some men on this. You may need to go with them to show them where you guys saw this kid. Do you mind doing that?"

"No, sir. Do you think this has something to do with Marcie and Penny's disappearance, Dad?"

"Mike, at this time every thing has something to do with this, absolutely everything," Tony said.

Claire and Tony finished dressing. In the kitchen they found Lindsay, Becky, and the boys having a big breakfast. "I hope you don't mind," Lindsay said. "They were hungry and I knew the two of you were tired."

"There's plenty," Mike said. "She can cook and she's used to feeding an army. She has kids too."

As everyone settled into chairs and coffee was poured into steaming mugs, they chatted easily. It might have been any other morning with company if tension had not been hanging in the air.

After breakfast they all cleaned up together, and Tony asked Lindsay if she wanted to go the station with him this morning.

"As a matter of fact, I would like to use your phone and then get started going to the different houses and I want to talk with Rose Muella. You said she's the one person who has seen this guy up close, right? Didn't the sketch come from her sighting of him?"

"We're not sure, but she did see someone. Her sighting was of someone strangely dressed, someone she had never seen before. The drawing is of that someone. Rose is the only one who has seen anything until today but Mike just told me about another possible sighting and I want him to look at that sketch. Does anyone know where it is?"

Lindsay retrieved it from the living room where she'd been sitting and looking at it earlier. She handed it to Tony and said, "Usually I would get more from a picture, but this is a drawing done by someone else and all that I get seems to come from the artist. So I can't really say whether it's him or not."

Tony looked at the drawing. "Rose may or may not have seen the kidnapper, but from the way it sounds he's someone we need to check out. This is someone new to our area, he was behaving strangely, and he did have something on the tips of his shoes. Remember the toe caps thing that we talked about?"

"Yes, I do, and it seems an odd thing to me that someone today would be wearing them. I wonder where he gets them."

Mike looked up from the sports page. "Hey, Dad, what are toe caps?"

"They are a form of decoration for the shoes that men used to wear a long time ago. Why?"

"What do they look like?" Mike asked with a note of fear in his voice.

"Most of the time they are little triangular-shaped things on the tips of very pointed shoes. Did the guy ya'll saw have something like that on his shoes?"

"He did, and he dressed like he was from a long time ago too, although he was clean."

Tony and Mike brought Lindsay up to speed on what they were talking about. Tony looked Mike in the eye. "Son, if you saw this guy again, would you recognize him?"

"Yeah, Dad, I sure would."

Tony laid the sketch on the table and tapped it with his forefinger. "Are you sure this is same guy that you and your buddies saw?"

Mike picked up the drawing and looked at it. "I'm sure Dad, it's him." he said.

"Are you sure, one hundred percent sure, Mike?" Tony asked in a serious voice. "There can be no margin for error here, son, you have to be very sure."

"I'm sure, Dad. You can call Jayme and ask him too. He saw the guy better than the rest of us."

Tony took the sketch back and looked at it. "Now all we have to find out is where he is and if this is the man who has those two little girls."

"Dad, he was in the area of the junkyard last time we saw him, if that helps any."

"Yeah, Mike, it does, but he could just be a customer that you boys made nervous. Understand? Maybe he was afraid someone was going to beat him up or something like that, and he was trying to show that he wasn't afraid of you. It could be anything like that."

"But Tony," Lindsay said, "if Mike and Rose saw the same person, isn't there a chance that he is the right one? I mean, this is a small town. How many strangers do you get here?"

"There is a chance, but it could be a coincidence. I have some other things that I need to do. Let's take it a step at a time. Hershel Owens is at the station. He has something that he needs to show me. I need to start there. Then we can go talk to Rose together if you want." Tony stood up and grabbed his radio and keys off the counter. "Let's go talk to Hershel first. Mike, you want to come?"

Mike stood and held the chair for Lindsay as she rose. As they walked outside Lindsay wanted to know the names of streets. "It helps to keep things straight in my mind. Since there are so many names, faces, and streets."

Lindsay, Tony, and Mike walked into the station and were greeted by Paula and Hershel Owens. He shook Tony's hand and looked at Lindsay and Mike. "Sorry, young folks, but this here is police business," he said as he steered Tony away.

After speaking with Mr. Owens, Tony assured him he would handle it personally and walked him to the door.

"You did a darn fine thing, Mr. Owens. This police department owes you a vote of gratitude." Hershel smiled and nodded as he left. Tony stood and watched him go as he shook his head. "Paula, did you get that specimen to John?"

"He's on his way, sir."

"One down and about four thousand things to go," Tony said as he walked over and picked up the mic on his desk.

He sent men to check out the area where Mike and his friends had seen the man in the sketch that Rose and the artist had put together. They promised to get back with him just as soon as they had checked out the area thoroughly.

"Don't leave anything undone over there, fellas. This is important," Tony said.

They all went out the door together.

"Paula, I'll be on my radio if you need me," Tony said as the door closed behind him.

"Let's go see the Wares," he said.

The day wore on for everyone, including Justina and Bill Ware. Jussy had to be sedated again since she could not cope with reality. Janet and Bill took turns sitting with her along with her mother, who had flown in. The waiting was the hardest part. Reading seemed to help, but more and more the articles that were piling up in the waiting room were about abductions. It was like a sore thumb, one that you never noticed till it hurt.

When Lindsay, Tony, and Mike walked into the hospital, everyone looked up at them. Most of the people in town knew by now who this stranger was and why she was there, and for the most part they were all for it. At this point in time, anything that might help would have been acceptable.

At the desk, Tony asked the nurse who was with Mrs. Ware. "Her husband is in with her now and that's her mother over there on the couch," the nurse said, looking over Tony's shoulder at Lindsay. Lindsay smiled at her, and for the ten thousandth time she felt like a spotted elephant.

Tony turned back to Lindsay. "Have a seat and I'll see what Bill wants to do. Maybe Jussy is up to seeing you, maybe not. We'll have to play this one by ear."

Lindsay headed for the couch, her mind full of the day's events. In her mind she knew that Hershel Owens and Mike had seen the man who had taken Penny and Marcie. She could feel the child with him all over the napkin. She had shuddered at the touch when she had held the tip of it in her hand. She had met with Rose and the feeling was the same as the one that she had gotten off the napkin. They were the same person. Now all she had to do was convince

Tony that they were one and the same. She wanted the answers, but she felt a dead end. Something had to happen. She needed some other information.

She smiled at Justines's mother, Emma Smythe, as she took the seat next to her. Mike sat on a nearby chair.

"You're the clairvoyant the police are using to help solve this, aren't you?" Emma asked.

"Yes, I am. My name is Lindsay. Are you Justina's mother?"

"Yes, and Penny is my only grandchild. Why would someone take my only grandchild? I just pray she is still alive," she said as she started to cry.

Lindsay put her arm around Emma. "Would you like to tell me about Penny? Would that help?"

For the next few minutes they sat in companionship and talked of Penny. Memories have a way of helping to heal a wounded heart.

Tony walked into the room where Justina and Bill had their heads together in prayer with Pastor Johnson. When they were through, Bill greeted Tony. "I've told Jussy and the pastor about Ms. Freeman and what she does. I also told them that I want to participate in this."

Tony turned to look at the others in the room. "Pastor, are you okay with this? I mean she is a Christian, I made sure of that a long time ago but I know that this is just outside the Bible, or so they say."

Pastor Johnson patted Tony on the back. "God has given so many of us unusual gifts. If this young woman can help and she is willing to, then I say by all means, let's let her try."

Tony looked to Jussy, who was crying softly. "Jus, are you up to this?"

"Yes, Tony, if it will help bring my baby home, I'll do anything."

"Okay, let's bring her in here. Let me warn you first, however, that sometimes she says things bluntly. Her heart seems to be in the right place though. She is usually pretty gentle."

Bill assured Tony that he had already filled them in.

Tony turned and walked to the door. As he opened it, he thought of something. Turning back to the room he said, "She doesn't have three heads, but she's getting a lot of strange looks from everyone. We don't want to insult her, so please just treat her normally if you can." They all nodded.

Again Tony turned to the door. Walking into the hall he motioned for Lindsay and Mike, who was sitting in the hallway talking to a very pretty nurse's aide. They both rose and walked into the room with Tony.

Lindsay greeted everyone and shook hands with Pastor Johnson. Then, walking over to the bed, she took Justina's hand in hers and looked into her eyes.

"I'm here to help you all that I can, but I need your help as well. Can we chat for a few minutes and maybe I can see your daughter?"

Justina nodded, and the tears came again. Lindsay patted her hand and looked behind her for a chair. Mike supplied one, and Lindsay sat down. She looked into Justina's eyes again and asked how she was feeling.

"I have good times and bad," Jus said. "Can you help find my daughter?"

"I hope so, but I need to get a feel for both of you. There needs to be some conversation between us so that I can feel you and then feel her independently. I hope that makes sense and I'm trying hard to be as gentle and socially acceptable as possible. Sometimes I tend to cut straight to the heart of the matter due to a lack of patience on my part and it comes across as being rude or unfeeling, but that is not how I mean it at all. I hope you can understand this and I don't hurt your feelings. That's not my intention. I just want to bring your daughter and her little friend home as soon as possible."

Justina nodded and said that she understood.

"Does your daughter have long hair, light with light-colored eyes?" Lindsay asked.

"Yes, she does."

"Does she have a mark on her left leg, like a birthmark? Something that she wants to hide most of the time?"

"Yes, yes she does." Justina was starting to get excited and so was Bill. No one knew about that scar. It was high up on Penny's thigh and she always wore her shorts long enough to hide it.

"Does your daughter bite her nails?" Lindsay asked.

"She does." Jussy smiled for the first time in days.

"Okay," Lindsay said. "These things are going to be hard for you to hear. I feel your pregnancy. Do you want your husband and me to talk this through alone or do you feel that you can be part of it?"

"No, please do not leave me out. I need to be part of it. I want her home and I want her to know that I helped in making sure that happens."

Tony reached into his shirt pocket and pulled out a tablet to take notes. For some reason, he licked the end of his pencil and then raised his eyebrows. *Ready,* he thought to himself.

Lindsay could feel him behind her, and she felt his readiness. She turned to smile at him and winked. He felt embarrassed at his fidgeting.

Lindsay looked at Bill, "Are you ready?"

"Yeah, I'm good. Let's do this."

They all seemed to know without the words being spoken that this was a painful time, when they would have to relive the events that had brought them all to this place.

"Okay," Lindsay began. "I may see what he saw when he took your daughter or I may see what he is seeing now. I have no way of knowing what I will get as I try to connect with Penny. Please feel free to say what you need to or ask me questions. This is not like a trance that can be broken by interruption. Just be yourselves since it will really help me to connect on the most normal level. I may only see what the girls are seeing, but I will be honest with you. Understand?"

Everyone nodded, and Jussy reached out a hand to Pastor Johnson and her husband.

"Carl, Bill, please," she said. "Okay, I'm ready."

Lindsay looked around the room. She let herself go. An image came to her.

"The dark is everywhere. I want my mommy and daddy. Why am I here?

"I have a feeling this is Marcie that I hear," Lindsay said.

"This man stood across the street and watched you, Justina, walk another little girl home about a week ago. You and Penny were walking past him about dusk and you were holding hands. You talked together about a play at school and the scent of baby powder was in the air. He saw you leave another child with her mother and turn and head back to your home. He wanted to take her then, but the timing was not right and you were there. He made his plan then. There is nothing you could have done to change the way things went. He has her in a place that should be dirty, but is not. This man is so neat and clean. They are not alone. Marcie is with them still.

"I hear, *'Time to come, time to come, tick tock, time to come.'"*

Lindsay looked up at Tony. "What does that mean?" she asked.

Tony shook his head. For the first time in his career he felt completely ignorant.

Jussy spoke softly. "I remember that night so well. I had been doing the dishes and the girls, Ashley and Penny, were outside playing when a feeling came over me and I ran outside to make them come inside the gate. I was so scared that I scared them. Penny and I walked Ashley home that night."

Chills ran over everyone in the room. This was a reality. This made Lindsay the real thing. There was no way she could have known this if she didn't have the gift.

Bill was looking at Lindsay. "Is there any way we could have stopped this before it happened? I have to know."

Jussy squeezed his hand tightly.

Lindsay looked at him. "There is nothing you could have done. His plan was too well thought out. He pumped little Marcie Anderson for details before he took your daughter. He knew just where her room was and he watched you and the patterns you live in. He knew, that's all there is to it. He just knew."

Bill was crying softly and he nodded as Lindsay spoke. He knew she was right, but the thoughts inside his mind would not let him rest. A man is supposed to be able to protect his family. How could he have let someone take his child?

Lindsay looked at him and said, "You didn't know he was there. There's nothing you could have done. I do believe that you would have given your life for her if it were possible."

Bill nodded again, then smiled. "Ms. Freeman," he said. "Would you please not do that?"

"What?" Tony said.

"She responded to my thoughts even though I didn't say them out loud. It's a little unnerving."

Everyone in the room laughed, including Justina.

"We're going to get your daughter back, you just hang in there," Lindsay said. "As soon as I know anything else, we'll call you." Something in her manner left no doubt in anyone's mind.

As Tony, Lindsay, and Mike drove away from the hospital, at each corner they could see the signs of a loving community coming together. Janet Anderson and her helpers had put signs for Marcie everywhere. Little Marcie's face was in all the stores and windows about town and at almost every street light, except one. Lindsay wondered out loud at that. Tony said that he didn't know why that one had been left out, but he would ask Janet. The street corner seemed to pull on Lindsay and she asked what the name of the street was.

"That's Hanover Street," Mike told her.

Lindsay turned in her seat and looked at Mike. "Where did you see the guy that you said acted so strangely, Mike?"

"About four blocks from here," he said, pointing north.

Tony looked at Lindsay. "Do you think that means something? I mean, do you want to go back there and try to get something off that area?"

Lindsay knew Tony had no idea how her ability worked, but she appreciated his trying to help her, so she nodded and Tony turned the car in the direction Mike had pointed. As they drove, Lindsay talked to Mike about what he and his friends had seen. She was hoping that he would remember something or say something about the man they'd seen that would trigger a thought in her mind.

As they drove the streets, they talked in general about the day's events. Mike talked almost absentmindedly about the day he and his friends had seen someone walking with his head down and his hands in his pockets. The man had been muttering, but none of them could hear what he was saying.

Lindsay asked, "Mike what made you aware of him?"

"Well, he was different and it's odd to see someone talking to himself. Dad had asked me to get my friends together and watch people. So we did. I guess that's the main reason why we noticed him."

Lindsay thought about what Mike had said. "You did the right thing and your sighting of this man and what Rose says he looks like seem to go together."

Suddenly Lindsay stopped talking. Her arms became covered with goose bumps, and she felt a tingling at the back of her neck, like when you are walking away from a dark place and get the feeling that someone is watching you or coming up behind you. She felt a flutter of an idea stir her gently and a scent seemed to float through her senses. This was the first time she had ever smelled something that was not in the physical. Her mind recalled a memory of a smell. To her it was warm sunny days and gentle breeze that lifted the beautiful scent of flowers through the air.

She turned to Tony. "What is that smell?"

"What smell?"

"Don't you smell that? It's like flowers and warm sunshine."

Tony rolled the window down. Mike did the same and both breathed in large amounts of air, trying to get a whiff of the scent.

"I don't smell anything," Mike said.

Tony looked at Lindsay, confused. "I'm not sure what you smell, but I don't smell anything different. So maybe what you smell is different for you and normal for Mike and me."

They drove past businesses and finally a used car place and then a junk-yard. Lindsay rolled her window down and sniffed the air. It didn't seem to come from outside. The scent was in the car. She rolled her window back up and the scent hit her nose again.

Tony and Mike looked at her. "Are you okay?" Tony asked.

"Yes, but I smell something sweet, and it smells like baby powder or flowers."

"Magnolia blossoms," Mike said.

"What?" she asked.

"Magnolia blossoms smell like that," he said.

They turned the corner, but as they drove on, the scent faded, as did the feelings that came with it. None of them realized that they had been with-in five hundred yards of the place where Marcie and Penny were being held.

"Lets go talk to Rose Muella again, I may get a more defined feel for him from her and Mike since it seems to be the same guy."

Tony turned on to the street where Marcie and Penny lived. They all looked at the houses as they passed them.

"Seems like a ghost town around here lately," Mike said. "This is summer. Usually there are kids everywhere on this street this time of the day."

Unspoken words hung in the air. Tony made one more turn at the corner, the same one that Roman Marsh had made when he walked the blocks of this neighborhood before he took action against these families.

As Tony pulled up to Rose's house, he said, "We should have called her first, but let's try it anyway. I wanted you to see the streets in the daytime. So even if she is not here we did accomplish something."

Rose was there, however. She was packing for a trip to California when she crossed the living room window. She saw the patrol car and recognized Tony right away.

Opening the door she greeted them. "Captain, how nice to see you again. Please come in."

Tony said, "You remember my son and Lindsay Freeman?"

She winked at Mike and took Lindsay's hand. "Welcome, please come in and have a seat. I'm surprised to see you again so soon. Is something wrong?" She directed them to the living area and a couch cluttered with suitcases and clothes. "Forgive my mess, I'm packing for a trip and as usual I'm running late. What can I do for you?"

Tony said, "Mike and his friends saw someone who looks like the sketch that you helped Ray Ross make. He didn't get a great look at him, but he thinks that it may be the same guy."

"Yes, that's what we came up with this morning," Rose said.

"Can you look at this sketch again and see if anything else comes to mind, so maybe Lindsay will get something about him from you as you speak," Tony said.

"Sure, Tony, you know I want to help." Rose told her story again. Tony was impressed once more by her eye for detail.

Lindsay watched her speak and felt the familiar thoughts as they went through her mind. She looked at Rose and said, "You still love your husband."

Rose smiled and said, "There's no keeping a secret from you is there?"

"Not much. Just ask my kids. Rose, did you notice a scent that day, something that hung in the air around you or around this man you saw?" Lindsay asked.

"Hmmm, well, come to think of it, the magnolia trees in the area were in full bloom around that time. The smell was heavenly. Is that what you mean?"

Lindsay smiled and looked at Mike. "That's exactly what I mean. Tony, that's the connection, the scent of magnolia blossoms. He likes the smell even though it makes him act strangely."

Tony looked confused. "I really don't care what makes him do what he does. I just want to catch him."

"But don't you see? If we know what sets him off, then we know when he might strike again. Rose, I want to hold your hand along with Mike's since he's not sure about the guy he and his friends saw. This way I can get a mental picture to make sure they are one and the same. Two sightings are better than one. That would tell us he is still in the area and starting to get sloppy in his work."

Rose looked at Lindsay. "How will you know?"

"Each thought process is independent, and you have that picture stored in your mind. Time may have faded it a bit, but it's still there. Mike too has a picture, and if they are the same or at the very least similar, then I will know."

"What do we have to do?" Rose wanted to know.

Lindsay stood. "May I?" she asked as she held her hand out to Rose and the other one to Mike.

Both Mike and Rose stood up and reached for her hand. Mike felt funny doing this. It was like a séance, and he couldn't wait to tell the guys.

"They'll get a kick out of it, won't they?" Lindsay said.

"What?"

"Your buddies, they'll get a kick out of this, won't they?"

"How did you know, I mean that I was thinking that, how did you know?" Mike was flabbergasted.

"Sometimes it just comes. I'm sorry, I had no right to intrude on your private thoughts."

"Gosh, I'm just glad they were ones that everyone could hear." Mike giggled, a little embarrassed.

They all laughed at that and it seemed to break the ice. Lindsay took Rose's hand as well as Mike's.

"Think about the man you saw and what was happening at the time that you saw him," Lindsay instructed.

Both did, and a moment later Lindsay had it.

"It's the same guy!" she blurted out.

Everyone looked at her. "Are you sure?" Tony asked.

"Yes, definitely, it's him. I'm sure."

"What now?" Both Rose and Mike wanted to know.

"Now we go back to that light pole and see what we get from that area. That makes two positive sightings in this area and that makes a target zone. Two kidnappings and two sightings. I'm impressed. Let's go," Tony said.

They took their leave and headed to the car. "Dad, can you drop me off at Jayme's?"

"Sure, but don't be a pest, okay? You guys go out and do something and try to stay out of trouble. Janet and Mac have enough on their hands without a bunch of teenage boys in the house," Tony said.

They turned the corner, and Tony pulled the car over to the curb, letting Mike out. Mike waved as they pulled away. Tony looked over his shoulder and then turned the car around in the middle of the street. "Let's ask Janet if she put a sign on that corner."

Lindsay nodded. "Good idea."

They parked and got out. Janet met them on the steps. "Any word?" she asked.

"No," Tony said, "but I need to ask you a question, if that's okay."

"Sure," she said.

"Did you put a sign up for Marcie on Hanover and Grove Street, there on the corner?"

"Yes, I did," Janet said. "I put them on every street corner I could walk to in this area, and then we canvassed the rest of the town with what was left over. I feel he must be in this neighborhood."

"Why?" Tony asked.

"Well, how would he have seen the girls if he wasn't around here?"

"That makes good sense, Janet," Tony said. He felt foolish that he had not thought of that himself.

"So to answer your question, yes, I put one there. Why, Tony?"

"It's not there now, and I wondered about it. By the way, I dropped Mike off to see Jayme. I hope it's okay if he stays for a while."

"Oh sure. And maybe that flyer just blew off. I'll put up another one today."

Tony and Lindsay headed back to the car. Neither of them spoke until they were seated and buckled in.

"Are you thinking what I'm thinking?" Lindsay asked.

"I think so. Let's go check it out."

Tony headed the car in the direction of the light pole. He slowed to a crawl and looked carefully around the it. Sure enough, there was no sign there.

"Let's stop," Lindsay said.

They both got out, and Lindsay walked to the pole and placed both hands on it. She could feel the coolness of the metal under her fingertips. The image of a man came to her. He was short and slight in build, with short hair of a reddish-brown color. He seemed angry. His intensity was almost overwhelming, and she had to pull her hands away from the pole.

She looked at Tony. "I think he took the sign," she said. "This feels almost familiar to me, in a sick sort of way. You know, once I get a feel for someone they become familiar." Lindsay wiped her hands on her jeans. She felt the need to get him off her, but he was now attached to her. The thought of it made her almost sick to her stomach. She had to embrace it, at least for now. Otherwise, there was no hope she could get him and the two small children at the same time. She couldn't leave him out there to do it again. Lindsay stumbled as that thought hit her, and she plunged into the light pole. Tony saw her and jumped from the car.

"Are you okay?"

"Yes, I just realized that I have to get him when I find Marcie and Penny, or I'll not get him at all."

"Jesus," Tony said, "how do you know that?"

"I just do, and I have a strong feeling that he's getting worse. Whatever that means."

Tony looked at her as a chill ran up his spine. They headed to the car together, both of them feeling that time was running out.

"Let's find John and bring him up to date on our progress," Tony said. They headed in the direction of the station house.

CHAPTER 42
Roman was getting worse.

He felt like he was losing a grip on his sanity. How could that be, he thought. *This is that Penny pet's fault. She's making me crazy with her attitude and her rebellion. She will not behave, and she's making Marcie pet act out too. Maybe I need to get rid of her. Maybe she just needs to go away, somewhere no one will ever find her. She could just disappear like smoke.*

He was having a hard time taking care of both of them since they cried all the time. Marcie had not been like that before. She had loved him prior to his getting her a pet. She had needed him before Penny pet had come along. This was all Penny's fault and he needed to find a solution.

Roman thought back to the night before. When he called them for dinner, they came right away. They were trying to be good. Then everything changed.

"Here, pets," he had said in his most gentle voice. "It's time to eat dinner, come, come, come." They had come, but he could see they didn't want to, hanging back until he had lost his temper.

"Come here, right now," he had shouted at them. Both girls had flinched, Marcie with her head down and Penny looking at him defiantly as they walked slowly into the living room where he was waiting.

"I want you in here to eat. You can't exist if you do not eat. Do you want to not exist?" he had shouted at them.

Penny had stared him down at this point and anger burned inside him.

"Stop staring at me," he shouted at her, waving his arms frantically in the air. Penny looked right at him anyway, eyes glaring, and shouted, "I want to go home. I want my mom."

Marcie felt panic. "Penny, please be quiet, please."

"No," shouted Penny. "I don't want to eat. I want my mommy and my daddy and when they find me they are going to kill you," she said looking straight at Roman.

Roman ran across the room and tried to grab her, but she'd been too fast for him and had taken off, running into the bedroom and scrambling under the bed. Roman, right on her heels, hit the floor and grabbed her by the legs, dragging her kicking and screaming out from her hiding place.

When she kicked him in the face, Roman grabbed her leg and pulled her along the floor into the bathroom where he ran the tub full of water. Reaching to grab her by the hair and protect himself at the same time, Roman felt himself losing control. He twisted his hands in her hair. Penny thrashed wildly on the floor and then in the air as he lifted her off the ground.

"Stop it," Roman had howled in a long drawn-out breath, shaking her until she was crying hysterically. She kicked harder and screamed louder. Roman shoved her under the hot water.

Marcie stood back, too scared to move until Roman did this. Then she lunged at him, trying desperately to grab for Penny under the water, burning her hands in the process.

Roman pulled Penny out of the water at the last possible moment, throwing her to the floor. Growling, he stormed from the room, pulling his hair and hitting himself in the face as he went.

Penny lay there, like a limp dishrag, steam rising from her clothes.

Marcie scrambled to her and held her close. Penny cried softly. "Marcie, I want my mommy. Please, Marcie, I want to go home."

Marcie could hear Roman in the other room. He was shouting and throwing things about. Dishes crashed into the wall and chairs were kicked over.

"Shhhh, Penny, be quiet. You can't talk to him that way. He will be mean to us if you do it again," Marcie pleaded, holding her hand over her friend's mouth. Penny just lay there on the floor, wet and crying that she wanted her mommy and daddy. The pink of Penny's skin was starting to turn a bright red.

Marcie sat by her in the puddle and cried too. "Me too, Penny, I want my mommy too."

When the outside door slammed, Marcie knew that for the time being they were safe, but she also knew he would be back. She had learned her lessons. She knew it would be worse when he got back. Until then they were safe, but there was much to do.

Marcie pulled Penny to her feet and pulled off her clothes. She rubbed lotion on the burns on Penny's skin. Penny cried out in pain and frustration. Marcie hung Penny's wet clothes over the shower curtain to dry just as Roman had shown her. Then she got Penny into some dry clothes and took her into the kitchen where the mess shocked them both.

"We have to clean this up or he will be really mad when he comes back," Marcie said.

"No, let's leave! Let's run away right now before he gets back," Penny said, pulling Marcie through the room toward the door. Marcie jerked back hard and Penny fell into her.

"No," she shouted, "don't touch the door."

"Why?" Penny asked.

"It will hurt you."

"How?"

Marcie told Penny about the time she'd tried to open the door. "It bit my fingers when I grabbed the doorknob, or at least that's what it felt like."

Penny looked at the door. She walked over to it and reached out a tiny finger in a pointing motion. As her finger touched the doorknob, she felt a jolt go through her finger and up into her hand. She jumped back, covering her finger with her other hand. "Ouch," she said.

"See, I told you," Marcie said.

"Why does it do that?"

"I don't know, but I never touched it again," Marcie said. "And the back door is nailed shut so we can't get out that way. All the windows are nailed shut too, and if he comes back and we're looking out the window, he gets like he was a while ago."

Penny's lower lip trembled and she started to cry again. Marcie pulled her back to the kitchen. "We have to clean this up before he gets back."

Realizing there was no escape, Penny looked at the mess and started to pick things up. The thought of not doing it crossed her mind, but her fear made her work harder and more diligently than she ever had before. The two little workers cleaned the kitchen and then turned off the lights.

They had eaten the scraps off the floor and drunk water from their bowl in the kitchen. Candy, cakes, and cookies were the only thing Roman gave them to eat, and the sweets were taking their toll, especially on Marcie. Since she'd been there the longest, her little body was already getting malnourished and she was starting to shake when she walked.

Tony and Lindsay spent the day driving around town and talking to different people. They stopped at the local dime store and bought an inexpensive handheld recorder for Lindsay to record her thoughts. At the end of the day they were tired, hungry, and frustrated, feeling as if they had accomplished little as they headed for home.

Walking into Tony's kitchen, the smell of food cooking welcomed them both. They realized they had not eaten since early that morning. Tony's stomach grumbled in protest as he greeted Claire.

"Hi, babe," he said as he kissed her.

"Hi yourself. Where have you two been all day?"

Tony ran a hand through his hair. "Everywhere. We've talked to everyone."

Lindsay looked beat to Claire. "You looked tired. Why don't you wash up for dinner and I'll bring a tray to your room?" she suggested.

"That's so nice of you. Normally I wouldn't even consider it, but tonight I think I'll take you up on it. Thanks again," Lindsay said.

Claire smiled at her as she watched her go. "Tony, how could you work her so hard? She looks positively beat," Claire said with a hint of concern in her voice.

"Me?" Tony said, shocked. "I'll have you know it was her. She's relentless and I'll bet she listens to her tapes before she goes to bed tonight. She's driven."

"Really?" Claire asked.

"It's almost like she's haunted by this guy now. It's weird and I'm not sure that's the right word for it, but I think she somehow feels him sort of as a part of her. Since this morning she's been saying 'we' when she talks about him. It's strange and kind of spooky, if you ask me," Tony said.

Claire looked at him. "You've taken up all her time so far. So I really have no opinion about her, to be honest with you." She looked hurt.

"This is an investigation, Claire, not a tea party. Our friends and neighbors are missing their little girls, and some guy is out there doing who-knows-what to them."

"I know, Tony, and I feel badly for them. I just want a chance to get to know her too. I know that sounds bad, and I feel terribly selfish for thinking this way, but I really can't help it. I was just hoping that tonight she would feel like visiting with us, or with me, for just a short amount of time. Never mind. I need to get your dinner. Forget I said anything."

Tony was angry. He was tired and hungry, and Claire was acting like a spoiled brat.

"Look, I'm going to take a shower. I don't have time for this. Don't bother her, Claire, or I promise I'll put her in a hotel. She worked damned hard today, and she needs to rest so she can do what she came here to do. She's away from her family, stuck in a town with people she doesn't know, feeling who knows what and trying so hard to prove her point. Leave her alone. Do you hear me?"

Claire sniffled, and Tony felt like crap.

"I hear you," Claire said.

Tony stormed from the room. "Damn it," he muttered under his breath. He hated treating Claire that way, but it wasn't like her to put herself first. Or was it? She had fought with his mom for years. Since they were kids and newlyweds, Claire always wanted to be the center of attention. And she was in Tony's world. But this was not about her. What the hell was wrong with everyone lately?

The phone rang. He looked at it on the stand next to the bed in their room. "Fuck it," he said and headed for the bathroom.

Within minutes Claire was outside the shower.

"Tony, John's on the phone, and he wants to talk to you about something".

Aha, Tony thought. *Here's a way to make Claire feel better and maybe score some brownie points with her.*

"What does he want?" he called out.

"John, Tony is in the shower and wants to know what you want," Claire said into the phone. She listened to the response. "Tony? He says he has something you need to see, something that came by FedEx today from FBI headquarters. Something about a guy who fits this guy's pattern."

"Ask him to come over here and show it to us."

"He heard you and will be here in about ten minutes," Claire said.

Tony poked his head around the corner. "And Claire, can you make us some coffee, sweetie, and maybe some dinner if there's enough. Let Lindsay know too. I'll be out in a few."

"Okay," Claire responded. She walked away happy and smiling. Tony knew it was wrong to indulge her. He also knew it was what saved his marriage and all the passion they shared. Keeping things strong in that department was no easy task. Most marriages fell apart within a year or so. He gave himself a mental pat on the back. "Good job old boy." He smiled and soaped up.

A few minutes later, Claire tapped gently on the door to Lindsay's room.

"Dinner," she called.

"Come in, Claire, please."

"I know you're tired, Lindsay, but John is coming over to show you and Tony something he got today. Do you feel up to meeting with him? I can tell them you're too tired if you don't think you're up to it."

"No, really, it's okay. I'm more frustrated than anything else. I'm used to working long hours." She paused. "We really haven't had much chance to get to know one another, have we?"

Claire smiled. "No, we haven't, but hopefully there will be time for that when you're done with what you're here for."

Lindsay squeezed her hand. "I hope so."

The doorbell rang and Claire turned to answer it. "See you out there if you feel up to it."

"Okay, be right there," Lindsay replied.

When Tony came out of the bedroom in his robe, he greeted John at the door with a handshake. Things were really getting better between them now.

"Hey, John, come on in," Tony said as he led him to the living room.

When Lindsay arrived, carrying the tray with her dinner, Tony and John both looked at it longingly. Claire saw the look.

"Oh my goodness. Where are my manners? Are you hungry? Come in, please."

Claire quickly set a place for all of them at the dining room table. After they ate, John started to talk about the new information he had.

"Tony, today I had an FBI pal of mine go back over some files and do some computer searching for me. It seems that about a year and a half ago in another town, not all that far from here, a little girl was taken. She was eventually let go and left in a men's restroom at a train station. This guy was young, dark brown hair, thin. We have a picture of him, but no one was ever able to put a name or age to that picture. The thing is, the picture is from a video camera, and you know how distorted those can be. We have him on video moving through the train station with the child. I have a gut instinct about it and I was hoping Lindsay might be able to confirm it. Tony, let's take a look at it."

When Lindsay nodded, Tony reached over to take the videotape from John and carried it into the living room. As he popped it in the VCR, the others assembled in front of the TV. With the remote in hand Tony pressed the play button. Nothing happened.

"Tony, I may be wrong but I think you have to turn on the TV first," John said.

Tony was tired and in no mood to joke around, but years of experience had taught him the only thing to do then was laugh.

"Up yours, Hanks," he said with a grin. Everyone laughed and the tension in the room was temporarily broken. After turning the television on, Tony sat down next to Claire and took her hand in his. It was a small comfort as well as a small apology, but it felt good to both of them. Claire squeezed his hand, and he answered her with a gentle squeeze of his own.

Immediately, horrifying scenes seized their attention. A little girl was being dragged into a bathroom by a rope that was tied around her wrists. Everyone in the room sat forward in their seats. John had seen it already, but he had not warned the others of how brutal it was.

Tony looked at Claire. The color had drained from her face, and a look of sheer terror was in her eyes. "Oh my God," she whispered. Reaching for the remote and pressing the pause button to freeze the scene, Tony said, "John, maybe this is too much for the ladies. You and I should watch this tomorrow at the station."

"No," Claire and Lindsay said together.

"Tony, I've seen worse, in person, and I'm the one who will know if this is him. I want to see it," Lindsay said.

Tony looked at Claire. "Honey, are you sure that you can see this?" Claire nodded.

"Okay." He pressed the button again. Now the child was being slapped viciously across the face, not just once or twice but several times. A man who fit the description of the suspected kidnapper of Marie and Penny was dragging her to the sink. He held her face over the sink and turned the water on. Reaching into the running stream, he splashed the child with water as her knees gave way under her, but they could see that she was still conscious. She continued to pull on the ropes that bound her. She threw her head about trying to avoid the water and the hands that were holding her head or slapping her. She was a small child who seemed unbelievably strong for her size and age.

Finally the man appeared to have lost his patience with the child. He drew his fist back to punch her, as Claire, Lindsay, and Tony all shouted at the same time, "NO." Grief and shock were mild words for what they were feeling as the scene on the television played on. Tears were in the eyes of every viewer.

When the child slumped to the floor, the man tied her hands to the sink leg and started stripping her clothing away. He looked down at her, and while no one in the room could see his face, they could sense the disgust in him. The man turned frantically around in the bathroom and seemed to be looking for something. He stepped over the body on the floor and reached across to the paper towel dispenser. Grabbing several handfuls of paper, he ran them under the water and threw them at the child with such force you could almost see her little body move.

Claire was sobbing softly. Lindsay walked over and sat next to her, holding her other hand and patting it gently. Still the scene on the TV played on. The man stood still at that point and looked down at the child. It was almost so unreal that it could have been a horror show on television or a slash-'em-up teen movie if the victim had not been so small and the image so distorted. The man drew his leg back and everyone knew what was coming next. With good aim, he delivered a kick to the child's body. The body moved with such force that it crumpled under the sink. Lindsay was sobbing now too.

Tony hit the stop button. "I've seen more than enough, John. Lindsay, is this our boy or not?" There was anger in his voice but they all knew at whom it was aimed.

Lindsay was about to answer, but John stood up. "Tony, there's more that you have to see."

"He does more to that poor child?" Tony asked.

John looked around the room. "Yes, I'm sorry to say he does. Ladies, if this is too much for you, I'm sorry. Please excuse us if you will. Tony, I have a feeling that you need to see the rest of this." John was so insistent that Tony turned again to the TV. The screen was mercifully blank.

Claire stood up. "I can't watch anymore. Just tell me, does that child live?"

"Yes, she does." The answer came from Lindsay, not John.

"You're right, Lindsay, she does live and was actually in pretty good shape when they found her."

"There's no need for me to see anymore, it's not him," she said. This shocked everyone in the room.

"What, are you sure?" Tony asked.

"Yes, I'm sure, and that means there are two men out there doing this."

"What, how do you know? Why do you say that?" John insisted.

"This man is dirty, actually he's filthy. He does not care for the child or the state he leaves her in. Our guy feels clean to me, something about the way this smells to me is different. My senses tell me this is not our guy. But the funny thing is I can feel our guy. It's like he is there somewhere, hiding." Everyone started talking at once.

"What do you mean our guy is clean?" John asked.

Tony said, "What do you mean hiding? What other guy?"

Lindsay held her hands up. "Our guy likes things that smell good, feel good to the touch. He has a fetish for softer scents. He would never, ever leave a child in this condition. He would want her to smell good, be clean, maybe too clean. I feel something about their hair is a major issue for him as well. He would never touch public lavatory faucets himself. Nor would he go in one if he could help it. I have a feeling that he would rather pee outside, to be honest with you."

Tony, John, and Claire just sat there looking at her.

Finally Tony said, "Blunt huh, you're not blunt. That's fucking blunt," he shouted pointing to the TV.

"Tony," Claire shouted. "Stop talking like that and stop shouting at Lindsay. This isn't her fault. This isn't getting us anywhere, and I know you're upset, but we have to be calm here and think this thing through."

Everyone looked up in amazement. Claire Miller, calm—now that was a shock.

"God, Lindsay, I'm sorry," Tony said as he ran a hand through his hair.

"No, Tony, I understand, really. Let's see the rest of the tape, John," Lindsay said.

"Are you sure?" He looked at all of them.

All heads nodded yes but Claire's. "Not me. I'm going to make some refreshments. Let me know when I can come back in." She left the room as the rest of them sat back down, and Tony started the tape again.

The child still lay on the floor. The man still stood over her and the wet paper towels still lay at his feet and across the small body. The movement on the screen made everyone in the room tense again. The man moved to the door, and reaching for it he pulled it open, then turned and looked at the small form on the floor. She didn't move. The man walked out, letting the door close behind him. Everyone in the room relaxed a bit but John. He knew what the others did not.

Tony looked at him with a question in his eyes. "Just watch," was all John said.

The door opened again at that moment and the same face peeked in. He seemed to look across the room. Not at the child lying on the floor, but deeper into the room, near the stalls, across from the urinals. At that moment a head popped out. Someone had been in there the whole time, watching. He looked at the man standing in the doorway. They nodded at each other and again the door closed.

The man who had been in the stall walked out slowly and knelt by the little girl. He brushed her hair back from her face in what looked like a gentle gesture. He got closer and seemed to be whispering something in her ear. There was a gentleness about him that almost made it feel like he was trying to help. If it were not for the nod to the man at the door, one could have thought that this man was salvation for the child.

Then the gentle man reached into his pocket and pulled out a large pair of scissors. Lindsay drew a sudden breath. Tony tensed and John just held his hand out toward them.

"Wait," he said, "watch."

The man gathered her wet matted hair in his hand and, taking the scissors, he cut it off close to the scalp. He was gentle in his movements, but the deed still had been done. He then stood and gently placed the hair in a paper towel he took from the holder. Arranging it neatly, he took his time and seemed to be talking to himself. The lips on the screen moved, but mercifully for the viewers there was no sound.

The child seemed to be moving now, and gently the man with the scissors knelt at her side again. Stroking her now short hair he spoke to her. Holding his hand over her mouth, he seemed to press her down. You could see him glance at the door every now and then. He was waiting for something. With scissors in hand he cut the rest of the hair off. Taking his time, he cleaned the area around her and dried her off with paper towels as well as he could. He seemed to be in no hurry. The viewers were spellbound by the horror in front of them.

Then the man stood and his mouth moved. The child had been moving, but now she lay still. Taking the hair and folding the paper towel around it, he neatly put it in his shirt pocket. He smoothed his hands down the front of his body and walked to the door. He turned one more time to the child and put his forefinger to his mouth in a sign of silence. She nodded and put her head down again. He blew her a kiss and was gone.

The viewers could see her lying there. Lindsay could hear her crying and feel her fear, though no one else could. The others just felt their own fear.

The child was so still that she appeared to be asleep. The tape ended.

John looked around the room. Lindsay seemed lost in her own world and tears were rolling down her cheeks. Tony sat still, too numb to move, almost too numb to breathe.

"What kind of animal does that to another human being?" Tony wanted to know.

John pointed to the screen. "That kind, the kind that we have here in this town. The kind that has those little girls."

Tony just sat there. Finally he said, "I don't know whether to hate him or thank him."

"Me either," John said. "On one hand he's gentle and good to her, saving her from the other guy and that torture. On the other hand he's an animal too. The other guy you just hate, loathe even, but with this guy you're not sure what to feel."

Tony looked at Lindsay. "You okay?"

"Yes, I'm fine, just shaken. Those poor children," Lindsay said.

"And Lindsay," Tony paused. "Which one do you feel we have here or do we have both of them?"

"The second one," she said slowly, "we have the second one and to be honest with you, I thank God for that."

Claire came back into the room with a tray of cookies and glasses of milk. "Is it over?" she asked.

"Not by a long shot, babe, but at least the film is," Tony said.

Claire nodded. "That's what I meant."

"Lindsay, is this guy close to us now? I mean, can you find him?" Tony asked.

"I hope so, but I have so many mixed feeling about him. He seems to be so many different places at one time that I have a hard time getting a fix on him. It's almost like he runs from one place to the next most of the day and I feel that the nighttime hours are the ones he has the hardest time with. That seems to be when his personality is the strangest. During the day he seems to fit in with the rest of the world somewhat," Lindsay said. "The nighttime hours, those are the problem."

Tony looked at John. "Where was that video taken?"

"About forty miles from here, due south."

"Same state?"

"Yup, same state. Our neighbors went through this too," John said. "The town was smaller and the station had installed those video cameras recently because of kids doing drugs in the bathroom. The only thing you can't see is inside the stalls and the urinals."

"Okay, in the morning, go down there if you will, and I'll take Lindsay around some more to see if she can get a handle on him from outlying areas. This guy needs privacy for all this activity," Tony said.

John nodded but he was looking at Lindsay, who was looking in shock at Tony.

"What?" Tony asked.

Lindsay still looked at him. "Say that again."

"Say what again?" Tony asked.

"The part about outlying areas, say that again."

"I want to take you riding around in areas outside the city limits because I think that this guy needs a great deal of privacy for what he does."

Lindsay closed her eyes. "Tony, one of you has seen him. Someone in this group has interacted with him."

"What, are you sure? I mean surely if we had we would know."

"Would you? Would you really?" Lindsay asked him.

"I think I would. God, I hope I would," Tony stammered.

"All I know is that I feel as if someone has seen him, talked to him," Lindsay said.

"Wait! Mike and his buddies saw someone fitting his description out on the feeder road. I have some uniforms checking out the area. It could be that. They are supposed to get back to me after a thorough search of the area. It's pretty busy out that way since it joins with the highway but it doesn't hurt to ask around."

"Okay," Tony said turning to John. "When you go down there tomorrow, talk to the officers and see what you can get from them that may not be in the case file. Just try to jog their memories a bit. It never ceases to amaze me what people will remember later that they forget in the heat of the moment. Find out if you can where he lived and how."

John nodded. "Will do. See you in the morning. Claire, thanks for dinner."

Claire, Tony, and Lindsay stood to walk John to the door. Saying their good-byes took time, in the typical southern way.

As the door closed, silence seemed to hang in the air.

Tony said, "I need some time alone."

Claire hugged him. "Be careful," she said.

She knew he was going for a drive. That's what he did when things got the better of him. Claire turned out the lights and headed the direction of her room.

That night, none of these four found peace in their dreams, but each felt the need to be alone and feel what it was they were feeling, to cry and be angry and not have to explain.

CHAPTER 43

Mac Anderson held his wife after having tucked in his sons, all of them, even Jayme.

The days slipped through his mind and he wondered just how many it had been. He could feel Janet next to him and her occasional sob in her sleep. Again tonight she had cried herself to sleep with her head on his shoulder. Two weeks, Mac thought. It has been two weeks and still no sign of Marcie. He lay there in the darkness, feeling inadequate, and prayed.

"Dear God, please hear my prayers. Forgive me, Lord, for my sins and make me pure enough for just this moment to come into your presence. God, someone has taken one of my babies, one of the gifts you saw fit to give me. I can't stand this, Lord. I hear you only give us what we can bear. I can't bear this, Lord. I know you don't make deals, but if you would just this one time make a deal with me I would forever be grateful. Please, Lord, take me instead. Bring my baby home, God, and take me."

A sudden intake of breath caught his attention. "No, Mac, please don't pray for that. I couldn't live without you," Janet cried.

"Oh, baby, I didn't realize I was praying out loud. God won't take me. He doesn't make deals like that. I'm just desperate, Janet, to do something to get Marcie back."

For the first time since the day that Marcie disappeared, Janet held him while his large shoulders shook as the sobs tore through his body.

"Baby, don't cry. Or better yet do, get it out and let me comfort you," Janet said. "Mac, you believe in God. Do you believe that God sends us angels to help in times like these?"

"Yes, I do." Mac sniffled and wiped his nose with his hand.

"Well, don't think I'm silly or anything or that I've lost my mind but I had a visit from an angel. I was praying for Marcie and Penny and a feeling came over me. There was someone there, Mac, and I heard but didn't hear that the girls would be fine. I don't really know how to explain it and it sounds silly to me as well but it happened."

"I believe you, baby, I do. I have to believe in something," Mac said. "Come let me hold you."

Janet climbed back into his arms and snuggled down close. Mac held her and felt a peace settle about the room. There were no words now, only silence but they really didn't need words. They just lay there and held each other. Slowly Janet's hands traveled over Mac's larger frame. He turned his head to look at her.

"Are you sure?" was all that he said.

Janet nodded and continued what she was doing.

Mac rolled to his side. Letting his hands explore the contours of her body, a form that he knew so well but had not touched in so long. The fire started in him.

Pulling her closer to him and tucking her under him, he again felt a sense of awe at how small she felt. He kissed her mouth first and then let his mouth travel over her body. She responded to him like she used to in years gone by when passion was almost what fed them. Mac felt her fingers on his skin, sliding slowly up his back and then tugging gently at the hair at the nape of his neck. He slid down farther to taste her. She responded in a movement of wonderful sensation as his tongue teased her. He was lost in the scent of this woman. He wanted to be a part of her. His hands moved expertly over her body. She was ready for him and yet he wanted to prolong this. Janet pulled him up to her. Mac meant to position himself over her but she slid out from under him before he could. She knelt on the bed in front of him and pulled the nightgown from her body. Mac was surprised by her actions. This wasn't like her at all but he loved it. Her skin glowed in the moonlight seeping through the curtains.

Mac reached out to pull her to him again. She brushed his hands away and positioned herself between his legs. Giving him a saucy look she bent and took him deep in her mouth. Mac gasped and pulled her head closer. It had been years since she had done this and now she had done it on her own. He was in heaven. His body was moving of its own accord. His hips were thrusting forward and his hands were stroking her hair. Janet slowly moved her fingertips up to find the fur that covered Mac's chest. He reached down and caught them in his own.

"Come here," he growled. "I want to be inside you."

Janet was easily flipped on her back by this large man. She giggled and squirmed as Mac covered her. He plunged inside her as she sharply drew in a breath.

"Oh, Mac," she cried.

They clung to each other and rode out the torrent of emotion and sensation.

Later they slept in each other's arms, at peace for the moment.

While the Andersons slept that night, in the Miller house the occupants tossed and turned, nightmares surrounding anyone who dared to drift off. In the hospital where Justina and Bill tried to sleep, nurses came and went at all hours. Even people who were simply following the story in the newspapers were having a hard time getting any rest. Across town, behind the junkyard, however, in a house that smelled of cleaning solution, two tiny figures shivered in fitful sleep.

Penny and Marcie huddled together out of desperation and fear. Marcie had a better idea of what to expect than Penny did, but she was just as scared, maybe more so since she knew how he would be when he got home. After cleaning everything they were hungry, but fear was a bigger demon and neither of them wanted anything sweet. So they climbed into their pallet beneath a chair and covered up as well as they could. Marcie instinctively wrapped her arms around Penny and held her close. Letting sleep claim them, they slipped off to a place where there were no Roman Marshes.

Roman had been angry when he left the house. Since the junkyard was closed for the evening, he had stormed around the yard with no fear of being discovered. He loved the cover of darkness, the feeling of moving about and no one knowing. Roman began to feel the tension in him ease as he inhaled deeply of the warm night air. He drew in again deeply, and his senses suddenly tingled and came alive. The scent was in the air. Roman looked around him, pausing in the direction of the house. The scent was there in the air and now he knew why: his pets, his darling pets created the scent. As he headed toward the little house and the sleeping children, Roman reached for the doorknob and then drew back sharply. He reached above the door and flipped the switch, chuckling to himself as the thought of all that power surging through some-one's body.

"That would be a jolt," he snickered.

Opening the door, he listened. No sound came from the darkened house. He walked into the kitchen prepared for a fight if need be to teach a lesson. When he flipped on the light, he felt tension build in him again. But as brightness filled the room, Roman smiled. His darling little babies had done a good job. Neatness met his eyes. Roman scurried around the room looking for signs of slovenly work. One sign and there would be hell to pay; he would tolerate no slackers. Instead, the room was as neat as if he had cleaned it himself. Roman felt a surge of pride. He turned off the light and headed through the darkness into the bedroom.

Marcie had awakened when the front door opened. Now she held her breath as the night-light in the bedroom came on. Roman stood in the doorway and watched the sleeping forms on the pallet next to the beds. The soft sounds of humming filled the air and Roman realized he was singing. *Run, run as fast as you can, you can't catch me, I'm the Gingerbread Man.*

As Marcie controlled her breathing, she remembered again how her brother Colton had helped her learn how to do this. Someday when she grew up and found him, she would tell him how he had saved her. When Roman turned and left the room, Marcie exhaled. She tucked her head against Penny's and drifted off to sleep, feeling for now all the safeness the situation would allow as she hummed the nursery rhyme, *Run, run as fast as you can, you can't catch me, I'm the Gingerbread Man.*

In the Miller house, Lindsay was struggling with the mixed things she was seeing and feeling. Her heart was racing, her mind reeling. She could feel the little girls, and she could feel the monster that was with them. Her stomach rumbled even though she knew she wasn't hungry. Her legs and arms felt cramped even though she was free to move them. She felt fear even though she was safe.

Suddenly the desire for a clean room entered her mind and made her stir in the bed. She sat up and put her feet on the floor as if to stand but then thought better of the idea. Lindsay knew what this meant. She knew she was going through what the inhabitants of a house somewhere near here were going through. Lindsay lay back and let the feelings come. She needed to see what the children were seeing. One thing worried her: she could feel only one of the children. Lindsay tried to control the fear and allowed the images to come to her. As she did this, she pressed the record button on her tape recorder and began to speak into it.

"A small room and hardwood floor, with windows that have curtains, can't see the pattern. The room is clean and for some reason I'm looking from the floor up. Cramped space and wood covering my head. Legs made of wood like chair legs. A large thing in the corner, no not really the corner but it feels that way from where I am. A window blows a breeze. Someone is coming, holding breath, listening. Oh my God, he is here. Hold still and be good, be quiet, make Penny be quiet." Lindsay felt herself trembling but she knew she had to go with this. *"He is there standing in the doorway, I know we cleaned the kitchen good, better than Vance and Jayme ever did. I hope we did, I hope he goes away, please make him go away."*

Lindsay took a deep breath as tears slid down her face. She knew she had them. She knew they were still alive but they were cold and hungry and a monster had them. Her heart was breaking for the two little girls she couldn't find. Lindsay slipped back into the space, and the images came to her. *"He's going away, we did a good job, he's going away."* Lindsay felt freedom coming to her. She knew that she could bring them home because she could feel them now. A feeling of peace and joy came over her and as she sat up a nursery rhyme played through her head but she couldn't quite remember which one it was. She reached for the door in the dark room and the scent of flowers in the air hit her hard. She sniffed the air furiously, trying to tell what the connection was. As she stood there in the darkened room, she let the new images come to her. A television was playing in the background and she had the feeling of long legs stretching out before her. There was a familiar smell but she couldn't place it; cars or car parts, oil and gasoline and the hint of magnolia blossoms.

Lindsay raised her hand and ran it through her hair. She could smell the scent again, oil and dirt. The feeling of satisfaction washed over her. Lindsay relaxed and let it come to her. She slowly walked backward to the bed and sat down again. She could feel the beginnings of arousal in her and wondered at that. She forced herself to stay with what she was feeling and tried to focus her mind on the eyes. Her feelings of arousal intensified and she hunched forward and gasped for breath. Then she was sweating and as she drew back with a feeling of revulsion she grabbed the trash can and vomited.

In the adjoining bathroom, she washed her face and rinsed her mouth but her desire to know who the sexual partner was drew her back to the feeling for fear that the children were being raped by this monster. Lindsay held her breath. As the face swam into view, she grabbed the countertop for security. She looked into the mirror and saw the face of a young man, dark hair with pockmarks and no facial hair. She realized that she was looking at the man who had Marcie and Penny. He had not raped them. He was just a kid. She blinked and the image was gone. Lindsay waited, praying for something else to come to her. Sometimes the mind is kind in that it gives time to recuperate from what one has seen before giving more.

Lindsay returned to her room and reached for the door leading into the hall, wondering if she would get more. But nothing came, so she opened the door and headed for the kitchen. A sound in the living area drew her in that direction. Tony sat hunched over a table covered with papers.

"I saw him," she said.

Tony looked up. He could see she was shaken. "Are you okay?"

"No, not really. But when I couldn't sleep, I just sort of lay there and let the images come to me. I guess fear had me up."

She told Tony all she had seen. Tony sat in fascination, rubbing his temples, and then looked sympathetically at Lindsay. "You poor thing, you have to live with that?"

"Yeah. That sucks, I know, but that is how we catch him. It sucks but it works."

Tony thought for a moment. "Lindsay, where is the tape you made?"

"In my room. Do you want to listen to it? I mean, that's why I taped it. I just let it come and listen to it later so that I can recall everything in real time."

"Real time?"

"Yeah, sometimes I don't remember what I say in that moment. I need to go back and listen, and sometimes going back and listening will bring up something new. So if I get stalemated I can use that to go forward again. It's sort of like a quick fix for writer's block. So do you want to listen to it?"

"Yeah, that might be a good idea."

Lindsay headed for her room. As she reached for the tape, she could feel moment behind her. Turning she saw a sleepy-eyed Becky standing in her nightgown.

"I want my daddy," Becky said.

Lindsay scooped her up and carried her into the living room, and placed her gently in her father's arms. "They're darling when they're little, huh?" Tony said.

Lindsay nodded, as she laid the tape on the table. "Do you need my recorder?" she asked Tony.

"No, I have one. I'll just go tuck her back into bed."

Lindsay sat in the big chair in the living room and let herself drift off to a light sleep. When Tony came back, he could see that as quick as that she was out. He turned off the lamp in the cozy room and covered her with a blanket.

Carrying the tape, he made his way to his workbench in the basement. He wanted to ask Lindsay what she meant when she said, "I saw him," but it could wait till morning. He couldn't sleep anyway; even the ride in the car hadn't soothed him like it usually did. He would listen to the tape. Maybe the answer was there.

CHAPTER 44
John Hanks started out in the early morning hours.

He was on the highway heading south, his mind going over the events of the past few days. He was a man of organized thinking, and was making mental notes for himself, including questions he wanted answered by the police officers he was going to meet. His heart was heavy and he felt frustrated at the stall in progress he seemed to be in. Lindsay Freeman seemed to be having better luck with this thing than he was. John hated inactivity. He wanted to make a difference here, and he felt the videotape had made a dent in things. But his mind would not let it go so that he could think through it clearly. He had never noticed a video camera in a men's room before. *Didn't that violate some law of privacy?* he wondered. *How had that tape come to be, and why didn't someone else know about it?* John had all these things running through his mind and the only answer he could come up with was that these were small southern towns. A lot went undone in small towns, southern or otherwise.

As he pulled up to the station, he shut the engine off, got out, and took off his suit coat. There was no need to go in there looking like some big-city guy, not if you wanted small-town answers.

John walked into the station and asked for the person in charge. The officer behind the desk looked him over.

"Have a seat over there. Who should I say wants to see him?"

John presented his ID. "I'm John Hanks, FBI. I need to ask him about a kidnapping case that happened here a year or so ago." The officer smiled and walked away.

Within moments a kind-looking man in his late fifties came around the corner. "I'm Captain Mike Lewis," he said, holding out his hand.

John stood and took the man's hand in his, giving it a firm shake. "Nice to meet you, Captain. I'm John Hanks from the FBI. I need your help, if you have some time to spare."

"I do, I do. I heard about your situation. Are you here from over Tony Miller's way?"

"Yes, sir, I am. I need to ask you about the kidnapping that happened here. We've watched the videotape but to be honest it left me with a lot of unanswered questions. Do you have anything else you can tell me about this case?"

"Sure. Come on in my office and have some coffee and we'll go over what I know."

For the next two hours they talked about Reese Keith, the violent man in the video. He was a known sociopath who had been in and out of foster homes and in trouble with the law most of his life. Mike Lewis didn't know the other man, but he was sure that the paths between the two had been crossing for a long time.

"Do you know where this Reese Keith is now, Captain Lewis?" John asked.

"Yes, sir, I sure do, and it's Mike," he said.

"Where?" John asked.

"He's dead. We found him buried in a hole about four months ago.

Funny thing is he seemed to have lived down there awhile. He had cans of food and gallon jugs of water, but eventually that ran out. The coroner said he starved to death. The ground above the hole was caving in, and some kids found his remains. He wrote some things while he was down there. Mostly they were the ravings of a mad man, but some of it made a little sense. He wrote about a brother by the name of Roman, but when we looked up what little bits of records we could find on Reese Keith, he didn't have a brother. In the foster homes, he may have met up with someone he felt was akin to a brother, ya know what I mean?" John nodded as Mike continued.

"Reese Keith was a bad man. He had quite a rap sheet. He was wanted for the rape of an elderly woman over in Warren County. The closest thing to a juvenile offense with him was when a little girl in our school system said he tried to get her to come to his old truck and look at some puppies. When she went he tried to pull her inside the truck, but she got away when she bit his leg."

"Did you ever check with the county homes about his foster placements?" John asked.

"No, sorry to say we never did. But you could." Mike took a notepad from his desk, wrote something on it, and passed it across the desk to John. "Mrs. Fields, over at the home, has all those records. She's been there about a hundred years."

John smiled and stood up. "Is there anything else you can think of, Mike?"

"Well, I can show you where the hole is, if you think that will help."

"I do believe it would," John said. "Let's go."

Mike stood and picked up his hat from the desk. As he walked out of the room he said to everyone, "I'm leaving. I'll be back in a while."

They both climbed into Mike's police car. As they headed out of town John asked who owned the land where Reese's body had been found.

Mike said, "It had belonged to the Marshes at one time but they left town to go live with Mrs. Marsh's sister. They left the house to Reese. He lived out that way and gave the previous police chief a hard time."

As they left the town they talked about the changes that police work had undergone. All the technology amazed Mike. John talked and Mike listened.

As they drove down pretty country lanes and over small hills covered with wild flowers, Mike told John about Birdie and Charles Marsh. "They were quiet folk that kept to themselves," he said. "They didn't go to church or any town socials, and it seemed that most of what you saw on the outside was what they were like on the inside, except Charles. He seemed to have a mean streak in him. From time to time, a neighbor would report him for shooting a dog or a cat. They never had any kids of their own, and the county counted on them in times of need to take in a foster kid or two. They were always obliging. They didn't have much money, and Birdie missed her family something awful. If you asked her how she was on those rare occasions when she came into town, she would always answer the same way. 'I miss my kin, and they miss me.' Then she would be on her way."

John asked if anyone had looked into their foster file to see if another kid had lived with them at the time that they had Reese.

"No, like I said, we never thought of it. Didn't seem to be no point. Reese was dead but to most it was good riddance. He was such a mean one we all just figured he finally got what was coming to him. Besides, he was strange. He was always talking about fallout shelters for the end of the world. He thought the commies were coming. He was always up to something."

They turned into the driveway of a dilapidated house. Its roof had fallen in from years of neglect. Mike led the way to the backyard. As John followed, something in him knew there was more here than met the eye.

Mike stopped and pointed to the ground where a hole showed. Tattered yellow police tape still surrounded the area.

John peered down inside the hole. "It looks like a net or something down there."

"Yeah, that was a net that had at one time been stretched over the top. I guess he thought he could hide down there and get out whenever he wanted to. I always believed that he got stuck down there and couldn't climb up or out. He must have been building this place as one of his fallout shelters for his end-of-the-world dramas that he claimed was coming. Hell, he had enough food and water stored in there to last him awhile. It did too. All we found were empty bottles and cans. He had some candle and pencil stubs and that old tattered blanket. He finished off all the resources he had. I guess his craziness finally got him in the end when this here net fell in and either trapped him in there before he died or covered him afterward," Mike stated.

"When we found him he was in a fetal position. It seemed like he must have just gone to sleep, never to wake up. He starved to death is what the coroner said."

John looked into the hole again. "Mike, I don't want to tell you how to do your job, but I have a feeling this was a homicide, not an accidental death. Someone put him in there, covered this net up with dirt, and left him to die. They may have meant to come back and get him, but they either forgot or changed their mind. How could he have climbed in there, covered the hole with the net, and then, from inside, cover it with the dirt and grass?"

Mike scratched his head. "Well, now that you say it that way, I agree with you."

They walked around the large opening in the ground, looking for clues and another way this could have taken place. Nothing came to mind. The view they had allowed for only one theory.

"I'll be doggone," Mike said as he scratched his head with his hat.

They walked around the rest of the backyard. A hundred feet away from the pit was a mound of dirt. Grass and weeds had grown over it, but to both men it looked like a man-made mound.

John grabbed a shovel from the shack in the yard and began to dig. As Mike looked on, the shovel dug into the old gumbo dirt. John was working up a good sweat. He stopped long enough to pull the shirt from his back. He went back to it, and after about thirty minutes of hard digging, he hit something that did not feel like dirt or rock, unless it was a big rock. John dropped to his knees and dug with his hands. Mike finally jumped in to help. The first skull was found right away and the second one, ten or so minutes after that.

Mike climbed out and ran to his car radio. "I need a team of officers out to the old Marsh farm right doggone now. Bring tape, shovels, and lights. Looks like we're going to be here awhile."

In a short amount of time the backyard filled with police officers. John and Mike handed the shovels to the first group with instructions to keep it going. They knew as soon as replacements arrived the shovels would be passed on, and that was fine as long as the area was completely excavated. They suspected the bones they'd found belonged to Charles and Birdie Marsh, but they weren't sure. A crime lab would be needed to determine that. The biggest fear was that more bodies would be found. Keith had a bad reputation for being mean, and whoever killed him must have been meaner. John and Mike needed to find out who that someone was.

John looked at Mike and said, "I need to drive over to the county home to talk to Mrs. Fields. Hopefully she has some answers about this family. I wonder what the hell went on out here."

"From the looks of things, more than you would put in a church bulletin. Come on, I'll drive you out that way," Mike said.

CHAPTER 45

Mrs. Ella Fields sat at her desk and looked at John and Mike.

She had at one time had a crush on Mike's daddy, but Mike Lewis Sr. had married Rebecca Toups and had six children. She had married Joe Fields and had her own family of four. She had been at the county home for more than fifty years. As John and Mike took turns explaining the story, she nodded in understanding.

"I remember those boys," she said.

"Those boys?" Mike asked.

"Yes," she said. "There were two that the Marshes took a shine to. One I understood, but the Keith boy I never did understand. His mother and father dropped him off on our doorstep on their way to seek fame and fortune in California. They told us he was a bad seed. We took him in and we even felt sorry for him, but what they said proved right in a short amount of time. He started out with pranks, like drilling a hole in the girls' changing room wall at school. We later found out that he charged the other boys money for a peek."

Mike and John laughed at this one.

John said, "He sounds pretty normal to me."

"That was in the beginning. From there he got progressively worse. He skinned the little cat that hung around and left him to die a terrible death. He set fire to the school on more than one occasion. He pushed another boy down a flight of stairs, causing him to break his leg in two places, then ran down the stairs and jumped on the boy's broken leg. At one time he grabbed a little girl and forced her to perform oral sex on him in front of a group of other kids. I'm sorry to say this about another human being, but for everyone concerned, the world is a better place without him."

"Mrs. Fields, you said, 'those boys.' Was there another boy involved here?" John asked,

"Yes," she said. "He was a boy we'd tried to place many times. To my way of thinking he was a sweet boy, but he never lasted long in any home we put him in. He always came back to us more bruised and battered than when we sent him. Then Birdie Marsh came in with Reese one day and I thought she was going to leave him. Instead, she said, 'My boy here needs a brother.'"

Mrs. Fields shook her head and continued. "It looked to me like Reese was the root of the problem 'cause Birdie looked like hell, but he just held her hand and smiled, and every now and then Birdie would flinch and ask again for another little boy. She had been a foster mom with us for a long time so I just took her to look over the boys we had. Reese picked out Roman right away. Since we hadn't been able to place him anywhere else, even though I was afraid for him I let him go. I saw Birdie a few months later and asked how she and the boys were getting along. She just smiled and said, 'I miss my kin and they miss me.'

"They moved away right after that and I never saw Birdie or Charles again. I heard about Reese from the newspaper and wasn't at all surprised, but I never did hear what happened to that other boy." Her eyes misted over with tears.

John could tell Ella Fields loved children and had tried to do her best even for the troubled ones. He reached his hand across the desk and laid his on top of hers, trying to give her some comfort.

"Mrs. Fields," he said slowly. "I hate to be the one to break the news to you, but we found two bodies buried out there on the farm and we think they are Birdie and Charles Marsh. It looks like they'd been there a long time."

Mrs. Fields gasped and her hands went to her mouth as the tears slipped freely down her face.

"Reese did it, didn't he?"

"At this time we don't know," Mike said.

"It could be, but he was found dead on the same farm," John said. "Do you have any information on the other little boy—what was his name?"

Mrs. Fields composed herself and said, "Roman, his name was Roman. There were several differences between Roman and Reese. The biggest one was the Marshes adopted Roman. They never did adopt Reese, in all the years they had him."

John and Mike asked at the same time, "Do you have a picture of him or something we could identify him with?"

She shook her head. "No, we never really had the money to take pictures of the children. Even if we did it would be more then ten years old."

John and Mike stood to go. "Thank you so much for your time, and we're sorry to have to be the ones to have to bring you this bad news," Mike said.

"Can I ask a question before you go?" She paused and took a breath. "Do you think Roman killed them all?"

John grimaced. "At this time we don't know what may have happened, but we'll let you know when we do."

CHAPTER 46

John and Mike left the county home filled with more information than they ever hoped to get.

They also felt like they had more questions than answers.

John looked at Mike and said, "I need a phone, a hot bath, some dinner, and a hotel room."

"You looking at staying on a few days?"

"Yeah, I don't see how I can do anything else. One good thing has come from this."

"Yeah, what's that?" Mike asked.

John said, "We know for a fact that Reese Keith doesn't have those two little girls."

Mike looked at him and smiled. "It's a blessing. Small, but at least we have one."

As they drove through town Mike pointed out the only motel, a Motel 6. He took John to the police station so he could pick up his car and then told him he could use the phone in his office. John walked inside and called Tony at home and filled him in on the events of his day. He promised to return as soon as he could.

As he hung up he heard Tony say, "Good job, John. We're counting on you, buddy."

CHAPTER 47

For Tony and Lindsay, the day had been a series of exercises in futility and neither felt they'd accomplished anything at all.

But that night, after John called, Tony turned to look at Claire and Lindsay, a hopeful expression on his face.

"John just told me that the violent guy from the videotape is named Reese Keith. He was found buried alive in a pit four months ago. Today, John found skeletons of two other victims he thinks will turn out to be Reese's foster parents. And here's the best part: this guy had a foster brother named Roman who the foster parents had adopted."

Lindsay narrowed her eyes as she looked up from her papers. "The name Roman feels right. What is the last name of the foster parents, did he say?"

"Marsh," Tony said.

Lindsay put the two names together, saying them softly to herself.

"Roman Marsh."

Again the goose bumps appeared on her skin and she shivered.

"Oh, my gosh! That's it. That's the name of the person we're looking for. Something feels wrong here but I have a strong feeling that's his name."

"What feels wrong about it?" Tony wanted to know.

"I'm not sure, but something is not totally right. I really can't get a lot of feeling on it but the name is connected somehow to the man who took the girls."

Wearily, Lindsay stood up. "I'm going to take a shower and try to get some sleep. Something seems to be closing in on me and I need some down time to prepare myself."

Tony and Claire could see the fatigue in her eyes. "Good night, Lindsay," they both said.

Lindsay made her way to her room. The hallway that led through the house was dark and images came to her of someone lurking in the darkness. She knew she was being silly, but she hurried into her room and flipped on the light as she shut the door. She looked around the now-familiar surroundings. The pink almost attacked her senses and she smiled at her silliness. What had she been so scared of, she wondered.

"Must be fatigue," she said to herself.

She pulled the covers of the bed back to expose her own sheets. "Two hundred and seventy count thread," she said to herself. "I love the feel of that. It's almost like luxury."

As she walked into the bathroom, she felt that feeling again. Someone was watching her, though she had no idea where to begin to look. Was it a real thing or was it in her mind's eye? She brushed her teeth and washed her face with the soft pink washcloth. As she applied moisturizer, she thought again of Roman Marsh.

"Where are you, Roman?" she said to the mirror. "Oh gosh, I spend more time talking to myself every day," she said as she stuck her tongue out at her own image. She giggled as she turned off the bathroom light.

Lindsay climbed into bed, letting herself enjoy the feel of the sheets and the coolness their extra softness provided. She turned to her side and turned off the light. Lying there in the darkness, she said her prayers. Her mind was traveling in many different directions at one time. Home, kids, travel, work—the list was endless. Slowly she drifted off to sleep. It was hours later when screams ripped through the silence. She heard them again and again. As she struggled from sleep, she realized the light to her room was on, and Tony was standing in her doorway with his gun in his hand.

"What happened?" he demanded.

"I don't know. I thought I heard someone screaming."

"You did. You heard yourself screaming. Are you okay?"

"Oh gosh! I'm so sorry. I must have had a bad dream."

Tony looked closely at her again. "Then you're okay?"

"Yes, I'm fine. A little bit embarrassed but fine."

"Good night then," Tony said as he turned to go.

He closed the door gently. He still felt the adrenaline pounding through his veins.

"Shit, that was weird. I know just how she feels. I want to scream too."

Tony went back to bed. In the darkness he heard Claire say, "Is everything okay?"

"Yeah, baby, everything is cool. Go back to sleep."

CHAPTER 48

The next morning when Bobby opened up his auto salvage yard at the usual time, Roman was nowhere around.

That was surprising because Roman was always around by the time he got there. Bobby had come to count on him in the short amount of time he'd worked there.

He walked out in the back. "Yo, Roman, you out there?"

There was no response. He walked into the mechanics shop. As he turned on the lights and pushed the button to raise the door, he heard a sound. Turning around quickly he grabbed a tire tool and raised it over his head.

"Who's there?" he demanded.

"It's me, Bobby. Roman. I had overnight guests that kept me up all night. I needed to get some shut-eye so I came out here. Hope you don't mind." Roman looked like hell.

"Drank too much, did ya?" Bobby teased.

Roman looked down and smiled. He felt like hell and he sure wasn't going to put up with Bobby's shit today.

Bobby looked at him again. "Go on home. Ain't nothing going on around here today anyway. Get some sleep and come on back tomorrow."

Roman looked at him. Home was the last place that he wanted to go.

"No, man, that's okay. I still have company and home is the last place I want to be. They're leaving around noon though, so if you don't mind I'll go then."

"Suit yourself." Bobby shrugged. He turned and walked back to his office.

Roman got up and walked into the bathroom. As he looked in the dirty mirror, he thought about the night before. He'd been so proud of his little pets. They had worked so hard to please him. The kitchen was as clean as if he'd done it himself. For some reason, even though that had pleased him, he felt something was missing. He missed Reese. He felt the need to make the trip to get Reese, but he was afraid of what Reese would do to his pets if they weren't on their best behavior all the time. He was still having some trouble with them now and then. He wanted to find a way to get his point across to them before he brought his brother home to live with them.

Reese had a tender side to him if you didn't rile him up, and Roman longed for the companionship of his childhood. He could see images of himself playing with other kids and being kissed good night by his loving parents. He remembered his mom bringing him a glass of sweet juice and a pretty pink sweater to wear as the day got cooler. He remembered playing on the porch with his toys.

Then the thought hit him. Those weren't his memories; those were someone else's memories. But whose, and how did he know them? Roman had sat up most of the night thinking about it. Finally, as he had taken himself to bed and seen the sleeping children on the floor in the corner, he remembered. Those were Marcie's memories. Marcie had the loving parents and the glass of sweet juice.

When Roman kicked the chair where the little girls were sleeping, they awakened with a start and then the screaming began. Roman ran around the house trying to get them to be quiet, but even though they stopped screaming, he couldn't get the sniffling to stop. So he'd left his own house again in a rage. He sat outside for hours watching the sun come up and longing for Reese. Today at noon he would go and get him. He would make Reese cross his heart and hope to die, stick a needle in his eye, promise that he wouldn't hurt the pets. He would make them behave and he wouldn't let them give Roman bad memories again.

Instantly, Roman felt better. He was going to get Reese and he would have an ally, someone on his side for a change. He walked into the office where Bobby was getting the day started. He was doing what he always did: stuffing his face.

Roman watched Bobby as he devoured the box of donuts.

"Have ya one kid," Bobby said as he stuffed another into his mouth. "There's plenty."

Roman looked into the box. *Plenty huh?* he thought. *Pig! All adults were pigs.*

Roman reached into the box with a napkin and took one of the glazed donuts. He carefully wrapped it up and then sat and watched Bobby as he ate another three.

"Get ya another one, Rommie. Boy your size needs to eat."

Roman carefully took another one with the last napkin on the counter. He again carefully folded the paper around it and tucked them both under the counter. "I'm saving them for later when my stomach wakes up."

Bobby reached into the box, looking for the last one, and finding nothing there said, "Finally got you to take more than one. I'll be damned. You've been here for three months now and you ain't never had more than one. You must be hungry today after getting no sleep last night. Well, I'm gonna go and get some breakfast. You take care of things round here for me, okay?"

"Will do," Roman said.

Roman laughed at him as the door closed. Bobby thought that Roman was laughing with him.

"Asshole," Roman said out loud. "The donuts are for my pets. I have to leave them alone all day and they are gonna get hungry. Besides, does that fat pig really think that I would eat after him? Ha! These are for my pets, my babies."

CHAPTER 49

Now that he had a plan, the morning hours passed slowly for Roman.

Life was so much simpler with a plan. He would go home at noon and feed his Marcie and Penny pets and then get on the road. He had made a list of supplies for Reese. Clean clothes, a length of rope, a shovel, lantern, and some shoes. Socks and underwear since he knew for a fact that Reese never changed his underwear unless you made him. A toothbrush and toothpaste in Reese's favorite flavor and some deodorant. He would need a bath and that was gonna be a chore, so Roman would get some soap and a towel. He needed to get some gas and check the oil in his old car.

Roman helped the time pass by cleaning the office and bathroom he and Bobby shared. They were almost spotless by the time Bobby returned from breakfast.

"Hey, kid, you've been busy. It ain't natural for a junkyard to have such a clean john. I think I'll go mess it up a bit," he said as he hitched up his trousers and closed the door.

Roman heard the fan come on. He knew the bathroom would be thoroughly fouled when Bobby came out. He also knew Bobby was going to be in there a while.

"Hey, Bobby," he said, "I'm gonna go on and go, okay?"

"That's fine, kid. Have a good one and get some rest. Tomorrow is Saturday and I need you to work all day."

Roman knew with Reese there he couldn't work; there was no way he could leave Reese home alone with his little pets till he learned to love them.

"I can't work tomorrow, Bobby. I have to take my company home."

"Shit," Bobby said, laughing at his own joke.

"Okay, call Waymon before you go. He's always needing extra money."

"Okay."

After Roman made the call, he headed out the door for his new adventure and his heart swelled at the thought of Reese. "It's gonna be great to see you, Reese, ol' boy."

CHAPTER 50

The girls were watching TV when they heard the old car Roman drove pull into the yard.

Marcie and Penny looked at each other in a state of panic as tears filled their eyes. They looked at the room. Marcie reacted first. She jumped up and ran around, putting things the way Roman wanted them to be. Penny grabbed the dishes they used and took them into the kitchen. Rinsing them quickly, she dried them on the clean towel. Some of the food came off on the white fabric.

When Marcie rushed into the kitchen and saw it, she burst into tears.

"Oh my gosh, we are going to get it," she cried.

"Why, what did I do wrong?" Penny said tearfully.

"Look at the towel. It's dirty." Marcie pointed to the dark stains on the bright white. There was no way to get it out before he came in and she knew it. She had tried in the past. Roman was going to be furious.

The girls waited, but as time passed and Roman didn't appear, both felt their anxiety reach a peak they could no longer stand. They moved cautiously toward the door. Penny walked to the window and slowly lifted one corner of the curtain. Marcie knew if Roman saw Penny, he would throw a temper tantrum for sure. Penny let go of the curtain just as carefully as she had lifted it.

"He's still out there," she said in a whisper, as if he could hear through the walls.

"Where is he? Can you see him?"

"Nope, but the car is there. Let's wait till he opens the door and then run out together. He can't chase us both at once and one of us might get away and get some one to help us."

"No, no!" Marcie knew her legs couldn't carry her.

Somehow Penny knew it too. She looked down at Marcie's thin legs that seem to shake all the time now.

"Okay, I know you can't run. And your face looks sick too. So you get his attention, and I'll run out the door. I'll bring someone back for you. I promise."

"No, no please, Penny. Don't leave me here," Marcie begged. "I need you. I wanna go too. Please don't leave me."

"Okay, when the door opens, we push him over and run. Make sure you keep running, okay? No matter what, just keep running."

Suddenly, Penny put her finger to her lips and motioned to Marcie to be quiet. They could hear Roman outside now, doing something. Penny lifted the curtains a bit to see him walking away from the house toward the car. He had things in his arms he was putting into the trunk.

Marcie grabbed Penny's arm. "Penny, we can't try to get away. If we do, he'll catch us and he can be really mean. He put me in a trunk of an old car one day. It was so hot and I was really scared. I don't want to go back in that old trunk ever again. Please let's not do this, okay?"

Penny would not budge. "No, I'm going home, Marcie Anderson. You can stay here if you want but I'm going home."

"Okay, I wanna go home too."

But suddenly the girls heard a knock on the door and then it opened and two napkins were tossed inside. The door was closed again as quickly as it had opened. The napkins fell open, exposing two glazed donuts Roman had taken from Bobby's box in the shop.

Penny screamed in rage and kicked the soft pastry. "I don't want donuts! I want to go home."

The sound of laughter met their ears. Then the car started and they heard it pull away. Marcie fell on the floor and curled into a fetal position and cried. Penny knelt and wrapped her arms around her friend.

"Marcie, don't cry. Someone will come to get us. Someone loves us, and someone will come. I bet your brother Jayme is looking for us right now," Penny said.

"No, he's not, he hates me. He wouldn't take me to the park," Marcie said through her tears. "I just wanted to go to the park, and then I wouldn't have been home for that man to get me. I just wanted to go to the park," she cried again softly.

"Marcie, you've got to stop crying. You don't look so good," Penny told her.

"I'm pretty," Marcie shouted at Penny, "pretty, pretty, pretty and you're just jealous, Penny Ware. You're mean and you're jealous."

Penny was instantly mad. "I am not! You are pretty but you look like you feel bad, and I'm pretty too. My daddy told me so."

The fire burned out between the two little ones quickly, as fires between children often do. Penny went and sat on the couch, but Marcie got up and walked to the bathroom. She looked in the mirror. Penny was right; she looked like she was sick. Marcie touched her face as she looked in the mirror. *I look like my mommy,* she thought.

CHAPTER 51
Across town Lindsay stood and looked in the mirror too.

I look like my mommy, she heard as she touched her face.

"Tony!" she shouted. "Tony, come in here."

Tony appeared around the corner. "What?"

"I've got them, I can feel the girls. Marcie is looking in a mirror and Penny is in another room. A room that is square with hardwood floors. Marcie isn't well. Something seems to be wrong with her. I can feel her limbs shaking. We have to find them soon. Something is coming, something bad."

"Okay, tell me what you see."

Lindsay took a deep breath. "Okay, I see a room, with curtains on all the windows. The room is truly square and there's little furniture in it. One of the girls has looked outside, and cars are everywhere. They must be in a busy place; it's a place with a lot of cars. I see Marcie's face in a mirror and I feel illness around her. Penny is mad and wants to go home. Oh, Tony, Marcie is sick. We have to find them soon. There seems to be someone they're watching, but I can't really get a good look at him. He's gone from them a lot."

Tony watched Lindsay and felt again that it must be horrible to live with all that in you all the time. He was amazed by what she could see. She was either the greatest con artist in the world or incredibly talented. He had to believe the latter of the two options. Certainly the accuracy of what she'd revealed so far supported that.

"Lindsay, you said that Marcie is sick. Can you tell how sick or what kind of illness she has?"

"No, she just feels weak and lethargic to me. It's like she has no energy and no reason to care. I don't feel a fever, however, and that's a good sign."

"Can you find them based on what you have now, what you know about them?"

"No, what I have is just how they feel. The thing is I don't think they know where they are themselves. That's a problem for me. If they could see something I could identify, then we could find that one thing and maybe find them. I need something more, something concrete."

Tony could see the frustration in her. He felt it too, but in his line of work frustration went with the job.

"Wanna go for a ride, maybe cruise around town or something? It could be that something that you feel now will tie in with something you get while we are out. Claire is making a special dinner for us, but we could go for a while."

They headed for the door as Tony shouted, "We'll be back in a while."

"Don't be long," Claire yelled from the kitchen.

Tony and Lindsay rode aimlessly for a while. In small towns it doesn't take long to drive from one side of the city limits to the other. It was driving up and down the city streets that took time.

"Let's go by the houses," Lindsay suggested.

She didn't need to say which houses; Tony just knew. He turned the car toward that side of town. As they rode in silence, Lindsay let her mind wander.

All the sudden she held a hand up. "Tony, something's coming, something bad, real bad. I can feel it as we get closer to the houses. Keep driving in that direction."

Tony felt panic welling up inside him. *God, please don't let something worse happen,* he prayed silently. He wasn't sure he could take it.

"Lindsay," he said, "it's not my house, is it?"

She looked at him and smiled. "No, Tony, it's not your house."

They drove past Penny's house and then Marcie's came into view. "Anything?" Tony asked.

"No, not yet. Keep going, okay?"

Tony continued down Third Street, cruising slowly and looking at things that he was familiar with from a new perspective. His eyes searched for things he might take for granted on any other day. Lindsay could feel something boiling just below the surface. Someone was moving about, something that was bad and meant to do harm. *Are these things to come or things that have happened?* she wondered. It seemed to be hanging in the air.

"Tony, I may be wrong, but I have a feeling he may take another child. Not because he doesn't have Penny and Marcie, but because he wants one who will do what he wants her to. I know that doesn't make much sense but that's what it feels like."

Tony looked at her. "Are you sure? Could it be because you're on the street where the other kidnappings took place? Or do you really feel that another child is going to be taken?"

Lindsay thought one more time before answering. "I have to say that he is going to take another child. A little girl who lives near here will be his next victim. Is there something about this area we have overlooked? Something that draws him to this part of town for some reason?"

Tony had no answer. In fact, he had asked himself that question a million and one times. "I don't know, Lindsay, I just don't know. Maybe John can answer that question when he comes back. He should be here in about an hour."

Lindsay wanted to go back to the house and wait for John. She knew that Claire would have dinner ready and she really needed to get out of the neighborhood so that she could be objective. Yet her thoughts wouldn't allow her to escape the questions.

"Tony, if I had something of his that I could hold I would know if the person that we think is doing this is really doing it or what he is thinking. I feel frustrated and confused most of the time. I can feel the girls some but not enough to know where they are. I can hear things but not enough to be sure of what I'm hearing. Does any of that make sense to you?"

Tony looked at her and again felt pity. "I have only known you a short time. I see what you do and I hear what you say but to me this is all out of the ordinary. You have to understand where I'm coming from. To you this is normal, natural since you've been doing it for a while now. But think back to when you weren't like this, if that is possible. Do you remember how it felt all of a sudden to be so different?"

"It was a nightmare for me, Tony. I lost family members over this. My grandparents and aunts and uncles didn't want me around anymore. My friends were gone. And I lost two years of my life; well, two years at least that I can remember. I remember being seven and I remember being nine. Everything in between that time is a loss for me. So please understand that I'm not this way by choice."

Tony could almost envision the little girl that she had been. Lost, confused, and afraid.

"How did you get through those times. Who took care of you?"

"I had the world's greatest mother. She and my brother are the reason I came out as well adjusted as I did. They took their time and loved me no matter what."

Tony smiled. "I can see the love in you. Does that surprise you?"

"No, not at all. You love your children. I can tell by the way you watch them, by the way you take care of your whole family. To me it's obvious too."

They pulled up in front of Tony's house and saw John's rental car. As they walked in the front door, Becky slid up to her father on short, white, cotton socks and banged into his legs.

He laughed as he picked her up. "You again! Why is it every time I come to this house I run into you?" he said as he nuzzled her neck.

She wrapped arms around him. "Cause I'm your bestest girl and you love me like marshmallows in your hot chocolate."

Becky giggled as Tony swung her around and tossed her in the air. Then he lowered her to the floor and patted her bottom as she scurried off. All eyes were on them and Tony blushed as he looked up.

"Gosh, I love that kid," he said somewhat sheepishly.

Claire beamed at him. "Dinner's ready, everyone. John's agreed to join us."

John nodded, "I haven't had a home-cooked meal in weeks."

They all headed to the dining room where Claire had outdone herself. Roast beef and vegetables of all sizes and colors met their eyes.

"Oh, Claire, this looks wonderful," Lindsay said.

Everyone agreed as they ate hungrily and shared some polite conversation as a break from their work. Tony noticed that John seemed to be inhaling his dinner.

"Hungry, John?" he asked.

"I've been full for fifteen minutes, but who knows when Claire will invite me back, and I never get food this good."

Claire smiled at him. "Thank you, thank you very much. John, maybe you should think of getting married. I know a nice woman I could introduce you to."

"Oh, no, you don't," Tony said. "Don't listen to her, John. Just keep eating and then run for your life. The last time someone said that to me I met Claire and ended up married and with all these kids."

Claire slapped at him with her napkin. Everyone giggled as John looked at Claire and said, "Do you have a younger sister? Believe me it takes a special woman to understand a cop's life."

"Alas, I'm an only child, one of a kind, but there are some really nice young woman in town."

John looked momentarily crestfallen. "One of the things about my life and my career goals is that there's no room for a wife and family. It's a choice I had to make and I made it, but it really does hurt sometime. Sometimes I miss it, times like these."

After they cleared the table together, Tony and John did the dinner dishes as Lindsay and Claire took some tea to the living room. They talked in comfortable camaraderie for almost an hour. Claire asked Lindsay about her family.

"I have two older daughters, and my son Jack is still very young. We are a close group." Lindsay looked around her. "Your family seems to be close too. You've made a wonderful home here. I can feel the love in this house."

"Becky was born here. Did I tell you that?" Claire asked.

"No, you didn't."

"I went into labor in the middle of the night. Tony thought we had plenty of time and so did I, but Becky had other plans. All the boys were here and up running about as Tony and I got ready to leave for the hospital. But suddenly my water broke and, only fifteen minutes later, Tony delivered Becky right there in the hallway with the boys looking on. Mike understood the most since he was the oldest. Tony put that wiggling, crying baby in his arms and he wrapped her in a towel. He lost his heart to her right then and there. That's why all the boys love her so. That's also why she's so spoiled."

Tears filled Claire's eyes as the memories came to her. "Those are precious moments to be treasured," Lindsay said.

"Tony and I have always been so close. And this kidnapping has made us even closer for some reason, even though he's working a lot of hours. We've had the best sex in years lately." Claire giggled.

Lindsay laughed. "I hear that a lot in situations like these. This sort of thing either makes love stronger or tears it apart."

"Tony's my knight in shining armor. He always has been, ever since high school. His mother hates me but that's okay. I try to like her but, to be honest, it's really hard sometimes."

Lindsay looked at Claire. "You know she treats you the way she does because she's afraid to be alone. She misses her husband and Tony is the only link to him. She doesn't really mind sharing him. But it seems to me, she feels like she'll be alone if she doesn't do things to make him see her. She feels like she needs to draw attention to herself, and the only time Tony pays attention to her is when she attacks you."

"I know. What should I do about it?"

"Include her. She needs to feel like she'll have a place to go in her old age, someplace where she's loved. She fears being stuffed away in a nursing home and forgotten. She wants to be needed, and I believe that would make her feel like she doesn't have to compete with you for his attention."

"How do I do that, when to be honest with you, I don't trust her, or like her very much?"

"Well, I would ask her opinion from time to time about the kids and Tony, to begin with. Even if you don't take her advice, it will make her feel needed, and I have a feeling that her love for them will make her give good advice. Let her watch Becky and the boys every now and then. Take her things, like plants since I know she loves them. That will disarm her some. I must be honest with you. In the time to come, you will be the primary caregiver of this woman. She will need you and Tony to build on a spare bedroom for her eventually."

"Mike goes away to college next year. She could use his room if it comes to that."

"It will come to that, and Mike will stay here and go to a city college not far away. She will need her own room done in her own taste. I think the pink rose room would work really well, since I have a feeling she is the one who did it," Lindsay said.

Claire laughed. "You are so right, she did."

"Well, tell her that you are going to leave the room that way just for her and that she should feel free to spend the night anytime she wants to."

"Oh gosh, you think she would actually do that, spend the night I mean?"

"She might just to test you. She would want to see if you just wanted her there as a baby-sitter. So in the beginning don't use that even if she offers, and Claire, you know how you've wanted to learn to knit. She's the perfect teacher, and she'll gloat for a while, but eventually she will become a friend."

"Oh, I don't know. I have a feeling that her hate for me runs pretty deep. If you think this would really work, I will give it a try. It's not going to be easy, but I'll try," Claire said.

Lindsay laughed and gently squeezed Claire's hand. "You can do it. In the long run it will be well worth it."

At that moment Tony and John came from the kitchen. "All done," they announced.

"Lindsay, John has been filling me in on some information about a man by the name of Roman Marsh."

Lindsay jumped up off the couch. The color drained from her face and she held her hand to her throat. "I can't breathe, I can't breathe," she stammered.

Tony ran for water and Claire helped her back to a sitting position. As the feeling subsided, Lindsay tried to understand what had happened. "John, why would that name and the feeling of the person it's attached to make me feel as if I'm gasping for air?"

"We think he buried his foster brother alive, and there's a strong suspicion that he may have killed his adoptive parents."

"I don't think he killed his adoptive parents, but I do think that he buried his bother alive. It seems to me that he knew about the parents but he didn't kill them," Lindsay said, as she took the glass of water from Tony.

"I also don't think he meant to kill his brother. It seems to me that he loved him. They had an argument, even a fight, but the love is there. Something is wrong with this man. John, would you say his name again."

John looked at her. "What?"

"Please say his name and his age for me, if you know it, so I can form an attachment with him.

"His name is Roman Jonathan Marsh, born Roman Jonathan Severson. He would be about nineteen years old, we think."

Lindsay looked at Tony. "He's your kidnapper. Be glad it's him and not his foster brother. The girls have a chance with him."

Tony ran a hand through his hair.

John looked at Tony. "Whew! Where do we go from here? Does anyone around here know a Roman Severson or a Roman Marsh?"

"I don't know, but I'm sure as shit going to find out."

Tony walked to the phone and called the station. After he hung up, he came back into the living room and sat down.

"We'll know something in the morning. John, do you think you can get a picture of this guy from your division?"

John nodded. "I can try, but some people with no priors are not in the system. That would be unusual for a guy like this but it happens. You have to understand something else here. If this guy has no priors we would need more evidence and concrete proof to get a conviction for the killings of Charles and Birdie Marsh and Reese Keith."

Tony nodded. He knew how the law worked and he loved it, even though he didn't always agree with it.

"Lindsay, you said you needed something more concrete before. Does this qualify?" Tony asked.

"It does. It tells me the things that I've shared with you already, but it will also assure me that we have the right guy when you catch him. I feel the catch but, Tony, something seems sinister about it, almost deadly."

"All catches of this kind are sinister, Lindsay," John said. "These guys never come along quietly or throw themselves at your feet and cry, 'I did it, please take me to jail.'"

Everyone laughed, but Lindsay still had a feeling that something bad was coming. She laughed, but the strain was evident in her eyes.

CHAPTER 52

Roman drove off in the direction of his past.

Reese was waiting and he couldn't wait to see him now that he had made the plans to go. As he thought of his life with Reese, the memories came flooding back to him in vivid colors.

Roman had gone to live with Reese and the Marshes from the county home. He had hated it there, but already he'd started to learn what to do to make others think he was conforming. He had been eight years old. Reese had walked up to him in the yard where everyone was playing.

"Hey, buddy, you wanna come home with us? We can share a room if you want. If not, you can sleep in the barn. What do ya say?"

Roman had looked at Reese and thought to himself, *Why not?*

So he had nodded. That was all the communication there had been at that first meeting. He met Birdie Marsh that same day. She was a quiet woman and had spoken only to mean old Mrs. Fields. Roman had known Mrs. Fields for more than a year at that time. He knew she would be glad to get rid of him, and she had done just that. Waved him off without so much as a good bye.

The Marshes had an old farm out in the country. They had chickens and pigs and a few other animals but mostly they had cats. The cats were everywhere and they had kittens all the time. Reese never really liked the cats but he always loved the kittens. In the beginning everyone got along okay, except for Charlie Marsh. Charles Marsh was a mean man and when he drank, it only seemed to make him meaner. Birdie and Charlie Marsh didn't exactly have a happy marriage or a happy family life. They had been married for twelve years and had no children of their own. They kept kids from time to time as foster parents for the state money they got for keeping them. It helped in the lean times, and most of the time was lean time.

Foster parents in that day and time, in back woods locations, didn't have to go through deep screening procedures. Anyone who had room could be given a child.

At the Marsh farmhouse Birdie slept in one of the five bedrooms and Charlie slept in another. That left three others for Reese and Roman, but they choose to sleep together. Roman liked Reese right from the beginning. He was funny and smart. Not book smart but people smart, street smart. Reese was only three and a half years older than Roman, but he knew a lot more about the world. Reese would sometimes get a faraway look in his eye and Roman would ask him about it.

"One day I'm gonna run away from here, Roman, and I ain't never gonna look back and ain't no one ever gonna find me either." He had looked at Roman that day long and hard.

"Hey, kid," he said, "don't ever let anyone call you Rommie. That ain't your name. You're Roman, do you hear me, you're Roman. You ain't no slouch and don't you let them make you one. You're Roman. Say it, say 'I'm Roman.'"

Roman didn't know what had Reese so upset but he did what he was told to do. "I'm Roman," he said, "not Rommie, never Rommie."

Reese had relaxed some after that day but things changed between them. They had become closer. Every now and then Reese would say that he was going to leave but that he would take Roman with him.

Winter at the Marsh farm was the worst time of year for everyone. The four were trapped indoors with each other and Charlie drank more, saying it was so he could keep warm. "Antifreeze," he'd mumble as he sucked on the bottle, then wiped his mouth on his sleeve.

It also was in the winter that Charlie picked on Reese the most. He never really got on to Roman but Reese seemed to be his favorite target.

"You boys turning faggot on me, sleeping in that room together when this old rundown heap of a house has all those extra bedrooms," he'd say. He started in the morning at the breakfast table and didn't let up till after the boys had gone to bed.

Roman was smart, book smart, and Reese was proud of him. Each day during the school year Reese and Roman would leave the house together and head off to school. Rarely did they arrive together. Reese took off to go fishing or something, but he made Roman go. Then they would meet up at the end of the day and hurry home to do chores together.

"Tell me what happened in school today, so as I don't get caught. Give me some of your homework and tell Ma it's mine, okay, Roman?"

Roman always did. He covered for Reese most of the time since it seemed that Birdie had a deeper affection for Roman. Reese needed all the protection he could get from Charlie, and Birdie didn't seem willing to offer it. Then one day things got even worse.

The school called and asked why Reese never came to school anymore. Charlie and Birdie were waiting when the boys came into the yard. Each had a handful of books and each claimed plenty of homework.

"Get in the backyard and get me a whippin' stick off the willow tree. I'm gonna tan me some soft white hide," Charlie sneered. "You boys been lying to me and your ma all along. The school called today and Reese here ain't been going to no school. Not only ain't he been going to school, he ain't been round here to help with the chores neither."

They had walked into the backyard scared out of their wits with good reason. Birdie seemed to be taking Charlie's side this time so there would be no protection at all forthcoming. Charlie staggered drunkenly to where Roman and Reese stood.

"Drop them drawers, boys. Let me see the shining white hide what lies all the time."

There was nothing to do but run or conform and both were too young to run. As they stood there in the bright daylight with their pants around their knees and that switch whistling through the air, the two foster brothers let the beginning of their release from reality start. Roman cried but Reese held it in. As the tears ran down Roman's face, Reese put his arm around him in a brotherly fashion. That little gesture had enraged Charlie.

"Fucking faggots!" he bellowed. "I'll teach you to be fornicating in my house."

He had broken several switches on Reese's backside that day. Roman had gotten his share but Birdie had finally stepped in, saying he was younger and easily led astray.

"Get your asses in the house and clean it from top to bottom. I want it to shine and don't you ask for nothing to eat till it's done. The Blessed Be don't cotton to bad kids. He don't have no time for faggots either. Get yourselves in there and get started and pray to the Blessed Be. Pray that he saves your damned souls," he shouted.

They had gone in the house together, blood running down their legs, but they cleaned till late into the night.

Roman stopped at a roadside park to clear the memory from his mind. His heart hurt and he felt betrayed. Reese had been his best friend and brother way back then, but time had changed that. Reese had always been the meaner of the two; most likely because Charlie and Birdie were meaner to him, yet Roman knew Reese had brought on most of his grief because he rarely did what he was told to do.

Roman wiped his face with a clean tissue from his pocket. Shaking his head, he got out and walked around the car. Squeals of laughter caught his attention, and he spun around to see three children playing a game of tag as their parents stood nearby. He had never had that, never had a parent watch him play or take him to a roadside park. Roman felt the tears slide down his face. He wanted that pretty picture to be his. He would take his pets to a roadside park and watch them play. He and Reese would do that together, just like a family.

As Roman watched the three children playing, he thought about his two little ones. They were going to be lonely without him today but he would be home tomorrow and Reese would be such a surprise for them. As Roman watched the children run back and forth, he felt uneasy. Something was wrong with that picture; something seemed to be missing. He couldn't quite put his finger on it but something seemed to irritate him about what he saw. Roman studied the pets. He watched the parents. Then he knew. Those parents had three pets, and he and Reese had only two.

Roman flipped the couple off as he headed back in a rush to his car. He was madder than he'd been in a long time.

"Some parents want it all. I'll show you," he shouted as he drove away.

The gravel spun in the tires as he peeled out. The couple called their children to them in a state of panic at the lunatic speeding past them. The man shook his fist at Roman. "You idiot!" he screamed.

Roman was back on the road heading toward Reese and the family life he longed for. As he drove, the memories returned.

Charlie was drinking in front of the fireplace on a cold December day when the two boys came in from school. Birdie was at the grocery store getting supplies because a bad storm was coming their way.

"Get your spoiled asses upstairs and get things ready in case we have to leave here. The storm is coming, and your ma don't want us stuck out here if we get any snow. We might be going to her sister's house for a week or so. Go pack your bags before the old bitch gets back or she'll blame me cause you ain't ready."

The two boys started up the stairs quietly, but then Reese poked Roman in the shoulder and said, "Race ya," as he ran up.

The thunder of their footsteps set Charlie off. He lumbered out of his chair and staggered up the stairs in pursuit.

Reese slammed the door to the bedroom as Charlie approached. The old man pulled himself forward, lunged against the door, and it flew open.

"What did you do that for, you little bastard? That's what you are, ya know, a bastard," he shouted at Reese. "No wait, you're a faggot bastard," Charlie started to laugh.

Reese shoved him and he fell to the ground. "Roman, run," Reese had called out.

But Charlie was in front of the door and there was no other way out. He got to his feet as the boys backed up.

"Now you're gonna get it. Now I'm mad," Charlie said.

Roman wanted the memory to stop. He slammed on the brake and pulled over to the side of the road. Taking long deep pull on his soda he swallowed and breathed deeply. But the memories seemed to have a mind of their own. Roman could see in his mind's eye Charlie staggering toward them. He could feel the fear again just as he had that day. Charlie grabbed Reese by his shirt collar and dragged him into the bathroom. He could hear Reese screaming and calling for help. Roman had thrown his small body at Charlie, trying to help his brother, but there was nothing he could do. Roman didn't know what was coming but Reese seemed to. He fought hard, pounding his fists and grabbing the door of the bathroom as Charlie dragged him inside. Charlie pulled back a fist and punched Roman in the face.

Roman awoke a few moments later to Reese's screams coming from inside the bathroom and the sound of grunting mingled with it. He ran to the door and pushed it open. There before him was Reese with his pants torn in pieces at his feet, bent over the toilet and Charlie standing behind him. Charlie's pants were around his knees and he was pounding away at Reese's behind. Roman just stood there as Reese screamed and Charlie grunted.

Screams of terror rolled out of Roman as he sat on the interstate and relived his memories. Charlie had turned to look at him and smiled. "You're next, boy," he'd said.

The Roman of today screamed again and again, sitting there on that lonely stretch of highway. He had screamed until his throat was raw.

Roman sucked down the rest of his soda and spit. The anger boiled inside him. He got out and walked around the car, slapping himself. Roman pinched himself real hard. "Stop thinking," he commanded.

"Stop it," he shouted out loud. "I want you to go away, go away, go away, go away," he shouted to his memory.

"You're making me mad," he threatened. "I'm gonna kick you. I'm gonna hit you right in the face. I'm gonna punch your lights out if you don't leave me alone.

Roman hit himself in the face. He kicked one leg with the other and pinched his arm so hard blood came to the surface. Jumping up and down he raced around in a circle. *Run, run as fast as you can, you can't catch me, I'm the gingerbread man and you are just a stupid old memory!*

Roman fell exhausted to the ground. He had won this round.

He got back into the car and headed toward Reese. His brother was going to be so proud of him. He had finally beaten Charlie. He could hardly wait to tell him.

Roman had put Reese in the "Behave Yourself Hole" more than a year ago, he thought. He really couldn't remember how long it had been, but he felt that enough time had passed and surely Reese had learned his lesson by now and would be nice to the pets. Roman wanted his little family to be happy. He wanted unity and love for his pets and he knew that Reese had it in him. He just had to find a way to make him let it out. Reese was gonna be good this time, Roman just knew it. The drive to the "Behave Yourself Hole" seemed to take forever.

Roman relaxed in the seat and leaned on the armrest. Finally he could see the town where he grew up and the light that he had to turn at to reach the old farm. Things had changed in the last year since he had been back. The town had grown and seemed busier. Roman maneuvered the back roads and turned onto the gravel drive. As the old feelings of home came back to him, he clutched the steering wheel tightly in his hands. Gritting his teeth, he had to concentrate so as not to push too hard on the gas pedal. His hatred for his adoptive father came rushing back.

"He's dead, he's dead," Roman said over and over to himself. "Reese made him dead. He hit him with the shovel and he's dead."

The car crawled slowly forward as the memories came rushing back.

Reese had changed after Charlie raped him. It wasn't the rape really, since that wasn't the first time it had happened. It was Roman seeing it, being a witness to it. That had not only made Reese meaner, but for a time he had withdrawn from Roman. Charlie had raped Roman too that day. Birdie had come home from the grocery store to see Roman crying in the kitchen on the floor. He had huddled up against the cabinets under the space where the desk was. Birdie sat there most of the time writing to her sister, and that's where Roman could feel her the most. She had put the groceries on the table and come to him. Kneeling down, she placed her hand on his shoulder and then cuddled him close.

"Roman, sweetie, what's wrong? Tell Mommy."

"Daddy, Charlie put his thing in my butt," Roman cried. "He did it to Reese too and Reese won't talk to me no more."

Birdie jerked her hand away from Roman and stood up.

"You're dirty?" she asked.

"Mommy, Daddy hurt me," Roman had cried again and tried to cling to her.

She backed up and Roman found himself crawling like a dog to her. Birdie turned on her heel and ran from the room. She found Charlie in the living room, sitting in his favorite chair drinking again.

"Roman was mine. You promised that he was mine and Reese was yours. You promised and you broke your word. Reese was yours for that terrible thing you have to do. You promised me and you lied to me."

"Shut up, woman. I take whichever one I want. Hell, I'll take you if I want. I pay for everything in the damn house, you included."

Birdie backed away at those words.

Charlie loved the fear in her face, and he staggered toward her. Dragging her to the bedroom the door slammed and the screams could be heard throughout the house. Birdie came out much later in her torn dress and ragged hair. She cried for days after that but she never challenged Charlie again. She never protected Roman again either.

Reese eventually forgave Roman for witnessing his rape. As time went on, the two boys increasingly shut themselves off from the adults. The rapes continued for the less dominant in the household, including Birdie. Her appearance changed drastically and then she just stopped caring all together. Food was no longer prepared, laundry was no longer done, and Charlie drank whenever he felt like it. Reese became more angry and hated life altogether.

Roman could see the changes and his own fragile little mind took a different path. While he longed for love and affection, Roman held hatred close to his heart. He shielded himself from love, and the anger that had always burned in his heart burned brighter. Roman closed himself within, hiding the gentle nature from everyone, including Reese. The boys spent hours and sometimes days at a time in the "Behave Yourself Hole" in the backyard as a form of intimidation. Charlie would put them there if either of them threatened to tell anyone about the things that went on in the house.

CHAPTER 53

Roman drove the remaining five hundred yards to the farm.

Something seemed different, as if someone had been here. He raced to the end of the drive that connected their farm to the one owned by the Handleys. Their daughter Clarissa had been the one Reese had turned to when he turned his back on everyone in the Marsh house. Roman hated her and he knew that secretly Reese hated her too. The one attraction she held was that she let Reese feel like a man at the tender age of fourteen. After years of abuse from Charlie, Reese needed to feel like a man and Clarissa let him touch her. Roman got to watch, but Reese never let him touch because she was his, all his.

Roman slowed the vehicle to a snail's pace. Again he felt a difference that seemed to hang in the air. At the end of the drive the difference came into view. There before him was bright yellow tape stretched across most of the yard. There were men everywhere and they had uniforms on. Roman looked around as he rolled to a stop. One of the men came over to the car as Roman rolled down the window.

"What do you want, kid?"

"What's going on?" Roman asked.

"You from here, boy? You live around here?"

Something inside set off a warning. "No sir, I'm from the next farm over. The Handleys. Did something happen out here?"

"Someone killed old man Marsh and his wife and one of his boys. Buried him in the ground while he was still alive. Looks like someone hit the old man and old lady with something big and heavy. Cracked open their skulls, it did. You hear anything about that?"

"You mean the Marshes, Charlie and Birdie, are dead?"

"Yup, deader than a doornail. Conked on the head and then shoved in that hole over yonder."

"The hell you say," Roman said.

"Yeah, and the boy was found in the other hole over there a few months back." The officer looked at Roman suspiciously as he pointed off in the other direction. "You sure you don't know nothing?"

"No sir," Roman said. "We kinda keep to ourselves over that way. I saw all the commotion over here and came to see what was going on. Ain't no one lived out here for a long time now. My sister had a crush on one of them and she ain't heard nothing from him in a long time either."

"Your sister at home now boy?"

"No, sir, she's gone off to school now. She ain't been around for more than a year." Roman's brain was working hard. He needed to find out who was in the other hole since that was the where he had left Reese. That was the "Behave Yourself Hole" and he knew that Reese had been the only one in there.

Roman thought to himself, *He must have gotten some help to get out and then killed the one that helped him. That was like Reese to bite the hand that fed him.*

"Officer, do you know who the other guy is that you found in that hole over there?" Roman asked, pointing to the "Behave Yourself Hole."

"From the stuff we found at that time, I believe he was Reese Keith, one of the Marshes foster kids. Did you know him, son?" the officer said with sympathy. He could see the shock on the boy's face. "Is that the one your sister liked?"

"Yes, sir," Roman stammered. His eyes filled with tears. *Who could have killed Reese? It's all my fault cause I left him in the "Behave Yourself Hole" where someone could get to him and kill him. It's all my fault.*

"You okay, boy?"

"Yes, sir. But did someone hit poor Reese on the head too, did someone crack his skull?"

"No, he was put in that hole and left there to starve to death. Terrible way to go, terrible. Someone did that out of pure damn meanness. Someone sure did hate that boy if it really was Reese."

"You mean it might not have been him?"

"Well, there's always a chance. He was pretty hard to recognize at that point and we didn't have anyone around that really knew him all that well to positively identify him. Say, you knew him pretty well. Do you think you could have a look at some pictures we took of the body?"

Roman had to know, he had to be sure. "Yes, sir, I knew him well enough. I ain't never seen a dead body though. What's he look like?"

"Well, he ain't all that pretty but you might be able to tell if it's him or not. You got a strong stomach, boy?"

"Yes, sir, normally I do. My ma says I have a cast-iron stomach."

"Sit right here. I'll be right back."

The officer walked over to a group of officers. Roman watched and waited and tried to think of what might have happened to Reese.

He knew what happened to Charlie and Birdie. He had been there the day Reese had finally had enough of Charlie's abuse and Birdie's crying. Charlie had been really mean that day. He had walked up behind Reese and dragged him into the barn. Roman wanted to follow but he knew what was gonna happen and that Reese would be mad if he watched. Still he wanted to see it, so he crept along the outer wall of the barn and peeked in a hole in the wood. Reese was on his knees in front of Charlie, and Charlie had his head laid back against the side of the barn. Reese was doing something that Charlie seemed to like, only he sounded like he was choking. Charlie had a pick in one hand every now and then he would raise the pick and say, "Keep it up, boy, or else."

The sounds continued, Reese crying out every now and then. Finally he got to his feet, spit something on the ground, and shoved Charlie back. Reese had never stood up to Charlie before and for the first time in his life Charlie was shocked.

"You old son of a bitch, suck your own dick. I hate you, Roman hates you, even Birdie, hates you."

Charlie tried to charge Reese, but his pants around his knees had tripped him up. Reese calmly walked over and picked up a shovel. He then walked back to where Charlie was, raised the shovel, and with all his might brought it down on Charlie's head. Reese hit him again and again and again. When he was done, he threw the shovel to the ground and turned toward Roman, who by that time had been standing in the doorway.

"How much did you see?"

"I seen it all, all but what he did to you," Roman lied. "Why did you hit him with that shovel?"

"Never you mind that, he's dead. That's all you need to know. He ain't never gonna bother us again with his nasty body. He ain't never gonna put us in the 'Behave Yourself Hole' ever again. He's one dead mother fucker. I killed him and I'm glad. Are you glad, Roman?" Reese looked straight into his eyes.

"I'm glad, Reese, glad he's dead."

The officer walked back to Roman's car, startling him from his memories. Roman had a strange little smile on his face.

"Okay, boy, let's go," the officer said as he opened the car door.

Roman got out and followed the officer to the hole. Memories swirled around his head, and he slowed his steps as he got closer to the hole. Walking up to the edge, he peered inside.

The hole was empty now except for Reese's belongings. Roman could see the empty cans of food he had left for Reese and the empty water jugs that lay on their side like a bad omen. Then, the officer held out some pictures. As Roman took them, he could feel a change in the air around him. Something sweet and strong drifted across his nostrils. He raised his head and sniffed the air. What was that?

"Don't ya just love the smell of them magnolia trees?" the officer said.

"Yes, sir, I sure do," Roman responded. "Is that what that smell is, magnolia trees?"

"Sure is boy. You said you lived here all your life, and you don't know what a magnolia blossom smells like?" the officer asked in a puzzled way.

"I've been away at school this year. I guess I just forgot," Roman said as he took the pictures that the officer held in his hands.

Roman studied the pictures and felt his throat go dry. Sure enough, it was Reese. Roman remembered what he was wearing the day he had hit him on the head, not too hard but hard enough to knock him out and shove him in the hole. There before him was Reese in his blue and white plaid flannel. He looked like he was sleeping, all curled up on his side like that. His head was tucked into his chest and he had his arms wrapped around his knees. The jeans that he had on were too short and baggy. Roman knew it was Reese right away, but he stared at the pictures, in a morbid fascination, taking all the time that he wanted.

Is that Reese Keith or Roman Marsh?" the officer wanted to know.

Roman looked up at him with a blank stare. "Yes, sir, it is."

"Well, which one is it: Reese or Roman?"

"It's Reese. He was taller and older than Roman. Who did that to him?"

"We don't know yet but we're gonna find out. You live right behind this house, don't you?"

The officer was testing Roman and he knew it, but tests were something he always did well. You just told people what they wanted to hear.

"No, sir, I live the next farm over," he said with confidence.

"You hang around then, okay, just in case we need to ask you anything else.

"Yes, sir, I hear you."

Roman turned to walk away. "Hey, kid, I need those pictures back," the officer shouted.

Roman thought about making a run for it with the pictures but he knew they would catch him. He turned and handed them back to the officer.

"Sorry about that. I forgot I had 'em."

As Roman got in the car and backed out, he looked one more time at the "Behave Yourself Hole." He didn't care about the one that held the bodies of Charles and Birdie Marsh but Reese was different. Someone had killed Reese. Now all his plans were ruined. No longer would he be able to have the happy little family he wanted. No longer could his dreams come true. He hung his head and cried as he backed out. The officers standing around the gravesite of the Marshes watched him leave. They felt sorry for him, finding out that his friend was dead like that.

CHAPTER 54
As Roman drove toward home,
he felt defeated.

He thought about all the dreams he'd made and all of them included Reese. He longed for him, missed him, and then just like that he dismissed him.

He thought back to the day Reese had killed Charlie. As Charlie lay there in the dirty hay of the old barn floor, Reese had told Roman he could never tell.

"The law will take me from you, Roman, and then we can't be together no more. You don't want that to happen, do you?"

"No, Reese, please don't let them take you away. Please take me with you if they do," Roman had begged.

"Roman, we're gonna live right here on this farm, and no one is gonna know if we don't tell them. So you keep the secret and I'll keep the secret and no one will have to go nowhere, okay?"

"Yeah, Reese, okay. Can I have my bed put back in your room again?"

"Sure you can, kid, sure you can. We can do that right now if you want to."

Roman and Reese headed in the direction of the house. Walking hand in hand they made a warm and fuzzy feeling come over Birdie as she watched them approach. Then she saw the blood all over Reese. She looked toward the barn but she didn't see anything. As the boys got closer and Reese reached his hand out to pull the door open, Birdie stepped back.

"Reese, what you got all over your clothes? Are you hurt?"

"No, ma'am, I ain't the one that's hurt," Reese said calmly.

"Then who's hurt, who's bleeding?"

Roman looked at Reese and he too saw all the blood all over his shirt, face, and hands.

"Reese, you made a mess."

"Reese, you better tell me what happened and you better tell me right now," Birdie had stammered.

"I killed him. I hit him with the shovel and now he's dead and I'm so glad. Are you glad, Birdie?" Reese asked in a threatening way.

Birdie had backed up. Maybe if she hadn't, things wouldn't have gone as far as they did, but it was too late for that now. Her hand flew to her mouth and she stepped back till she came up against the wall.

Reese started toward her as Roman said, "Just tell him you're glad he's dead, just tell him quick before he makes you dead too."

Birdie didn't have time to say anything. Reese grabbed her by her hair and started dragging her to her bedroom.

"Go outside, Roman, and start digging a big hole. Daddy Charlie is gonna get in his own 'Behave Yourself Hole' while I get some of Mommy Birdie."

Birdie started fighting Reese, but by this time he was bigger and stronger. All the times that she had let Charlie do whatever he wanted to Reese came out in his attack on her. Roman ran for the door because he didn't want Reese to kill him too. Birdie fought him like a wild woman, but Reese raped her and then tied her up as Roman watched through the window. He had flipped her over and did to her what Charlie had been doing to him for years. Roman never felt sorry for her. He never cried and he never would. Both of them deserved what Reese did to them. Reese hit Birdie on the back of the head with a lamp when he was done with her. Then he carried her to the hole that Roman had only just begun. They worked till the sun started to come up and then they threw them both in.

"Should we say a prayer to the Blessed Be for them so they won't come back to get us?" Roman asked.

"No, they don't deserve no prayers. Prayers are for good people like you and me, Rommie."

"Don't call me Rommie, don't never call me Rommie. I'm Roman, you said so," Roman shouted at him.

"That's right kid, I was just testing ya."

Roman thought about Reese and the Marshes until he came to the same roadside park he had stopped at earlier that day. It was dark now and the lights were on, making weird halos around the street lamps. He thought about the wasted day and wondered what his pets were up to. Parking the car, he got out and stretched. As he walked toward the building to use the bathroom, he thought about the little pets that had played here earlier. Did they use the bathroom too, he wondered?

"Pets always have to use the bathroom," he said out loud.

As he headed back to his car, a thought hit him. He could still have three pets. Maybe they would behave better if he had three. Those pets today seemed to be good and they looked like they were having so much fun together. Maybe that was the key to happiness with families and pets, have a lot of them. Roman thought about his Marcie and Penny. They loved him so much and they were always so good but they never smiled. Maybe they would smile if he had another one. Maybe he could find one more that would make his little family complete and they could come to the roadside park and play and laugh and squeal together and he could watch them. That was all he really wanted anyway, just to watch them and to see them happy.

A much happier Roman got back in his car and headed for home to be with his pets and to help them find a family. He got about ten miles before he pulled over to sleep for the night. His mind was clear and the demons of his past no longer haunted him. He gave no thought to the two little girls who were home alone. He gave no thought to a murdered set of adoptive parents or a murdered foster brother. He slept the sleep that comes only to those with a free and clear conscience.

CHAPTER 55

Marcie and Penny spent the day alone and that was fine with them.

They talked and played as little girls do. The door was the only restriction to what they wanted, that and Roman's idea of a menu. Marcie was tired, so she rested most of the day. Penny played with her toys and chatted as Marcie lay near by. As the evening wore on, both girls crept into the kitchen.

"I want some soup," Marcie said.

Penny looked up at the cabinets. "I can reach it if you know how to cook it."

Marcie nodded. "Try it Penny. When Roman gets home, he's gonna be plenty mad but I don't care. I don't want another piece of cake or a cookie. I just want some soup."

Marcie started to cry. She lay down on the kitchen floor as Penny pulled a chair to the cabinets. Climbing up she opened the doors and looked inside. Canned soups of everykind were there along with bread and peanut butter.

"Hey, Marcie, do you want some peanut butter and jelly?"

"No, I don't want anything sweet. I just want some soup."

"Okay, what kind do you want?"

"The one with noodles and chicken and yellow water. Chicken noodle, my mom calls it."

With the mention of her mom, she started to cry. Penny climbed down in a hurry, a can in her hand, and helped Marcie up and into a chair at the table. "How are we going to get it open?" Penny wanted to know.

"I know how, give it to me. Jayme taught me so that I would leave him alone."

Penny handed the can to Marcie. As she stood to walk over to the counter she faltered just a bit. Holding onto Penny and the counter, Marcie made her way to the can opener. As the can spun around, the smell of the soup made her feel better.

As their dinner warmed on the stove, the two little girls bowed their heads. "Dear Jesus, please take Roman away and bring someone to help us. Jesus, we will be real good if you will do this for us. I just want my mommy and daddy, please God."

The tears slipped down their little faces as they said, "Amen."

They ate their dinner and watched TV. What a joy it was to have Roman gone. "Maybe he will stay gone," Penny said.

"No, he always comes back. But Penny, I really want my mommy. I need her, I don't feel so good."

"Yeah, I know. We need a phone. Do you know your phone number? I want my mommy and daddy. What if they think I'm gone forever?"

"Roman says they can go to the home and get another little girl. Maybe Roman's right and they gave you to him so they could go and get another little girl?"

"My mom and dad love me, they don't want another kid, they just want me. My mommy told me so. That's why I don't have any brothers or sisters cause they just want me," Penny said.

Penny was starting to cry. Marcie felt bad for being mean to her.

"I'm sorry, Penny. I know your mom and dad love you. It's just, why don't they come and get us? Why don't they call the police to come and get us away from Roman?"

"They will. They called them for you when you were gone. The police were everywhere. They came to our house and talked to my mom and dad. My dad said he would shoot them if he caught them."

"What did my dad say?"

"Your dad cries a lot," Penny said as she looked down at the ground. "Your mommy cries even more. She sits in the rocking chair and cries and everyone can see her."

Marcie threw herself down on the sofa and cried for her mommy and daddy. Her daddy was a big man. He shouldn't cry. Big guys didn't cry, did they?

"I know, let's break a window and climb out," Penny said excitedly.

Marcie raised her head. "Do you think we can?"

"We can try. I can throw a chair through the window and we can climb out. Come on, Marcie, let's try it."

"What if it doesn't work and Roman finds out we broke a window?"

"It's gonna work. Come on, you'll see." Penny's confidence was contagious.

The girls ran to each window. Marcie's illness was really taking a toll on her body and she lumbered more than ran. But each window they checked was not only nailed shut but had little windowpanes about eight inches square. As they went from window to window, they started to become disheartened.

"Let's try it anyway," Penny said.

"No, if it doesn't work he is gonna know and you saw how mad he gets. I don't want him to get mad at me," Marcie said in a scared voice.

"I want to try," Penny shouted. "You're a scaredy cat. That's why you're still here but I want to go home so I'm gonna try it."

With that Penny hoisted a chair high above her head and with all her strength threw it at the window. There was a loud noise as the chair fell short of its target. Penny ran to it and picked it up again. This time Marcie lumbered toward it too, and both girls heaved it up and threw on the count of three. The darkness from outside leapt into the room like an invader. The girls jumped back and the glass shattered. Five of the glass panes were broken but the wood dividers held tight. Penny grabbed one and pulled. Other than cutting her finger, which she quickly put in her mouth, nothing happened.

Marcie pulled her to the bathroom and ran her hand under the water as the blood flowed freely into the basin. Marcie put a Band-Aid on Penny's finger. It was a Flintstone Band-Aid and it thrilled Penny. She held her finger up and wiggled it back and forth.

"That's as good as my mommy does it."

"Marcie if we don't get out of here, we'll always have each other, right?" Penny's voice revealed her fear even if her actions didn't.

"Yeah, we'll always have each other," Marcie agreed and hugged her friend.

The experience they were stuck in was fast robbing these two of their childhood. It was time to go home.

Marcie and Penny headed back to the broken window. Looking at the mess on the floor, they started to cry. Marcie reacted first. She ran to the kitchen for a dustpan and the broom. They cleaned up the broken glass as good as they could, but the curtains on the window still billowed in from the night breeze.

"What are we gonna do?" Penny wailed.

"I don't know but we better think of something or he is gonna be really, really mad."

The nighttime breeze was cool. It felt good as it brushed across their skin. All of a sudden Penny started dancing around in the gentle breeze. She enjoyed the way it felt on her skin. Marcie caught the feeling and she danced too. They held hands and danced around just like they did in ballet classes on Tuesday nights. The moment was euphoric, and the girls giggled and bowed to one another.

The moment was ripped apart by the opening of the front door. Doom and destruction was home.

CHAPTER 56

At the Miller home, Lindsay and Claire were in the kitchen preparing dinner when the doorbell rang.

Claire had resolved to try to get closer to Tony's mother, Ruby, and had invited her to join them for dinner and to spend the night. Thinking the doorbell meant Ruby had arrived, she paused before opening the door to put on her most welcoming smile. But the image that showed through the curtains let her know that she was wrong. It was a policeman in a uniform illuminated by the porch light. Claire opened the door.

"Good evening, Mrs. Miller. Is the captain here, ma'am?"

"Yes, he is, come in, come in. You're letting the mosquitoes and June bugs in."

Billy stepped inside. In his hand was a tiny plastic baggie about the size of half a sandwich. Claire could see something white in the baggie.

"Tony," she called over her shoulder, her eyes never leaving the bag or its contents.

Tony came around the corner. "What? Oh hey, Billy, what ya got there?"

"Sir, this just came back from John Hanks. He asked me to bring it out to you right away. He said Ms. Freeman would be most interested and to give you this piece of paper."

Tony took the paper. "Come on into the living room."

The note from John said: "Tony, this is back from the lab. It's the same blood type we found in Penny Ware's bedroom. It came in from Hershal Owens, along with the license plate number of the car that left it behind. He swears he got it right. Said his mind was good as his eyesight. I ran the number and it belongs to a Charlie Marsh. Call me at the hotel if you want to do something about this tonight. Otherwise, I'll see you in the morning."

After thanking Billy and letting him go, Tony read the note one more time before putting it aside. He looked at the bag containing the tissue and thought of something.

"Lindsay, can you come in here for a moment?" he called.

Claire frowned at him, "Tony, dinner is almost ready and your mom is coming over. You and Lindsay aren't going to run off, are you?"

"Claire, this is a kidnapping investigation. What if it were Becky? Would you want me to take time out for social niceties or would you want me to go and find our daughter?"

Claire instantly felt awful. "I'm sorry, Tony, it's just that one night I would like the evening to go by without something dreadful happening."

Lindsay came into the room. "You bellowed, oh exalted one?" she joked.

Claire laughed in spite of herself. Tony grinned and said, "That I did."

"Remember when you told me that you needed something more concrete?"

"Yes. What have you got?" she said, instantly interested.

"Let's go in the living room."

Sitting on the sofa, Tony handed the bag to Lindsay. "Well, Billy just delivered this. It came from . . ."

"A man who lives near Penny Ware's house," she finished.

"Yes, go on."

"The blood belongs to the child, but the man around it is Roman Marsh or what I have come to know as him. He was feeling very intense and full of himself. He was proud of the fact that he brought so much pain to the family. He liked being the center of attention."

Lindsay paused and Tony waited. "Tony, something is wrong, terribly wrong. We have to go! Get up, get up now!"

Tony stood up, not knowing what to do. "Go where, Lindsay? Where should we go?"

"I don't know, but he's in a temper, raging and he's violent. He's mad at them, both of them."

Lindsay was on her feet stumbling around the living room. Tears were in her eyes and she was holding her hand. "Ouch," she said as she stuck her finger in her mouth.

"Blood, there's blood everywhere. Someone's bleeding. Wait, it's not bad."

Lindsay stopped and looked at Tony. "One of the girls has a cut, minor, but that's what he's mad about. They broke something and he's in a rage over it. Oh my God, Tony, we have to do something."

Claire came rushing in with a pad and pen.

"Lindsay, calm down and just let the images come. I'll write down what you say, but don't stall it. Just let it come."

Lindsay looked at her. "Okay, I see a man coming through a doorway. He feels defeated by the day but bolstered by his new idea. He's looking at a window that's billowing with curtains. The girls broke a window. He's mad, storming around, screaming at them and calling them names. Both of the girls are hiding from him or trying to. The place is small where they are, small and there isn't much furniture in it."

"Lindsay, can you see anything I can identify?" Tony asked.

Lindsay stood still and seemed to be staring off into space.

"I see the inside of a house. He is storming about and now he seems to be looking for something. I see walls; there are walls with no pictures. I see one window that has curtains that billow so that must be the window with the broken glass. I see a room that seems to go somewhere the girls don't want to go. There is a light on in another room but I can't see what it is."

"Lindsay, what do you smell?" Tony asked. The scent of things had been so important in this case that he just had to ask.

"I smell motor oil. I know that sounds funny but that's it. Gosh, Tony, I'm so sorry," Lindsay said in such a way that Tony knew she was suffering.

"Okay, we need some help over here. We need some others who know this town well and can help me brainstorm what you see," Tony said as he got up and headed to the phone.

He called Mac first and then Bill. Both agreed to come and listen.

"Bill, how is Jus?"

"She's doing a little bit better. She says an angel told her that her little girl is coming home soon. So she seems to be better."

"I hope that angel's right," Tony said. "See you soon."

Claire got up and called Ruby.

"Mom, how big is that roast you're bringing?"

"The darn thing could feed an army. Why?"

"Tony's invited two more for dinner. Mac and Bill are coming over and I bet John Hanks from the FBI ends up here too."

"Okay. Don't worry, there will be plenty. Make some vegetables and cornbread. We'll stretch it like God feeding the masses with two fish and five loaves of bread."

Claire laughed. "See you soon?" she asked.

"You betcha," Ruby said.

CHAPTER 57
Roman was indeed in a rage.

He felt as if he had been betrayed. His pets had misbehaved yet again.

"Why won't you be good? Why?" he screamed at them. "You make me so mad, I hate you!"

Penny squared her shoulders, marched up to him, and shouted, "I hate you too, and you're ugly!"

Roman was shocked by her outburst. "You better go sit down or you'll be sorry."

"No, and you can't make me. My daddy is going to find you and kill you with his gun. I hate you, hate you, hate you!"

"You are making me mad," Roman said again in a strong voice.

"So what? If I make you mad, let me go home to my mommy and daddy. Let Marcie go home too."

"Nooooooo," Roman crooned. "You aren't going home. I will take you to the pound if you don't behave."

"I don't care. Any place where you aren't is good for me," Penny said, then stuck her tongue out at him.

Marcie drew in a deep sharp breath. "Oh, Penny, we're gonna get it now."

Roman walked toward Penny.

"If you touch me, I'll bite you, you hear me, Mr. Ugly. I'll bite you." Penny shook her finger in Roman's face.

Roman reached out and slapped her hard right in the face. Penny's little body literally flew through the air. As she landed on the floor near the broken window, she let out a scream that ripped the night air apart. Dogs howled in the distance and Marcie screamed in her place near the sofa. Penny lay there crying out loud with her mouth wide open.

"Shut your ugly mouth," Roman said.

Penny tried to do what she was told, but her crying continued softly.

Marcie slipped around Roman to get to her. As she wrapped her arms around Penny and helped her sit up, Marcie looked at Roman. "I hate you too and I don't care if you kill us but I hate you."

"Oh you hate me, do you? You don't know what it is to hate someone yet, but when I'm done with you, you will."

Roman stormed from the house. He went to the garage and crawled back into his car. As he started the motor, he realized he'd left the door unlocked. Pulling the car out of the garage to park it in the yard, he saw Penny and Marcie make a run for it. They both dashed into the yard and started running. Roman was older, taller, and just as scared as they were. He had them in a less than a minute.

Towing both girls back into the house by their hair, Roman said in a low and threatening voice, "You will never leave me, do you understand? You love me, you need me, and that is the way things are going to be or I will get mad and we all know what happens when I get mad, right? Go in the bathroom and brush your hair and wash those faces. I don't want no dirty faces in my house."

Penny and Marcie couldn't do anything but cry and obey. They walked into the bathroom together and did as they were told.

"Marcie, what are we going to do?" Penny cried.

"Penny, please be nice to him for just a little while, okay?"

"Okay, but I don't want to. I want my mommy."

"But if you'll just be nice to him, you'll see he can be nice right back and that makes things better."

Roman sat in the living room. Reality was slipping away from him as he allowed his memory to take over. The little girl in the train station had been a better pet. She had behaved and she loved him.

"Maybe I should go get her back," Roman thought out loud to himself.

What had made her behave, Roman wondered? Why was she good and these two pets were so bad. He would sleep on it, he thought. That's what he needed, sleep.

Roman left the car running in front of the house. He left the lights on and he left his clothes on as he lay down on the sofa and went to sleep.

Dreams of little children playing at a roadside park haunted his mind. He saw them with pretty dresses and ribbons in their hair. They were waving and smiling at him and he was happy. Then the dream shifted and the pretty little pets playing in the park were making fun of him, sticking their tongues out at him and mocking him. He moaned in his sleep and turned over on the sofa.

The two little beings that huddled in the corner watched him and waited in fear. Penny held a cold cloth to her swollen eye. The bruise was turning a dark purple and her eye was swelling to the point of being closed. She cried out every now and then as Marcie touched it.

Marcie pulled Penny into the bedroom with a finger to her lips. "Shhh or he'll wake up. Let's just go to bed and tomorrow will be better. Tomorrow be nice to him, please, Penny."

"I will, I promise," Penny cried.

They cuddled up together on their pallet on the floor. Blessed release came in the form of sleep.

CHAPTER 58

The group in Tony Miller's living room went over Lindsay's statements as written down by Claire.

"Tony, what do you think all that means? I have to be honest here, I have no idea what to look for," Bill said.

Tony looked at everyone as he rested his forearms on his knees. "Okay, something is here that we're missing. We're too close to this, so we need to brainstorm this whole thing. Something is coming and I don't have to be clairvoyant to know that."

Mac nodded his head. "I've been thinking the same thing."

"Okay, then we have to make sure that we cause what happens. Does that make sense to everyone?"

"No," Janet said. "What if we do the wrong thing and bring about a change of events that cost us the lives of our daughters?"

"I just don't think we have any other choice. I want to do something to force this guy's hand, to make him show himself. He likes to be the center of attention. He wants someone to notice what he does. We're doing all of that.

The thing is to not do that, to make him come out so that we can see him and hopefully catch him," Tony said almost desperately.

Bill nodded. "I agree. This waiting for him to do something else is killing me. I need something to happen."

"Chances are that he'll do something himself soon but I'm tired of waiting too."

Suddenly Lindsay stood up. "Tony, something's happening," she said as she fingered the tissue in her hand. She'd been holding it since she realized it was a link to the girls. Janet sat next to her on the couch.

"What? What's happening?" Janet asked.

"There's fighting in the room. The girls are fighting with him, not physical yet but one of them is shouting back at him and that seems to be making him mad. He's storming about. Leaving, wait, he's coming back. This is so confusing."

"Take your time, Lindsay," Claire said.

"Okay, there's anger and water, and someone is crying."

Janet jumped up. "I can't listen to this, Mac. I want to go home."

"No, Janet, we have to do this. We have to find Marcie soon. I have a feeling that time is running out. Please sit down and listen."

She sank back down on the couch.

Lindsay squeezed her hand. "It's quiet now."

"How do you live with this?" Janet asked her.

"I do it for the girls. Remember this, Janet, if you remember nothing else. There is always hope. Till the very last minute rely on your faith and know that there is always hope."

Janet squeezed her hand again and smiled. "Thank you for being here, for coming."

"Sure thing, sweetie," Lindsay said.

They sat and talked for a time, all of them going over and over the notes that Claire had made. Ruby and Claire fed everyone and worked side by side in a wonderful new companionship. Tony watched them come and go into the kitchen.

Mike smiled at his dad as he saw him smile at the two retreating figures. "It's cool, huh, Dad?"

"Cool for sure, Mike, cool for sure."

The others had note pads in their hands as well. They all copied down what Claire had written and studied them together.

"Dad, what about what the guy we saw out on the feeder road? Did we ever find out anything about that?" Mike asked.

"Yeah, I have a couple of uniforms canvassing the area, showing off the sketch and asking questions. So far nothing has come of it. I'll check on it again tomorrow at roll call," Tony said. He made a note on his own pad.

Finally Tony decided to call it a night. "Okay, it's getting late and a tired brain doesn't storm well. Take the notes home and every now and then think about them or just take a few minutes to look them over. If you get anything, anything at all, call me."

They all stood to go, and each one hugged Lindsay good bye.

But as Bill hugged her, Lindsay stepped back and looked at him hard. "You've interacted with him."

"What, who, me? Interacted with who?"

"Roman Marsh. You've interacted with Roman Marsh," Lindsay repeated.

"Of course I have, he took my daughter," Bill said in a shocked tone of voice.

"No. I mean he's someone you've met. Someone you've talked to. Look at the picture again, please, Bill. Tony, show Bill the picture, the drawing. He's the one, the one I saw interacting with Roman Marsh."

Tony looked at Bill.

Bill started to get nervous. "Are you saying I did this. That I had this madman kidnap my daughter?"

"No, not at all. Bill, relax," Tony said. "Lindsay feels that one of us has met him, talked to him, or had some form of interaction with him."

Bill took the drawing in his hands. There was a spark of recognition, but try as he might he wasn't able to remember where he had seen him.

"I know him, you're right. I just can't remember where I met him."

Tony nodded. "That's just the sort of thing we need to work on."

Bill agreed and headed for the door.

"It's time for some shut-eye. Mom, do you want me to drive you home?" Tony asked.

"No, I'm staying the night in Mike's room."

Tony was surprised. "Okay, what is going on here?"

"Lindsay showed us the light. We're a family," Ruby said.

"And your mother is a better cook than I am," Claire said.

"I'm not touching that and you aren't tricking me into it. I'm going to bed. Anyone who wants to sleep here can. This place is starting to feel like a hotel with revolving doors anyway."

They all laughed as Tony headed toward his bedroom.

The ladies talked until late into the night, then bid each other good night. That night sleep came to those who felt they were doing something to bring about an end to the crisis. It's funny how even if you don't solve the puzzle, as long as you are working on it, you can rest.

CHAPTER 59

The next morning was Saturday and it was a grand one.

The sun shone brightly early in the day. It was a glorious day. The latter part of June in the deep south was usually hot, but today there was a wonderful breeze that seemed to come out of the north, and everyone in town seemed to be up and out early doing yard work or errands.

Ashley Griffon also wanted to be outside. She missed her friends, but children are so resilient that they bounce back better than adults do. She did her little girl chores that her parents insisted she do and ate her breakfast as she was told.

"Ashley, brush your teeth before you go outside," Barb Griffon said.

Ashley made a face at her mother's back as she headed into the bathroom. "Brush your teeth, Ashley; make your bed, Ashley; clean your room, Ashley," she said in a mocking tone of voice.

"I heard that," Barb said.

"I heard that," Ashley mocked and then laughed.

She did as she was told and then headed for the door.

"Backyard, young lady," her mother shouted from her room.

"Mom, I want to play with Laura, and she can't come in our backyard because of Brutus."

"I don't care, backyard or not at all."

Ashley headed for the backyard. "Can I put Brutus in the basement?"

"Yes, go ahead."

Ashley ran out the back door, letting it slam. Her mother shook her head.

The kidnappings were almost like an undertone. The reality was the kidnapping, but the day was so beautiful it gave the appearance that all was right with the world. Barb's mind would spin if she tried to keep the crisis involving Marcie and Penny in her thoughts constantly. She felt as if she was betraying them or their parents, who were her friends, if she didn't. She felt guilty for enjoying the day, guilty as she watched her child play in the backyard.

"Please, God. Do something," Barb prayed silently.

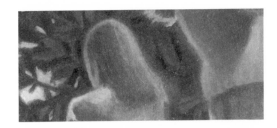

CHAPTER 60

Roman woke with stiffness in his back and neck from sleeping in a bad position.

He felt sore all over, and that made him mad. He sat up and rubbed his neck and lower back. His memory started to come back to him and Roman felt the urgency of the night before. He ripped open the front of his pants and worked himself into a sweat. He needed the release because that was the only control that he had now. His pets were controlling his life, not the other way around. He needed control and he needed it now. He pulled hard on his body, jerking, groaning, and demanding from himself what only he could give.

Finally, the blessed release came to him, and he put his head back and took several deep breaths. He was sweating even though the day seemed wonderfully cool for this time of year.

Roman had a plan that would give him the control he needed. He wanted to take his pets to the roadside park to play, but he couldn't trust them till he took their strength. And Roman knew how to take their strength. Just like Delilah had taken Samson's hair to take his strength in the Grand Book his momma had read to him when he was a little kid. The Blessed Be had an answer for everything.

He sat forward to think things through. He had always taken hair from his pets at the end of his time with them, not at the beginning. This time had to be different. If he was to keep them, he had to make them behave. He had to take their strength. Roman stood up and walked into the bedroom.

"Little pets," he called out softly. "Little pets, it's time to wake up. We are going to be good today, right?"

Marcie opened her eyes first. Penny followed sleepily.

"Pets, we are going to do something together today. Today we are going to learn to be good so that we can go to the roadside park. Does that sound like fun to you?"

The girls looked at Roman and then at each other. To Penny this sounded like a chance for escape; to Marcie this sounded like a chance to play outside and get some fresh air.

They crawled out slowly, stretching as they came. Standing before him, they felt self-conscious. Marcie rubbed her eyes and then headed for the bathroom. She reached back and grabbed Penny's hand when she realized that Penny didn't follow.

They washed their faces and brushed their hair. When they were done, they walked back out into the living room. Roman was waiting for them. He called them to him and had them turn around and face the other side of the room. Both girls were nervous and they started to cry.

"No, no, it's okay, really. We are just going to trim your hair a bit and then go outside to the roadside park and play. Doesn't that sound like fun?"

They nodded in almost perfect unison. Roman reached for the scissors and started with Penny, since she was the hardest one to deal with. He gently lifted her long tresses of blonde hair and cut just below the ears. Penny reacted violently. She jumped away from him and ran her hand over the back of her head.

"You cut too much! My daddy will be mad because you cut too much," she cried.

"I cut too much because you moved. Come here and let me straighten it out," Roman demanded.

Marcie started to cry. "Don't cut my hair, Roman, please. I'll be good, I promise. Please don't cut my hair."

Roman made a grab for Penny. He held her by her neck and cut wildly at her head, nicking her several times in the process. Penny thrashed about and screamed. She kicked at him and tried to bite his hand or arm or whatever she could reach. Roman tossed her from him and looked at what he had done to her. She looked terrible with little tufts of hair sticking up here and there. Then Roman stood and walked up to Marcie. With the scissors in one hand and a determined look on his face, he stood before her.

Marcie cried softly. She turned her back to him and stood there as Roman gently took the long auburn hair in his hand and cut it off.

He then cut the short hairs shorter. Soon she looked like Penny. Both girls walked into the bathroom and sat on the floor. They laid their heads on their arms, which were folded over their knees. Roman saw what he took for defeat and he knew he had won. He triumphantly walked out of the house. He took the tresses of hair to the garage and added them to the others he kept stashed in his glove compartment.

"Ah, sweet memories," he said, as he rubbed the fine texture across his face.

He was in heaven and all was right with the world.

CHAPTER 61

As Lindsay stood in the bathroom and stared into the mirror, she could see tiny figures that looked as if they had been terribly mistreated.

She picked the scissors up from the counter and felt the urge to cut something. Grabbing paper from her note pad, she cut wildly at it. Tiny pieces fell to the floor, but what Lindsay saw was hair falling. Long strands of blonde and brown hair with red highlights in it. Lindsay cried, and slowly slipped to the bathroom floor. She sat on the cool tiles and cried because she knew she was too late to save them yet another indignity. She knew that if what she saw was right Roman had cut the girl's hair. He had cut it short, butchered it.

She stood up as a thought came to her. Reaching for the phone, she called home.

Marie answered in a sleepy voice. "Hello?"

"Marie, it's Mom. How are things?"

"Good. Jack is at his dad's and things here are pretty quiet. How are you? How are things going there?"

"Not too good but hopefully something will break soon."

"Mom, don't let this thing do you in, okay? We still need you here."

"I won't. I just wanted to hear the voice of someone who isn't involved."

"I love you," Marie said.

"I love you too," Lindsay whispered into the phone before she hung up.

Lindsay walked into the kitchen. "Claire, can I use your car today? I need to get out and ride around alone so I can feel things from my own point of view. The whole cop thing is getting too invasive for me."

"Sure you can, Lindsay. Let me get you the keys. Do you feel you know your way around here enough to venture out alone? I could go with you if you want."

"No, really, I need to go alone so I can get some work done, if you don't mind."

"No, I don't mind at all, I'll get you those keys now," Claire said. "Oh, Lindsay, do you want some coffee before you go? I can put it in a to-go cup for you if you want."

"That would be wonderful."

She went to her room to change into jeans and a tank top. As she walked out the back door, the brightness of the sun greeted her and tried to coax her into a feeling of lightheartedness. The morning thoughts of the two girls weighed heavy on her mind and while she embraced the sun, the urgency of the situation pulled on her.

CHAPTER 62

As Lindsay rode through the small town, she looked at all the people.

Such a pretty day had brought them out in droves. She wanted to get a feel for the way they lived. She had to know this town so she could know the one person who didn't fit. Roman was that one person. He was an out-of-towner who would never fit in here. His life had been too traumatic from the little she knew about him. There had been a time when she thought perhaps the first child was dead, but the second one lived. It was the only reason she agreed to come. Never again would she recover a dead child. Those days were in the past. Her heart couldn't take it any more.

As she drove past one shop or bakery after another she saw hometown values, southern style. Her heart longed to belong to something like this but rarely was she ever totally accepted. There was always a hint of who or what she was hanging in the air, getting between friendships and communication. She had tried keeping what she did a secret, since she lived in a small town. The secret had gotten out. Many relationships had fallen by the wayside due to her ability to know if someone was lying.

Lindsay passed the elementary school. No children were there now, but she could hear the memory of laughter in the air. The elements of days gone by and all the children who had played there hung heavy and sweet. Little smiling faces popped into her mind's eye as she drove slowly by. Her strongest prayer for this community was that it was not forever scarred by this incident. Hopefully, parents would still let their children play outside and run to one another's homes after school.

Jackie was rarely left alone to play outside and he never got to ride his bike to a friend's house unless his mom or one of his sisters could see all the way there. He was a child who lived in the know: he knew and he felt the dangers often. Still he seemed to be a happy child, playing and laughing easily and loving with a deepness that most adults envied.

Lindsay turned on the street where Marcie and Penny lived. She drove past their homes and could hear their joined laughter hanging in the air. As she drove by Marcie's house, she waved to Janet sitting on the front porch and pulled over to the curb.

"Good morning, or should I say good early afternoon?"

Janet got up and walked to the car. "Hi there, how are you doing? I see you found a car and a few moments of freedom for yourself."

"Well, I needed to get away from all the police stuff. Sometimes it's necessary to do what I do."

"Are you finding your way around okay?" Janet asked.

"You know, sometimes as I drive these streets I feel as if I have lived here for years."

"I hope we've made you feel welcome. I didn't mean to offend you last night. It's just that sometimes they talk about my daughter as if she never existed or like she is not someone they love."

Lindsay patted the hand that lay on the car doorframe.

"It's okay, really I do understand. You know, this is not the first time I've done this, but sometimes in order to be effective we have to stay detached so that we can do our jobs."

"How do you live with all of this and still seem so normal?" Janet asked. "I mean, you seem just like me or one of my friends. I can picture you living here, walking your son to school or being on the PTA."

Lindsay nodded. "That's what allows me to blend in, and back home that's exactly who I am."

Janet tried to understand. "It's like being a cop, isn't it?"

"Well, no, not really, in the legal sense. But in every other sense I guess you could say it is. I have to deal with things like they do or go crazy. Although I think Tony is a little closer to this than he normally would be."

Janet shook her head to the negative. "No, Tony knows everyone in this town. His father was the police captain a long time ago, and Tony grew up here. He would be personally involved no matter whose child it was."

"Wow, now that has to be hard. To watch your friends go through something like this and never be able to rest from it. I thought he was so attached to these two little girls that he felt like they were family. I guess I was wrong there."

Janet giggled. "I guess that happens from time to time but not too often."

Lindsay laughed too. "Oh yeah, it happens. Just ask my ex-husband. He'll tell you how wrong I am and just how often."

Both women laughed. "Well I'd better get going or I won't see all I want to before lunchtime."

Janet waved as Lindsay drove away and looked up to the heavens. "Please, Lord, please let something happen soon. I miss my daughter."

The Lord must have had a busy day, because prayers were going up all over town for Marcie and Penny.

As Lindsay drove by the hospital, she saw Bill pushing Justina in a wheelchair to the car parked in front of them. She slowed down and watched as he helped her in. "They must be going home," she said to herself.

The town was small so making "the rounds," as Tony called them, wasn't hard and didn't take long. Lindsay had made what Claire called the big circle in no time at all.

As she turned the car back toward the Millers' house, she felt a pull—someone or something was pulling on her. She reached into her pocket and pulled out the tissue Billy Cohrt had brought over the night before. She had taken it from the house, and even though it was police evidence, she didn't feel bad. To her it was a link to the two precious souls she was looking for.

Her radar was up, her senses tingled, and she just let them come. Something was wrong. She had the feeling someone was in the car with her. she looked over her shoulder. No one was there, other than another motorist behind her who just waved and politely waited for her to go.

"Gosh, this is a small town. At home someone would have flipped me off."

Again she felt the feeling. She turned first one way on the street, then the other to see if the feeling intensified. She turned back the other way when she felt the feeling diminish and headed in the direction where something was happening. Her mind was working furiously and she found herself holding her breath and gripping the steering wheel with white-knuckled strength. Her eyes were on the road before her but her senses were tuned into the surrounding area. She realized that she knew where she was.

"This is Penny and Marcie's street. Oh my God, is he going to take another child from this street?"

Lindsay pulled over to the curb and looked around. She slowly got out of the car and walked just a few feet from it. Looking around she saw homes that were just like all the rest. Nothing was different other than something that hung in the air. The air was rich with the scent of magnolia blossoms and the sun was shining brightly. There was a feeling of family in the air and something else. Lindsay stood very still and then she knew; danger was nearby. Lindsay turned and ran toward Janet's house.

"I need a phone, please I need to use your phone," she yelled as she got close enough to see Janet, who was still sitting on her porch.

"What's wrong?" Janet said as she stood up.

"Phone, I need a phone, please let me use your phone."

Janet ran inside and got the portable. As she came back out, Lindsay was turning slowly in a circle with her hands held out before her.

"Are you okay?" Janet asked her with concern in her voice.

"Tony Miller, will you please call Tony for me." Lindsay was feeling panic coming to her.

Janet quickly dialed the number and handed the phone to Lindsay.

"Tony Miller here."

"Tony, it's Lindsay."

"Oh, hey, Lindsay, I was just going to call you. The guys I had checking the feeder road have something to report and I wanted to know if you would be interested in hearing it. They say it's not much but it could be a start."

"No, Tony, listen to me. I'm over near Janet and Mac's and something's coming, something's wrong. Please come here," she said in a rush, "please come now. I can feel him!"

"Feel who? Lindsay, calm down, take a deep breath, and tell me what's going on." Tony was getting excited himself.

Lindsay took that deep breath and started over just as Mac came outside.

"What's wrong?" he asked Janet.

Janet tried to explain to Mac as Lindsay tried to explain to Tony. Since Janet knew very little and had to guess at the rest, she held a hand up to Mac and said, "Just listen."

Mac, Janet, and Tony all got the same story.

"Tony, I'm here at Janet and Mac Anderson's home, using the phone. I was driving around town and all of a sudden I could feel something, I could feel him. He's on the move and he's in this area. Tony, I think he's going to take another child, right here in the same neighborhood."

Tony had it then.

"I'm calling John. I'll be right there. Lindsay, don't you do anything until I get there. Do you hear me? You're not a cop, you're a civilian and I'm responsible for you."

Tony hung up and ran for his own car, calling as he ran. "Claire, call John and tell him something's going down over near the Anderson house. Get him there and tell him I'm on my way."

Claire looked at Tony. She saw the cop in him. He wouldn't answer questions right now so she did as he asked and ran out the door behind him. She heard his tires squeal at the corner as she ran out the door and cut through Ms. Hemple's backyard.

A couple blocks away, Mac ran into his house and came out with a handgun.

"I'm going too. Janet, go back in the house," he said as he ran after Lindsay who was running down the block toward her car.

"No, she's my daughter too."

As he ran right behind Lindsay, he shouted. "Where?"

Lindsay pointed to the brick home, the only one on the block. The white tiles that outlined the windows stood out like a neon light.

"Are you sure? That's Barb and Hal Griffon's home. Are you sure?" Mac asked.

"Yes, backyard, child with brown hair and light green shorts. Hurry, he has her!" Lindsay screamed.

The football star that he was came back to Mac as he ran through the side yard and jumped the gate. His heart was pounding, and the gun in his hand was held in a death grip.

Hal Griffon came running through the house and charged out the back door. "Mac what the hell is going on, what . . ."

Then he saw it. There at the back fence all the way in the corner was his own worst nightmare.

He hit the soft earth running, screaming, "Stop!"

Barb came out of the house, saw what was going on, and screamed at the top of her lungs, "Noooo, please, God, no."

Janet ran to her as Mac charged the man on the other side of the fence.

CHAPTER 63

Roman had made his mind up the day before to get another pet.

That way he could have three of them at the roadside park just like the man who had been there showing off. He was really proud of himself for finding a way to take the prideful ways from his pets, a way other than the way Charlie had used. His way didn't hurt them, it just showed them who was boss. Sometimes parents had to do that to their pets. Sometimes there was just no other way.

Roman had played with his souvenirs in the garage for the longest time. He held them lovingly in his hands and stroked their softness. He crooned over and over to himself about love and family and being a part of it all. He wanted happiness, and now he had found a way. As he walked back into the house, his pets were still sitting where he had left them more than three hours before, although their heads were raised now. They looked at him and then down again.

"Good pets, you have finally learned your lesson. I hope you'll continue to be good now," he said somewhat smugly. The only sound that met his ears was that of sniffling.

"I'm going out for a short time. We need another pet for our family so that we can go to the roadside park and play. You'll be happy then, do you hear me? You *will* be happy."

Both of the girls nodded and said, "We will be happy. We promise."

"Good," Roman said and turned to walk to the door. "Oh, there's breakfast in the kitchen. I couldn't get what you normally eat, but you'll have to eat all of it, or you can't go to the roadside park. I will leave you here and take the other pet."

"We will, we'll eat it all," they said, because going was better than not going and they both wanted to see who the other pet was going to be.

There was no doubt in their minds that he would bring another one home. As the door closed they both stood up and walked into the kitchen. There before them was McDonald's sausage and egg biscuits. Both girls ran to it and stuffed it in their mouths as fast as they could. They drank the fresh orange juice and laughed as it dribbled down their chins. Feeling much better they cleaned the mess up and went into the bathroom to look at what Roman had done to them. Penny's was the worst because she had fought him, but that was her way—she was a scrapper. As they looked into the mirror, their eyes filled with tears.

Marcie said, "At least it won't hurt when I comb my hair now. My mommy won't have to put it up in a ponytail anymore."

Penny looked at Marcie and nodded. "Yours looks better than mine. Marcie, please fix mine."

She was crying hard now and her little shoulders shook. Her nose ran and she wiped it on her sleeve. Marcie took the scissors from where Roman had left them the night before and started working on it. The cut places on Penny's head had bled some. The blood had dried and matted what was left of her hair, making it look worse than it should have.

"Let's wash it first. I'll be real careful. I won't hurt you."

"No, I'll get soap in my eyes," Penny cried.

"No you won't. Here, we'll put this rag over your eyes, and you won't get soap or water in them. That's how my mommy does it."

The two tiny figures bent over the sink and washed Penny's hair. Marcie felt sorry for her and was extra gentle.

The soap bubbles turned a dark red in Marcie's hands like the color of bricks, as she sang, "Penny's hair is gonna get washed, gonna get washed, gonna get washed. Penny's hair is gonna get washed and look real pretty," to the tune of "This is the way we wash our clothes early in the morning."

The sadness hung in the air as the two tried to make the best of a bad situation.

Marcie worked on Penny's hair for a long time. They let it fill the day and take up time, since that was all they really had anyway. Today they had more than ever, only at the time, they didn't know it.

CHAPTER 64

Tony came running around the corner just as Mac charged the man at the back fence who had Ashley Griffon in his grip.

He was pulling her by her hair toward the fence and she was screaming at the top of her lungs. Hal was right on Mac's heels, trying to keep his heart in his chest as he saw his daughter lifted off the ground and pulled over the fence. Mac never missed a step. He grabbed the fence in one hand and hurdled over it as Roman lifted Ashley into a football hold and took off running.

Roman's heart was beating. He had never been so scared in all his life. Things were not going the way he wanted them to lately.

Tony and Hal were right behind Mac as Roman turned in full stride and threw his car keys at them. The keys hit Tony full in the face, slowing him quite a bit. Ashley wiggled, squirmed, and screamed in Roman's grasp. He reached down as he turned toward the side road and slapped her hard.

She put her hands to her face and screamed, "Daddy, help me!"

Mac could take no more. The gun in his hand was heavy, and he felt its weight as he dove at Roman, taking him down hard. Ashley fell to the ground and rolled away.

Roman jumped to his feet and faced Mac. "If you shoot me, you'll never get your pet back. She will die right where she is and it will be all your fault."

Tony came running up behind Mac. "Give me the gun, Mac, this isn't the way. We have him now. It's just a matter of time before we get Marcie back."

Mac looked at Roman. He wanted to shoot him. He wanted it deep in his soul but Tony was right. Mac turned to hand his gun to Tony but as he did Roman took off running. Mac aimed and fired. Roman had left him no other choice.

Roman's body spun in a complete circle as he fell to the ground. The sound was deafening in the small alleyway. The women standing at the fence screamed as Tony ran over to Roman, lying there on the grass. Hal ran to scoop his daughter in his arms, then grabbed Mac and gently took the gun from his hand. The barrel was still hot to the touch.

"It's over, buddy. You saved my daughter from a fate worse than hell. There is no way I can ever thank you."

Hal hugged Mac in a bear hug embrace as Tony stood and looked at them. Roman struggled to rise, clutching his left elbow and screaming in pain. Tony had his foot on Roman's shoulder and would not let him up. The wound was not bad enough to kill him but it did stop him rather effectively.

Blood was everywhere as Claire ran around the gate toward her husband. She could see that he was bleeding and she had heard the shot but had not witnessed it. Her heart was in her throat as she ran toward Tony, but he held up his hand to stop her from coming closer.

Mac grabbed her as she ran past him. "I'm okay babe, it's just a scratch, really," Tony said.

Claire could see him and that was enough.

"Take her back. Everyone get back," Tony said.

Mac and Hal moved with Ashley and Claire back toward the Griffon yard. The neighbors were filling up the alleyway, and as Tony looked up he came face to face with John, who had been there the whole time with his gun drawn just in case Tony needed backup. He had never said a word. He knew this town needed Tony to be their hero and once again he was.

Tony smiled at him. "Call an ambulance and some backup to take this scum bag."

John smiled and said, "Will do."

Tony reached down and turned Roman over. He pulled him to his feet and then with one hand cuffed him to his free arm.

"Oh, by the way, asshole, here's your keys," he said, and he held the keys up and dangled them in the air.

Roman jerked his shoulder trying to free himself. Tony increased his pressure and held up their joined manacled hands.

"You aren't going anywhere, so stop your struggling before I let those three fathers over there have you."

Roman looked around him and for the first time he noticed the alleyway was lined with people. The largest group stood at Barb and Hal's backyard gate that led into the alley. Ashley, who had been scooped up by her father, buried her face in his neck.

"Daddy why did that man do that to me, what did I do?"

"Nothing, baby, you didn't do anything. He's a bad man. Daddy has you now, you're okay."

Barb took her daughter from her husband and cuddled her close. As she turned to walk back into the yard, she saw Janet Anderson with her arms around Mac. She walked up to him and placed a hand on his face. "There is no way that I can ever thank you for what you did for us. God surely will bring your little girl home."

Tears slipped down Mac's face and Barb brushed them aside as she kissed his cheek.

Janet reached a hand out to touch Ashley. "Are you okay, baby?"

"Yes, ma'am," she said as she held on to her mommy.

The backyard was filling up fast with policemen, and radios were crackling in the background. The ambulance attendants, along with John, took Roman away after Tony had transferred the handcuff to John's wrist. He had repeatedly asked him where Marcie and Penny were but Roman never said a word.

Claire ran to him and took him in her arms. "I'm okay, babe, really. It's just a little scratch and maybe a broken nose," he said as he fingered the lump that was coming up.

Claire sniffled and said, "I'm so proud of you. I have never seen you in action like that before. Is this what your days are like?"

"No way, this is an extraordinary situation. Mac is the real hero. Did you see him hurdle that fence?"

Claire nodded and laughed. "No wonder he got that football scholarship."

Tony laughed again and draped his arm around Claire and led her toward the gate. A round of applause went up as he passed the people who had gathered to see what had happened. Tony and Claire waved at them and smiled.

Lindsay rushed up and hugged them both. "Congratulations. Did he say where the girls are?"

"No, we couldn't get him to talk, so I had John take him on to the hospital. Hopefully we can get something out of him there."

Claire looked up at Tony. "This isn't over yet, is it?"

"No, baby, not until Marcie and Penny are safely back home. I made a promise to Janet and I intend to keep it."

"You go, both of you. I'll stay here and help with things," Claire said.

At the hospital, Tony and Lindsay had to push their way through a crowd of reporters and television cameras to get to where Roman was being held. The doctors were working on his arm when they arrived.

"He's gonna lose that arm," one of them said.

Tony walked over to Roman and asked, "Are you Roman Marsh?"

"Yes, sir," Roman said.

"Has he been read his rights by anyone?" Tony turned to look around the room.

John was sitting in the corner and said, "Yeah, I read them to him, but he wouldn't answer me."

"Roman Marsh, do you understand the rights that were read to you, and do you want an attorney to be here with you?"

"No, I don't want an attorney. Why did you shoot me?"

"Just for the record, I didn't shoot you. Are you sure you don't want an attorney?"

"No, sir, I don't need one." Roman said with a confused look on his face.

"Roman, do you know what an attorney is?" Tony asked.

"Yes, sir, he's one of those people that tells everyone that you didn't do what you did."

Everyone in the room snickered, even Tony.

"Okay, let's get a social worker in here and find out what he knows or is capable of knowing," Tony said.

The emergency room doctor broke in. "Do you mind if I finish with him first?" His tone was less than accommodating.

Tony felt instantly foolish. "No, doctor, sorry about that. It's just that we have two little girls out there somewhere waiting to be found."

Roman tried to sit up as he repeated in horror, "There are two little girls waiting to be found? Where are they? Let me help you look for them. I'm a good looker."

The look on his face was genuine and his concern seemed to be the same.

"Roman," Tony said gently, "can you tell me where those two little girls are?"

"No, sir, but I can help you look for them. I'm a good looker. Reese could never hide from me for long because I have a way about me."

Tony was shocked; he had been so sure. John was on his feet next to Roman across from Tony.

"Son," he said, "are you telling us that you didn't take those two little girls? Are you saying that you didn't take Marcie Anderson from her home while she was playing outside on the front porch? Is it your story that you didn't break into Penny Ware's home in the middle of the night and take her from her bed? Is that what you're telling us?"

"No, sir, I didn't take no two little girls. All I have is pets. Just two pets is all, no little girls."

Tony and John looked at him as he lay there with blood all over his arm, and for just the briefest moment they believed him. But they had seen him in the video and the resemblance was amazing. John was thinking that maybe Roman was setting himself up for an insanity plea to try to get away with it.

Tony was madder than he'd been in a long time. He squared his shoulders and started again. "Roman, what you're telling me and what I know to be true don't really go together. Are you lying to me for some reason? because if you are things will only get worse."

Roman shook his head back and forth. "No, sir, I would never lie to an officer. That would get me in big trouble. Everyone knows you don't lie to an officer."

"Okay, guys, that's it for a while. Let me get him cleaned up and stable before you talk any more," the doctor said.

"Am I gonna bleed to death?" Roman asked, getting more nervous and trying to sit up.

"Out, everyone. This is a hospital, not a police station."

The doctor was getting upset. Tony and John didn't need that. They would need his help again later.

Tony walked to the door, but John hung back and spoke to the doctor. "This prisoner is in my custody. I stay, but I'll be quiet."

The doctor nodded and went back to work on Roman's arm. The pain medication was starting to wear of, and Roman had to be sedated again. That was fine with him, but Tony hated the thought of it since it would be that much longer before they got to interview him. He looked over his shoulder one more time as he went out the door.

Lindsay was waiting in the hallway. "I hate hospitals. After working in them for all these years you would think I would feel at home in them but I don't. Something about them makes me think of death."

Tony nodded. "Me too. Lindsay, we have another problem. Roman says he didn't take the girls. From the look on his face he seemed genuinely concerned. He offered to help us look for them. Said he was a 'good looker.'"

"He's lying, Tony, you and I both know that. He's lying or he's more messed up inside than we thought."

"Yeah, well, the doctor is working on him in there and won't let us talk to him anymore. So other than his personal effects we have nothing to go on."

"What are we going to do? We can't just let him get away."

"Lindsay, he's a suspect in a multiple kidnapping. He's not going anywhere right now. John is in there with him. He won't let Roman out of his sight, no matter what. So don't worry about that."

"Tony, what about those two little girls out there waiting for this mad man to come home? Remember, I told you Marcie isn't feeling well. We have to get to them, we have to find them soon."

"I know, I'm working on it. I want to go through his things, but I can't legally until someone explains his legal rights to him."

Lindsay started to interrupt but Tony held up a hand. "Yes, John read him his rights, but he doesn't seem to have the ability to understand them. He's slow or something. We need a social worker in there with us to help him understand."

"Tony, you said you have his things. Can I get a look at those things?"

"Not until he's read his rights and understands them so he can be officially arrested. I know it stinks but that's the way it is."

"Tony, can I as a civilian look at those things? I mean I'm not a cop so there's no legal problem. I'm just someone who has an interest."

Tony looked at her and paused for a moment. "Lindsay, this is a hard thing to say, but I just don't think that I can allow you do that. Do you understand?" He'd spoken very slowly and deliberately.

"Oh yes, Tony, I understand. Absolutely and without any doubts at all."

Tony nodded and walked away. He turned at the end of the hallway and looked back at her. "Lindsay, I don't want you to go in this room right here for any reason at all, do you understand me?"

"Yes, Tony, I understand," she said, sounding exasperated for anyone listening.

Lindsay waited until Tony rounded the corner and then she slipped into the room. Inside were bags and bags of personal belongings. She started going through the bags one at a time until she noticed they were arranged in alphabetical order by patient name. She smiled to herself. "Just like I would do it."

When she found the bag containing Roman's things, blood was everywhere. She looked around the room and found a box of gloves hanging on the wall. Lindsay opened the bag and poured the contents out on the table. Her senses were assaulted as she staggered back at so much information at once.

Images of Roman came fast and furious. She saw his youth and some of what he had been through. She saw the death of his parents and knew why Birdie Marsh had been killed and how. The visions caused her to stagger backward and look for a place to sit. Finding nothing, she climbed up on the table and sat down. But all the images she got were of Roman; nothing about the girls.

Lindsay took the gloves off and gently touched the clothing that was free of blood smears. There were more images of things she would love at some other time to delve into but this was not the time. She stored some of the images and others she let go. Finally, just when she thought she had been wrong, she got them. Images of Marcie and Penny running away from someone. Anger in Roman, intense anger. Lindsay feared for the safety of the two girls. She allowed more of Roman's images to come to her. They came in spurts, not the flow she was used to. There were images of things she recognized and things she didn't. She stored them all for future reference, as she knew she would need later. For now, all she wanted was Marcie and Penny and their whereabouts.

Unfortunately, nothing concrete came through, nothing she felt she could give the police or FBI to work on. Her lack of success was frustrating, and now she was stuck with all those images. It was giving her a terrible headache so she stepped back from the table. The last thing that she got was about cars, lots and lots of cars, but the headache was taking over and Lindsay knew that anything she got from this point on could not be trusted. It would be mixed with her own pain and her own prejudices and that wasn't fair to anyone involved.

She put the things back in the bag and tied it closed, then picked the gloves up off the table and threw them into the hazardous waste receptacle. The idea came to her as she stood there in the room feeling frustrated.

Opening the door with a determined swing, she stormed into the hallway. Tony was nowhere in sight, so she walked back down the corridor toward the examining room. John was seated across from the table Roman was stretched out on. She watched the doctors work on his battered arm as she went to John and leaned in to speak into his ear.

"John, is there a way that I can interview Roman?"

John motioned with his chin in the direction of Roman and shook his head. "He's in their hands and it looks to me like it's going to be awhile."

Lindsay leaned around the doctor and saw where they were in the process. "Nope, they're going to be stitching up soon and then put on a cast and then he should be all ours."

"How do you know that?"

"I've been an ER nurse for a long time. In fact, I've been all over a hospital and believe me when I say he's almost finished."

"Okay, cast him," the doctor said in the background and Lindsay smiled at John. "Told ya," she said. "Now can I interview him?"

"Let me talk to Tony first. Of course, you're not a cop or a social worker but you are a nurse and maybe, just maybe that will be enough to justify it." John watched as the casting team came in to work on Roman.

"How about if you look in the hall for Tony and see what he says. I can't leave Roman alone for even a minute."

Lindsay nodded and headed for the door. As she opened it, Tony peeked his head in and motioned her to come into the hallway.

"What did you find out, anything?"

"I got lots and lots but most of it's not all that useful."

"You might be surprised what's useful, believe me."

"Well then, later we need to go over it. Right now I have another idea. I want to interview Roman, and John said since I'm not a cop or a social worker there might be a problem but that I'm a nurse so there might be a way around it. He isn't going to talk to anyone but me, Tony, believe me."

Tony looked at her. "Lindsay, believe me I want to find those two girls just as bad as you do, but we have to be careful here because if things are not done a certain way, a lawyer with any grit to his grain might be able to get him off on some technicality. We don't want him getting away to do this again, that is if he is the one who did it."

"Oh, he did it," Lindsay stated firmly. "That's something I'm sure of. I did get images of the two little ones from him. He has them hidden somewhere, Tony. Please let me talk to him, please."

Suddenly a loud banging noise and the sounds of scuffles came from the room. People were shouting and running about inside. Tony drew his revolver, pushed Lindsay out of the way, and stormed into the room. John was on the floor pinning Roman beneath him. The doctor and one of the nurses lay on the other side of the room. The doctor's hand had been slashed; blood dripped from it. The nurse slowly sat up, stunned and crying. John was struggling to hold Roman down as Tony ran toward them. They grabbed him together and pulled him roughly to his feet. As Tony and John walked him past Lindsay, they both looked at her and in unison said, "No!"

Lindsay knew that there would be no arguing with them now. But she also knew she had to come up with a way to talk to him. That seemed to be the only way to find Marcie and Penny.

CHAPTER 65
Marcie and Penny had a long day.

They had waited in fear for Roman to return, but when he didn't, they knew something was wrong. Late into the evening hours they waited. Marcie could do no more than sleep, so Penny played on her own most of the day. Time and again she went to the window that had the broken panes and peeked out as the evening breeze moved the curtains. Penny would check on Marcie and hold her hand but Marcie never really moved very much.

"Marcie, please get up. I'm lonely. Please get up. I want you to play with me."

"I can't, Penny. I don't feel good. I want my mommy. I don't feel like playing."

Penny went into the kitchen to make some soup for Marcie but she couldn't use the can opener.

"Marcie, if you open the can, I will make you some soup."

"I don't want soup, I want my mom."

"Marcie, I can't get your mom but I can make you some soup. Please don't cry. Soup always makes us feel better. Please open the can for me. I want some too."

Marcie pulled herself up to try to help Penny. As she got up walked she shook terribly. Penny helped her into the kitchen. Marcie opened the can and Penny heated the soup. The two little girls sat in the kitchen and ate at the table. They talked of going home and being able to play outside. Penny wanted to play on the swing in her backyard.

"My dad can put one up for you too if you want Marcie."

Marcie shook her head firmly. "When I get home I'm never going to leave my house again."

After they ate they walked into the living room and looked longingly at the sofa. The TV was a constant reminder of what they couldn't have.

"Let's just go to bed, Penny," Marcie said.

Penny looked at the couch and the TV. "Let's watch TV for just a little while, Marcie, please."

"Okay, but if Roman comes home and the TV is on, we're going to get in trouble. We have to turn all the rest of the lights off and be real quiet."

Penny nodded and went into the bedroom to get Marcie a pillow and a blanket. She came back and lay down on the other end of the couch.

The TV played on and on until late into the night. Roman never came home.

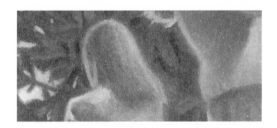

CHAPTER 66
Tony was busy with other things.

Now in custody at the police station, Roman bounded back and forth between enraged psychopath and docile child. There was little Tony could do with him other than to lock him up. They had been at him for hours when the nurse from the local clinic showed up with orders from the ER doctor to medicate him. Tony knew that once he took the medication he would sleep for hours.

"Please just one more question," he said to her as she set the pill before Roman.

"No!" Roman screamed and shoved the pill into his mouth.

Tony grabbed him. "Where are those two little girls?" Tony shouted.

Roman shouted back at him. "I don't have two little girls. I only have pets!"

"Where do you live, Roman?" Tony asked for the umteenth time.

"I live at Bobby's house, I told you," Roman shouted back.

John grabbed Tony and pulled him from the room. "Tony, man, you have got to get hold of yourself. He's gonna file abuse charges against you and he's gonna walk."

Tony shook John's hands off. "I want that bastard, but I want those little girls more."

"I know, buddy, but we have to do this the right way. To make it stick, Tony, do it right."

Tony nodded. It was near midnight and he knew he wasn't going to get anything else out of Roman tonight.

"I'm going home; you do the same. Let's pick this up tomorrow morning."

"Tony, what about letting Lindsay talk to him?" John asked.

"No, no way. You saw him at the hospital. He's crazy, and we have no way of protecting her if he goes off."

"We could set her up behind a two-way mirror. We could have officers outside the door and watch every minute. He's not gonna break, Tony, because in his mind he is telling us the truth. He has no idea what we want from him. She may be our only way. Think about it, then ask her and see if she's willing after what she witnessed earlier today."

Tony looked at him for a long moment. "Okay, I'll ask her."

"Night, Tony, get some rest. You look like hell and you smell ever worse and I just know that nose is broken."

Tony fingered his nose. The bandage hurt and it distorted his eyesight. "Yeah, I'm out of here."

He made it home long before John made it back to his hotel room. John stood and watched Roman for a long time. He was looking for a kink in his suit of armor.

CHAPTER 67
Lindsay awoke early the next morning and hurried to the kitchen.

Tony sat there looking much the worse for the wear. Claire was fussing about him, getting his breakfast and applying a cold ice pack to his nose.

"Morning, all," Lindsay said.

"Morning," Tony grunted.

Claire looked up and smiled. "Good morning, Lindsay. You look fresh as sunshine. It's a beautiful day, isn't it?"

Lindsay looked out the window and smiled. "Yes, it is."

"Coffee?" Claire asked.

"Hmmm," Lindsay nodded.

Claire poured her coffee as Tony studied Lindsay's silence. "Okay. You can interview him behind a two-way mirror. But if he gets squirrelly you're out of there. Do you understand me?"

"I do. You won't be sorry, Tony, really."

"Go change. I can't take you there in your bathrobe."

Claire laughed out loud. "I know this is going to work."

"I agree with you, Claire," Lindsay said, reaching out her hand to clasp Claire's.

Tony stood and walked out of the room to dress. He was not in a good mood. He wanted Marcie and Penny back. He had made promises and he intended to keep them.

Within the hour he and Lindsay were headed to the station. As they arrived, they saw John's car parked outside.

"Did he sleep here or what?" Tony said to no one, but Lindsay answered him just the same.

"Yep, he did," and then she smiled.

Tony smiled too. "Thanks, Lindsay, for being here. He would have gotten another child if not for you."

"You're welcome. It's what I do. Now, let's go get those babies back so you can put them in their mommies' arms."

Tony stood there, temporarily dumbfounded. "How did you know?"

She turned and laughed at him. "Oh ye of little faith. I know you, Tony. I know the promise you made to Janet and Justina is some of what drives you."

"How did you know I made the promise?"

"There, I cheated. Janet told me," Lindsay said.

Tony followed her into the station. His laughter could be heard throughout, and it set the stage for the day. Prior to that moment all inside had waited anxiously to see what kind of mood he would be in.

The interview was set up. Roman had agreed, and John had everything ready to go. Tony looked at John and nodded as he came in.

"I knew it!" John said with a large smile.

CHAPTER 68

At the police station, Lindsay sat in the room Tony and John had prepared.

She could feel them outside watching and that feeling gave her some security. She stood and walked over to the big mirror. She and Tony had come up with a signal; two taps on her side and he would tap once so she would be sure he was there. She tapped and waited. Tony tapped back. She smiled and nodded.

Lindsay had no idea what she was waiting to meet: a mad man or a child so badly abused he had lost all control. She felt out of her element, untrained and honestly scared. She felt a little foolish for feeling that way since she knew that just beyond the mirror a battery of police officers stood ready to come to her defense. She wanted to do this. She knew this was the only way. Yet she felt the weight of all that rested on her ability and the outcome of this interview. She had the opportunity to help bring those little ones home and once again give her gift some credibility.

She was the one who always said, "There is always hope, until the last moment there is hope."

Now she had to stand behind that. Her mouth was dry and her hands were sweaty. The tingling sensation started again and she knew the time had come. She could feel him coming. As the weeks had passed, she had come to know what this man felt like, what he smelled like, and even what he dreamed.

She stood as the door opened and two officers stepped into the room accompanied by the man who had caused all this. Roman walked towards Lindsay and looked at her directly in the eye. She longed to look to the big mirror for comfort, but she stood her ground and hung on to the aversion she had toward him. She knew better than to let him see it. She knew what he most wanted was to be loved and mothered. He wanted a family and someone to hold him in a position of love and respect.

Roman held his hand out to shake hers. She really didn't want to touch him. He felt like a pedophile but that was why she was here. She needed to learn the location of Marcie and Penny. Time was running out. Only Roman had that information.

As Lindsay took his hand, her skin crawled and the hair at the nape of her neck stood on end. His hand was warm to the touch. He grasped her hand in his and shook it gently. He felt small to her, small and very dangerous. Images started to come to her faster than she was prepared to handle and she let his hand go and stepped back.

She took in his appearance. Even though he was standing there in his jail garb with his arm in a sling, he had an air of dignity about him that was unmistakable. He held himself erect and seemed warm and friendly toward her, but that was only on the surface. She could see instantly why he had Tony and John confused. He seemed genuine to her as well. It was only when she dug under his exterior that she could see the difference. He raised his head and sniffed the air. She watched him and named him right then and there; he was scenting evil to its deepest level.

He continued to look at Lindsay as she gestured to the chairs that had been placed in the room for them. He walked over to one and looked at it as if to assess it. He reached into his shirt pocket for a handkerchief, but all those things had already been taken from him. Instead he pulled out a tissue.

"I don't like tissues. They're cheap. But this will have do," he said.

He shrugged his shoulders and wiped the chair with his tissue. Then he looked at the tissue and around the room for a place to put it off. Seeing none he wiped his hands on it and turned the chair toward Lindsay. He then did the same thing with the other chair and they both sat down. Holding her hands in her lap, Lindsay looked at him. He smiled the most pleasant of smiles.

"Are you a police officer?" he asked.

"No, I'm just here to talk to you, to see if I can help everyone, including you. Do you mind talking to me?"

"No, not at all. I'm used to talking to doctors."

"Roman, I'm not a doctor, but I would like the chance to talk to you if that's okay with you."

"What do you want to talk about?" he asked

"Well, why don't you just tell me your side of things since I think you know you're in a lot of trouble."

"I really don't know what you want to talk to me about. I have told them, those cops, everything they want me to say and they won't let me go. I have pets to feed. I need to go home. What's your name?"

"It's Lindsay."

"Just Lindsay?"

"Yes."

"I like your name."

"I like yours too, Roman," she said. Lindsay paused. "Roman, what do you know about the two little girls that are missing?"

"I don't know nothing. Honest, Lindsay. They keep asking me but I really don't know nothing."

Lindsay knew that he knew where they were but she suddenly had the feeling that maybe she was asking him the wrong question.

"Roman, tell me about you."

"What do you want to know?"

"Well, I want to be friends, and friends know a lot about each other. So tell me about you."

"You first," Roman said suddenly.

Somehow Lindsay knew that a lot of what she said would have a great bearing on what he told her about himself.

"Well, I have children and I work. I believe in God and go to church. I have friends who I hope love me. My house has three bedrooms and two bathrooms."

"I have a house," he said.

"Really? Tell me about it. I love my house. How about you?"

"I like mine okay, but it's not where I want to live forever. I want to live in the mountains. I have seen the mountains, you know. Someday I'm going to take my pets and head up to the mountains. I'm gonna let them play at the roadside park on the way."

"Oh, you have pets? So do I. Tell me about yours."

"I have two pets. Mine don't always behave so well but they love me a lot."

Lindsay felt instantly removed from the situation. Something he said had moved her worlds away from here. She looked up at him as he studied her.

"What's the matter?" he asked.

"I love my pets," Lindsay said tenderly. "I have Edgar, Haydon, and Squeak."

Images of Marcie and Penny swam before her eyes. She was onto something but as of yet she didn't know what it was.

She tapped twice on the table hoping that Tony would understand.

"I have Marcie and Penny," Roman said. Lindsay looked up suddenly. Her sudden movement scared Roman and he sat back.

"Oh, Roman, I'm sorry. I didn't mean to scare you. I just love those names. Marcie is my favorite name. How did you know that?"

Lindsay's mind was working. She could imagine the flurry of activity his words had caused, just beyond the mirror.

"Oh, I didn't know that," Roman smiled. "I didn't name them really. They came to me with those names, but I like them too."

"I have two cats and a dog, Roman. What do you have?"

"I have two pets, that's all, just two pets."

"I love my pets. I keep them at my house. How about you, do you keep your pets in the house where you live?"

"Yeah, you can't be too careful with pets these days. They are always trying to run away. They could get hit by a car, you know?"

"Yes, I know. I live in a small town, Roman. Where do you live?"

"Oh, I live at Bobby's," Roman said. "He has a house out back that I get to live in for working for him."

"Really? That's great. Do you keep your pets there with you?"

"Yeah, Bobby don't know that I have them since he said no pets and all but I keep them anyway. I always wanted pets. Me and Reese used to try to get pets when we was little and Ma and Pa would always cart them off. So now I get to keep my pets inside cause Ma and Pa are gone away."

"Roman, until we get this all straightened out and you can go home, would you like me to go and feed your pets?"

Roman thought this through. "I think that would be real nice of you, Ms. Lindsay."

"Okay, I need to know how to get to your place and what your pets like to eat."

"They only eat sweets. They don't like nothing else and I don't make them eat what they don't like."

The nurse in Lindsay knew instantly what was wrong with Marcie. Since she had been gone the longest, she was suffering the most from malnutrition.

"Roman, I have to go soon so if you would just tell me how to get to your pets, I'll be sure to feed them till you can do it yourself."

Roman looked at her and started to cry. "Please don't leave me, don't go away. Everyone always goes away from me."

"I'll be back. I'll come to see you when I can, when they let me," Lindsay said. "I'm going to go and feed your pets now."

Roman leaned into her as if to whisper in her ear. "Okay, go to Bobby's place and go out in the back and don't forget to push the button on the door or it will bite you. I made it do that so no one can take my pets."

Lindsay still had no idea where Bobby's was. "Roman, where does Bobby live?"

"Oh, he lives by all the cars."

"The cars?" Lindsay asked.

"Yeah he lives by all the cars, all the old cars where people put them when they don't want them no more. Like the country home." Roman laughed at his little joke.

Lindsay stood to go. "Bye for now, Roman. You take care."

"Bye-bye, Ms. Lindsay."

As Lindsay walked to the door, it was opened from the outside by the two officers who had brought Roman in. Tony and John stood just beyond them.

"I know where they are, he told me where they are." Lindsay was excited, and Tony and John strained to hear what she was saying.

"Where is Bobby's place, a place where there are old cars, lots of them?"

"There's Bobby's Auto Salvage Yard out on Highway 87," said Tony.

"How far is that?" John asked.

"About twenty minutes from here. Let's go."

Tony, John, and Lindsay started out the door. A host of police officers were hot on their heels. Tony wanted them along just in case they were wrong about Reese, and he was alive and well and helping Roman. Since from what they knew of Roman there was no way he could have masterminded this all by himself. Lindsay had told Tony about Marcie and Penny's diet and what she thought was wrong with Marcie now.

"We have to get them back today, Tony, no matter what!" Lindsay said.

Tony nodded and slammed the door to his patrol car.

The drive took less than twenty minutes. As they came up on Bobby's Auto Salvage Yard, Lindsay could feel them. The girls were there, scared and not feeling well, but there just the same.

As Tony turned on to the property, he realized the junkyard was closed. Tony squealed the tires to a stop and jumped out of the car. The officer who came up fast behind him did the same thing.

"Cut that lock," Tony shouted to him.

The officer ran around to the trunk. He grabbed the bolt cutters and raced to the big gate. With a snap the lock was gone, but as the gate swung open a loud siren pierced the air.

Lindsay covered her ears as Tony gunned the motor and raced to the back of the yard. There a house stood alone and seemed odd in the desolation of all the abandoned cars.

Tony was the first one out of the car, followed by Lindsay and John. He raced to the front door.

Lindsay called out, "Tony, wait!"

But it was too late. He had grabbed the doorknob and the bolt raced through his arm. He jerked back and swore out loud.

"Tony, go slowly. They're in there but they're scared to death. Go slowly, Tony, please."

Tony looked at everyone standing behind him. "Surround the house and stand back. Don't do anything unless someone comes running out of that house at you directly. Everybody hear me?"

They nodded. "Lindsay, who's in there?" Tony asked.

"Just the girls, Tony, honest. Unless someone is in there who is dead, I feel only the girls."

"Okay, let's go." Tony walked to the door and stood looking at it.

Lindsay reached around him and pushed the button Roman had told her about.

"Sorry about the jolt. I forgot."

"Oh, that's good," Tony said sarcastically.

She turned the doorknob and pushed the door open. The room came into view. Tony was the first one in, his revolver drawn. John was right behind him. He too had his gun drawn.

"They're children, gentleman," Lindsay said and she pushed past them. They looked at each other and shrugged their shoulders.

But their quick search of the house produced nothing. "They're not here, Lindsay, no one's here," Tony said, looking at her in a strange way.

"I can feel them, Tony. I know they're here somewhere."

As she walked into the kitchen, Lindsay could hear the faintest of sounds. She walked softly around the room. As she came to the sink, she paused. Slowly she bent and touched the door of the cabinet under the sink. She knew and she slowly pulled the door open. There before her was Marcie Anderson. Her face was buried in her hands and her hair had been cut short. Lindsay reached forward and touched her.

"Marcie, it's time to go home, sweetie. Can I take you home to your mommy and daddy?"

Marcie slowly looked up. She desperately wanted to go home, but she didn't know this lady and the last time she went with someone she didn't know she ended up with Roman. Still the lady smiled at her and she wanted to trust her.

"Tony," Lindsay called softly. "In here."

Tony came around the corner and the minute Marcie saw him she started to cry. She reached her arms out to him and he took her. He gently cuddled her into his arms and cradled her close.

Tony looked over her to Lindsay and silently said, "Thank you."

"Marcie, honey, where's Penny?" Tony asked.

"She's in the water closet, over there," Marcie said, pointing in the direction of the door that stood in the kitchen off to one corner.

Lindsay walked to the door. Slowly she opened it and peered inside. There was Penny tying to put on a brave front. She stood with her little hands on her hips and glared at the door. She would have pulled it off if her bottom lip hadn't quivered so badly.

Lindsay bent down and smiled at her. "Hello, I'm Lindsay and you must be Penny. I'm here to take you and Marcie home. Would you like to go home?"

With that Penny jumped into her arms. "Yes, ma'am," she said.

When the officers outside came in to let Tony know that all was secure outside, he told them to radio for an ambulance. "Girls, would you like to ride in an ambulance?"

Both of them nodded.

While they waited for it to arrive, Tony punched out some numbers on his cell phone and waited for an answer.

"Hello," Mac said.

"Mac, this is Tony. I have someone here who wants to say hi to you."

Tony handed the phone to Marcie. "Daddy, I want to come home."

Mac let out a whoop that his whole family heard. "Yes, baby, you come home now. We all want you to come home. Are you okay?"

"Yes sir," Marcie said. "I'm sick and Mr. Miller is going to take me to the hospital in the ambulance. Will you and Mommy come see me there?"

"Yes, baby, Mommy and I will be there. I love you."

"I love you too, Daddy, and I won't never be bad again."

"Baby, you're not bad. You're Daddy's angel."

Tony took the phone and said, "Tell Janet to get those arms ready. I have a beautiful package to put in them."

"Will do, and Tony, thank you," Mac said.

The next phone call was to the Ware's residence.

"Hello," Justina said.

Tony placed the receiver next to Penny's ear.

"Hello," Justina said again. "Is someone there?"

"Mommy," Penny cried. "Mommy, it's Penny. Mommy, Mr. Miller found me and he's is going to let me ride in an ambulance."

Justina put her fingertips to her lips. "Oh my God, Bill, Bill!" she screamed.

Bill came running. "What, Jussy, what's wrong?"

All she could do was shake her head and cry. She handed him the phone. Bill feared the worst but his fears were quickly put to rest when he said, "Hello."

"Daddy!" Penny said into the phone.

"Oh my God, Penny, is that you, baby?"

"Daddy, Mr. Miller is going to let me ride in the ambulance with Marcie. We're going to the hospital. Do you want to go, too?"

"Yes, baby, Mommy and I want to go."

"Mr. Miller, my mommy and daddy want to go for a ride in the ambulance too. Can they?"

Tony took the phone. "We'll see you at the hospital, Bill."

As Marcie and Penny were being lifted into the ambulance, Tony looked at the attendants with a twinkle in his eye. "Can you stretch the rules and go lights and siren to the hospital?"

"Sure we can, just this once."